ARCADIA
FALLS

ARCADIA

FALLS

KAI MEYER

Translated from the German by

ANTHEA BELL

BALZER + BRAY
An Imprint of HarperCollins*Publishers*

Also by Kai Meyer
Arcadia Burns
Arcadia Awakens

Balzer + Bray is an imprint of HarperCollins Publishers.

Arcadia Falls
Copyright © 2011 by Kai Meyer
Translation copyright © 2014 by HarperCollins Publishers
All rights reserved. Printed in the United States of America.
www.epicreads.com

Library of Congress Cataloging-in-Publication Data
Meyer, Kai.
  [Arkadien fällt. English]
  Arcadia falls / Kai Meyer ; translated from the German by
Anthea Bell. — First U.S. edition.
      pages   cm
  "Originally published in Germany in 2011 by Carlsen Ver-
lag"—Copyright page.
  Sequel to: Arcadia burns.
  Summary: "Rosa and Alessandro go on the run from killers"—
Provided by publisher.
  ISBN 978-0-06-200610-3 (hardcover bdg.)
  [1. Organized crime—Fiction. 2. Supernatural—Fiction.
3. Shape-shifting—Fiction. 4. Vendetta—Fiction. 5. Love—
Fiction. 6. Sicily (Italy)—Fiction. 7. Italy—Fiction.] I. Bell,
Anthea, translator. II. Title.
PZ7.M57171113As 2014   2013014512
[Fic]—dc23   CIP
                                                 AC

Typography by Sarah Hoy
14 15 16 17 18   LP/RRDH   10 9 8 7 6 5 4 3 2 1
❖
First U.S. Edition, 2014
Originally published in Germany in 2011 by Carlsen Verlag.

CONTENTS

SCARS

"IF WE WERE SCARS, our memories would be the stitches holding us together. You couldn't cut them apart, and if you did, it would tear you in two."

"But my memories hurt," she said. "I want to forget. There's so much I just want to forget."

"How are you going to do that? Everything that's happened to you is still happening today. Once something has begun, it doesn't end. There, in your head, it never ends."

A FAREWELL

Fundling's funeral.

It was too hot for a Wednesday in March, the wind too sandy, the sun too bright. The hilly, caramel-colored landscape flickered, as if the procession of black figures had strayed into a mirage.

Rosa was trying to block out her surroundings. And all sensations except for the feel of Alessandro's hand in hers. He was crossing the graveyard beside her. She felt his closeness in every pore.

The only trees among the graves were cypresses. The vaults of rich landowners rose along the broad main avenue, the families who had once ruled this country like kings. Now everything here belonged to the Carnevares. Their vault was the largest and most magnificent of all. Its door was wide open.

Rosa and Alessandro walked right behind the casket and its six silent pallbearers. She had chosen to wear a plain, dark dress that fit closely over her hips, lacy stockings, and flats. Alessandro's black suit made him look older than he was, though a shirt and tie suited him better than most other boys she knew. It probably helped that everything he wore was custom made.

At the head of the short funeral procession—apart from the two of them, there were only a few of the domestic staff of Castello Carnevare, people who had known Fundling since he was a little boy—the priest entered the shade of the porch. The pallbearers raised the casket by its gold handles to slide it into an opening in the wall. Fundling was not a member of the Carnevare family by birth, only a foundling of unknown origin. But Alessandro had made sure that every last honor was shown to him, as if they had been real brothers.

Iole also entered the funeral chapel with Rosa and Alessandro. She had exchanged the summery white that she usually liked to wear for a dark skirt suit. A strange girl, too eccentric for her fifteen years, Iole was getting prettier every day. Her short black hair framed delicate features, and her huge eyes were black as coal. Lost in thought, she was drawing a little heart with the toe of her shoe in the dust on the marble floor.

The priest began his funeral oration.

Rosa had known for days that this time would come. This standing and waiting for the moment when the finality of what had happened couldn't be denied any longer. She wanted to be angry with the doctors who hadn't realized that Fundling might come out of his coma and have enough strength to leave his bed without help. With the nurses who hadn't kept watch on him carefully enough. Even with the men who had finally found him, not far from the hospital but deep enough in a crevice in the rocks for the search to have lasted two whole days.

She would have liked to talk to Alessandro now. All at once she was afraid she might never hear him again, because everything seemed so transient, so impermanent. Wasn't this more proof of that? She had only recently lost her sister, Zoe, and her aunt Florinda. And now Fundling too. Who was going to guarantee that Alessandro wouldn't be next? And here they stood wasting time.

The priest said a last prayer in front of the burial place in the wall. Then they came forward, one by one, to say good-bye.

Rosa's turn came directly after Alessandro's. She tried to remember something that linked her to Fundling, a moment, something personal that he had said to her.

All that occurred to her was a remark she had never understood: *Have you ever wondered who's in the gaps in the crowd?*

Why did she think of that, of all things, just now? Why not think of his smile—*had* she ever seen him smile?—or his sad brown eyes?

They're always there. Around us, but invisible. It's only in a crowd that they're visible.

She pressed her fingertips to her lips and touched the cool wood of the casket. That felt like the right thing to do. A little clumsy, but right.

Iole laid a photograph of Sarcasmo, Fundling's black mongrel dog, on the casket's lid. Then she rubbed the back of her hand over her eyes and left the chapel with Rosa and Alessandro. After a moment's hesitation, Rosa put her arm around the girl. Iole rested her head on Rosa's shoulder. The fabric of Rosa's black dress felt moist and warm under Iole's cheek.

Alessandro's hand clutched Rosa's a little more firmly. "Over there." He was looking to his left and nodded at three figures standing in the shade of a cypress well away from the others. "Are they out of their minds, showing up here?"

Through the stone forest of crosses above tombs and statues, Rosa saw a small woman whose short hair barely reached the collar of her beige coat. Something flashed on her breast. Rosa remembered a locket. She had never seen Judge Quattrini without it.

Across the distance between them, the judge returned her glance. She was flanked by her two assistants and bodyguards, Antonio Festa and Stefania Moranelli. They both wore their leather jackets open, and anyone could see the straps of their shoulder holsters.

"What do they think they're doing here?" Fine black hairs were rising from Alessandro's collar and up to his throat.

"They're just here to watch." Rosa hoped she wasn't wrong. When they had gone to the hospital morgue to identify Fundling's body, there had been a fierce argument between him and the judge. She knew exactly how Fundling had died, he had told Quattrini angrily. So what was the point of an autopsy? "Taking him apart like a boiled chicken," he had said.

The top part of Fundling's wound had been visible under the edge of the sheet that the forensic team had used to cover him. They had opened his rib cage and then stitched it up again. Yet it was obvious what had happened. Fundling had dragged himself out of the hospital—no one knew exactly how he had managed to do that, after lying in a coma for five months—and had fallen into a crevice in the rocks. Police officers had—finally—found him there.

Rosa had listened to Alessandro and the judge shouting, then she went away without a word. He had caught up with her in the parking lot, still in such a furious rage that the argument went on there, without Quattrini. He and Rosa never yelled at each other. But they knew each other's tones of voice well enough to know when a difference of opinion threatened to turn into a serious problem.

By now that confrontation was forgotten. But it didn't look as if he could accept the fact that Quattrini and her assistants, of all people, were turning up at Fundling's funeral.

Just when he was about to go over to the judge, Rosa held him back. "Don't do it."

"I'm the *capo* of the Carnevares. My people wouldn't expect me to put up with this."

"If you want to impress them, get a bigger hat than theirs or something like that. But don't get yourself in trouble for anything as silly as this."

Iole confronted the pair of them. "Stop fighting or I'll pretend to faint. Maybe I'll scream a bit, too." Dark tracks of mascara were drying on her cheeks.

Rosa put her arms around Iole.

Sighing slightly, Alessandro ruffled Iole's hair, dropped a kiss on the nape of Rosa's neck, and took her hand again.

"Let's get out of here." Panther fur was receding under his clothes.

A little later they reached the graveyard gate. Several vehicles were parked on the small lawn. A dusty track wound its way down the hill. The delicate fragrance of lavender rose from the valley.

The Alcantara helicopter stood a little way from the cars. It had flown Iole in from Isola Luna. She was now living on the bleak volcanic island with Rosa; her tutor, Raffaela Falchi; and the clan's lawyer, Cristina di Santis. The young attorney had taken over the work of the late Avvocato Trevini with zest. After the destruction of the Palazzo Alcantara, Rosa could have chosen one of the many luxurious villas among her family's vast real estate holdings, but she liked the island. It had also been a present to her from Alessandro. He spent a great deal of time with her there; they saw each other more often now than they had in the past.

Rosa gently took Iole's shoulders. "Will you be all right?"

The girl nodded. "I'll be giving Sarcasmo lots of hugs."

Rosa kissed her forehead. "I'll be back tomorrow."

Iole nodded and then walked over to the chopper. The pilot put his newspaper down and started the engine. He waved good-bye to Rosa.

Hand in hand, she and Alessandro watched as the helicopter took off and eventually dwindled to a tiny dot in the cloudless sky. More mourners were leaving the graveyard. There was no sign of the judge. Had she and her assistants disappeared through a side entrance?

"I searched Fundling's room," said Alessandro abruptly.

During the months Fundling had spent in a coma, Alessandro hadn't touched his things, and Fundling's room at Castello Carnevare had remained locked.

"There was all kinds of weird stuff in there. I put it in a box in the trunk." They had decided to disappear for a day right after the funeral, get away from the clans and all their businesses, maybe stay in a beach hotel in the southeast of Sicily: go on a diving expedition, dine at sunset with a view of the sea and the vague sense that Africa was there to the south.

Slowly, they walked back to their cars. Rosa's anthracite-colored Maybach gleamed in front of the dusty panorama of hills—she never touched her father's Maserati these days, although like all the other Alcantara vehicles it had survived the palazzo fire intact.

She had left the windows down; no one was stupid enough to steal a car belonging to the head of a clan. And if anyone wanted to put an untimely end to her with a car bomb, closed windows weren't going to stop him.

Her glance fell on the driver's seat. A crumpled note lay on the black leather.

"Is that from her?" Alessandro breathed out sharply. It sounded like the snarl of a beast of prey.

Rosa took the piece of paper out of the car, closed her fist around it, and walked behind the vehicle so that it would screen her from the eyes of the people on the grass. Most of them seemed to be in a hurry to leave.

She smoothed out the note and skimmed the few words.

"What does she want?" he asked as she put the note away.

"A meeting with us."

"No way."

Her chin jutted out stubbornly. "Is that an order?"

"Just common sense."

"If she showed up here in person, it must be important." He was about to interrupt her, but she laid a finger on his lips. "She knows something."

"That's why she's a judge. She knows a lot about Cosa Nostra."

"I don't mean that. Her note gives the name of a place and says she wants to speak to us. And then the word *Arcadia*. With a question mark."

He looked darkly past her toward the graveyard.

"She didn't hear about that from me," said Rosa.

"I know she didn't."

"Or—" She fell silent, biting her lower lip.

"What?"

"The Hungry Man. When I went to see him in prison . . . The rumor is, he's not being closely guarded—on instructions from very high places. But maybe she's overridden those instructions. She could have been listening in on our conversation."

Alessandro rubbed the bridge of his nose. Even before he could reply, she came to a decision.

"I'll talk to her."

"Not again."

"And you, too."

He snorted scornfully.

"She knows about it," she whispered insistently. "About us, about the dynasties. Don't you want to hear what she has to say?"

He clenched his fist and slammed it into the roof of the car. Under his breath, he let out an impressive series of curses.

"San Leo," she said. "Is that a village? She wants to meet us at the church."

"There's a San Leo up in the Monti Nebrodi. It's two hours' drive from here. An hour and a half if we step on it."

"Who's driving?"

"Which of us drives *faster*?"

She kissed him, bent down into her car once more, took her iPod out of its holder, and emerged back into the open air.

"Your car," she said. "But my music."

THE WAREHOUSE OF SAINTS

THEY HAD LEFT THE little town of Cesarò far in the distance and were following the winding road higher into the Nebrodi Mountains, when Rosa remembered Fundling's things in the trunk.

Fever Ray's "Keep the Streets Empty for Me" was booming around the interior of the black Porsche Cayenne. The bass didn't have to be quite so low to drown out the quiet purring of the engine.

> *I'm laying down, eating snow*
> *My fur is hot, my tongue is cold.*

Rosa adjusted the volume. "What exactly is in that box?"

Alessandro looked in the rearview mirror longer than was really necessary on the lonely mountain road. There was no one following them.

"In all these years I haven't seen Fundling with a book in his hand more than once or twice," he said. "I always assumed reading didn't appeal to him. He tinkered with cars a lot, repaired things—practical stuff. I never thought someone like Fundling took any interest in books."

"And now you've found a library in his room?"

He shook his head. "A handful of books, yes, but that's not it. Fundling collected stacks of catalogs. Lists from antiquarian booksellers all over Italy. Not glossy brochures from mail-order companies, but photocopied price lists, even a couple of handwritten ones. He must have written to dozens of small businesses to ask them to send him their lists."

"So he was looking for something. A particular book. Or several."

"Looks like it."

"Do you know what he was after?"

"No idea. I packed up most of his papers and brought them with me. I thought we could check it out together when we have time. As I was flipping through the papers, I noticed that he'd put checks beside a lot of titles, circled some of them several times. Maybe there's some kind of system behind it, and we'll find out what sort of books in particular he was after."

"Not books full of pictures of cars?"

"Definitely not. I brought the few books he did have lying around, along with the papers. They're nonfiction about ancient catastrophes. The fall of Pompeii, the end of Sodom and Gomorrah."

Their glances met before he had to look forward again at the next hairpin turn. "Atlantis?" she asked.

He shrugged his shoulders. "That too."

"You once told me Atlantis was another name for Arcadia."

"I said that's what a lot of people *believe*. But there's no evidence. Atlantis could be all kinds of things. No one really knows anything about it. And even if Arcadia and Atlantis were one and the same place, what difference would that make today? And why would someone like Fundling be interested? He wasn't an Arcadian himself."

She hadn't met Fundling many times. He was odd, and somehow attractive at the same time. He was good-looking, in a dark, almost Asian way, but in Sicily, with its many North African immigrants, that was nothing unusual. It certainly wasn't what gave Fundling his special aura.

The road ran along a steep slope. Chestnut trees and gnarled holm oaks clung to the rocks, and woods of beech and maple grew in the valleys below. Again and again *trazzere*, dusty cattle tracks, branched off the paved main road and disappeared into ravines, or led by a winding route to remote farms. Trying to summon help here if you had an accident was not a pleasant idea. Too many bad films.

"You don't have to drive so fast," she said, as he cut one of the hairpin turns again. "We can keep her waiting if she gets there before us."

"I want to get it over with, and then never have anything to do with Quattrini again. If any of the other families find out we've been meeting her, we're dead."

Of course, *omertà*. The law of silence. Rosa concentrated on a random point in the mountainous landscape. "Who cares? They wouldn't be the first to want us out of the way."

Alessandro slowed down on a short stretch of straight road. To their right, the slope fell steeply away. There was no guardrail, only knee-high blocks of stone at intervals of a few yards apart. Farther down, Rosa saw an illegal garbage dump, one of thousands all over Sicily. The mountain farmers probably got rid of their trash there when, yet again, no sanitation truck made its way into this barren wasteland.

Alessandro stopped the car and turned to her. "We're going to see this through together, okay? Quattrini can go to hell for all I care, but if you think you ought to speak to her, then I'm with you."

She smiled. "To make sure I don't do anything stupid?"

"When you do something that other people think stupid, you usually have a good reason for it." He leaned over and kissed her. Her hand went to the back of his head, and she buried her fingers in his hair. She felt the chill of the snake rise in her, but kept it under control. By now she could deal with the metamorphosis. No more unwanted shape-shifting. Or not usually, anyway.

Finally Alessandro put both hands on the steering wheel and stepped on the gas. Smoothly, almost silently, the car started moving.

She switched on the stereo, and the song started again. Eagles were circling the peaks of the Monti Nebrodi, hunting for prey to feed their young.

The Porsche Cayenne went around another bend. Rosa closed her eyes.

"Over there," said Alessandro. "That's it."

Seeing the lush green of these mountains, Rosa almost forgot the bleak, ocher land that was the property of the

Carnevare clan. It was as if Sicily wanted to use this spot to show it could be as fertile as anywhere in Europe.

San Leo was nestled among the fissured rocks of an impressive massif. The backs of the houses on the outside of the village were set against a steep wall of rock, giving it the look of a medieval castle.

Alessandro steered the Cayenne through a paved square with a stone well in the middle of it into an alley between the tall walls of houses. There was hardly anyone in sight. At a few windows, curtains made of colored strips of plastic wafted in the breeze as the car drove by. Even the wooden bench outside the only bar in the place was empty. Surely the old men of the village would normally have gathered here.

They drove through the shady maze of buildings and left San Leo behind. After a few hundred yards, they saw the church rising to one side of the village among precipitous rocks. The road leading up to it was in good shape. Beyond it there was another, broader road running down the mountainside.

There was a board out front with information about the healing spring to which the church owed its location. A kind of warehouse with a roll-down door rose behind the building.

A black BMW with tinted windows was parked outside the church, one of the cars available for the judge's use. Stefania Moranelli was leaning against the door with her arms folded, looking at them. She was a slender young woman, still under thirty. On some days she tied her long black hair back in a ponytail, but today it was loose and falling over her well-worn leather jacket. She was attractive in a severe way, with pronounced cheekbones and a wiry build.

The judge and her second assistant were nowhere to be seen.

"Your friend doesn't stick to the speed limit, does she?" said Alessandro morosely, as if he felt it an insult to his honor that Quattrini's people had shaken off his pursuit.

"If she upholds the law, you don't like it," said Rosa, smiling, "but when she breaks it, you don't like that either." She stroked his hand and got out. He followed her, but a moment later when Stefania Moranelli brought out her gun, he seemed to regret it.

"Hands on the car roof," Stefania ordered.

"Oh, great," he said, but did as she asked and promptly burned his hands on the sunbaked metal.

Rosa was fairly sure that the order didn't apply to her, but she put her own arms out and held her hands above the car roof to keep Alessandro from feeling even worse. The bodyguard patted Alessandro down, noticed the glance that Rosa cast her, and understood. She came over and subjected Rosa, too, to a cursory search.

"Thanks," whispered Rosa with her head half turned away, so that Alessandro couldn't see her lips moving.

A smile flitted over Stefania's face. She pointed across the courtyard. "The judge is waiting for you by the spring behind the church."

Alessandro looked darkly at the buildings. "Why here, of all places?"

"She comes here to pray. Once a week."

"To—" He interrupted himself, shaking his head. When he looked at Rosa, she shrugged. She hadn't known that Quattrini was so devout. Well, she thought, it was none of her business.

Stefania stayed with the vehicles while Rosa and Alessandro crossed the quiet courtyard. An eagle rose from the rocks behind the church with a screech of outrage. The mountain winds howled in the cracks and crevices of the mountainside.

Antonio Festa met them behind the church. He had shaved his hair so that it was only a millimeter long. A scar began under his left eye and continued up to his eyebrow. His right hand was resting on the shoulder holster under his jacket. Rosa greeted him briefly; Alessandro said nothing. The icy glance that he and Festa exchanged showed where the lines were drawn.

There was another square behind the church, bounded on the right by the warehouse, on the left by the church, and the far side of it ended at a rocky wall. Water from the mountain spring splashed from a stone basin at chest-height to a larger basin on the ground. The judge was kneeling beside it with her hands folded and her eyes lowered. She finished saying her prayer, stood up, and came over to them. Alessandro reacted coldly but courteously to her greeting. Rosa hoped they could manage to conduct this interview in a civilized way.

Quattrini told her bodyguard to wait outside, then led Rosa and Alessandro into the warehouse through a side entrance. Festa did not look happy about leaving his boss alone with the two of them. But he obeyed her order, ostentatiously drawing his gun and walking out of the building to keep an eye on the access roads.

There was a smell of sawdust and paint inside the warehouse. Huge figures of saints made of wood and papier-mâché stood under lengths of clear plastic film, lined up like a silent company of soldiers. Most of them were placed on structures like litters. Some were as much as nine feet tall, with folded hands and suffering glances turned heavenward. Even from the entrance, Rosa could see several versions of the crucified Redeemer, four statues of the Virgin Mary, some with and some without her child; she didn't recognize most of the others, presumably local saints who the deeply religious people of Sicily carried through the streets in their annual processions. Rosa had not witnessed any of these festivals, and knew about them only from TV reports and stories. Thousands of people would throng the decorated streets of cities and villages alike on festival days, following the statues.

"Rather impressive, aren't they?" Quattrini led the two of them farther into the warehouse of saints. "This is where the processional saints' figures for all the local villages are kept."

"Why in San Leo?" asked Rosa.

"Because of the spring. Healing powers have been associated with its water over the centuries. Years ago the Pope himself visited San Leo and blessed the village and its church. Since then all the neighboring communities have wanted to be allowed to store their statues here. For that, they'll even endure the long trip to transport them through the mountains. And it brings in a good income for the village."

"Does it do any good?" inquired Alessandro.

"Does what do any good?"

"The water. I mean, that's why you come here. Don't say you've never tried it yourself."

If his tone of voice annoyed Quattrini, she didn't let it show. "A few drops of water are not enough on their own to save a soul from purgatory. Not mine, not yours." Her hand went to the locket on her breast.

"Why are we here?" Rosa didn't want another argument between those two. The scene in the mortuary appeared graphically before her mind's eye. "You were bugging my conversation in the prison, weren't you? If the Hungry Man—"

"So you really still call him by that name?" Quattrini tightened her lips in a humorless smile. "There have been bosses with less resonant nicknames. But as for bugging your conversation, I couldn't use a word of it in court." She was standing at the foot of a statue of the Madonna that, under its covering of transparent plastic film, looked double the judge's size. "A document issued by the minister of justice forbids me to keep watch on any high-level prisoner without his personal permission. Many of the gentlemen in the government have much to lose if a former *capo dei capi* washes their dirty laundry in public."

Rosa couldn't take her eyes off the gigantic figure of the Madonna. Somewhere under the warehouse ceiling, pigeons were cooing. Their fluttering wings beat against the wooden roof. "You did it anyway."

The judge nodded. "I learned a long time ago that here in Sicily, we have to get by without any support from Rome. Too many of my colleagues have paid for their obedience with their lives. I'm not prepared to do that yet. I've declared war on Cosa Nostra, and you have chosen the weapons."

Alessandro didn't move a muscle. The belief that judges like Quattrini were his mortal enemies had been drummed into him since early childhood. And Rosa understood. Hour after hour of police interrogation, the first time when she was only twelve—she knew all about that. Her dislike of everyone who claimed the law and morality as their own was as strong as his.

All the same, she liked Quattrini. The judge had protected her from the law several times. In return, Rosa had passed her aunt's documents on to her, had ended her family's human trafficking in illegal emigrants from Africa, and had put a stop to the Alcantaras' involvement in the drug trade.

Quattrini slowly walked over to Alessandro, who was looking at her darkly. "Have you ever read Tomasi di Lampedusa's *The Leopard*?"

He shook his head.

"Lampedusa recommends that all young men leave Sicily by the time they're seventeen at the latest. Otherwise, he says, their characters will fall victim to what he calls the Sicilian weakness." She stopped in front of him; she was a good head shorter than he was. "You came *back* to Sicily when you were seventeen. What does that say about you? And what else has to happen before you realize that you can't control the Mafia?

Rosa understood that long ago, whether she admits it or not. When you go under, do you want to drag her down with you?"

He was going to reply, but Quattrini didn't give him the chance. "I've asked Rosa, more than once, to give me information about you. She'd sooner die than go behind your back. But what *you* are doing, Alessandro, is a kind of betrayal. You don't expose someone you love to such risks."

For a moment it looked as if he would lose his self-control. Rosa was ready to intervene if necessary. There was already a stirring beneath his skin as the panther fur fought to come to the surface. Sometimes his metamorphosis into a predator was like an explosion and couldn't be held back. However, Alessandro kept himself reined in. A thin film of sweat glistened on his forehead as he fought down his seething emotions.

"What do you want from us?" he asked quietly. "Why were we asked to come here?"

But Quattrini hadn't yet finished what she wanted to say, and Rosa was beginning to wonder whether she had been wrong. Whether the word *Arcadia* in the judge's message had simply been bait, bringing them here so that she could have a serious talk with them, as if they were two difficult children. She didn't have much experience with that kind of thing.

"You both grew up without your fathers," the judge went on. "One of them dead, the other far too busy committing crimes to take an interest in his son. Do you want the same thing to happen to your own children? Your grandchildren? Look at the members of the clans. How many men get to be grandfathers before a bullet finishes them off, or they're put behind bars for the rest of their lives? Are you going to protect other people with your silence, just to have someone or other inform on you in the end? *Capi* may be powerful for a while, but they have one big problem: They can easily be replaced. What became of your forebears? How many of them died a natural death? And how many of them succeeded in spending their whole lives with those they loved?"

Rosa had clenched her jaw so hard that her teeth were beginning to ache. Strangely enough, now of all times she found herself thinking of Fundling again—one more death she had seen for herself in her few months in Sicily.

Alessandro took a step back, as if Quattrini were breaking out in an infectious rash. But Rosa noticed that the harshness had left his eyes. For a moment it looked as if he would make concessions.

Then, however, he responded in a tone of such strong dislike that it shocked even Rosa. "You talk and talk, but the fact is you're not saying anything that could help us. You might as well be telling a sick person: Why don't you just get better again? It's not that easy, and you of all people should know it, Judge Quattrini. What did you expect? You thought you'd give us some good advice, and immediately we'd say: Yes, right, why didn't we see it that way all along? You stand there making a speech, talking about proper behavior and responsibility, about morality and what you think is right and what is wrong. But you represent only the law, and it's not our law. It was made in the north, in Rome and Milan and all the cities that have grown rich by exploiting the land here in the south.

Your law is the law of the victor, and it is supercilious, arrogant, and couldn't care less how people have survived in Sicily for hundreds of years. My father committed crimes, terrible crimes, yes—but does that mean I have to be like him? Do I have to make the same mistakes? And do you seriously expect me to walk away from my family and begin again somewhere else?"

Quattrini held his gaze and smiled. "But I know that you've been playing with that very idea yourself for some time. What about the hundred thousand euros you withdrew from your bank accounts? And the two tickets for the ferry? One for you, one for Rosa." She looked from him to Rosa, then fixed her eyes on his again. "Yes, Alessandro, I know about that. I'm a judge. It's part of my job to know about these things."

Rosa touched his hand. "Is that true?"

He had bitten his lower lip, and she hoped the taste of blood wouldn't bring on another transformation. Briefly, he looked down, then nodded. "I deposited the money and the tickets somewhere safe. Just in case we're left with no option but to disappear."

"And when would you have told me about that?"

"If and when it became necessary. I meant it only for an emergency. In case we have to move quickly at some point."

Quattrini nodded. "That's the truth, Rosa. The tickets he bought are open-ended. And they are in the same names as the false passports he's had made for you both. By an extremely gifted forger from Noto called Paolo Vitale."

Alessandro's expression was stony.

"But," Quattrini went on, "none of that particularly interests me. Nor am I interested in knowing where you've hidden the money and the papers. It only shows me that you realized, long ago, what a fix you're in. That you know perfectly well neither of you can survive as *capi* of your clans. Sooner or later someone will—"

She was interrupted by a squeal, not particularly loud, but as penetrating as the rasp of chalk across a blackboard. The sound came down from above, from the rafters of the warehouse twenty-five feet above their heads, and was accompanied by the agitated fluttering of the pigeons.

One of the metal skylights had been opened with a squeal of its hinges. A slender figure stood out against the clear rectangle of sky, a woman with long hair.

When she plunged into the depths below her, arms outspread, Rosa saw that she was naked.

Even as she was still in the air, her limbs changed shape, brown feathers covered her skin, and her feet curved and came apart in claws the size of hedge shears.

By the time she reached Quattrini, and buried the judge under her, the woman had become a gigantic owl.

HARPIES

WITH ITS WINGS OUTSPREAD, the creature sat enthroned on Quattrini, threw its head back, and with a grinding sound buried its hooked beak in the judge's breastbone.

Alessandro let himself sink to the floor and disappeared from Rosa's field of vision. A moment later, he'd already become a panther. Scraps of his black suit sailed down to the floor as one paw ground his tie into the dust. He leaped forward, rammed the body of the gigantic bird with all his might, and tore it away from Quattrini. Amid roaring and the wild beating of wings, the owl and the panther collided with the tall statue of the Virgin Mary, knocked it over, and were buried under it. But the statue, made of plaster and wood shavings, was not as heavy as it looked. Alessandro was already crawling out from under it, while it took the owl two or three seconds more to free its wings.

Rosa had just decided not to change shape, and tend to the judge instead, when she heard more wing beats from up above, too loud to be coming from the panic-stricken pigeons in the rafters. She looked up and saw a second man-size bird swooping down. Its huge claws were already closing around her as she turned into her snake form and eluded its grasp. Quick as lightning, she slipped aside, raised her amber-colored snake's head, hissing, and prepared to bite her aggressor, but it swept her away with a wing the size of two car doors. Rosa had feathers between her teeth and snapped her jaws shut, but she lost her hold on the creature as she was flung backward. She slid across the floor and collided with a plastic-wrapped saint, got caught up in the plastic, and was out of commission for several seconds.

When she had freed herself and raised her head, she saw other statues falling and bursting apart in clouds of plaster dust. There were pigeons fluttering everywhere now. Alessandro and the first huge bird of prey were locked in a furious fight, surrounded by a white haze, pigeon feathers, and shreds of plastic wrap.

The second owl, however, was sitting in triumph over Quattrini. The judge looked up uncomprehendingly at her blood-stained breast, and then at the creature. The bird's claws were digging into her flesh. No sound came from Quattrini's open mouth as the owl snatched her up, dashed her to the floor again, and then rose into the air with her.

Rosa wound her way forward, then shot up and landed on the back of the enormous bird. Her golden-brown scales rubbed against bristling plumage. She tasted strange blood, and cursed the fact that her fangs had no venom glands. She still had no idea exactly who or what she was fighting.

The owl let go of Quattrini, but could not attack Rosa with its claws or its wings. Rosa dug her fangs even deeper in the back of the creature, but could only scratch the skin. Her adversary's protective feathers were too dense.

She was distracted when Alessandro, hissing angrily, was slung past another line of statues, collided with the wrecked remains, and lay there on his back for what seemed like never-ending seconds. The first owl emerged from the clouds of plaster dust and came down to ground level, wings spread like a cloak, obviously injured but not mortally wounded.

Rosa lost her balance, slipped to the floor, eluding another heavy beat of those wings, and was beside Alessandro a moment later. The front part of her body reared up to protect him, her snake's skull a yard and a half above the ground. Her eyes went from one owl to the other; her hissing was more aggressive than ever before. She would fight for him to her last breath.

But then he moved again, struggled up, and was standing beside her.

The giant owls came no closer. One of them stood there in the haze of dust, feathers ruffled, chest heaving with the effort it had made. The other looked down at the judge, but did not strike again.

Quattrini was dead. Her eyes, wide open, stared into a void. Feathers and streaks of plaster drifted in the dark pool of blood around her body.

The first owl uttered a shrill cry, then rose from the floor and flew up into the rafters. The second followed, weaving slightly in the air, but then regained control and disappeared through the skylight and out of the warehouse. A moment later there was a clattering from above, as the owl reappeared in the skylight, snatched a pigeon neatly out of the air with one claw, and flew away with its prey.

Rosa and Alessandro stood in a column of light filled with falling dust and sawdust. After catching their breath for a moment, they returned to human form. They were both naked, and Alessandro was stained with the judge's blood. Rosa quickly made sure that apart from a few scratches he was uninjured, and then, although unsteady on her feet, she hurried over to Quattrini's body and knelt down beside it. Her eyes were drawn to the terrible wounds. She tried to look away; this was not how she wanted to remember the judge.

Alessandro swore. "Those were the Malandras."

"Who are they?"

"Aliza and Saffira Malandra. Harpies. They're sisters. No one likes to tangle with their family—unless it's to hire them as contract killers."

She looked up. "What happened to Festa and Moranelli?"

As soon as the words were out of her mouth, the side door of the warehouse was flung open. Antonio Festa raced in, pistol drawn, drenched in sweat as if he himself had just had to fend off an attack.

"Those birds . . . totally crazy," he gasped. "We must get to the church—"

He stopped short when he saw the two naked young people, splashed with blood, beside the motionless judge.

With a cry of rage, he raised the weapon. "Get back! Keep away from her!"

Alessandro was about to take Rosa under the arms to help her get to her feet, but she had already jumped up. "It wasn't us."

"Back!" shouted the bodyguard again. He walked slowly toward them and stared at the body. "What the hell have you done to her. . . . Oh, my God!" He groaned when he saw the wounds.

"It wasn't us," Rosa repeated as she and Alessandro took another step back.

"Flat on the floor! On your stomachs, hands above your heads!" He called to his colleague. "Stefania!"

The young police officer's footsteps approached over the square outside. When she entered the warehouse, she stared first at Rosa and Alessandro, unable to make anything of their nakedness and all the blood. Then she saw Quattrini on the floor. "No," she whispered. Several pigeons took off from the rafters and flew past her into the open air. "What have you done?"

"We were trying to help her!" Rosa strode angrily toward the two of them. "While you were outside there—"

A shot whipped through the air, left a notch in the concrete of the floor right in front of their feet, and ricocheted away, whistling.

"Not another step!" shouted Festa. "And lie down, you bastards!"

Alessandro touched Rosa's arm. "Come on, let's do as he says." He crouched down and lay flat on his front. She could hardly suppress her indignation, but after a moment's hesitation followed suit.

Stefania had sunk to her knees beside the judge, and was closing her eyelids with the palm of her hand. "Why did you do it?" she asked quietly, without looking at either of them.

"She wanted only good things for you."

"We had nothing to do with it," Alessandro protested. "It was—"

"The birds, maybe?" Festa interrupted him. The bodyguard was never going to believe them.

Alessandro turned his head slightly until he could look Rosa in the eye. She was waiting for his signal. Changing shape in front of the police officers would be the easiest way out.

"Got the cuffs?" Festa called to his colleague.

"In the car." Stefania couldn't take her eyes off the dead woman. Her face was filled with grief and rage.

"Get them. I'll keep an eye on these two."

She shook her head, then rose to her feet and took her cell phone out of her pants pocket with her left hand. "I'll call for reinforcements. Neither of us should stay alone until they arrive."

"I can deal with them," replied Festa.

Alessandro's glance said, *Wait a moment. Soon.*

Stefania looked back at the judge's injuries. "No one did that to her with their bare hands." Her head swung around, and she stared at Rosa. "And what happened to your clothes?"

"They wanted to be rid of them," said Festa, getting his word in first. It was easy to see that he would have loved to pull the trigger.

Rosa indicated what was left of Alessandro's suit with a nod of her head. "And first we tore them to pieces in order to—in order to do *what*? Swallow them?"

Festa looked at the scraps of fabric. For all his tough attitude, it was obvious that Quattrini's death had hit him as hard as his colleague.

"How about the owls?" asked Rosa. "You saw them yourself."

The police officer inclined his head. "So?"

"Those damn birds were six feet tall!"

The bodyguards exchanged glances, as if they now really did doubt Rosa's sanity. Could she be held responsible for her actions?

"Their totems," whispered Alessandro. "The Malandras set a couple of ordinary birds of prey on them. Harpies can do that. The way you can talk to the snakes in the glasshouse, the way I can talk to the big cats in the zoo."

Shit. This was not good.

"Watch them," Stefania told Festa, tapping numbers into her cell phone, and after a last glance at Quattrini she went to the side door.

Alessandro made one more attempt. "Someone wanted it to look as if we had killed the judge." He raised his head to look at Festa. "That's why they didn't kill us too."

It wasn't hard to guess the motive for the attack. Someone in the Alcantara or Carnevare clan was tired of taking orders from eighteen-year-olds.

"Shut up!" Festa sounded exhausted now. The aggression had almost entirely disappeared from his voice. He turned his head and called over his shoulder, "Bring those damn handcuffs back!"

The only sound was a faint rustling.

When Festa looked ahead again, he saw a black panther racing toward him. The big cat flung him backward and dug its teeth into the police officer's wrist. Festa let out a cry, dropped the pistol, and was paralyzed by fear for several seconds.

Outside his field of vision, Rosa became a snake and glided past a row of saints to the doorway. When Stefania rushed in, alarmed by Festa's cry, Rosa was already beside the wall there, coiling herself swiftly around the bodyguard's legs and up her body, wrapping herself around Stefania and then falling to one side with her. The gun was still in Stefania's hand, but she was so tightly caught in Rosa's reptilian coils that she couldn't take aim.

Festa reared up under Alessandro, who let him rise a little way and then, with an impressive roar, thrust both his forepaws against the man's rib cage. The police officer fell flat, and the back of his head struck the concrete floor. He immediately went limp, all resistance gone.

Alessandro returned to human form. His face was distorted with pain; too many metamorphoses, performed too fast, were draining his strength. Rosa had to concentrate to maintain the tension of her serpent body. Stefania would not struggle free, but she was still holding the pistol, and there was no way Rosa could get her jaws within reach of it.

Alessandro felt for the pulse of Festa's carotid artery, breathed a sigh of relief, and took his pistol. Rosa's serpent head was up in the air right in front of the policewoman's face. There was pure horror in Stefania's eyes.

Alessandro went up to them, took the gun from Stefania's hand, and told Rosa, "Keep hold of her a moment longer."

He went back to Festa, stripped his jacket off, and searched for his keys. He hurried out into the square with them, but soon came back with the handcuffs from the police car. He cuffed one of the unconscious Festa's arms to the litter for carrying one of the statues of saints, and came back to Rosa, who loosened her coils enough for him to handcuff Stefania's wrists together behind her back. Then he pointed her pistol at their prisoner.

Rosa dropped to the floor and changed back, in less of a hurry than before in an effort to keep the pain within bounds.

"What are you, for God's sake?" asked Stefania hoarsely.

Alessandro ignored her. "We'll have to take her with us."

Rosa stared at him. "Where?"

"She called for reinforcements. Festa will tell them a load of confused stuff about a panther and an attack by birds, which may gain us a little time. He wasn't watching when we changed. He'll probably have one hell of a headache when he wakes up, and he won't be entirely sure what happened to him."

"You're not human," whispered Stefania.

Alessandro seemed to be on the point of giving her an explanation, but then let the subject drop. He turned back to Rosa. "They'll be searching the whole island for us within an hour."

"We can't run away from the entire police force of Sicily. Romeo and Juliet, sure, but now Bonnie and Clyde, too?"

"You'll have to turn yourselves in," said Stefania.

"We never touched a hair on the judge's head," Rosa snapped at her. "And that's the truth."

"Then you'll be able to give proof of your innocence."

Alessandro assumed a scornful expression. "Your people have been looking for something they can pin on us for months. This will be low-hanging fruit to them. I can tell that you believe we killed her."

"We can't take her with us," said Rosa.

"No, it would be abduction," the policewoman confirmed.

A smile was playing around his mouth. "We're Mafia, remember?"

"I have no idea *what* you two are. At least you're not stupid. And it would be damn stupid to make me go with you. The police come down even more heavily on hostage-takers than—"

"Than on the alleged murderers of a judge?" He waved the idea away. "Just be quiet, okay?"

"Alessandro," Rosa said imploringly.

"I'm not going to prison," he said firmly, and managed to sound gentle in spite of everything. "Certainly not for something I didn't do. You aren't either, I'll make sure of that."

"This isn't just your decision, it's mine as well." She went over to the place where she had changed shape the first time, doing her best not to look at Quattrini.

Rosa's clothes lay there intact, the advantage of being a Lamia. With shaking fingers, she put on her underwear and the black dress. Fortunately she hadn't chosen high-heeled shoes this morning. She could already see herself in the papers in her mourning outfit: *Mafia Princess on the Run.* Gorgeous.

Then she hurried back to Alessandro, took one of the pistols, and gestured at the motionless Festa. "Put his clothes on. I'm definitely not going anywhere with you like that."

He managed to smile and gave her the second pistol as well, confident that she would keep Stefania at bay, then set about removing the police officer's jeans and T-shirt. Finally he put Festa's leather jacket on. None of the garments fit him perfectly, but they were better than nothing.

"First we have to get out of here," he said.

Stefania's tone of voice was increasingly insistent. "Our people will hunt you down."

"One more reason to get away from here." He gently touched Rosa's arm. "If we can show her that the Harpies exist, maybe she'll help us."

Stefania nodded in the direction of his gun. "And you think that's the way to persuade me to trust you?"

Rosa scrutinized the young police officer. Her face showed what a shock the judge's death had been to her. And who could tell what would happen after she'd had time to think about the transformations?

Once again Rosa went over to Quattrini, touched her cold forehead, and then, tenderly, her right hand. Finally her glance fell on the judge's little pendant. Hanging on its narrow chain, it had slipped to the floor between her head and her shoulder, and was lying in the blood there. Rosa took it between her thumb and forefinger, and briefly thought of looking inside. Instead, she undid the clasp, rubbed the medallion clean on her dress—not on the judge's coat, she felt that was important—and put it around her own neck.

Finally she stroked the dead woman's hair. "Thank you for everything," she whispered.

When she rose to her feet, she felt the gazes of the others resting on her. Stefania looked unsure of herself, while there was understanding in Alessandro's eyes. Rosa let the pendant slide down inside the neckline of her dress, and felt it warm on her skin.

When she was back beside him Alessandro gave her a quick kiss. He smelled of fresh blood, and against her will the snake stirred inside her.

"Let's go," she said.

IN THE MOUNTAINS

"IT'S MY FAULT," SAID Rosa after a while. "I made Trevini stop my people from drug trafficking. He warned me that they wouldn't like it."

And that wasn't all. She had put an end to the human trafficking of the African refugees on Lampedusa, and she had tried to limit the arms deals. As she saw it, those were the rightful decisions of the head of a clan. But to the clan itself, that meant betrayal. Now she was paying for it.

"It's just as likely that the Carnevares were behind it." Alessandro was sitting at the wheel, driving the black Porsche down a narrow mountain road into a wooded valley. "A lot of them would like to be rid of me. Cesare was the most honest of them; he never concealed the fact that he thought the family would be better off without me. The rest of them are only just crawling out of their holes now."

Stefania was sitting on the backseat, handcuffs on her hands and feet. They had found another pair in Quattrini's car and put them on the policewoman before they left. She didn't say a word about the transformations. Maybe you learned that kind of thing at the police academy: Keep calm, however weird the situation.

"Tell me something," she asked from behind them. "If your

own families want to get rid of you as soon as possible, why didn't you listen to Quattrini and opt out of it all? What good does it do you, being the target of a horde of contract killers? Is it the money, all that luxury? Expensive cars like this? I don't understand."

Rosa didn't really understand too well herself. She had originally come to Sicily to put a few thousand miles of the Atlantic between herself and her past. But she had found the past waiting for her on this island. Instead of overcoming the trauma of her rape and abortion, she had had to face her family history. After the murder of her aunt Florinda, she had found herself head of the clan whether she liked it or not. And that wasn't all: She had found out about her grandmother Costanza's greatest crime, her secret pact with TABULA. It was like a family curse. Finally, Rosa had discovered that her father Davide, who she had thought dead for years, might still be alive and, if so, had personally ordered her rape by Tano Carnevare. Last, but by no means least, was her inheritance as a member of the Arcadian dynasties, her entirely unexpected ability to take the shape of a gigantic nine-foot-long snake.

The whole damn Atlantic hadn't been wide enough to make her forget her old problems. And now she was saddled with a vast number of new ones, all because of her family and its origins. So Stefania had asked a good question. Why was she doing this to herself? Why hadn't she called it quits long ago and left Sicily?

She supposed she'd probably already missed the moment when she could have jumped off the moving train. Probably on the day when she first looked into Alessandro's emerald-green eyes. And not in her wildest dreams did she think of sacrificing her love for him. Not even in exchange for a life without the Mafia—a life without him.

Was that the answer to Stefania's question? Or just *one* answer?

Alessandro had another. "My father allowed my mother to be murdered," he said. "Then he was killed himself, by those he trusted most. That's the only reason I became *capo* of the Carnevares. And now Fundling is dead, too. I can't simply give up, or there would never have been any point to it all."

In the shifting light and shade of the lonely road through the woods, Rosa looked across at his handsome face. Maybe that was the one facet of his character that she would never entirely understand: his vehement insistence on the fact that he *must* lead the Carnevares. That it was both his birthright and his duty. He had fought so hard to reach that position.

"What about the forged papers?" asked Stefania. "Aren't they your tickets to a new life?"

"They're only for an emergency."

Had he ever really meant to discuss it with Rosa? Would he have involved her in the discussion at all, before it was too late?

The policewoman laughed softly. "And when do you expect that emergency to come if not now?"

His hand closed hard on the gear lever, and suddenly he slammed on the brakes. Rosa was flung forward against her seat belt.

"Hey!" she exclaimed.

"Sorry," he murmured, and got out of the car. Rosa was afraid that Stefania might try escaping through the driver's open door. She snatched the pistol up from the floor in front of her seat and spun around. Over the barrel of the gun, she and the policewoman stared at each other.

"You won't shoot me," said Stefania. "You're not a murderer."

"Where would you go in the middle of the mountains, with your hands and feet cuffed? I don't have to shoot you to stop you. You can't get out of here. So sit back again and keep your mouth shut."

Alessandro opened the trunk and searched through the box inside. He had already conjured up a substitute license plate with a fake number from it before they left.

A moment later he was on the backseat beside Stefania, a piece of cloth and a roll of adhesive tape in his hands. She protested vigorously as he gagged her, taking care that she could breathe easily through her nose.

"Do you really have to do that?" asked Rosa.

"Do *we* have to listen to this stuff for the whole drive?"

"Then we shouldn't have brought her with us."

He closed his eyes for a moment, as if forcing himself to calm down. Then he said, "We're not going to hurt her. She's the only one who will believe us if we can prove that the Malandras killed Quattrini. She's seen what we are."

"If that's all it will take—we can show everyone else, too."

"And then they really will believe we killed her. They'll

point the finger at us and fix it to burn us at the stake." He pointed to Stefania. "She'll be okay. She gets on my nerves, but she's not necessarily our enemy."

Rosa's mouth twisted. "So that's why you *gagged* her?"

Stefania mumbled something into the cloth, raised her cuffed hands in protest, and then let them drop to her lap again.

"She'll survive," he said, getting back behind the wheel.

Rosa looked behind her with a resigned expression, put the gun away, and leaned back in her seat. The car began to gather speed.

"About those tickets and passports?" she asked after a while. "Why didn't you say anything to me about them earlier?"

"Because I didn't want things to turn out the way they have. I didn't want the decision of whether we stay or go hanging in the air between us."

"You don't want to run away from this at all."

"I'm not letting myself be simply chased away. I misjudged Quattrini, and I'm sorry about that. For some reason or other she took a great liking to you. And now she's dead because her murderers want it to look as if we killed her. That wasn't spontaneous. It was planned well in advance."

Stefania managed to utter a furious groan, and then lay down on the backseat. She had obviously decided to reconcile herself to her fate for now.

"Why did they do it?" he wondered aloud.

"To be rid of us."

"They could have just killed us. Maybe those two Malandras would have done it. And there'd have been a hundred other possibilities."

"They want to get rid of us but not kill us?" Rosa shook her head. "That doesn't make sense."

"Which is why I'd like to have an explanation."

Rosa was feeling guilty about the judge's death, and she was burning with rage toward the murderers. For the first time she thought she understood what had been driving Alessandro all this time. First revenge for the death of his mother and Cesare's treachery. Then revenge on the men who had raped Rosa. His urge to exact retribution had always seemed a little strange to her, but now, with the judge's dried blood under her fingernails, she finally understood it.

An exclamation escaped her. "Oh, fuck!"

"What?"

"Iole and the others. If it was the Alcantaras behind all this . . . if there really is something like a coup going on, they're not safe on Isola Luna."

"None of your people take any interest in Iole," he said reassuringly.

"But they take an interest in Cristina di Santis! She knows about all the deals, all the agreements, all the sources of income from the Alcantara businesses, both legal and illegal. And she's right there with Iole and Signora Falchi on Isola Luna."

"There's a cell phone in the glove compartment. Call them and tell them to keep their eyes open."

Rosa opened the teak glove compartment and took out one

of Alessandro's iPhones; he had several, none of which could be traced back to him. Impatiently, she let the direct line to the villa on the island ring until the automatic voice mail picked up. Then, searching her memory, she tapped in the number of Iole's cell phone.

She heard the ringtone at the other end twice, then Iole took the call.

Rosa breathed a sigh of relief. "It's me."

"I always keep the refrigerator door closed," Iole assured her. "And I haven't given Sarcasmo any chocolate—well, not much, anyway. And I haven't been ordering anything over the internet, or not today, not yet. And I've been really polite to Signora Falchi, even if she says I wasn't. Anything else I might have done wrong?"

"Iole, listen to me very carefully. You're back on the island, right?"

"Since fifteen minutes ago."

"Is there anyone else there? Apart from Cristina and Signora Falchi and the security men?"

"Haven't seen anyone."

"Are you in the house?"

"In the strawberry room."

"Can you go to the window? Look toward the south over the sea from there."

"Wait a minute . . . yes, I'm there now."

"Is there anything in sight? Ships? Helicopters? Anything?"

For several seconds there was silence at the other end of the line.

"Iole?"

"Three boats. Coming closer quite fast."

"Fuck."

Alessandro glanced at her anxiously. "What's going on?"

"Iole, look very hard now. Are they really coming to the island? Heading straight for Isola Luna?"

"Looks like it. It's not the mail delivery, is it? I'm expecting a package of—"

"Do you know where Signora Falchi and Cristina are right this minute?"

"Old Falchi is running around in quite a state, looking for me." Iole's girlish laughter sounded as carefree as usual. "I took her for a ride. Well, a bit of a ride anyway. And Cristina is reading some kind of papers." She laid emphasis on that, as if she'd caught the Alcantaras' legal adviser doing something immoral. "She's *always* reading, all day long. When she isn't on the phone."

"Listen. You must promise me something. I mean really promise. On Sarcasmo's life, and your uncle's, and—"

"I'm not a baby, Rosa. I know what promising means."

"Go to the kitchen and pack up all the food you can find. Everything that can be eaten without cooking it. And water. All the water you can carry. Then go find Cristina and Signora Falchi, and hide with them."

"Cool."

"No. There are men on those boats who may want to kill you all. That is *not* cool, understand?"

"Okay."

"You'll need a really good hiding place."

"Like the old bunker down by the moorings?"

Rosa had strictly forbidden Iole to go down there. She might just as well have written a friendly invitation to her to drop in any time she liked.

"Sarcasmo ran into it," the girl defended herself, "so I had to look for him. I couldn't leave him all alone there, could I? But I was only in the bunker that once. And just for a few seconds." She was lying, but at that moment Rosa could have hugged her for her incorrigible curiosity.

"Take flashlights with you. And plenty of batteries. You only have a few minutes. The security men will try to hold off the men from the boats." If they hadn't been bribed, if they weren't on the way to the villa themselves. Shouldn't think that out to the end. Shouldn't always assume the worst. "Did you understand all that?"

"Food. Water. Flashlights. Sarcasmo. Cristina . . . and Signora Falchi, supposing I can find her."

"No *supposing* about it."

Iole giggled. "And then all of us into the bunker. Roger and out."

"Alessandro and I will be with you as soon as we can."

"Got it."

"Look after yourselves. And Iole? I love you."

"Love you too. But listen, when you're dead can I make you into a purse? A snakeskin purse. You'll be very old by then, and so will I, and I guess I'll like that sort of thing. Ugly, but kind of chic. Can I?"

Rosa smiled.

Iole hung up.

THE *GAIA*

It began before they reached Milazzo. But when they left the commercial district and approached the city center it became almost unbearable.

Rosa suspected every car of containing spies; every radar trap seemed like the watchful eye of a pursuer. Pedestrians seemed to be staring through their windows, especially at the red lights. She tried to tell herself that it was the expensive car, not its occupants, that drew all eyes, that she was only imagining things, and in reality no one was paying them more than a brief moment of attention. But by now paranoia had her firmly in its grip.

There were no radio announcements yet of the judge's death, no news that two suspects were on the run, but the investigation must be in full swing by now. Their fake license plates wouldn't keep them from being identified for long. And having a prisoner in the backseat didn't improve matters.

"We'll have to take her gag off," said Rosa, as twilight plunged the streets of Milazzo in dark red light. "If anyone sees her, we're done for."

They had told Stefania to stay lying on the backseat and not sit up. Rosa had no idea what they would do if she sat up anyway. No doubt Stefania herself was wondering the same thing.

Alessandro disagreed. "She'll bring half the city down on us if she screams."

"Every time we stop at an intersection I almost have a heart attack," said Rosa. "And how about people in buses and trucks? They can see into our car even when they're driving." She turned to look at the backseat, and saw Stefania watching them. "If we take the gag off, will you promise to keep your mouth shut?"

Alessandro made a face. "Oh, come on, Rosa."

The policewoman nodded.

"You won't call for help?"

Stefania shook her head.

"I trust her," said Rosa.

"You don't. You don't trust anyone."

"Well, we can't drive on like this."

He thoughtfully chewed his lower lip, nodded, and pulled the car into a shady parking spot. Not far away there was a newspaper kiosk, but the view of the man inside was blurred by the magazines dangling in foil wrappings from its canopy. A fruit seller was taking empty crates out of his shop and stacking them on the sidewalk; a stray dog lifted its leg against them after the man had gone back inside. No one seemed to be taking any notice of the black Porsche.

Rosa leaned back between the seats and loosened Stefania's gag. A few of her hairs had caught in the adhesive tape, but she didn't even flinch as Rosa tore the whole thing off with a strong jerk.

"Thanks," said the policewoman, a little breathlessly.

"You won't scream?"

"Promise."

"Or do anything else silly?"

"No. Do you by any chance have some water?"

Alessandro's expression darkened. "We had to leave the picnic basket behind." His voice dripped with sarcasm. "But maybe Rosa will loosen the cuffs on your hands and you can get a snack from the shop over there."

Rosa moved back into the front seat, keeping an eye on the police officer. She couldn't get out through either of the back doors; Alessandro had switched the child lock on.

He stretched, snapped his fingers, and sat up straight, clearly slightly uncomfortable in Festa's jacket. Then he threaded the car back into the traffic.

"We're nearly at the harbor," he said.

Rosa fiddled with the radio until she found a local station. By now she had tried half a dozen, but none of them were broadcasting police reports in the news bulletins. "Why aren't they saying anything about us?"

"To give you a sense of security," said Stefania. "They want you to think they don't take what happened very seriously."

"The murder of a judge?" said Alessandro. "Oh, sure."

The sea shimmered ahead at the end of the street. The closer they came to the harbor, the more distinctly they could see the masts of many sailing boats, black lines against the sunset glow of the sky.

Alessandro's 130-foot yacht, the *Gaia*, lay at anchor there. Rosa had set out from here last October on her first expedition to Isola Luna, after Fundling had picked her up outside the Palazzo Alcantara. The memory of him was beginning to hurt. It was the last thing she could deal with right now.

Outside the yacht harbor, a broad road with a promenade on one side ran along the water. Tall palms grew at the roadside. The *Gaia* was moored close to the exit from the harbor basin, next to another yacht of similar proportions. The other boats by the landing stages were smaller, although most of them cost as much as a comfortable single-family home.

Beyond the harbor, on the other side of the road that ran along the shore, was a square with a tall fountain in it. Their view of the square was a wide, open one, with no police cars in sight.

Alessandro drove past the *Gaia* without stopping. They came within fifty yards of the yacht, but saw nothing suspicious.

"They're here, though, aren't they?" asked Rosa.

Alessandro slowed down slightly as he observed the yacht in the rearview mirror. "What makes you think that?"

"Just a feeling."

Stefania sat up a little way and looked through the side window. "They're sure to be concentrating on the ferries and airports."

"Your people know about the yacht," said Alessandro. "If they haven't been here yet, they could turn up at any moment."

"Maybe. Or maybe not."

"Meaning?" asked Rosa.

"She's trying to trick us," remarked Alessandro.

Stefania let out a sigh. "I shouldn't have to tell this to you two, of all people. Our unit is severely understaffed. We can't be everywhere at once. The Mafia became fairly transparent some time ago; you have far fewer secrets than you think. But there are simply not enough of us. In theory, we could lay our hands on half of Cosa Nostra within a single week. But as long as we don't have enough operational forces, there's no chance of that happening. That's why it's sometimes better to tolerate some of you and keep a watch over them, rather than alarming you all and then seeing you slip through our fingers and go underground, never to be seen again. Every Mafioso worth his salt has a ship or at least a boat lying in some harbor or other. If we were to watch them all day and night, we'd have to commandeer the services of every traffic officer in all Italy."

"But to your people, we're Quattrini's murderers," said Alessandro. "You'd think that would give us some kind of special status."

Rosa nodded. "A message posted in the next issue of the police trade union journal."

"And if the police aren't waiting on board for us, then the others may be," he finished.

"The people who took you for a ride?" Nothing in Stefania's face or voice showed whether she believed that or not.

It was certain that someone had it in for Rosa and Alessandro and wanted to get them out of the way, using Quattrini's murder as a means to that end. But who? And what were they going to do next?

Rosa was more concerned about Iole than herself. She

hoped that by now she was in the abandoned war bunker under the island with the two women, getting on their nerves.

"Let's wait until it's dark," suggested Alessandro. "If they haven't done anything by then, we'll go on board."

He parked the car in the road along the seafront, almost a mile from the yacht harbor. Here the Porsche fit in unobtrusively among the other expensive cars.

Alessandro called the number for the bridge of the yacht. Meanwhile Rosa kept her eye on Stefania. The policewoman was still sitting quietly in the backseat, pushing a few dank strands of hair off her forehead with her cuffed hands.

After a couple of seconds the call was answered. Alessandro frowned, but nodded at Rosa hesitantly. She still didn't feel like breathing a sigh of relief. But the *Gaia* was their only chance of reaching Isola Luna.

After he had finished the conversation, he summed up the gist of it for her. "That was the first mate. He says they haven't noticed anything unusual. So far there haven't been any police on board, and the crew are there except for the cook—it's his day off. They can organize a few men to go to Isola Luna with us, if we want."

"Killers," said the policewoman scornfully.

"And you still trust the crew?" asked Rosa.

"I'd swear that the captain's an honest man. I'm not so sure about the others. But we don't have a choice." For a moment there was an indecisive silence. "They'll call if anything strange happens. The *Gaia* can leave at any time. All the same, I'm in favor of waiting until it's dark, just to be on the safe side. An hour, or an hour and a half would be better. Until then let's watch the harbor and see if we notice anything."

Rosa looked out to sea. It was as if ink were flowing from the horizon into the water, slowly coloring it black.

"Okay," she said reluctantly. "Then we'll wait."

At that moment Alessandro's phone rang.

"Iole," he said, checking the display. "Or someone using her cell phone."

Rosa snatched up the iPhone and took the call. "Hello?"

"The Dallamano purse factory here."

"How are you doing?"

The connection was bad, with a scratchy sound on the line. Iole's voice sounded lower than usual, and she was whispering. "I know those men. Some of them are our people. Alcantaras."

"Are you sure?"

"Absolutely sure."

"Are you in the bunker?"

"Cristina and Signora Falchi are down there. I couldn't get a signal, so I came out again. I can see a couple of them. They're at the moorings. Two boats are anchored here. The third must be somewhere else. Maybe in the bay on the south coast."

"Make sure they don't see you."

"I'm not stupid."

Rosa had never been so glad to hear Iole's voice before. At this moment, she could have let her go on babbling for hours.

"I just wanted to tell you they haven't caught any of us,"

said the girl. "Sarcasmo is here with us, and we have enough to eat for a few days. Chocolate and cookies." Iole paused for a moment, then there was a rushing and crackling on the line. "They *are* your people. They shot the watchmen."

Rosa closed her eyes and let her head drop back against the neck rest. "Go back into the bunker at once. Don't get caught. We'll try to reach the island tonight."

"Do you think that's a good idea?"

"We don't have a better one."

"I don't want anything to happen to you and Alessandro. We're fine. We're safe in the bunker. None of them know their way around. Did you know how huge it is?"

During World War II, Isola Luna had been an advance military base meant to repel German attacks. Rosa herself had never been in the bunker, but Iole, who had spent six years as a hostage and was not afraid of the dark, had obviously explored most of the underground fortress long ago.

Rosa urged her again to look after herself and the others, then ended the call.

Alessandro turned to her. "Everything all right?"

Rosa turned her eyes away. "We're screwed."

"Amen," said Stefania.

AMBUSHED

"Look at that!"

The cry from the backseat of the car pulled Rosa out of her thoughts. They were driving around the area by the yacht harbor for the third time, looking for a place to park closer to the *Gaia*. All the streetlights and car headlights were switched on; the sky had changed from dark blue to black. Neon signs cast ugly lighting over plastic chairs on the sidewalks.

Rosa turned to her left and saw a snack bar with a phone number over it in digits as tall as a man. The flickering bright red sign over the door said AMERICAN PIZZA. An Italian wearing a cowboy hat was loading flat boxes into the trunk of a Fiat.

"That's not pizza," said Alessandro, with deep conviction, "that's mushy dough with melted rubber topping."

Stefania shrugged her shoulders. "Fills you up, though."

"You police officers have no civilized culinary tradition."

"Most of all we have no time," retorted Stefania. "I can't remember when I last sat down at a table to eat."

"But eat something like that?" Rosa couldn't take her eyes off the fake cowboy. "American pizza? In Italy?"

"My pistol comes from Germany. My jeans come from Turkey. My mother comes from Morocco. So?"

54

Alessandro grinned. "What's the world coming to if not even the police maintain old Italian values?"

"Says Mister I-studied-in-the-States-and-I'll-tell-the-spaghetti-eaters-back-home-what-it's-all-about."

"Calm down," said Rosa. Was she, of all people, acting as peacemaker now? Crap, they really were in a jam.

Stefania looked over the back of the rear seat. "Damn. We've passed it now."

"I noticed the number," said Alessandro.

"I'll do everything you ask."

"That's why it's called being taken *hostage*."

"I haven't eaten since yesterday evening. Quattrini wasn't exactly thoughtful about these things. If she wasn't hungry herself, why would anyone else be? And did I mention before that I didn't sleep all night?"

"Why not?"

"Because I had to get bloody *cameras* into place in the graveyard. Satisfied?"

"There wasn't much to film."

Stefania let her head sink back against the upholstery. "I could be sitting comfortably in the surveillance van right now, evaluating the video and eating American pizza."

Alessandro tapped a number into his cell phone. "Hello? I want to order pizza. Three pies, with extra cheese and onions. American pizza, yes." Stefania was beaming, but then he said, "For delivery to a yacht in the harbor. On the left at the exit from the basin, you can't miss it. The name's the *Gaia* . . . G-A-I-A. And at ten on the dot, please, no earlier, no later.

Can you do that? Okay, thanks." He ended the call and immediately made another.

"Can I speak to the captain now?" he asked. "Well, okay. Tell him there's a change of plans. I'll come on board alone. At ten exactly. And don't be surprised to see me looking rather odd. Yes, a disguise. How do we know who's watching the yacht? So don't shine a spotlight in my face before I reach the rail, okay? Thanks. See you then."

Rosa glanced at him sideways, and slowly shook her head. Stefania leaned forward between the seats. "What a waste of three good, nourishing pizzas."

"Lie down. Please."

She did as he said. "Hear that? It was my stomach."

Rosa nodded. "Pretty loud, too."

"Can we stop talking about food?" asked Alessandro.

"There," said Stefania. "There it goes again."

"We can gag her."

"I'll eat the gag."

He looked at the time, and turned into the square beside the harbor.

Behind the lights in the portholes of the yacht, shadowy outlines were moving, but never up in the saloon or in the private cabins. The crew were staying on the lower deck, although no passengers were on board. There was nothing to suggest that everything wasn't the same as usual. No suspicious persons at the moorings, certainly no police officers.

"How much longer?" asked Stefania. "He's going to be late."

Rosa pointed forward. "There he is."

The pizza delivery man's Fiat braked by the promenade with its warning lights blinking. The driver with the cowboy hat jumped out, took three boxes from the trunk, and walked over to the *Gaia*.

"If they have any sense," said Stefania, "they'll take the pizzas and eat them."

"Unless I'm mistaken," replied Alessandro, "there's going to be so much adrenaline spilled on board that no one will have any appetite left."

A narrow strip of steel began to unfurl down the side of the yacht—an extendable boarding ladder. The steps were covered with thick carpet.

Rosa narrowed her eyes. "That's not the captain up by the rail."

"No," whispered Alessandro.

"Anyone I know from the crew?"

"You know them, but not from the *Gaia*. Those are men from the Castello. They're on guard."

"Oh, great."

Stefania sat up slightly so that she, too, could see the yacht. "An ambush?"

"Something like that. They knew exactly why they couldn't let me speak to the captain. He'd have warned me."

Rosa clenched one hand into a fist. "Suppose they shoot the delivery man?"

The policewoman snorted. "Then it'll be another death on your consciences."

For a moment Rosa thought that Stefania had gone too far.

Black down appeared on Alessandro's hand as he gripped the steering wheel, but then it disappeared again under the sleeve of the leather jacket.

Time for her to do something.

"Rosa, no!" Alessandro swung around. "They won't hurt—"

Too late. Her fist landed, hard, on the horn. The key was in the ignition, the lights were switched on, and a loud, hooting wail immediately rang out over the harbor area.

The pizza delivery man stopped just before he reached the stairway and looked at his car. The men behind the rail of the yacht changed their position to get a better view of the street.

Rosa pushed the car door open. She had meant to shift shape as she got out, but it didn't go as quickly as she had hoped. Instead, she landed on all fours on the asphalt, and the metamorphosis started a split second later. Like a golden rope covered with scales, she shot out of the dress as it fell off her, slid into the street, hoping there would be no car speeding along at that moment, and glided over to the promenade. Headlights caught her as she went the last few yards, but then she was already on the sidewalk, winding her way around the palm trees and along the dark quay to the yacht.

The pizza delivery man had turned to the *Gaia* again. Motorists probably hooted at him all the time. Ahead of him the snow-white hull rose like the wall of a glacier, and the distant streetlights reflected off varnished steel.

From the ground, Rosa could see the face under the cowboy hat. This wasn't the same driver as the one they had seen outside the snack bar. The one she was looking at was older, at least thirty. He wore a jacket like his colleague's, with a white shirt under it—and something else under *that*. He was far too warmly dressed for a mild Sicilian evening in March.

She was still two yards away when she saw the pistol in his waistband.

"American pizza!" he called up the stairway. The rail of the yacht was several yards above the moorings. Impossible to recognize anyone up there from this angle. "You ordered from us."

From below, Rosa saw that he had a second gun in his right hand, under the flat pizza boxes. He was either crazy, very brave, or convinced that reinforcements would arrive at any moment.

Not her problem anymore. She had changed shape to help an unsuspecting pizza delivery boy out of a mess. But whoever this guy was, he must have intercepted the real delivery man. All hell was about to break loose. She hastily set off back to the promenade.

Everything suggested that this was an operation carried out in great haste. Probably by Stefania's colleagues. Presumably a great many fingers were hovering rather nervously over the triggers of guns.

Rosa sped up even more, and had to leave her cover. She catapulted herself forward in thrusting loops.

Suddenly she heard shouting and a car revving behind her. Shots rang out. The next moment a searchlight flamed in the night sky. Its beam of light swept just past Rosa, bathing the deck of the *Gaia* in dazzling brightness. At the same time tires squealed on the road along the seafront, doors were flung open, a voice speaking through a megaphone called on the men aboard the yacht to give themselves up. Masked figures stormed toward the moorings. Rosa just managed to coil around the foot of a palm tree before they all raced past her and went to the aid of the fake pizza delivery man.

What with the lights, the voices, and legs all around her, she feared she might lose her sense of direction. The exchange of shots by the water became more violent, and she saw the muzzle flash of guns more and more frequently, but when she looked at the yacht once more, none of the attackers were on board yet, because there was firing from above them, and the metal stairway was just being drawn in.

She hoped her honking hadn't attracted anyone's attention to the Cayenne. It was standing among a number of cars on the other side of the multilane road, not far from the end of a side street. Rosa wound her way between two unmarked police cars, unnoticed by several men who were directing the operation only a few paces away.

Stefania had lied to them. Her unit was far from under-staffed. Plainclothes investigators had probably been keeping watch on the yacht since that afternoon, intending to give the signal to attack now, after nightfall. The pizza guy must have been a godsend. Maybe they had hoped to get one of their men on board to prevent the stairway from being pulled back in.

Rosa's coils swept across the road, where all traffic had now come to a standstill. Someone shouted what sounded like, "Hey, there's a snake!" but no one seemed to take him seriously. She reached the other side, unharmed, and slid on past and under the stationary cars. The Cayenne must be the next car, or the one after that.

The driver's door was open. Alessandro had gone. The backseat, too, was empty. Rosa reared up and glanced across the road. Had he followed her, in human form or as a panther? Either would have been madness. A snake, even a snake nine feet long, could pass unnoticed in all this chaos, but no one could overlook a panther.

"Rosa!"

The door of a silver Volvo beside her was pushed open. Alessandro leaned far over the seat and signaled to her. Her clothes were lying on the floor in front of the passenger seat. She pushed her coils into the car, and was just getting the end of her snake body into it when he slammed the door.

"Sorry," he murmured remorsefully, when he noticed that he had nearly closed it on her tail. He was busy hot-wiring the ignition. "I saw that you'd turned around."

She crawled up on the seat and returned to human form. A glance over her bare shoulder told her that they were alone in the car. There was nothing in the back but the carton from Fundling's room and the crate with the fake license plates in it. "Where's—"

"In the trunk. She planned to make off the moment you were gone. She attacked me from behind and tried to get the gun away from me."

Rosa was still dazed by her swift return to her own shape,

but she knew she had to pull herself together. With nervous movements, she picked up her underwear and dress and slipped them on.

The engine of the Volvo started. The harbor was enveloped in a haze now, maybe from a smoke bomb. Muzzle fire was still flashing; sirens were sounding. The helicopter she had heard hovered high above the *Gaia*, flooding it with bright light.

Slowly, Alessandro sat back, so as to avoid attracting any unnecessary attention. They still had a chance of getting a head start on the police.

Rosa pulled the hem of her dress down over her thighs, and saw that her fingernails were growing back. Alessandro put the car in gear and stepped on the gas cautiously; he didn't want to rev the engine.

"The people on board wouldn't have harmed the delivery guy," he said. "They thought it was me, and they obviously want us alive. Otherwise the Malandras would have killed us."

The Volvo cruised along the seafront road at a leisurely tempo going south, fell into the traffic behind some other vehicles, and passed a half-constructed safety barrier just before the crew of a patrol car could close it. Obviously the operation carried out by the anti-Mafia unit had also taken the local police force by surprise.

"If Iole was right," said Alessandro, "and it was men from your clan who occupied the island . . . and if the men aboard the yacht really were from the Castello—"

"Then the Alcantaras and the Carnevares are in league with each other against us," she finished his sentence, her throat dry. It all seemed perfectly logical now.

"They commissioned the Malandras to kill Quattrini so that there'd be no one left we could ask to protect us," he went on. "Not even the police."

"But an alliance between your family and mine means a new peace pact. A new concordat." As she spoke, the ends of her forked tongue grew back together. She shook her head. "I thought they wanted to get rid of us so exactly that thing would *not* happen?"

"There must be more behind it. We're not just dealing with a few traitors who've had enough of us. There's something much bigger going on."

In the trunk, Stefania kicked the backseat, with much crashing and banging, but with no success.

Rosa knocked dry snake scales off her forearms, folded the sun visor down, and watched the slits of her pupils turn back to human eyes in the makeup mirror.

THE GAPS IN THE CROWD

A CLEAR, STARRY SKY stretched above the slopes of Mount Etna. The volcano was quiet that night, and no smoke rose from its peak. Rain clouds often gathered on the sides of the mountain, but there were none in sight now. The lights of a few villages shone in the distance, but here, at the end of a bumpy path through the fields, only the stars sparkled, silvery gray in the darkness.

The Volvo was parked between black rocks. Solidified lava covered large parts of the volcanic slope, and tangled grass and bushes grew on many parts of it. By day sheep and cattle grazed here, but by night only the blades of grass moved in the wind. Away from the main roads at the foot of Etna, there were only narrow paths for the few farmers who cultivated crops on the meager soil between lava fields and expanses of scree. Most tourists kept to the eastern and southern sides of the mountain, where there was accommodation for hikers and people traveling through the area. But here to the west, the land was bleak; scarcely anyone lived outside the few villages. Remote farmhouses lay in ruins, their silhouettes merging with the rugged lava crests.

They had stopped to get a few hours' sleep. Alessandro had threatened to gag Stefania again if she didn't keep quiet in the trunk. He refused to let her lie on the backseat again, and for the moment Rosa didn't object. Stefania had lied to her at least once, and she took that badly. Tomorrow they would have to decide whether it would be better to let the police officer go free.

They had pushed their seats as far back as possible, but it was still pointless to even think of sleeping.

Alessandro held Rosa's hand as they looked up at the mountain through the windshield. The peak of the volcano couldn't be seen from here; rising ground lower down obscured their view. Here and there, porous lava structures were visible in the moonlight, looking like the waves of the sea frozen as they broke.

Weariness and lack of sleep combined made Rosa edgy and impatient. She switched on the interior light of the car.

Alessandro stretched. "Shall we drive on?"

Shaking her head, she reached over to the backseat and transferred Fundling's things to her lap. She felt around for the lever to adjust her seat, and sat upright again. In that position, the box came up to her breasts and was uncomfortable to hold, so she opened the door, dumped it on the ground beside the car, and took several books out. Putting them on her lap, she began leafing through the volumes one by one.

"*When the Seas Were Gods,*" she read aloud, shaking her head. "*The Model of the Hollow World. Hand-Ax and Magic Staff. The Cosmic Orient. Great Cataclysms. Creation in Reverse.*" She handed the books to Alessandro, who made a face as he took them. "Surely he didn't read all these, did he?"

He examined the covers. "Looks to me like most of them are a few decades old." A glance inside confirmed his suspicion. "1972. 1967. 1975. Were people then more gullible about such nonsense than today?"

"There are some notes in this one. Is that Fundling's writing?"

He looked at the handwritten notes in the margin of the text. "Could be. I don't know for sure."

She continued paging through the book. The appendix contained a long bibliography. Many of the titles had a cross beside them; a handful had been encircled. She put the book to one side and took another stack out of the box.

Snakes in the Sky. The Deluge. The Last Days of Ur. And then, unexpectedly, she found a title in one bibliography that rang a bell with her.

The Gaps in the Crowd by Leonardo Mori.

"Does that mean anything to you?" she asked, holding the page out to him.

"No. How about you?"

"Fundling once said something like that to me. When he was picking me up to take me to the *Gaia*, before our first expedition to Isola Luna."

"Gaps?"

"Gaps in the crowd. All pretty vague. He believed that there are often empty spaces in crowds of people, spaces that stay empty however great the crush around them. And he thought those spaces move about."

"So?"

"He called them the gaps in the crowd. Then he said they aren't really empty. It's just that we can't see who's occupying them." She closed the book and put it with the others. "I think he was afraid of them. They're always around us, he said. Always there, but we can't see them."

In the faint interior light of the car, Alessandro looked at her skeptically. He seemed older than usual, more reasonable. "You and I would agree that that's nonsense, wouldn't we?"

"Sure—like humans who can turn into animals, as I'd have said if you'd asked me six months ago."

He tapped one of the books. "Atlantis. Extraterrestrials building the pyramids. What do you bet we'd find something about the yeti and the Loch Ness monster if we spent awhile reading this stuff."

"I didn't say I believe in it," she retorted sharply. "Fundling talked about it, that's all." To avoid the temptation to argue with him, she opened the next book, running her finger back down the titles in the bibliography to the one that had caught her eye. *Mori, Leonardo: The Gaps in the Crowd—New Truths about the Cataclysms of Antiquity.* And a publisher: *Hera Edizioni.* The line was encircled in felt pen. No other title stood out in the same way.

She unloaded the second pile of books on Alessandro's lap. He groaned. Then she leaned out of the car to keep searching the box. She found another two or three books, but *The Gaps in the Crowd* was not among them. Instead, she took out the many catalogs from antiquarian booksellers that Fundling had collected. At a loss, she looked more closely at a few, and leafed through them.

She found something in the eighth or ninth catalog. Under a thick stroke of yellow highlighter, she saw the entry: *Mori, Leonardo: The Gaps in the Crowd—New Truths about the Cataclysms of Antiquity. Privately printed by Hera Edizioni.* Plus the year of publication, a comment on the condition of the copy, but no picture of the cover. However, it was expensive: 2,500 euros.

"Wow," she whispered. "Privately printed means—"

"A tiny print run. Something between a couple of dozen and a few hundred copies."

"Hand-numbered, it says here. Copy number eighteen."

Alessandro opened his door and got out, carrying the tottering piles of books around the car, and letting them drop into the carton on Rosa's side. "Listen, this is all very well, but we have worse problems than Fundling's eccentric taste in reading."

"How can someone who doesn't read at all have eccentric taste in reading?"

"I only said I never *saw* him reading. How would I know what he got up to in his own room? We didn't always spend twenty-four hours a day together." He lowered his voice; there was a regretful note in it. "In fact we very seldom did."

She looked in more of the catalogs, but Mori's book was listed only in that one. The antiquarian bookshop was called the Libreria Iblea, and was in Ragusas in southeast Sicily.

Alessandro stretched his legs outside her door, keeping a watchful eye on the nocturnal landscape of lava rock, and strolled back to his side. He was just behind the back of the car when he let out a low-voiced exclamation. "Hey!"

In alarm, Rosa reached for the pistol, but then he was standing beside her again. "Everything okay?" she asked. Her heartbeat thudded in her ears.

He nodded, crouched down, and held out several photographs in the faint interior lighting. "They were lying on the ground outside. They must have dropped out of the books when I was carrying them around the car just now."

There were seven or eight of them, sticking together slightly. They must have been lying pressed close together in one of the volumes for some time.

He handed them to her one by one, looking at them in sequence first himself. The first photo was really made up of two black-and-white pictures that Fundling had obviously fitted together on a copier. One showed Fundling as Rosa had known him. The second was of a man in what looked like his late thirties. He had short dark hair, a high forehead, and he wore a jacket and sunglasses. Fundling had placed the photographs side by side so that the horizon was on the same level. At a fleeting glance you might have thought that the two men were standing next to each other.

The rest of the photographs, all of them in color, showed the same subject: a large building against hills scorched by the sun. The wording over the entrance looked old-fashioned, no neon-lit letters, just a painted sign illuminated by two lamps mounted on the upper rim. HOTEL PARADISO. Two of the pictures had been taken at night, the others in daylight. Under the last photograph two more came into view, not glossy copies like the rest but in sepia and taken from old brochures, or perhaps from newspapers. The building was the same, but the landscaping around it was different. In one picture a horse-drawn carriage stood outside the hotel. There could have been half a century between that photo and the later ones.

"Here!" Rosa pointed to one of the color photographs. "That's your car, isn't it?"

A red Ferrari stood outside the hotel, and she could read part of the license plate.

Alessandro nodded. "Fundling must have taken the pictures. He often went out in different cars from the garage at the Castello. When he was old enough my father and the others were always sending him on errands. I'd guess he had a forged driver's license as he was seventeen. That was when I was away at boarding school in the States. He probably took the Ferrari out quite often—I can hardly blame him."

Rosa rolled her eyes.

Alessandro smiled. "He must have taken the pictures on one of those drives."

She leafed through the photos again. "What do the words *Fundling* and *hotel* make us think of?"

"My father's men rescued him from a burning hotel when he was small."

"After setting it on fire themselves in the first place. How old was he then? Two?"

"And you think it was this hotel in the photos?"

"Doesn't look like it ever burned down."

"It could have been rebuilt."

She held up one of the two old photos, and the one with the Ferrari so that they were side by side. "Same facade. No one would bother to rebuild such an old place exactly the way it was before, right down to the window frames. Doesn't look like it was under a protection order as a historical monument, either."

Alessandro took the books out of the carton again, one by one, and shook them out. He found no more photographs. "Wait a minute," he said. "There was something else with them. Kind of an album or scrapbook." He rummaged among the remaining booksellers' catalogs in the carton, and finally took out something that, at first sight, looked like a photo album covered in brown artificial leather. When he opened it, however, they saw no pictures, just newspaper articles stuck into the pages.

Rosa sat sideways on the passenger seat, put her feet on the bottom of the doorway, and drew her legs almost to her chest. Her dress slid up over her pale thighs, but that didn't bother her. Alessandro was still sitting by the door of the car with the scrapbook open in front of him. He leafed through it with one hand, and absent-mindedly stroked her calf with the other. Together they read the captions and the bold lettering of the article headlines.

"He was trying to find out what happened back then," said Alessandro.

"What *really* happened," she said, without taking her eyes off the press cuttings. Most of them were short reports from daily papers, and at the end there were three in English from something that called itself the *Global Gnostic Observer*, and appeared to be a tabloid for aficionados of UFOs and Atlantis.

What they all had in common was their subject, although they differed about the facts. Or in the case of the *Global Gnostic Observer*, what it claimed were the facts.

The first articles were the most objective. A married couple had been murdered in a hotel in the country around Agrigento, a town on the south coast of Sicily. No names were given, and there were no other details, either about the Mafia or any other possible killers. All the cuttings said was that police inquiries were ongoing.

The second report was about the murdered couple's small child, who had obviously disappeared from his parents' room while the crime was being committed. There was no mention of any fire, but this time the name of the hotel was given. The Hotel Paradiso.

Several other reports gradually went into details of the mysterious case. According to them, the murderers had entered the room through the balcony. As there was no way of climbing up to it, the criminals must have scaled the three floors by some other means.

The next report had appeared only four weeks later. There was still, it said, no trace of the child. One of the investigators said the murderers had probably taken the little boy with them and simply abandoned him somewhere. The chances of finding him were few and far between. Exposed in the open, such a small child would be easy prey for wild animals.

The case became really interesting, however, in the articles published by the esoteric paper. It revealed the name of the dead man, in huge letters: Leonardo Mori, "the highly esteemed scientific writer and guest columnist of the *Global Gnostic Observer.*" Which in Rosa's opinion was no great tribute to his scientific reputation. And the photograph that Fundling had copied along with his own came from one of those articles.

There was no information about the dead woman, but this report mentioned for the first time that the couple had not been shot or stabbed; instead, it said they had been "dropped to the ground from a great height."

Alessandro ran his finger over the paper, as if that would bring a hidden truth to light. "What do they mean, 'from a great height'? Thrown off the balcony?"

"Well, not off the dresser."

Smiling, he gave her a kiss.

Rosa picked up the scrapbook, paged through, and came to the last article, which was also the longest and was once again taken from "the specialist international journal for the borderline sciences, occult phenomena, and pre–space age archaeology." It read like that, too.

This time the authors resorted to their own stock of theories. According to them, Leonardo Mori and his wife had not been killed by human beings at all. Credible witnesses—none of them named—said that on the night of the murder, two gigantic birds had come flying out of the darkness. They had smashed the windows of the hotel room with their vast weight, snatched the unfortunate couple from their beds, and carried them out into the open in their claws. They had not simply thrown Mori and his wife over the balcony but carried them a good hundred yards up in the air. Then the giant birds had let go of them both. The impact had inflicted fatal injuries; the article did not refrain from recounting the appalling details. Finally one of the creatures had flown back into the room, seized the little boy, and then carried him off.

Asked what the birds had looked like, one of the eyewitnesses replied, "They were owls. Owls the size of men."

Rosa looked at Alessandro.

"Saffira and Aliza Malandra were too young at the time," he said, "but their clan has been known for generations for taking on contract killings. Particularly if the goal was to create confusion and divert attention from the Mafia."

"Did they ever work for your father?"

"No idea. But if the boy who disappeared really was Fundling, then I can't think of any other reason why he finally ended up with us. The Harpies probably didn't know what to do with him. Most of the Malandras aren't what you might call masterminds; they just carry out orders. They'd have taken him with them to make sure they weren't getting anything wrong."

"And your mother saved him."

"From that point on, yes, the story rings true. Or that's the way she told it to Fundling and me."

"But why would your father have given the order to kill Mori? He must have found out something. Something that didn't sit well with the Carnevares."

"The truth about the dynasties?"

"It's a possibility."

"And what do the gaps in the crowd have to do with it?"

"Maybe nothing. Or maybe they do. Again, I've no idea. As long as we don't know what's behind it, all this is just assumptions." Rosa remembered something else. "And Salvatore Pantaleone once said something about gaps in the crowd. About them and about TABULA. It was just before his death." The former *capo dei capi* had mentioned both terms in the same breath, and now she wondered whether that had been more than just coincidence.

She continued flipping through the scrapbook, but there were no more articles. What it contained seemed to be all that Fundling had been able to find out about the case.

"He must have decided, at some point, to look for the hotel where my father's men allegedly rescued him." Alessandro turned to Rosa, still squatting on the ground, and ran both hands over her thighs. She put the scrapbook down and stroked his hair.

"This is getting crazier by the minute," she said softly. "As if what's happened to us wasn't crazy enough."

His dimples deepened. The green of his eyes was unfathomable. "The crazier everything around us gets, the more normal I feel. Mafia boss at eighteen? Shape-shifter? In love with obviously the craziest Rosa in the world? None of it compares to the craziness out in the world."

She kissed him on the forehead, the tip of his nose, and then pressed her lips to his. Their kiss was long and deep, while his fingers slowly wandered up her bare thighs, touched the hem of her dress, and were soon on her hips.

A police siren howled somewhere in the distance, far away in the darkness. It was not for them, but the sound roused their hostage in the trunk. There was loud banging, and they heard a muffled shout.

"Damnit," whispered Rosa. "I'd almost forgotten her."

"Down the coast we'll sell her to an Algerian gangster," said Alessandro, raising his voice and speaking in the direction of the trunk of the car. "Maybe he'll put her in his harem."

That prompted a muted tirade of curses and insults.

Rosa bent her head. "*Down* the coast? What about Iole and the others?"

"I don't think your people will occupy the island for long." He kissed her knees in turn. "They wanted to keep us from hiding there. The police will probably turn up there sometime, too. If no one finds us there, they'll all go away again. If we can think of a way to help Iole before they do, then we will. But for now the three of them will have to manage on their own."

Sometimes it was so easy for her to read his eyes—yet sometimes she wasn't sure what to make of him. "But you don't want to run away either. Or we'd have been on the way to Syracuse long ago, to pick up those tickets and the forged papers."

"That would just confirm what they expect of us. They think we're weak. They think we don't deserve to be the *capi* of our clans."

"You can't drop it, can you?"

"How about you?"

She sighed quietly. "Fundling saved our lives. I think we owe him this."

"You want to go to that hotel. To Agrigento. And then what?"

"He tried to find out more about his parents and their murder." Rosa lowered her eyes, moistened her lips with the tip of her tongue, and sought Alessandro's gaze again. "The least we can do is put his real name on his grave."

THE GIFT

In the gray light of dawn, they stopped not far from a village. It was less than thirty miles from here to Agrigento and the coast, but they wanted to stop for a break outside the city. They couldn't risk using one of the resting places on the 640 expressway; too many people, too many curious glances. So they had turned off the main road and driven a little way into the hills. Now the Volvo was standing on the outskirts of an olive grove, with both front doors open. A few yards away, lost in thought, Rosa was listening to the chirping of the cicadas. Lizards were waiting for sunrise on the pale rocks.

She knelt on the bank of a narrow stream winding its way down the slope between bushes, scooped up water in both hands, and did her best to wash herself. In films, that looked romantic; in real life it was merely uncomfortable, cold, and far removed from what she thought of as hygiene. She wasn't compulsive about washing, but a toothbrush and soap were starting to seem like unattainable luxuries.

Alessandro had gone into the village a few hundred yards downhill to buy some breakfast. With any luck, there would be a grocery store already open. All the money they had came from the wallet he had found in Festa's leather jacket, just under a hundred and fifty euros. They would have to get by on that for now.

She rubbed her teeth with her forefinger and clear water, gargled at length, and washed the sleepiness out of her eyes. At some point last night, when Alessandro had continued refusing to let her take the wheel, she had nodded off for a while.

Now she caught herself scanning the sky again and again for birds of prey. The gray clouds seemed to press down on her like heavy weights. The cry of any bird made her jump. The graphic accounts of the death of the Moris were troubling her more than she wanted to admit.

As she stood up she caught her tangled hair in some twigs. Finally she lost patience, tore herself free, and left a strand of blond hair behind on a bush. She was already on her way back to the car when she thought better of that, and went back to remove the loose hair from the branches.

The worst of it was that they couldn't be sure *who* was hunting them down. An image of dozens of big cats prowling the hills in search of them appeared in her mind. And the Panthera weren't the only Arcadians who bore them a grudge. There were only a few Lamias in Sicily, but Rosa had relations in the north, in Rome and Milan and Turin, and maybe they had set out for the island well before now. Then there were Harpies. And perhaps also Hundinga, the Hungry Man's canine mercenaries, who had set fire to the Palazzo Alcantara.

As she approached the car again she saw Alessandro emerging from the bushes a little way below. He was carrying a pale green plastic bag and had two bottles of water jammed under his left arm. She ran to meet him and reached him halfway, in the middle of the strip of tangled meadow just below the olive trees.

"Did anyone see you?" she asked.

"I shot everyone I met on the road."

"Glad to hear it."

"There was no one in the store but the woman at the cash register, and she was around a hundred years old, hard of hearing, and half-blind. Outside, a few workers drove past in a van, but they didn't pay any attention to me." He held the bag out to her. "Bread, cheese, and a few wilted lettuce leaves for the vegetarian among us. A knife, a daily paper—I haven't looked inside yet, but we're not on the front page."

"Toothpaste?"

"Who needs it?"

She crossed her arms over her breasts. "No more kissing from now on."

"Will gum do?"

"Not a chance."

He put the plastic bottles down, searched the bag, and brought out a tube of Colgate.

She hugged him. "My hero."

The toothbrush was followed by a hairbrush. "For girls," he said. "Pink, with glitter."

"How well you know me."

He went on searching. "Something for headaches. Band-Aids. More adhesive tape for our guest." Triumphantly he brought out something bulky. "And this."

She looked at the brown box. "Chocolates?"

"Take a look inside."

She took the flattish box. Heavier than she had expected. "A diamond ring?"

"Open it."

She opened the lid. The smell of chocolate met her nostrils. "Oh!"

"I'm sure it will suit you."

She grinned. "That is *so* romantic!"

"I'm afraid they didn't have one in pink."

A staple gun. Worked by compressed air. With a magazine for eighty steel staples.

"This is the most beautiful gift in the world," she said, taking it reverently and feeling the grip and the release trigger. Perfect for driving five or six staples into someone's skin at top speed.

He watched as she went up to the nearest tree, put the stapler against its trunk, and pressed the release three times. With a few steps, he was beside her, tenderly touching her hips. "That's the smile I've missed these last few days."

She turned her head and looked into his eyes. "Now the Natural Born Killers can tackle anything." She waved the stapler in the air. "No ordinary gun can compete with this!"

"But we're innocent," he said a little more thoughtfully. "The couple in the movie weren't."

She stroked his cheek. "We're not the good guys," she said gently, "and you know it."

He pointed to the stapler. "Anyway, they didn't have a ring, or I'd have bought that."

"Now I should give you something, too."

His glance held her far more strongly than his hands. "I just want to be with you for always. Whatever happens."

She put her outstretched hands on his shoulders, stood on

tiptoe, and kissed him. Suddenly he laughed. "Give me that thing." Only then did she notice that the stapler was against the nape of his neck.

"Don't you trust me?"

He drew her close again. He had already taken off his jacket, but he still smelled of leather. At this moment everything about him aroused her.

They fell to their knees together and lay side by side in the grass. Not far away the plastic bag rustled in a morning breeze. Little goat-bells rang down in the village. In the trunk of the Volvo, Stefania woke up and shouted for breakfast.

Rosa stripped off Alessandro's T-shirt, kissed his sunburnt skin, his ribs, the gentle curves of his muscles. He tasted salty; she liked that, too. She opened his jeans, pulled them down, and caressed his thighs.

Alessandro's hands felt for the zipper at the back of her dress. She slipped out of the black fabric and pressed close to him. His tenderness almost broke her heart, as if there was nothing to lose, nothing to fear. Only the two of them in the grass under this tree, in this nameless place.

She trembled as he pushed her panties down over her thighs. She couldn't help watching him, every one of his movements, every glance, every rise and fall of his rib cage. At that moment she wanted to keep him this close to her forever, just to hear him breathing. She placed her hand on his chest, felt his heart as if through a membrane. An unnatural clarity surrounded her whenever they were together, as if she could see him more keenly, smell him better, taste him more intensely than anything else she had ever experienced.

She wasn't a romantic; she had never thought much of visions of flowery meadows and sunrises. So it surprised and disturbed her to find herself feeling things that would once have made her turn up her nose. And that now, when she was in one of those visions herself, it felt entirely real and unforced.

Her own heart seemed to wander through her body under his hand; she was throbbing and pulsating all over. The snake in her went on dreaming. Rosa had learned how to manage it. No involuntary transformation. Everything under control.

Alessandro whispered something into her hair, and the sound of his voice was as firm as everything he did. Her lips followed the muscular sinews under his skin from shoulder to throat, sought his mouth, kissed him until she was almost breathless. Her tongue seemed to tingle and then to burn, but it was still her own tongue, not the snake's, and that aroused her more than ever. When she opened her eyes, their glances met, and they both had to laugh, but it deprived their passion of none of its intensity.

His hands moved over the curves of her small breasts, held her waist, moved lower again. She slowly rolled over on her back. Her fingers were in his hair, were holding his shoulders. Now he was above her, entirely human, and she responded wildly to his urging, wrapped her legs around him, and for a while she no longer felt pale and small and thin, but beautiful and strong, and so happy that she could have wept.

"What have you been doing all this time?" asked Stefania, as Rosa opened the trunk. The policewoman narrowed her eyes, dazzled by the sunlight. "I thought you'd gone off and left me behind."

Rosa felt a slight pang of conscience when she saw the policewoman lying in the fetal position. Her ankles were still handcuffed together, but she had freed her left hand, and only the right hand was in an iron loop. That didn't give her much more freedom, but at least she could scratch herself if she felt like it.

"You shouldn't have lied to us," said Rosa.

"I didn't. How was I to know they were bringing in a special unit? I wasn't there when they made that decision."

"Understaffed, you said. Not enough people, you said." Rosa held out two *tramezzini*, white-bread sandwiches from the village store. "Here," she said. "We don't hold a grudge. Well, not much."

"I do," Alessandro called back. He was sitting behind the wheel beside the open driver's door, looking at the maps he had found in the side pocket of his seat.

Stefania took the sandwiches and began eating. Rosa put a bottle of water in the trunk for her.

"You can't leave me in here all day," said Stefania, munching. "Do you have any idea how bloody hot it gets?"

Rosa had thought of that, but not, so far, of any solution. In the end they would probably have no option but to load her into the backseat again. Or let her go.

She leaned against the left-hand rear light of the Volvo and looked down at their captive. "What was she like? In private, I mean."

"Quattrini?"

Rosa nodded, brought out the judge's pendant from under her dress, and turned it between her fingers.

Stefania stopped eating for a moment when she saw the locket around Rosa's neck. "Have you looked inside it?"

"Not yet."

"She never told us whose picture she kept in there."

"She liked cats." Rosa remembered her first conversation with the judge in the Pantheon Hotel in Rome. "But she'd run over a good many of them hunting down Mafiosi. She told me so when we first talked."

"So you know everything that matters about her." Stefania unscrewed the bottle with her left hand, but didn't drink from it. "She'd have done anything to stop the illegal trading the clans were engaged in. She was beside herself with fury when your *capo dei capi* was released from prison and allowed to go back to Sicily."

The return of the Hungry Man was still very recent, but by now it was in the media. Only in brief reports, however, as if it wouldn't really interest anyone much. As long as the politicians who controlled television and many of the newspapers in Italy owed their careers to making deals with the Mafia, a lot of dirt would go on being swept under the carpet. The early release of the former "boss of the bosses" from prison was another setback to the judiciary, and a victory for corruption and nepotism. Rosa could understand why that had given Quattrini sleepless nights.

"Did she have children? A husband?"

"She was divorced, had been for years. No children. She lived only for her job. Three cheers for every cliché there is about cops." Stefania blinked again as she looked up at Rosa. "Don't you think this is odd—we're talking about her as if she were a friend we had in common? I mean, although you and I are on different sides."

"I'm not on the same side as the *capo dei capi*," Rosa contradicted her, shaking her head.

"But all the same, here I am, bound and gagged in the trunk of your car."

"Do you have a better idea?"

Alessandro spoke up again from in front. "One that doesn't include the words *let me go* or *give yourselves up*."

"You two are digging yourselves deeper and deeper."

"Yes, we noticed. But we've run out of alternatives."

"Then what are you doing in Agrigento?"

Rosa sighed. She leaned over the wing of the car in Alessandro's direction. "She was eavesdropping on us," she told him.

Stefania kicked the lining of the trunk. "This bloody thing isn't soundproofed. Can't help that, can I?"

The maps rustled, and then Alessandro got out of the front seat and came around to join them at the back of the car. "You'll never understand it," he told Stefania. "You'll never understand things like loyalty to friends and family—"

"Oh, do you mean the family that got you into this mess? That's doing all it can to make everyone think you two murdered Quattrini?" The policewoman uttered an icy laugh. "You can bet they'll know what to think of your loyalty, I'm sure of that."

"Want another sandwich?" Rosa asked.

Stefania shook her head. She and Alessandro engaged in a duel of staring each other down, but neither of them seemed willing to fight on to the end.

Finally, he turned away and glanced down the slope at the yellow-tiled roofs of the village. "I need new clothes. Not from here, though. Let's keep going, and maybe we'll find something on the way."

Rosa looked down at her own black dress, worn as mourning, although it was not so very different from what she usually wore. However, she was coming to feel like the leading lady in the old French film *The Bride Wore Black*. At the moment she'd rather be wearing jeans and a T-shirt. Okay, black jeans, and a black T-shirt.

Alessandro made for the driver's seat of the car. Rosa cast Stefania a last apologetic glance and was about to close the trunk over her when she noticed something.

The policewoman crawled a little way forward, but it was too late.

"Shit!" Rosa exclaimed.

"What is it?" asked Alessandro.

"She has a cell phone there."

"She has a *what*?" With a couple of swift steps he was back, looking down at Stefania in the trunk. He pushed her aside roughly, struck away the hand she was trying to raise in self-defense, and pulled the flat cell phone out from under her thigh. Cursing, he tapped the keys, but the display stayed dark.

"Dead," he said.

Rosa took the phone from his hand. "The question is, how long has it been dead?"

"Who were you calling?" he asked angrily.

"Santa Claus," replied Stefania.

Rosa got between them. "That's enough. Leave this to me."

"That stupid—"

"We'd have done the same in her place."

"So I suppose that makes it all right?" he said. "And she really means well by us?"

"No, she doesn't." Rosa bent down and picked up her stapler from the grass where she had left it when she handed Stefania her breakfast.

The young policewoman looked at her grimly, but now there was a touch of uncertainty in her expression.

Rosa pressed the stapler to her calf. When Stefania tried to push it away with her free hand, Rosa took her forearm and held it tightly. "You were making calls, right? When did the battery run out? How long have they been able to locate us?"

Stefania tightened her lips.

Rosa pressed the release. The steel staple snapped shut on the policewoman's jeans, just missing the skin and stapling the leg of the jeans to the carpeting in the trunk. "The next one will go into you."

Alessandro shot her a glance of mingled surprise and concern. But she wasn't going to lose her nerve, no matter what.

"You were right," she told Stefania. "We won't shoot you. But I promise I'll staple each of your fingers to the trunk floor separately—then we'll be able to do without the handcuffs.

Unless I get an answer. Right now."

"Are you really surprised that the clans want to get rid of you two?" asked Stefania. "You want to be *capi*? Then don't act like kids who don't want to go to bed. You don't have a chance! You'll never get away from this island, and there's no place to hide here where someone or other won't find you. If not my people, then yours. Which would you rather?"

Rosa's finger curled slowly around the stapler. "What did you tell them? And how long was the phone switched on?"

The policewoman snorted softly. "Kiss my ass."

The staple shot into Stefania's thigh.

She suppressed a cry of pain, but uttered a curse between her teeth.

"How long?" asked Rosa again.

Alessandro was running both hands through his hair. "Wait," he said.

"Why give it to me if you don't want me to use it?"

"Leave this to me."

"What's your problem?" she asked him angrily. "Exactly what do you think you could do better?"

She wasn't really angry with him. She wasn't even angry with Stefania. She just felt so helpless in the face of circumstances over which she had hardly any control.

He turned to their captive. "You spoke to Festa, didn't you? You told him we were on our way to Agrigento. Am I right?"

Stefania closed her eyes, took a deep breath, and then nodded in silence.

Rosa lowered the stapler. Suddenly she felt exhausted.

Cold sweat was running down her throat into the neckline of her dress.

"All he'll know is the name of the city," Alessandro told her quietly. "There are probably a hundred hotels in Agrigento. Any number of tourists visit it every year to see the excavations. Festa has no idea where we're going. We didn't once mention the hotel by name."

Rosa managed a faint nod. The stapler seemed to weigh twenty pounds when she picked it up and grabbed it out of the trunk.

She went to the passenger door, threw the stapler on her seat, and took the small, sharp knife that Alessandro had bought for the bread and cheese out of the bag. With the knife in her hand, she went over to Stefania again.

The policewoman's eyes widened.

Alessandro tensed.

Rosa bent over Stefania's legs and pushed the point of the knife under the staple. With a slight jerk, she levered it out of Stefania's flesh and her jeans.

Then she took a step back, looked Stefania in the eye once more, and closed the trunk over her.

THE HOTEL PARADISO

THE VOLVO ROLLED SLOWLY up a steep road, too narrow for two cars side by side. From time to time they passed places where one vehicle could pull into a bay to avoid oncoming traffic, but they were alone on the road with no one coming in the opposite direction.

"Everything okay?" asked Alessandro. He hadn't taken his eyes off her since they'd started out.

Rosa steered the car around the last bends in the road. She had taken the wheel without a word when they left. Her face must have spoken volumes.

"Everything's fine," she said.

"You seem kind of relaxed."

When was that damn hotel finally going to appear? They must be nearly there. The GPS hadn't said anything for several minutes, probably intimidated by Rosa's mood.

"You did exactly the right thing," he said.

"Yes, sure."

"You're beating yourself up."

"I'm wearing Quattrini's locket around my neck while I cart her bodyguard through Sicily in the trunk of a car, driving a staple into her leg now and then." She raised both hands in pretended innocence. "Why would I have a guilty conscience?"

"The wheel."

"What?"

"Your hands. The wheel."

"Oh." She grasped what he was saying and grabbed the wheel just before the car could overshoot the next bend in the road.

When they had rounded it the hotel lay ahead, a few hundred yards below the top of the hill. Dusty winds and the salt air had weathered the facade, which was as gray as the wood of the shutters at the windows. The sun burned down from a blue sky, but the closed shutters made it look as if the building had something to hide. People didn't take their families to places like this on vacation.

The house might once have belonged to a large land-owner, not a magnificent villa, but attractive enough to impress the local farm workers. There were annexes to the left and right, with smaller windows and tiny balconies. The Harpies must have come down on one of the upper balconies there when they snatched Leonardo Mori and his wife. There were brown tiles on the roofs, and one of the chimneys had half collapsed.

Near the driveway up to the hotel there was a swimming pool now filled to the brim with rotting leaves and twigs, and old car tires. "Welcome to our oasis of well-being," commented Alessandro.

Rosa parked in the shade of a chestnut tree not far from the entrance. They had folded down half of the backseat before they left to create an airway to the trunk. Air-conditioning from the front of the car made Stefania's situation more bearable; with the engine switched off, she wouldn't have lasted long in this heat.

"This won't take long," said Rosa over her shoulder, but the only response was silence. Stefania was still attached to an iron ring in the trunk by one handcuff; she wasn't going to run away from them.

They got out of the car, went along the path to the front door, and looked around once more. The front courtyard of the hotel ended in a cliff, beyond which the slope of the mountains dropped steeply away. A good six miles farther off, they saw the ugly tower blocks of Agrigento rise on the other side of the hotel. The famous excavations in the Valley of the Temples could not be seen from here, but there was a good view of the Mediterranean, its turquoise waters reaching to the horizon.

Together, they went through a glass door into a foyer with furniture from the 1960s. There was also a stale cooking smell. An elderly man with a few long strands of hair combed sideways over his bald patch rose from behind the reception desk. His smile was not unfriendly.

"Good day," he greeted them. "Signorina, Signore, welcome to the Hotel Paradiso. How can I help you?"

"You have a beautiful view here," said Rosa, nodding over her shoulder at the entrance.

He was visibly pleased. "Thank you, Signorina. We're very proud of our view. The Paradiso has an eventful history, but our location has always been a great asset, allowing us to make the most of what we can offer." His old-fashioned phrasing sounded a little stiff, but it suited him. "I could give you a pretty room with a view of the sea. If you book for several nights, there will be a free bottle of our house wine thrown in."

Alessandro placed one hand on the reception desk. "We really just wanted to ask you for some information."

The old man's smile did not disappear, but it lost a little of its warmth. "If you want the best route to the expressway, then you must go on along the—"

"No, but thank you," Rosa interrupted, handing the photocopied picture of Fundling and Leonardo Mori over the reception desk. "We're searching for a friend. Could you take a look at the men in this picture and tell us if he has ever been here?"

Alessandro put a twenty-euro bill from Festa's wallet on the desk beside the photo.

The man was still gazing at them, his eyes moving from Alessandro to Rosa. Only then did he glance at the money, and finally at the photograph. "Hmm," he said.

There was a faint clattering sound in the distance. A tractor? There was a cool, tingling sensation in Rosa's fingertips.

The old man placed a hand stained with age spots on the bill, and without a word put it away under the desk. "Signor Mori," he said when he looked up at them again.

Rosa shook her head and placed her forefinger on the side of the photocopy showing Fundling. "This is the man we mean. The younger of the two."

"Signor Mori," he repeated.

Alessandro and Rosa exchanged a fleeting glance.

"To make ourselves perfectly clear—"

The old man interrupted Rosa with a swift gesture that seemed to come from nowhere. On the desk the muscles of Alessandro's arm tensed visibly. "That will have to be enough," the man whispered.

Alessandro took a second twenty from his pocket. Rosa was almost sure that it was the last of their money.

The reception clerk pushed it away, shaking his head. "It's not as simple as that."

"What's so difficult about it?" Alessandro did not bother to conceal his impatience. He was only here to do Rosa a favor, and she knew it.

"Not because of that," said the man, bending his head and tapping the bill. "I'll be in trouble if I say any more."

Rosa picked up the photocopy and held it in front of his nose. "We're not looking for Leonardo Mori, we're looking for the young man in the picture. Was he ever here or not?"

"You *are* looking for Signor Mori," he said, deliberately slowly. "At least, he registered here under that name. I don't remember the man in sunglasses, but if you say his name is Leonardo Mori, very well. Is the young Signor Mori related to the older one?"

Rosa lowered the photocopy. "He spent the night here?"

"Did he ask for any particular room?" asked Alessandro.

The reception clerk let out his breath noisily. Rosa saw that the long hairs in his nostrils showed for a moment. He bent forward, nimbly appropriated the second twenty-euro bill, and put it away. "He asked for a room on the third floor."

"The one where Leonardo Mori had been attacked?"

The old man shook his head. "No. There were two things he wanted: a view of the courtyard, and a room as close to the elevator as possible. We never talked about the other Mori, the older man."

"Why close to the elevator?"

"Well, because of his wheelchair, I assume."

Rosa's jaw dropped.

The man looked at her thoughtfully. "Are you two from the media as well? I'm sure I've seen your faces somewhere. On TV, maybe? You seemed familiar as soon as I saw you come through the door."

Alessandro's nod was too fast, but the reception clerk didn't seem to notice.

"Do you have an appointment with him?" asked the old man. "There's been a lot of coming and going."

Rosa nudged Alessandro's foot with hers. "When was he here? How long ago?"

"I can call him for you."

Alessandro leaned forward and placed his hand on the telephone behind the counter. "That won't be necessary."

There's something odd going on here, thought Rosa. Suddenly she wanted to pinch herself and wake up in the seat of the Volvo, still on the way to Agrigento.

The old man took an alarmed step back. "Please leave now. Signor Mori can call you himself if he wants to speak to you."

Rosa was breathing in warm air, but what she breathed out was icy. As if her insides were turning into a deep freeze. She had to pull herself together, had to get herself back under control.

"He's *here*?" she hissed. "Now, at this moment?"

The engine she had heard before was louder now. Outside, car doors slammed.

Alessandro went to the entrance and looked at the front yard. "We've got to get out of here."

Rosa stared at him, then at the door, then at him again. "How can Fundling be here? We saw his corpse." If she had had time to think about it, she could probably have answered that question herself. But she was forced to fight so hard against the emergence of the snake from within her that she didn't fully understand, not until Alessandro was beside her again, taking her hand.

"Back exit?" he shouted at the alarmed old man.

The reception clerk pointed to a door behind his desk. "Down that corridor."

"Come on." Alessandro was going to pull Rosa along, but she had already caught up with him, ran to the desk, and pushed the door behind it open. Beyond it lay an office from which a second door led into a long corridor.

"They took us for a ride," she managed to say, her throat dry. "All this time. Beginning with Quattrini." If Fundling was really in this hotel, only three floors above them and alive, then who or what had they buried in the graveyard? Only a casket full of bricks again, as in her father's case?

Alessandro reached the rear entrance for the staff a couple of seconds before her. He was going to push it open when they heard hushed voices on the other side. "They're waiting for us out there," he whispered. "They'll have surrounded the whole damn hotel."

She shook her head. "Then they'd have gotten here before

us, and they'd have caught us as we left the car."

She went past him, took a deep breath, and pushed the heavy metal handle down.

There were indeed men outside it. They both wore white chefs' uniforms, and they were smoking. They looked at Alessandro and Rosa in surprise.

"Only for the staff," one of them began. He was as dark skinned as his colleague. Probably North Africans.

"Come on," Rosa called to Alessandro, and then they ran past the startled hotel cooks and out into the open air. There was a broad strip of coarse grass behind the building, verging on wild undergrowth. Beyond that, the slope rose again, thickly overgrown with *macchia*.

"Fundling and Quattrini must have hatched this plot together." As they ran over the rough meadow, she pushed out the words breathlessly. "We thought we were standing in front of him in that damn morgue, and he was alive the whole time!"

Alessandro didn't reply, but kept looking right and left over his shoulder, back at the hotel. Any moment now police officers might appear around the corners of the annexes.

"But I don't understand," she gasped hoarsely. "Why would he get involved with something like that? And what did *she* get out of it?"

"Witness protection. He'd already worked for her as an informer. Maybe he wanted to disappear and begin again somewhere else."

She let out an incredulous laugh. "What, *here*?"

Now there was shouting. When Rosa glanced back, she saw Antonio Festa at the open rear doorway and several police officers storming out into the open air with him. The two North Africans had dropped their cigarettes and looked as if they wanted to disappear into the wall so that no one could ask about their work permits.

"Stop where you are!" roared Festa.

"He wants his jacket back," said Rosa.

"Then maybe he won't shoot any holes in it."

Another three yards to the bushes.

A shot shattered the silence over the mountain slope.

"Stop!"

They reached the undergrowth and flung themselves into it. Twigs scratched Rosa's skin, and something sharp just missed her eye. She felt as if she had landed in barbed wire. She struggled another step forward, plunged into the bushes, and in her snake form slid out of her black dress. The fabric was left hanging in the branches behind her. Briefly, she turned back once more, took Quattrini's pendant in her reptilian mouth, and threw it to land on the dress, so that it wouldn't be lost. Festa would find it and take care of it. Then she looked around for Alessandro.

In panther form, he easily broke through the dense branches of the bushes. The men could not have seen the two of them shifting shape; they were too far away. But it would not escape their notice that something large and black was moving through the undergrowth.

The next moment, however, Alessandro's instincts were

those of a panther. He slunk over the ground, ducking low and skillfully using the smallest gaps in the bushes. Rosa stayed beside him while they made their way as fast as they could up the slope.

Once again shots rang out, but this time they were no longer just a warning. Festa and the others were hunting down the supposed murderers of a judge, the abductors of a policewoman. They would have no qualms shooting with live ammunition.

The rampant shrubs and bushes covered a large area of the slope. They offered protection to Alessandro and Rosa, and kept their pursuers from following them. Rosa would have liked to glance back at Festa, but she didn't dare. She would have had to stop and put her snake's head through the branches. It was too much of a risk.

So they fled on up the mountain, toward the wild and uninhabited hinterland of Agrigento.

THE LAW OF SILENCE

THE POLICE SEARCHED THE slope for them for hours, backed up by a helicopter circling above the mountain and the surrounding valleys. Early in the evening the chopper was taken out of operation. A little later the uniformed officers also returned to the hotel, with scratched hands and faces, and in a bad enough mood to keep them from continuing the search for the time being.

As long as Rosa and Alessandro were still in animal form, they had the advantage over the police. Their pursuers had been looking for two teenagers, not animals. It was possible that Stefania, once liberated from the car, had thought it more sensible not to talk about the unusual qualities of her abductors. And Festa and the others would have chalked it up to the heat in the trunk anyway.

North of Agrigento lay the large nature reserve of Macalube di Aragona, sparsely inhabited and crisscrossed by only a few paths. The police would likely assume that the couple would want to reach one of the nearby major roads as quickly as possible; the 118 and 189 probably had checkpoints set up on them already. It might have surprised the officers to know that, instead, Rosa and Alessandro were still on the mountain above the Hotel Paradiso.

Rosa, in snake form, lay coiled on a flat stone, well camouflaged by the sunbaked surroundings. From here she had a good view of the hotel several hundred yards farther down the slope. With the vision of a snake, she had less depth of focus, something she'd had to adjust to. In human form she would have seen more detail around the building, more of the comings and goings that went on until late in the afternoon. Only then did the activity begin to slow. The police officers assigned to keep the hotel under surveillance stayed in their cars, one or another of them walking around the hotel now and then.

Alessandro had not yet shifted back, either. She enjoyed his agility of movement as a big cat, the play of muscles under his gleaming fur. Even metamorphosis couldn't banish the mocking sparkle in his cat's eyes. If Rosa looked at him long enough with her amber gaze, she noticed a faint quivering of his sensitive whiskers, as if he saw something in her that touched him deeply. The longer she knew him, the less important it seemed whether he faced her in human or animal form. She loved the majestic panther as much as the boy with the dimpled smile.

When twilight finally began to close in, Rosa decided to shift back. She wound her way down to the ground where the bushes would shield her from anyone looking up from the hotel. She returned to human form, lay first on her side, then had a good stretch, and finally leaned her bare back up against the rock. She drew up her knees, clasped her arms around them, and watched Alessandro's own metamorphosis begin. In his human shape, unlike her, he still had all the cuts and scratches he had suffered as he escaped through the bushes.

"Let me see," she said, finding a wound on his hip. He was about to lick the injury, just as he would have done in animal form, but then the reflex went away, along with the remnants of his big-cat existence. Rosa leaned forward and looked at the cut in his skin. It was not deep. The wound that had opened up to show fresh blood when he shifted back would soon close again.

"It's okay," he said, sitting down beside her and putting an arm around her shoulders. She nestled close to him, and felt him trembling slightly again.

It was cooler now in the evening, and they had had to leave their clothes behind in the undergrowth lower down. Soon their only option would be to shift shape again, so that they could bear the cold better.

"Do you think he's really down there?" she asked. "Somewhere in the hotel?" There were lights in only a few of the windows, behind closed shutters. If the man at the reception desk was correct, Fundling's room was at the front of the building, with a view of the courtyard, and invisible from where they were now.

"I'm beginning to think that just about anything is possible."

"Yes, the way the police arrived so quickly would prove that." Rosa had had hours to think about it all. "That scene at the morgue, the stitching in his chest, a dead Fundling who wasn't really dead at all, the whole farce . . . Quattrini *must* have known about it. It could well have been her own idea." The memory of the judge aroused mixed feelings in her: grief, and a reproach that she couldn't quite express in words yet. "If we were really to believe that he was dead, then she had to show us his body. He played dead; maybe they anesthetized him for a little while. But anyway, he wanted us to think he was dead. And then he went on with his research here at the hotel where his parents had been murdered. Quattrini would hardly have sent him to stay here of her own accord, so it must have been what he wanted. And of course Festa and Stefania knew about it as well, and in fact they probably helped to get the whole thing under way. So when Stefania was in the trunk of the car and overheard us planning to go to a hotel in Agrigento, she knew which it would be. We didn't have to mention the name out loud. She called Festa, and he knew at once where to find us. Our one stroke of luck was that he arrived a little later than we did. Otherwise we'd have run straight into his arms."

Alessandro nodded. "Do you think Fundling was afraid of me?"

"Because he worked for Quattrini?"

"He broke the law of silence. All the clans would have killed him for that. He must have come out of his coma, walked away, and—"

"No," she interrupted him. "No one just gets out of bed after five months in a coma and walks away, even if he's in shock. The old man mentioned a wheelchair. So Fundling still can't walk by himself, he's probably very weak. Other people in his situation would spend a year in rehab. I guess Quattrini had him under observation the whole time, probably by an informant in the hospital. And when there were signs that he was coming out of his coma, they got him out of the place in secret, and then made it look as if he'd run away of his own accord and fallen into that crevice."

"Which never really happened."

"They made it all up to cover his tracks. And laying him to rest in your family vault was supposed to underscore the whole story. Everyone would have thought he was dead, even you."

He nodded, downcast. Fundling's distrust had hit him harder than she would have thought possible.

"Hey," she said quietly, sitting up. "Who knows what was going on in his head? He'd suffered a bad gunshot wound; he just lay there for almost six months. We don't even know if he was conscious but just couldn't communicate. Anyway, there was plenty of time for him to persuade himself of all kinds of possibilities." When she herself lay awake at night, everything that went through her mind seemed perfectly logical. Only in the light of day did it turn out to be exaggerated and nonsensical. Had Fundling been doing something like that for *five whole months*?

"Right," said Alessandro. "Well, everything suggests that the old man in the hotel was telling the truth. Because otherwise Festa wouldn't have found us. So Fundling must be down there."

She looked down the slope to the hotel. Its shape was gradually blending into the darkness, and the air was becoming cooler and cooler. Rosa had goose bumps for some time. "We can't go and talk to him. That's exactly what they're waiting for."

He slowly shook his head. "Why would we, anyway? He obviously doesn't want to see us."

"All the same, there's one thing I'd very much like to know."

"Mori," said Alessandro. "That's really bothering you."

She leaned forward, hugging her legs close to her upper body. "Why did your father give orders to have Mori and his wife killed?"

"Mori must have found out something. Something that my father wanted to keep secret at any price."

"He and Cesare had already done something like that once. When he almost exterminated the Dallamano family."

Divers working in the Strait of Messina for the Dallamano clan had discovered several statues dating back to classical antiquity, including one of a panther and a snake. At which point Baron Carnevare and his cousin Cesare, as his adviser, had the Dallamanos murdered. Only Augusto Dallamano had escaped them. Quattrini had enrolled him in her witness protection program, and secretly got him to Sintra in Portugal after his evidence in court had done a great deal of damage to several other clans. The Carnevares themselves, however, had escaped any prosecution because the baron had taken Augusto's niece, Iole, and was keeping her imprisoned as a hostage.

If it were now to turn out that Leonardo Mori had been murdered by contract killers working for the Carnevares, it was safe to assume that there had been reasons like those behind the massacre of the Dallamanos. Had Mori come upon information about the Arcadian dynasties in the course of his research?

Rosa shifted position on the uncomfortable, rocky ground. "That book he wrote, *The Gaps in the Crowd* . . . could it have been about the dynasties?"

Alessandro looked at her. "I know what you're planning."

"We don't have any clothes, any money, or any car. It's making me crazy that we can't help Iole. I can't even call her. But while we're stuck here in Sicily we might as well try to find out the truth. It's all connected somehow. From Mori and the gaps in the crowd, to the dynasties and the statues in the sea, all the way to Evangelos Thanassis and TABULA."

"And TABULA and your father," he added, coming to the point that troubled her most.

She lowered her gaze. "If my father really is still alive, then I have to find him."

"I thought I was the one who went in for revenge."

She looked at him sadly.

"Sorry," he said, "that was stupid of me."

"No, you're right. I have no idea what I'd do if I met him. Maybe it would be enough just to ask him *why*."

"That's not enough. Because the answer would only hurt you even more. In the end, when all's said and done, you'll wish him dead. And he deserves it."

"Just once I want to look him in the eyes."

"And then you'll kill him."

She was trembling with the cold now. Everything he said was the truth. She wanted to see her father suffer for what he had done to her. And it was possible that that might make a difference, but much more likely that everything would stay the way it had always been. She would still be the same, and so would the world around her.

But it would be without him. Without Davide Alcantara. Something that made taking the next step worthwhile.

"We need new clothes," she said, "and a car."

"To go to that antiquarian bookshop in Ragusa?"

"Only for a look at the book. Unless Fundling gets there first."

He glanced away from her and back at the hotel, a cluster of pale lights in the darkness.

Above them there was a screech, then a flapping of wings quickly coming closer.

She raised her head. Something was diving down on them out of the night.

"Harpies!"

Rosa shifted to her snake form.

THE SISTERS

Huge claws seized Rosa's reptilian body and snatched her from the ground. Out of the corner of her eye, she was able to see a second giant owl plunge out of the night sky and come down on Alessandro. He had shifted into animal shape only a moment after Rosa, but the Harpy caught him still in human form, dragged him up by his shoulders, and let go of him again when he changed into his panther shape. Rosa was flung around, and lost sight of him. At the same time she realized that she was already thirty or forty feet above the ground, and the owl was carrying her higher and higher.

Vertigo and the darkness robbed her of any sense of direction. She writhed in her adversary's grasp, trying to concentrate entirely on those monstrous claws. They were the only fixed point in her wild flight through the night. Rosa let her reptilian skull hang down, swung herself back and up into the belly of the giant owl, where she dug her fangs deep into the creature's plumage.

The Harpy uttered a fearful screech and staggered in the air, her wings beating out of time with each other. Rosa lost her sense of direction again when the owl dropped a little ways, so suddenly that Rosa hissed in panic, and as she did so tore her fangs out of her opponent's body.

A split second later, she realized that it would kill her if the Harpy let go of her—or if she made the Harpy fall to the ground. As long as they were so high in the air, Rosa was dependent on the Harpy. It was a fallacy that because snakes were so supple, they had no bones; a crash landing from this height would smash her skeleton, just like any other living creature.

Worse than her disorientation was her uncertainty about what had happened to Alessandro. Had the first Harpy carried her away so that the second could attack and kill him? Were more Malandras diving down on him at this moment?

She writhed in the grip of the owl's claws. But her attack was too aimless, and a beak the size of an ax pecked at her. To do that, the Harpy had to bend forward, and it somersaulted in the air, making Rosa lose her sense of balance again.

She gave up for the time being, and let her body dangle with the wind shaking her head and her tail, while the Harpy stabilized her flight and carried her through the night. Rosa could see the ground beneath her now; she guessed at the shape of the trees and bushes, branching gray on a gray background, that might be waiting thirty or fifty yards below.

She bent her head far enough around to be able to see the group of lights that was Agrigento behind her in the distance, and the surface of the Mediterranean Sea shimmering in the moonlight. The owl was flying inland, farther into the deserted hills. Ahead of them lay nothing but darkness.

Soon they started losing height again as they approached a bare rise in the ground with something on it that Rosa thought, at first, was a house. Angular, unlit—but too small for a building.

A transport van. The vehicle was parked in the dry grass at the end of a narrow path. It looked like an armored van, no windows, dark paintwork, and it was not too dark to work out why the tailgate was wide open.

The owl flew a quarter of the way around the hill, and began a swift descent, making for the back of the van and the square, black opening in it. Rosa thought briefly of shifting shape, but decided it was not a good idea. Broken arms and legs were the last things she needed at this moment.

The owl let out a warning screech, raced at wild speed for the tailgate, let Rosa swing back in the air for a moment—and let go of her.

The movement sent her straight into the open steel van. Once again she lost all sense of up and down, only thinking that the impact would hurt like hell—and at that very moment she crashed against the van's interior.

Fuzziness sucked her down into endless darkness, as if in a whirlpool. It was so tempting simply to give up. However, she fought against the pain and the risk of falling unconscious, and she succeeded in coiling her body and then shooting forward again to the opening at the back of the van.

The Harpy landed in front of the opening from above, wings spread wide. Rosa thought she wanted to bar the way out with her wings, but then she realized that the wingtips were curling around the open steel doors, and suddenly jerked them shut.

Rosa was still moving as she changed shape; her coiling became stumbling, and then her shoulder hit the right side door. It hurt a lot, but she had rammed that door out again; the left door was firmly in place, but there was a small gap open on the right. She pressed herself against it from the inside, while the Harpy's wings blocked the gap from the outside. They both pushed and shoved; sometimes the gap was only a finger's breadth, then it was wide enough to get a leg through it. As a snake, Rosa could have passed through to the outside, but that would have meant taking pressure off the inside of the door, and she would inevitably have been caught and squashed.

The gigantic owl raged and hissed, her beak pecking at Rosa through the opening to drive her back. But Rosa was not giving way and increased her pressure on the door when her bare feet got a better grip on the floor of the van. There was a burning pain in her shoulder now, going all the way down to her legs, and she sensed the approach of the moment when she simply could do no more and would have to give in.

An earsplitting cry came from outside the van. The next moment there was no resistance anymore. Rosa let out a groan of surprise as the right rear door gave way and swung open. The owl had retreated slightly but was not climbing in the air. Instead, it was staring at a point on the crest of the hill. Rosa tried to keep her footing, but she slipped and fell to the earth. She landed on stones and grass, and tried shifting into snake form, but she was too weak. Everything about her hurt, so she merely struggled to get to her feet. She braced herself against the closed left door as she stood up, and followed the direction of the Harpy's gaze.

Alessandro shot out of the dark. In his panther's jaws, he was carrying something that swung back and forth with every leap he took. Something pale. Oval. With a shock of blond hair.

The Harpy cried out again as the big cat spat the bundle out on the floor. Wide eyes looked up from it. The mouth was half-open. Blood shone on freckled cheeks.

Rosa felt hypnotized by the sight of the dead Malandra sister. At the same time, she pressed herself closer to the steel door of the van. The Harpy spread her wings to fly and was about to rise from the ground, but Alessandro moved too fast for her. He covered the last few yards with one mighty leap, and they collided.

Quick as a flash, he rammed into the owl's feathered breast, flung her back, and landed on her. She pecked, but her beak met only empty air. Roaring, he opened his mouth and dug his teeth into brown feathers. His jaws closed around the Harpy's neck, while hysterical screeching emerged from her throat, followed by a strained hiss.

Rosa ran to him. "No!" she cried.

Alessandro growled, so much a predator that she shuddered. But then she placed a hand on his silky fur, felt that it was drenched with blood, and said, "You've beaten them. You don't have to do this."

The Harpy shifted shape under him. Her wings folded down beside her body and merged with a delicate figure. The mighty bird turned into a feathered girl, perhaps a young woman, it was hard to tell her age just yet. Then the feathers disappeared back under her skin, and the beak dissolved into a mouth. She was the image of her dead companion, also freckled, with a pointed chin and a straight nose. Rosa had expected to see fear in her face, but instead it was full of hatred. Alessandro had killed her sister. One glance was enough to know that she would not beg for her life.

The panther's jaws slowly withdrew from her neck, but only slightly, so that they could snap shut like lightning again and tear her apart.

Rosa's bare skin was gleaming with sweat, and her knees threatened to give way. But she couldn't help looking at that angry face and trying to find answers. Who had sent her? Why had they been wanted alive, instead of being killed at once, like Quattrini?

Their prisoner was only a few years older than Rosa herself, at the most in her early twenties. Strands of blond hair clung to her head and face.

"What's your name?" asked Rosa.

For an answer she got a grimace. The young woman was not yet entirely aware that she had changed back, and part of her still thought she was an owl.

Alessandro growled ferociously.

"Your name," Rosa demanded.

"Aliza Malandra."

"Who gave you this contract?"

Feathers began to cover Aliza's face. Immediately the

panther's jaws shot forward to encircle her slender neck. The feathers retreated again.

Rosa had an idea. Staggering slightly, she went to the front of the van, opened the passenger door, and looked on the floor in front of the seat. An open duffel bag lay there, with crumpled clothing spilling out of it. Rosa tugged at the catch on the glove compartment, which seemed to be jammed. She hit the front of the compartment hard with her fist, and it promptly sprang open. Inside, she found what she was looking for: a silver hypodermic needle in a short syringe. A glass vial containing a clear fluid was screwed behind it.

Anyone trying to catch and abduct Arcadians needed something to keep them from shifting shape at an untimely moment. It was not surprising that the Malandras had some of the TABULA serum with them.

She came back with the needle and syringe, and gave Aliza a double dose of serum. Only when her body was no longer changing did Alessandro stop baring his teeth.

"Who gave you the contract?" Rosa asked again.

"Go fuck yourself."

"Alcantaras? Or Carnevares?"

A scornful silence.

Rosa crouched down beside Aliza. "When we lock you in this van and take off, we can take your sister's head with us— or we can leave it lying out here for stray dogs and wild cats. Which would you prefer?"

Aliza bit her lower lip. There had been blood on her mouth before, perhaps her own, perhaps Alessandro's. But Rosa could see no new injuries through his black fur.

She bent over their captive. "Who was it?"

"Your own clan," whispered Aliza, blinking tears out of her eyes. "And his."

"But you were told not to kill us?"

"You deserve to die for what you've done to Saffira."

"What was your contract?" Rosa pointed to the van. "Where were you to take us?"

Aliza closed her eyes. "The dynasties are hunting you," she said quietly. "In the end there'll be nowhere left for you two to hide. *He* will come back, and Arcadia will awaken."

BREAKING WAVES

THEY FOUND NOT ONLY the sisters' clothes in the duffel on the passenger seat of the van, but also their cell phones and their cash, just under four hundred euros. Rosa was a bit shocked to realize how quickly she had grown accustomed to the wealth of the Alcantaras over the last few months, life in villas and every imaginable luxury. Now that all of that had been taken away from her in a single stroke, this money regained the value it would once have had for her, back in her drafty apartment in Crown Heights. Four hundred euros felt like a small fortune.

She held the bills fanned out in her hands and stared at them thoughtfully, until Alessandro reminded her that they could get by with that sum for a while but that they could not buy the book in Ragusa, nor could they turn the clock back a couple of days. If they ever reached Ragusa they'd have to think of something.

She took the Malandras' clothes out of the bag, expecting them to stink like birds' nests. Instead, they smelled of perfume and were as black as her own things. She slipped into a pair of slim pants, cuffing their long legs, and a fitted blouse. Then she pushed a black dress back to Aliza through the viewing panel to the rear of the van. A small plastic bag of pills right at the bottom of the duffel reminded her, fleetingly, of

Valerie and the Suicide Queens. She opened the front passenger door of the van and threw the little bag out.

Alessandro had had to get into the driver's seat naked. Rosa handed him a T-shirt from the duffel so that he could wipe away the rest of the bloodstains with it. "Maybe I ought to drive," she said. "Someone might get suspicious, seeing a naked man at the wheel."

"The windows are tinted glass. No one will notice."

"Well, *I* get interested when I see you." Not just because she liked his body, but because the smell of blood seemed to intensify his powers of attraction. She, too, was finding it difficult to suppress her animal nature. After each metamorphosis, a little more of it seemed to stay with her.

Was that how the first hybrids had come into being? Not the mongrel creatures bred by TABULA in its laboratory, but those Arcadians who one day, for no apparent reason, had been caught in transition from one body to the other, and kept features of both species? Ever since Alessandro had first told her about the hybrids, Rosa kept thinking about them. Heaven knew there were plenty of other things that she ought to have had on her mind. But the idea of ending up as a freak, half human, half snake, troubled her more than she liked to admit.

When she looked around the cab of the van, she found a blanket behind the driver's seat. She dragged it out and offered it to Alessandro. With a sigh, he draped it around his hips. "Happy now?"

She nodded, grinning, and investigated the glove compartment again. There was nothing to provide any information about whoever had hired the Malandras. Basically, it didn't matter which member of her family had given them up. Her second cousins, the female directors of the Alcantara bank? One of the business managers of her Milan companies, women whose names she could never remember? Or had they all ganged up to forge a new concordat with the Carnevares?

Shrugging her shoulders, she closed the glove compartment. "Eight vials left."

"That'll be enough," he said.

"What are you planning to do?"

"I'm making sure that she tells us everything."

Rosa didn't care for his tone of voice. Once again, she heard too much of his other side in it, the ruthlessness of a Sicilian *capo*. There were times when she liked the hint of danger in him, the subliminal threat to everything and everyone. Today, however, that note in his voice made her feel queasy.

"How are you going to do it?" she asked.

"Leave that to me."

"How, Alessandro?"

He started the engine.

The fastest way to Ragusa was down the 115, along the coast, but there might be roadblocks there. So instead they drove through the night into the interior along winding mountain roads—endless hairpin turns on bleak, rocky slopes, interspersed now and then with small vineyards. Glowing eyes observed them from bushes and roadside ditches.

Not until daybreak did they turn toward the south coast

again. When the red light of dawn rose over the Mediterranean, the van was parked on a deserted sandy beach close to a village called Scoglitti. A little farther east, on the other side of a sandy promontory, stood a lighthouse beaming the last of the night's signals out to sea.

Rosa was sitting alone in the front of the van, adjusting the volume of the radio to loud and then soft again in turn, and wondering over and over again what they were doing here. What *she* was doing here.

She heard muted voices from the back of the van. Alessandro was asking questions; Aliza was cursing or screaming.

Rosa bit her nails, and she hated it. Hated the nail-biting, the inactivity, her own indecision. Most of all she hated the moral conflict going on in her mind. She didn't understand it herself. Aliza had torn Quattrini to pieces. She was a cold-blooded murderess—her cute freckles didn't change that. She had slung Rosa into the van in midflight, not caring whether she broke all her bones. Aliza deserved no pity, and it was some time before Rosa figured out that pity wasn't what troubled her so much.

Her inner turmoil had nothing to do with the young woman in the van behind her. It had to do with Alessandro. He was hurting Aliza, after injecting her with another dose of serum and tying her up. He was acting like a torturer—or at least that was how she imagined it, because to her own annoyance she couldn't bring herself to climb out of the cab and watch. Hell, she only had to push back the flap over the viewing hatch and take a look through it.

But she sat there, biting her nails, feeling useless and childish. It wasn't fair to blame him. He was doing what had to be done to keep them alive. He was doing it for her, for Rosa, far more than for himself.

Yet all the same she couldn't get her head around it. She loved him. And she knew him well enough to know that he had demonstrated the ruthlessness necessary for a *capo* to survive much earlier than she did. He had defeated Cesare, disposed of several other adversaries, and only a few hours ago he had killed Saffira. Rosa wasn't judging him, of course she wasn't. She herself had shot Michele Carnevare and never for a moment regretted it.

But Aliza's screams were getting to her, and it didn't help to turn up the sound on the radio again, roll down the window, and hold her face in the cool breeze coming off the sea.

Nothing helped.

What was going on in the van behind her was right and wrong at the same time. It might help them both to survive this business intact. She just wondered whether it might not also leave traces that wouldn't show until much later.

Finally she took one of the two cell phones out of the duffel bag, got out of the van, and went a little ways along the beach with the phone. She came within a few yards of the breaking waves and sat down in the sand. Streaks of cloud striped the scarlet sky like muscle fibers. Dawn had never looked so much like raw meat before.

She dialed Iole's number, not for the first time since they set off in the van, and let the phone ring until her voice mail picked up. She didn't dare leave a message; she didn't know whether the police might be listening in on Iole's connection somehow. Better if it looked like an unknown caller. Iole would draw the right conclusions and call her back on the number of this cell phone as soon as she could.

If the men hadn't found her in the bunker on Isola Luna. And if she, Cristina, and the tutor were still alive. If. If. If.

Rosa drew up her legs, linked her hands behind her head, and pressed her chin down on her knees so hard that her lower jaw hurt. As she did so, she looked out to sea in dawn light that on any other day she would have thought beautiful. Today, she thought of nothing but wounds, pain, and death. Even the smell of seaweed reminded her of decay.

The beach was deserted, not a human soul in sight. Somewhere beyond this sea lay Africa. She had never been there, had never even thought of going to see it. But now she suddenly wanted to. She would have loved to leave right away.

Behind her, the rear door of the van slammed shut. She didn't turn around, but waited in silence until Alessandro reached her side.

He was wearing jeans, some kind of cheap imitation brand, and a printed T-shirt. They had bought two each of those items at a stall kept by a Moroccan street trader, a man who sold his trashy wares to truck drivers and commuters early in the morning north of Gela.

"She's told me everything," said Alessandro quietly, sitting down cross-legged beside her. He spoke matter-of-factly, no triumph in his voice.

She looked out to the sea again, asking no questions, letting herself drift on the flow of her melancholy mood just as the gulls out there drifted on the rocking waves.

"It's exactly as we thought," he went on, letting his hands rest in his lap. "The Carnevares and Alcantaras got together and hired the Malandras. They were to take us to the Castello. My people"—he sounded contemptuous, but not angry—"occupied it while we were at the graveyard. They probably didn't have to touch a hair on anyone's head. Most of those I could rely on were at the funeral as well. I only hope nothing's happened to any of them."

"No one would let himself be killed for you," she said quietly. "No one but me."

It was like a vow that she had never put into words before.

I'd die for you.

And I for you.

Alessandro kissed her, then leaned back and propped himself on his elbows in the sand. "The judge was murdered to isolate us. Everyone was to think we killed her. The families must have found out, only a little while before, that you were in touch with Quattrini."

"Who told them?"

"The same person who told them that she'd be at the funeral. Someone from her unit was open to a bribe. But I believe Aliza when she says she has no idea who that informer could be."

"Festa? Or Stefania? It could be anyone, probably ten or twenty others in her unit."

He nodded. "Anyway, their plan worked. We can't turn to anyone now: not the other clans because they think we were working with Quattrini and not the police because they're convinced that we murdered the judge. Now they can sit back at their leisure and watch the Malandras hunt us."

"And because the anti-Mafia cops are after us, our people find out the latest from their informants about where they think we are."

"Right now they should all be groping around in the dark. The police don't know anything about this van, and the Malandras won't find us in a hurry."

She looked him in the eye. "So how about Aliza?"

"We'll have to get rid of her somehow. And in a way that keeps her from putting anyone on our tail."

"I'm not going to let you kill her. She can't defend herself. It would be murder."

A smile flitted over his face. He didn't look like someone in the middle of a conversation about the life and death of a human being. "I know."

"I mean it. We're not about to kill anyone who doesn't attack us first. I'm going to defend myself, just like you, but I won't watch you going over to her in this van and—"

"Do you believe that of me?"

"I have no idea," she said truthfully. "A little while ago, when you were in the back of the van there with her, I'd have believed a great deal of you."

He looked out at the sea. Wave upon wave rolled into the sand in front of them not two feet away. "I'm not a murderer," he said after a while. "Or not as I understand the word."

"I know—there have to be good reasons. But aren't there always?"

"You saw what they did to Quattrini. You were there."

"And I'd have killed Aliza on the spot if it would have saved Quattrini. But I can't get into that van and kill someone lying tied up on the floor in front of me."

"She isn't tied up. She's simply sitting in a corner. I haven't touched her. All I threatened to do was feed her sister's head to the seagulls."

"Seriously?"

"Did you think I'd beat her up? Or stick needles under her fingernails?"

"I'm not so sure what I thought."

"She finally caved in when I said we might hand her over to TABULA."

"You did *what*?"

He smiled faintly. "That's what they think of us. That we're hand in glove with TABULA—you in particular. Someone must have leaked the fact that your grandmother did business with TABULA. Like Florinda, and finally, they assume, you yourself. That's why your family is so bent on showing the dynasties that they disown you. They're putting on a big show of remorse, promising to atone for the errors of their leaders."

"The lying hypocrites!"

"Who knew about your grandmother and TABULA?"

She realized what he was getting at. "Only you and me, a number of people who are dead now—and the Hungry Man."

"Aliza is convinced that he's going to take over. When he comes back everything will change, she says. Then the dynasties will be able to drop their masks and live as they lived in the past. Hunting human beings, enslaving them, or—"

"Eating them when they fancy human flesh," she finished his sentence for him. "We've heard that a hundred times before. As if the world would go back to the days of antiquity, just like that."

"So far, the dynasties themselves have opposed it. Some were for the Hungry Man, some against him. But if he's succeeded in winning over the last doubters, then there'll certainly be changes on the way."

"But why would he suggest that I'd made a pact with TABULA?"

"Very likely all he had to do was tell them what your grandmother did. The furs of Arcadians in the Palazzo have been burnt or buried, but perhaps he knows something more. Or maybe a few cleverly spread rumors were enough. Your family couldn't do anything but crawl to him."

"I've met him, though. I spoke to him when he was in prison. He wanted us to be his allies, not his enemies."

"Then he's changed his plan. Or his notion of an ally isn't the same as ours."

"You mean because the Malandras were supposed to take us alive?"

"He needs us for something," Alessandro said. "Seems like we're no use to him dead. This new concordat between our families must suit whatever mischief he has in mind. Because

otherwise the Panthera and the Lamias would have been more likely to tear each other apart than unite in an alliance."

"When I saw him, he wanted me to promise him something. In return, he lifted the death sentence on you. He said that the day would come when he asked me a favor."

"A *favor*," he repeated scornfully. "Oh, sure."

"There's something he wants me to do for him. That's why he wants to get his hands on us as soon as he can."

There had been reports in the media of the imminent release of the former *capo dei capi*, but the Ministry of Justice had not given the precise date. To avoid a lot of publicity, or so it was said. It was perfectly possible that the Hungry Man was already free. And back in Sicily.

"He'll have all his opponents liquidated," said Alessandro. "The police will write it off as conflict between Mafia clans. A few criminals more or less, who's going to mind that?" He slowly shook his head. "But what does he want from us? Why the two of us?"

"The statues," she said. "Maybe they're the key to it all. He must know their significance. For some reason he knows more about Arcadian history than most of the others."

"He's been in prison for thirty years. No prison library is that well stocked."

"Then someone outside did the research for him. Someone who knew exactly how to go about it. Where to begin. How to go to the right source for finding out about events that took place thousands of years ago."

Their eyes met.

"Leonardo Mori," Alessandro whispered.

Rosa jumped up. "You think he's the link between old Arcadia and the dynasties of today, between the Hungry Man and . . . Fundling?"

They hurried back over the sand to the van. Aliza didn't even let out a squeak when Alessandro started the engine and drove back down the narrow road to the beach.

A few minutes later they passed Vittoria and turned onto the expressway for Ragusa.

SIGISMONDIS

A FEW MILES FROM the city, Rosa tried reaching Iole once more. No answer. Only her voice mail.

"Damnit."

"Can you try the hotel again too?"

She raised an eyebrow. "Hotel as in Hotel Paradiso?"

"Ask to speak to Signor Mori. The old guy at reception said there was someone wanting to speak to him all the time. It just might work."

After Rosa had directory information connect her, a woman's voice answered. No, there was no Signor Mori among their guests. Yes, she was perfectly sure of that. However, she'd be happy to take Rosa's name and number, and call back if any such person arrived.

Rosa ended the call. "She's lying."

Alessandro looked attentively in the rear and side mirrors. "The police will already have told them what to do. They probably moved Fundling to a safe house long ago."

Rosa stared out the window, not sure what to make of it all. Alessandro was strictly observing the speed limit to make sure they didn't fall into a radar trap.

There was knocking on the bolted flap of the peephole to the loading area. Without opening it, Rosa called over her shoulder, "What do you want?"

Aliza knocked again. Not violently, but in a slow, almost comfortable rhythm.

Rosa put the cell phone down and opened the peephole just a crack. "What is it?"

An owl's eye the size of a coin appeared in the crack, bloodshot, with a huge black pupil. In the next moment it changed back into the eye of a young girl with sandy lashes and freckles.

"You won't get away with this," she whispered, barely loud enough to be heard over the sound of the engine.

Rosa was going to close the peephole again, but Aliza thrust a bird's claw as sharp as a knife through it. It was not an attack, only a blockade.

"You killed my sister. My family will kill you for that. Our contract isn't in force now. You'll die as she did."

"Great," replied Rosa. "Thanks for the information."

"All the Malandras will be hunting you. Look up at the sky. Maybe they're up there already. If you can't see them, that doesn't mean they're not around. It definitely doesn't mean that."

"Okay."

"She's only trying to frighten us," said Alessandro.

"Get your finger out of there or I'll cut it off," Rosa told Aliza, annoyed.

The long, horny claw bent enticingly, like a witch's finger. So ugly.

"They'll find you. There are many more of us than you think. We Harpies are everywhere."

Rosa pushed the peephole shut with all her might. The claw got wedged in it, but stayed in bird form. Rosa repeated that three times, before Aliza took her finger away. There was a blood-stained edge to the steel flap now.

"And *I* wasn't supposed to hit her," growled Alessandro.

Rosa angrily kicked the duffel bag in front of her seat. She was wearing sneakers that had belonged to one of the sisters, but she wished she had her sturdy steel-toed shoes on.

"Can't she just keep her mouth shut?" she hissed furiously. "And that whispering! Who does she think she is?"

"A monster with a bad manicure."

"I hate birds. I didn't even have a parakeet when I was little."

"Snakes eat birds."

"Damn right."

A grin spread over his face. "But they both lay eggs."

"*I* don't lay eggs."

"That remains to be seen."

For a moment she was speechless.

He laughed out loud, and she punched his shoulder with her fist. "Idiot." Playfully, she punched him again. He stepped on the brake to avoid driving off the road.

There was a loud clattering in the back of the van as Aliza lost her balance.

Rosa beamed. "Let's do that again. Come on."

He braked again.

Clattering. A furious curse.

And again.

The van was parked under tall trees on a steep slope. On the other side of a ravine lay Ibla, the picturesque Old Town of Ragusa, with its alleys, flights of steps, and baroque palazzi. Church towers rose out of the jumble of yellowish-brown gables and walls. No one had ever taken the trouble to remove old TV antennae, and so they lived out their lives in rusty oblivion, side by side with gargoyles.

The front doors of the van were open. Alessandro stood outside, one hand shielding his eyes as he looked down at the city. Rosa was sitting cross-legged on the passenger seat as she listened for the ringtone again. She was about to put the cell phone aside when another idea occurred to her.

She rang the number of her secretary in Piazza Armerina and was not surprised to get only the answering machine. She quickly entered the number code and listened to the recorded messages.

The first voice was Iole's.

"Hey, it's me. No idea when you'll get to hear this message, but it's just after six here on the island. Just after six this morning, that is. Everything's the same as usual. I guess we're safe for now. Sarcasmo's the best dog in the world, he never makes a sound; it's like he knows exactly what's at stake. Cristina's divided up all our supplies again, she did that twice already—*rationing*, she calls it. I don't know about that. Anyway, that's how she passed her time until finally she found some kind of papers. There's a whole archive down here, umpteen file folders, old books, all kinds of stuff. She's reading the papers now. And Signora Falchi isn't getting me down half as much as I thought. She's kind of okay really. Worries far too much and tries not to let us notice. You can imagine how good she is at acting . . . okay, I have to go now. You two didn't turn up here last night, so something must have kept you. I hope nothing happened to you. I really do hope that very much. I'll call again later, here or wherever. *Ciao*."

Rosa went over to Alessandro. Only when he looked at her in surprise did she realize that she must have a huge grin on her face.

"Everything okay?" he asked.

"She's fine. They haven't been found yet. Or at least, not by first thing this morning."

"I hope she'll watch out. They're not stupid. Maybe they'll think of listening in to the machine as well."

As they talked, more recorded voices were babbling away: two journalists who were brash or stupid enough to assume that, even in flight, Rosa would take time to give them an interview.

The fourth message was less than half an hour old. "Eva here," announced a young woman's voice, and it made Rosa prick up her ears. "I heard on the radio that you have problems right now, so probably this isn't so important to you. But you did say I was to call at once if I found anything out. And I have. I think it could be what you're looking for. I don't want to put it all on a recording, so just call me back when you have time. You can always reach me over the next few days. I'll be either here or at the uni. You have my number. Talk to you soon."

A flock of pigeons was circling over the Old Town. Alessandro looked expectantly at Rosa.

"Eva called," she said.

"Eva?"

"I told you about her." She lowered her voice to make sure that Aliza, in the back of the van, couldn't hear her. "A student from Palermo. I hired her through an employment exchange on the internet. She's checking up on all the Nobel Prize winners and contenders over the last decade."

In Sintra, Augusto Dallamano had advised her to put TABULA at the top of the list in her search for leads. If it really was a secret organization carrying out experiments on live Arcadians, then there must be some top scientists among its members. Since TABULA had more than enough money and influence, it could have recruited eminent experts who hadn't found such lucrative employment elsewhere, or who had been disappointed in traditional scientific research at the universities.

So Rosa had hired the student to check up on all Nobel Prize winners since 1950 working in the fields of animal and human reproduction, genetics, and biochemistry. Who had fallen out of favor with other scientists and committees? Who had expressed dissatisfaction with lack of funds, or had come into conflict with the law by carrying out banned experiments? Eva had put not only the prize winners under a magnifying glass, but also the far greater number of scientists who had had their Nobel Prize hopes dashed.

Alessandro ran a hand through his hair. "At the moment TABULA is the least of our problems."

"I'll call her back, anyway. Maybe I'll catch her still at

home. If everyone thinks I'm hand in glove with TABULA, then I ought to at least find out all I can about its members."

"Hurry up, then." He nodded toward the maze of streets in Ragusa Ibla. "It's not really safe here. Too many people who might recognize you."

"Eva heard something about us on the radio."

He swore. "Then it's starting with a vengeance now. We'll have to start thinking what we—"

Rosa interrupted him with a gesture when directory information picked up. She asked to be connected to Eva's number in Palermo. The student picked up the phone after the fourth ring.

"Eva, hi. You know who this is, don't you?"

"I . . . yes, sure. Hi."

"Do you have any problems if we talk on the phone? I mean because of what you heard on the radio."

"It was on TV as well just now. No, no problems. You paid me in advance, so that's okay."

"Good, thanks. The police haven't been to see you, have they?"

The student's voice rose a little higher than before. "Been to see me? What would the . . . oh, shit, you're not dragging me into it, are you?"

"No, I promise. Listen, I don't have much time. What have you found out?"

Rosa didn't know Eva personally, but she had looked at her Facebook profile. A few harmlessly cheerful photos of travels with friends, none of them outside Italy. Favorite books that

Rosa had never heard of. Links to music videos of obscure indie bands.

"Well then," began Eva, a little nervously, "I went through all the years one by one. Of course there were a whole lot of prize winners in the fields you mentioned. But either they work in respectable institutes and write books and articles regularly about their current research, or they're dead. Quite a number of them are dead, in fact. I managed to check the precise dates of death of all the ones who seemed important and where they were buried. Nothing suspicious so far."

During her conversation, Rosa had moved a few paces away from Alessandro, who was still gazing down at the city, and she could tell from the look on his face that he liked her plan less and less. Although what she had called a plan on the grand scale hardly qualified. While Alessandro was to watch the van with their prisoner in it, Rosa was going to find the antiquarian bookshop and try to get a look at Leonardo Mori's book. So far, so good—as long as the bookseller didn't recognize her because he'd been watching TV this morning.

Eva was sorting through papers of some kind. Rosa imagined a crowded desk, thickly covered with papers, books, empty plastic bottles, and teacups. "Next I looked at the scientists who, in spite of being written up as likely Nobel winners, had walked away empty-handed. Specifically any of them who then expressed their annoyance in interviews and open letters. I mean the sort you'd pick if you wanted to hire a competent specialist inclined to overestimate himself, a man with a hot temper, and get him to do secret experiments. And that's what you're after, right?"

"Roughly speaking, yes."

"In the end I was left with a group of five or six scientists. All men. Well, they would be, wouldn't they? People who just can't accept it if they felt they've been treated unfairly. Instead of going on and getting better results—"

"Only the names, Eva. Please."

"I tried tracing all their careers, dug up death announcements, et cetera, et cetera. And in the end there was only one man left."

"Really? Only one?" Rosa hadn't expected that. She had thought she would be facing a list of ten or twenty names that might, with a lot of luck, get her a little further. But only a single man?

"A guy called Eduard Sigismondis. Born in Latvia, but seems like it's been ages since he was seen there. He studied in Moscow, Helsinki, and Paris. He'd be eighty-one now—if he's still alive, which isn't certain. I didn't find any announcement of his death, but no sign of life from him either in almost thirty-five years. He could simply have disappeared and died at some point. Or maybe he's vegetating in an old folk's home and thinks his urine bag is a setup for experiments."

"How did you land on him?" A man eighty-one years old didn't strike her as a very promising key to the mystery of TABULA.

"He fits into the framework perfectly. He was one of the early pioneers of the Human Genome Project, and—"

"Eva, I have no idea what you're talking about."

"He cloned animals. He was cloning them years before that famous sheep. Officially, Dolly was the first successful attempt at a clone, but Sigismondis did the same thing much earlier. Or so he said, anyway, and obviously several of his colleagues confirmed his account. But above all, he experimented with crossing different species—you know what I mean, rats with guinea pigs, dogs with cats, apes with—"

"Human beings?"

"That was what ended his career. He'd begun by conducting most of his experiments in secret, and he had some really surprising results, early success with splitting genes and so on. That was what made him a hopeful for the Nobel Prize. But when it turned out that there were gaps in his documentation, and rumors began circulating that he'd broken all kinds of scientific and ethical taboos, everyone dropped him. He cited freedom of research, even the ancient principles of alchemy, saying that the ends always justified the means. He probably made a spectacle of himself on various occasions. A real troublemaker, and not a very nice guy. After a while he simply disappeared, and a little later pictures kept by his former assistants made the rounds. Photos of interspecies creatures that he'd bred in the laboratory, really nauseating sights. I can point you in the direction of some websites where you can see his work. Or at least part of it."

"Thanks, that won't be necessary."

"I'll finish the job by putting a file together—then you can make up your own mind whether you want to look at more or not." Eva sounded amused to think that a woman wanted all over the country on suspicion of murder might shrink from looking at photos of animal experiments. "One way or another, we've hit the bull's eye with Sigismondis. First his name disappeared from all lists of nominations, applications for financial backing, and outlines of international projects. Then he kind of dissolved into thin air. Assuming he didn't fall into a hole of some kind, and no one has ever found him, I'd guess he hasn't given up his research. He's gone on working somewhere or other, under a false name, maybe in a country that doesn't take ethical controls too seriously. The Soviet Union, North Korea, Cuba, East Germany—there was quite a wide choice at that time. Or else he simply has an enormous garage. But he certainly must have had financial backers for his work—and they had deep pockets and a burning interest in his experiments." Eva stopped for a moment, got her breath back, and added, "Only please don't ask me who the hell takes an interest in dog-headed human beings. Or cows giving birth to human babies. What's for certain is that the backers were really sick characters."

"You're absolutely sure?" asked Rosa. "I mean sure that it can only have been Sigismondis?"

"Of course there are plenty of deranged scientists around. But among those who almost made it to the very top, and then stumbled at the finishing line because of their lack of scruples, Eduard Sigismondis easily takes first place. So if you're asking me, yes, I do think he's the man who fulfills all the criteria you mentioned to me."

"If he's still alive."

"That doesn't really make any difference. Could be he's dead by now—all the same, he may have had two or three decades since the scandal to get his filthy business done, before death finally caught up with him."

THE ANTIQUARIAN BOOKSELLER

ROSA FOLLOWED A WINDING alley uphill. Now and then the cupola of the Cathedral of San Giorgio appeared behind the rooftops of Ibla, then disappeared from sight again. A cream-colored cat looked sleepily down from between terra-cotta pots on a wrought-iron balcony. The cobblestones were as smooth as if they had just been polished. When a boy clattered past Rosa on a Vespa, it seemed as inappropriate in the purity of these surroundings as if he were racing the scooter through a living room.

She was still wearing jeans and a blouse belonging to one of the Malandra sisters, and although both fit her well, she didn't feel comfortable in them. She had also found a large pair of sunglasses in the glove compartment and put them on. The rubber soles of her shoes squeaked on the cobblestones with every step she took, as if she were in a gym. She felt as if she was being watched from a window through half-open shutters. But aside from the boy she hadn't seen a single soul, nor did she see anyone at the windows or behind the inevitable plastic curtains hanging over the balcony doors.

A piece of paper taped to a well told visitors the history of Ragusa Ibla. The print was just large enough for her to decipher the first two sentences as she passed it. It said Ibla had been built on the ruins of an ancient city of the Siculians, the native inhabitants of Sicily. Rosa had seen the caves where they buried their dead at what seemed like the end of the world, in a place that she would always link with Alessandro. After the Siculians, the Greeks had taken possession of the island, founding their settlement of Hybla Hera on the mountain here. Later the name became Ibla.

The antiquarian bookshop was on the first floor of a corner house. Its dusty shop window was barred. A sign with the inscription LIBRERIA IBLEA in plain lettering hung over the entrance. There were all kinds of books on display in the window, most of them as brown as the tuff stone that had been used to build a large part of the Old Town. It was as if everything here had in fact been turned to stone: the houses, the window display, even the cat sleeping by the window.

And the old man sitting at a table in the shop fit seamlessly into this stony scene. He did not move so much as an inch when Rosa came in. His skin was the color of parchment, and so were his pants and the vest he wore over his shirt. He had a magnifying glass in one hand and was examining the pages of an open folio volume through it.

The shop was crammed to the ceiling with books, most of them from a time before there were brightly colored book jackets. The bindings that protected the pages looked like used baking paper. There was a door open in the back wall of the shop, giving Rosa a view of more rows of crowded shelves and glass display cases.

She greeted the man as she came in, but he didn't look up.

She opened and closed the door again, and waited for him to react to the sound of the bell ringing. Nothing.

"Excuse me, please," she said, taking off the sunglasses, "is your shop open?"

"How else would you have been able to open and close the door twice, scaring my neighbor's cat? My neighbor is fond of her pet, she won't like that." He went on studying the microscopic words on the pages. Not made of stone after all, she thought. Good.

"If the doorbell scares animals I guess not many people come in here."

"As a rule, those who do are notable for their good manners." Sighing, the old man put his magnifying glass down, half turned in his chair, and inspected her. "You will find what you're looking for, Signorina, in the bookstore three streets away, just past the cathedral."

"Are the booksellers there friendlier?"

"I haven't yet had the pleasure. I don't sell paperbacks and gift items."

She decided to be nicer to him. Genuinely impressed, she looked around. "This place is like our library at home."

His smile was slightly condescending, but he did seem a little more interested now. "You have a library?"

"Most of the books in it date from the time of my great-grandparents. Or their great-grandparents."

"Fancy that. A young lady from an old family of well-educated book-lovers." He sounded mocking, but less dismissive now. He even got off his chair and came a step toward her. "How can I help you?"

Rosa's eyes fell on a stack of catalogs beside the old-fashioned cash register. They were the same edition as the one they had found in Fundling's possessions. "I'm looking for one particular book."

"I see."

"You listed it in your catalog." She pointed to the stack by the cash register. "*The Gaps in the Crowd* by Leonardo Mori."

The expression on his face didn't change, but the long pause before he spoke again told her that he was surprised. "An unusual choice for a young lady of your age."

"You don't know me," she replied, smiling.

"And what, if I may ask, aroused your interest in that work?"

"My grocer doesn't ask me why I want cauliflower and not some other vegetable."

He went over to the cash register and picked up a copy of his catalog. He knew his way around the leaflet and opened it to the page listing Mori's book. "Not a cheap volume," he said, as if he were seeing the catalog entry for the first time.

"I know. Is it really such a rare book?"

"Indeed it is. Once, years ago, there was talk that a new edition would appear on the list of one of the larger publishing houses, but then it never came to anything because, to this day, no one knows who holds the rights."

"Because the author was murdered?"

"You're well informed."

"May I look at it?"

He put the catalog down again, then nodded slowly. "I suppose that can't do any harm. Come with me."

She followed him into the back room, which was so full of books that it felt oppressive. The smell of old paper and printer's ink had something heady about it, setting off the same reaction she would have to an intense floral perfume. Up to a certain point she found it intoxicating and sensuous, but after that it turned her stomach.

The bookseller opened another door. At the end of a corridor only a few yards long there was a door consisting of a set of bars. Beyond it lay a room much larger than the other two. An air conditioner under the ceiling was humming. There were no bookshelves here, only many high desks arranged around the center of the room in a semicircle. Every desk had a small lamp over it, and a single book lay on each of them.

The old man pressed a button, and all the reading lamps came on. Their dim yellow lights were all carefully pointed at their books, and there was a table beside the door with a box of disposable gloves on it, as well as a magnifying glass and another box containing white face masks like those worn in hospitals.

"I'll admit," she said, "there wasn't a room like *this* in our library."

"There wasn't?"

She hesitated before she answered, but then thought that she might as well tell him the truth. "It burned down. Along with the house."

He got between her and the locked, barred door, as if afraid that her mere presence might set fire to his precious volumes.

"It wasn't my doing," she said.

"No," he replied. "Presumably not. It's just that I'd like to know whether you can really afford the purchase price."

"May I look at the book first?"

He slowly stepped aside, and pointed through the bars at one of the books. "It's that one, over there. *The Gaps in the Crowd*."

A nondescript volume without a dust jacket, only a brown binding with plain typography stamped on the front.

"It doesn't seem like much from here," she said. "Can I look inside it?"

"First I have to ask you again: Can you afford that book?"

Only two days ago she could have bought this entire street with her family's money, including all the books and all the cats in it. Now she had exactly a hundred euros in her pocket, and even that didn't belong to her.

"I'm afraid I don't have enough cash on me," she said.

"Of course not. But if you give me your credit card, I can check it. There's a device for reading cards at the front of the shop."

"I don't have my credit card with me, either."

"That is certainly a problem."

"So you aren't going to show me the book?"

He smiled. "Most certainly not. The books in that room are worth a small fortune. It would be very irresponsible of me to let just anyone leaf through them, wearing out the binding and the paper."

"Very well," she said, forcing a smile, "I'll tell you what

it's all about. I'm a student, and I'm working on a dissertation about"—here she hesitated for a moment—"about natural catastrophes in fiction."

He made a face as if the sound of the words hurt his ears.

"And their effects on human sensitivity to climate change," she added.

"I see."

"Leonardo Mori's book is considered one of the best studies of accounts of disasters in classical antiquity, or at least that's what my professor says, and I'm interested in finding out whether authors have ever used it as a basis for their novels." Rosa had never seen the inside of a university, and the only books she had read were tattered paperbacks at home in New York. She felt like a one-legged man being pushed out to play on a football field.

The old man might be a prickly loner, but he wasn't unworldly. "So you were lying to me," he pointed out.

"I'm sorry."

"You never really had enough money to buy the book."

"No. I'm sorry, I mean I really am. But I thought if I asked you whether I could just look through it you'd never let me."

"And you were right."

"Does it help if I say please nicely?"

"I'm afraid not."

She could have shifted shape, strangled him in her serpentine coils, and slipped into the room through the bars. For the first time she cursed herself for not really being the unscrupulous criminal who was wanted all over Sicily.

"Can I give you my professor's phone number, so that you can call and confirm that I was here? He's never going to believe me if I tell him you've put the book in prison. With no visiting rights."

For the first time one corner of his mouth twitched. Maybe she was in luck, and he was about to have a stroke.

"Would you do that?" she asked again.

He took a deep breath and nodded in the direction of the front room. "Come with me a moment, and I'll tell you something about the book. Maybe that will be a help in your research."

He sounded friendlier now. That gave her a glimmer of hope that her plea for sympathy might work after all.

Taking care not to overdo the pathos, she followed him into the front of the shop, where he pointed to the only chair. "Sit down."

She did so, while he leaned against the cash register with his arms folded.

"What do you know about Leonardo Mori?" he asked.

"Only that he was murdered. Presumably murdered, anyway. Under rather mysterious circumstances."

"He and his wife died," the bookseller confirmed. "The couple had a child who disappeared without trace at the time. The little boy is probably dead as well."

"A sad story."

"But you knew that already, didn't you?"

"To be honest, yes."

"Then I'll tell you something that you don't know yet. You

can make it a footnote in your dissertation if you like."

She waited, as he hooked his thumbs into the shapeless pockets of his pants and looked past her at the window display. Only now did she notice that the dim light in here bathed the shop in eternal twilight.

"Mori was obsessed with major catastrophes—deluges, volcanic eruptions, earthquakes. He spent years working on his book, traveling all around the Mediterranean to see the most important sites with his own eyes. You know the kind of thing: Pompeii, Santorini, of course Mount Etna, as well as the former Carthage, Uruk, and a few dozen other locations. He thought they were all parts of a greater whole. The subtitle of his book is *New Facts about the Cataclysms of Antiquity*, but it's much more than a collection of factual accounts. Of course he did collect facts: the numbers of victims if they were known, geological reports by experts, anthropological theses about the consequences, and so on and so forth. But what interested him most—and that is what makes his book so fascinating—were the eyewitness accounts. There are more of them than you might think. The ancient Greeks and the people of Mesopotamia, North Africa, and elsewhere, left written reports. People then were much the same as they are today. If we have the bad luck to be present at some truly overwhelming disaster, we feel an enormous need to talk about it. Look at all the books that have been written about September Eleventh. Or the tsunami in Southeast Asia. If you've experienced something like that personally, you want to talk about it, and usually you'll find an audience eager for every detail.

Mori knew that very well. He'd written a great deal of nonsense for journals in the course of his career, stuff that you, as a budding scholar, wouldn't touch with a ten-foot pole."

There was something challenging about his smile. The suspicion hadn't disappeared from his face, but he seemed to like the sound of his own voice.

"Mori confined himself to the catastrophes around the Mediterranean," he went on, "probably because that was where the great civilizations that left written records were to be found. In the end he had collected a vast number of accounts, but that wasn't enough for him, and he extended his field of research to the modern era. He was particularly fascinated by the great earthquake of Messina in the year 1908. Thirty thousand dead within minutes. While he was reading all those accounts, drawing up a catalog of them, and comparing them with one another, he noticed something that they had in common. Something that a great many writers and historians of classical antiquity had documented again and again and again."

"The gaps in the crowd?"

The bookseller nodded. "What exactly do you know about them?"

"Not much. Someone told me about them once. About places in large gatherings of people that always stay empty, moving through the crowds like something alive. 'Who is in the gaps in the crowd?' he asked me. That was all."

"Had he read Mori's book?"

"Possibly."

"As a rule there's mass panic when catastrophes of that order happen, powerful human movements thronging the streets of burning or flooded cities. And that, at least according to Leonardo Mori, is when the existence of gaps in the crowd is most clearly visible. 'Who is in the gaps in the crowd?' is a quotation from his book. Mori asks that question several times, but even he finds no satisfactory answer to it in the end."

"Did he have a theory?"

"Mori was not a scholar. Ultimately he was only a sensationalist scribbler, but one with a certain talent for choosing his subjects, and extremely persistent. The mystery of the holes in the crowd never lost its grip on his imagination. He was convinced that they were not chance phenomena, but living beings—that's what he called them. Invisible powers, not harmless observers but entities that had caused all those catastrophes."

She thought of something she had heard in Sunday School lessons as a child. "Like the angels sent by God to destroy Sodom and Gomorrah?"

"Mori was not a Christian believer. As far as I know he didn't believe in God. Not in the *one* God, and certainly not in his angels."

"But?"

"Who knows what he believed in? Maybe the pagan gods of antiquity, Zeus and the rest of the Greek deities on Mount Olympus. Jupiter and the Roman gods. In the end, all myths are the same: They're always about beings who are greater than we are, older and more powerful and merciless."

Feeling uncomfortable, she shifted position in the chair. "Mori really thought that those invisible beings caused earthquakes and volcanic eruptions? That they were responsible for such disasters?"

The old man nodded. "And he thought that in a way, crowds of people made them visible by flowing around them. It still happens, he believed, in modern times. He found eyewitness reports of the 1908 earthquake that matched other accounts that were two or three thousand years old, almost word for word." The bookseller's narrow lips looked as if they had been drained of blood. "At any rate, it's certain that Mori is dead. He died mysteriously. And at the time of his death he was working on a second book that was to be the next step in his presentation of his case. I don't know exactly what it was, but probably some subject on which he had only touched briefly in *The Gaps in the Crowd*. In his new book, he wanted to develop that aspect in more detail. He claimed to have found echoes still reverberating in the present day. To people alive now who are deeply interested in that history." The bookseller's gaze was piercing. "He'd dug up something or other. Something so sensational, it convinced someone that Leonardo Mori had to be silenced once and for all."

BREAKING IN

SHE FELT DIZZY WHEN she stepped out into the open air: the catalog leaflet that the old man had given her in one hand, Aliza's cell phone in the other. She had to call Alessandro as quickly as possible.

She hurried back to the well she had passed on the way to the shop, sat down on the steps, looked at Aliza's list of numbers, and called her dead sister Saffira's cell phone. Alessandro answered after one ring.

"Everything okay?" he asked.

"Sure." His anxiety made her smile. "I've only been to a *bookshop*."

"While half of Sicily is looking for you."

Apart from Rosa there was no one at all in the little square with the well. All the same, she shifted along the circular step surrounding the well until she was at the back of it. Through her sunglasses, she had a view of the windowless wall of a house. In a whisper, she told him everything that she had learned from the bookseller.

"Let's speculate for a moment," he said after she had finished. "So Mori wrote that book about the gaps in the crowd. For some reason it falls into the hands of the Hungry Man while he's in prison, and he decides that Mori is the right man

to find out more about the history of the Arcadian dynasties for him. The Hungry Man claims to be the reincarnation of King Lycaon of Arcadia, but you and I both know that's nonsense. He's just a megalomaniac *capo* exploiting the myth of the Arcadians to regain power. Right?"

"But we're only assuming that Mori worked for him."

"Mori certainly meddled too much with matters that had nothing to do with him. He wasn't a political journalist, or someone who wrote about economics, so I can't imagine that he stumbled into some kind of Cosa Nostra business. There must be more than that behind it, or my father would have set a couple of human hit men on him, not the Malandras. The fact that Mori was killed by Harpies can really only have been a warning—my father's warning to the other Arcadians, to the Hungry Man, or who knows who else. Someone must have talked to Mori about the dynasties. What he found in old books can't have been enough to get him murdered."

"That's just more speculation," Rosa objected.

"My father hears about Mori's research and decides to put a stop to it. Maybe to harm the Hungry Man if Mori has been working for him, maybe just to preserve the secret of the dynasties. The Harpies kill Mori and his wife, and get Fundling to my parents. Later on, Fundling begins taking an interest in his origins, finds out that the hotel in Agrigento never burned down, and so he comes upon the story of the Moris' child who disappeared. In secret, he collects more and more information, at first only about the two Moris, but then also about the subjects that were on Mori's mind. When

Fundling comes out of his coma, and the judge has taken him to a safe place, he asks her to put him up in the very hotel where he"—Alessandro hesitated—"where he's now doing, well, whatever it *is* he's doing."

"Whatever it is, yes." Rosa groaned and sat back against the little wall enclosing the well. "If we want to know more precisely what happened, we have to take a look at Mori's book. Maybe that could get us further forward."

"Or maybe Mori kept the really interesting things for the second book, the one he was working on when he was killed."

"We'll see."

Alessandro said nothing for a moment. "You're not planning to get back into that bookshop and steal the book?"

"Can you think of a better plan?"

His reply was drowned out by indistinct shouting.

"What's going on there?" she asked, alarmed.

"Aliza. She's been rampaging in the back of the van ever since you left, raising hell."

"Can anyone hear her?"

"There's no one for miles around. She keeps shifting shape—it can't be healthy. But she has stamina, you have to give her that. When you're back we have to get rid of her whether you like it or not. She's nothing but trouble."

She didn't want to have this conversation with him again, particularly not on the phone, so she changed the subject and said that she would stay in Ibla until the evening. As soon as the old man left his shop, she was going to try to get the book out. The way back to the van would take her almost an hour, she said, and it wasn't worth going there and then back to the city. Secretly, however, she was afraid that Alessandro might persuade her to change her mind.

"I don't like it," he said. "I'd rather be with you."

"One of us has to stay with Aliza. And the chances of getting into the shop are far better for a snake than a panther."

"Promise me you'll look after yourself."

"And you do the same. Aliza is still dangerous."

After they had hung up, she held the phone uncertainly in her hand, then put it in her pants pocket. Another few hours before darkness fell. She had to retreat to some place where no one could recognize her.

She glanced up at the sky above the Old Town. No birds anywhere, no owls. If Aliza had been telling the truth, and the other Malandras were searching for them, at least they hadn't yet followed them to Ragusa.

Looking down again, she strolled along the streets, and finally found a park. She took off her clothes among some bushes, became a snake, and coiled up behind a rock.

She slept until twilight fell.

The old man locked the door of his shop and pulled a grille over it. Dragging his feet, he moved away downhill, a leather briefcase in one hand, a canvas bag full of books in the other. Rosa—now in human form again, her blond hair untidy and her blouse crumpled—waited until he had disappeared around the next bend. Then she approached the corner building where the shop stood.

After one last look down the street she turned into the narrow alley beside the shop. There were bars over the windows on the first floor of the building, and those of the back room, with its valuable collectors' editions, were too far above ground level for her even to look in.

After twenty yards she came to a wooden door that probably led into a backyard. It was locked from inside with a chain and secured by a padlock. She couldn't climb over it because the wall was too high. However, there was a small gap under the door, presumably for the neighbor's cat.

She looked cautiously in all directions, saw no one in the alley, and shifted shape. Winding her way out of her heap of clothes, she slithered through the gap.

The yard was tiny, just large enough for an old bicycle and a drying rack. Clotheslines with dripping sheets hanging from them stretched above her head. There were two doors at the back of the yard. One was barred and led into the shop; the other was a door to the neighboring house. A light was on in a second-floor window there. The sky was not entirely dark yet, but the last of the day's brightness hardly reached this walled corner of the Old Town. The distorted sound of music on a radio came from somewhere.

Rosa pushed her snake's head back through the gap, and taking her clothes in her mouth pulled them out of the alley and into the yard. She hoped fervently that the bookseller's neighbor wouldn't look out the window at this minute and see the giant amber-colored snake among her laundry.

A brief investigation revealed that the back door of the

shop had several security measures in place. Only the small window, also barred and a good six feet above ground level, could give her access.

She slowly wound her way up one of the iron posts outside the door. Once at the top of it, she pushed her head over to the window at an angle, and then, exerting all her strength, hauled the rest of her reptilian body after it. Finally she was lying, closely coiled, on the windowsill between the glass and the iron bars outside it. Hoping that the radio would drown out the noise, she pressed her scaly body against the pane as hard as she could. It gave way and fell with a clink of broken glass to the floor inside the room.

Rosa stayed where she was for some time, expecting an alarm to sound, or the angry neighbor to appear. Only when all remained calm did she glide through the broken window into the room, reach the floor, listen once more for suspicious sounds, and then return to human form.

She was standing, naked, in the gloom of the back room. Faint twilight fell through the little window looking out on the alley, just enough to show her the semicircle of reading desks. With every step she took, she worried about crossing some kind of barrier that would switch on the lights, or about touching hidden sensors on the floor.

She found the book and switched on the little lamp above the desk. After one last glance at the barred door into the corridor, she opened *The Gaps in the Crowd*.

It was a bound book, printed on high-quality paper, and as far as she could tell unblemished. Hesitantly, she leaned forward and breathed in. It smelled new, as if it had never been opened before.

The title page had Mori's name, the title of the book, and the year of publication. Right at the bottom of the page the name of the publisher was given in small lettering: *Hera Edizioni, RG.* The two capital letters stood for Ragusa. Of course: Hybla Hera, the city of the Siculians. Hera Edizioni.

On the next page the details of the firm included its address.

It was this one: The house where she was standing.

And then she realized that she had spoken to the publisher himself a few hours ago. The old man had known Leonardo Mori personally.

Her fingertips shook slightly as she opened the book at the table of contents. Each chapter dealt with a historical catastrophe, and the names of the chapters were the places where they happened. At random, she read several of the names. Sodom and Gomorrah. Alexandria. Carthage. Santorini. Sicily.

And somewhere among them, Arcadia.

She turned the page and skimmed the prologue, then the beginning of the Sicily chapter. It seemed to be about the eruption of Mount Etna as well as the earthquake of Messina.

The chapter about Arcadia began like this:

Arcadia may have been many things in its eventful history, but one thing it certainly was not: the earthly paradise to which the myths of later generations—

A sound in the shop beyond the door.

Rosa switched off the lamp on the reading desk and closed the book, but she kept her finger between the pages.

A horizontal line glowed under the wooden door at the end of the corridor. The light had been switched on in the room beyond it. Dragging footsteps. The old man had come back.

She heard him moving about in the front room as she tip-toed back to the window. Throwing the book out through the broken pane would make a noise. She didn't want to run any more risks. Without further ado, she placed it open on the floor and tore out the pages of the chapter on Arcadia.

The footsteps were coming closer.

She left the thin pile of pages where they were, and tried lifting one of the reading desks to haul it over to the window. It was very heavy—and creaked as she put it down again.

The old man stopped.

Rosa became a snake.

The door into the corridor flew open. Light flooded through the bars.

She snapped up the Arcadia chapter in her mouth, coiled her way up the reading desk, pushed off, and shot the last part of the way to the window. She managed to push her head and the crumpled paper in her mouth through the bars, and hastily pulled the rest of her body after it.

The old man called something. His footsteps reached the door. Keys clinked.

Rosa pushed her way out into the open air, afraid of getting stuck in the bars over the window, half in the room, half outside it. But then the weight of the front part of her body hauled the rest after it, and she fell to the yard below.

She heard the old man pushing the door open and hurrying

into the room. He must have seen her; perhaps he had even seen the paper in her reptilian mouth.

She reached the ground, and hissed as the whole weight of her body buried her head under it, glided out from under her own coils, and wound her way over to the door of the yard. Her clothes were still lying there in front of it. She tried frantically to push them through the gap in the door with her head, without losing her grip on the pages of the book.

The bookseller was fumbling at the outside door. Security lock after security lock snapped open.

Leaving her clothes behind, Rosa pushed herself through the gap and into the alley, and raced away over the paving stones with the Arcadia chapter between her teeth. She wound her way at high speed along the bottom of the wall of the house, away from the door to the yard, away from the old man whose outline she could see in the light from the corridor as he stood motionless, looking the way she had gone in the darkness.

THE ARCADIAN INHERITANCE

WHEN ROSA REACHED THE van, Aliza was dead.

"What happened?"

Alessandro raised both hands, warding off her criticism. "She tried making a break for it."

He was wearing clean clothes, the second set they had bought from the street vendor in Gela. His hair was wet; he must have washed himself as best he could with water from one of the plastic bottles.

"And that suited you just fine, right?" Rosa was breathless, naked, and had just stumbled through thorny bushes into the little clearing on the mountain slope. She had gone most of the way back as a snake, without realizing how stressful that would be. Right now, she wished for any other animal shape—to be one of the Panthera, the Harpies, the Hundinga—anything but a damn Lamia. With no legs.

Alessandro's nerves were on edge, too. "Hell, she attacked me!"

"She was locked up. In a steel box. Like—" She fell silent, took a deep breath, and scrutinized him. "Did anything happen to you? Are you hurt?"

Shaking his head, he dismissed her question. "First she cracked up completely, letting out bird cries that could probably be heard all the way to Ragusa. Then she suddenly went deathly quiet. I tried to look through the peephole from in front, but it was too dark. She'd wrecked the interior lighting. What was I supposed to do? I went around to the back and opened the doors just a crack. That's when she attacked."

"You've been wanting to get rid of her the whole time. And you knew perfectly well that I wouldn't be back in a hurry. This is just great." Furiously, she took a step toward him. "I told you I wouldn't go along with anything like that."

He was about to respond, but she waved his reply away. She toyed briefly with the thought of opening the doors at the back and looking at the body, but then remembered that she was still stark naked and went to the front instead. She flung the pages from Mori's book onto the seat and rummaged in the dead sisters' bag. A little later she slipped into a black stretch dress and sneakers that were at least one size too large. Then she emptied the bag and threw the pages, badly battered by now, into it along with the Malandras' wallet, the rest of the serum, and the syringe.

She heard Alessandro doing something at the back of the van. She walked around to him and saw that one of the doors there was open; she couldn't help glancing in.

Panthers were not squeamish killers. She had already seen how Alessandro dealt with opponents, and it was never a pretty sight. But what had happened in the van made her recoil a couple of steps. The bag fell into the grass beside her.

Alessandro had climbed into the loading area and seemed to be looking for something. The only source of illumination was a cigarette lighter that he had found in the glove compartment. The little flame flickered in the evening wind from the valley, casting more shadows than light.

"What happened?"

"What does it look like?" he asked, annoyed.

The inside of the van stank of blood, feathers, and worse, a combination of a slaughterhouse and a rundown chicken shed.

"She didn't want to give in," he said. "She was rather . . . irritated."

"You did *that*? With your *teeth*? Fuck, Alessandro, how—"

"Blaming me is a big help right now, thanks."

Shivering, she stepped from one foot to another outside the van. "Can you tell me what you're doing there? You're not *cleaning up*, are you?"

"We can't drive around with a corpse and a severed head."

"Let's look for another van. Or travel by train. Why not?"

She was not sorry about Aliza. The Harpy's murder of Quattrini had been positively bestial—and she had done it for money. But yet again, Alessandro's efficiency as a killing machine scared her. She was with the boy she loved so much, and at the same time she saw a little more clearly, every day, the killer instincts in him surfacing whenever his Arcadian heritage was awakened.

But was she any different? She had killed Salvatore Pantaleone, and only recently Michele Carnevare too. And then there were the Hundinga mercenaries when the palazzo burned down. She was no better than him—and certainly no more humane. It was time to accept that.

"I'm not sitting in that van anymore," she said. "Let's get out of here."

He jumped out of the loading area, landed on all fours—the smell of blood kept the beast in him awake—and stood upright. Carefully, he wiped the soles of his shoes on the grass.

"Going where?" A final cat-like spark died away in his eyes. "Someone or other will find the van in this mess. With our fingerprints and hairs all over the interior."

"They already want us for murder. This won't make matters any worse." She smoothed down the dress and picked up the duffel bag. Then she walked past him and slammed the back doors of the van. The stink still hung over the clearing, and she had an unpleasant feeling that it would follow them wherever they went.

When she turned, he was facing her. "What I told you is the truth," he said quietly. "I wasn't waiting until you were out of the way to . . . to do that. You mustn't think that of me. She attacked me, and she'd have killed me if I hadn't been faster than she was."

She laid one hand on his cheek and felt how cold it was. "I shouldn't have said that just now. It was just the long wait in the city, then the difficulty of getting hold of Mori's book. The bookseller saw me—I mean he saw me *as a snake*—and I have no idea if that's bad or not. He knew Mori, and maybe he knows all about Arcadia and all about us. Let's just hope he keeps his mouth shut, so that he doesn't get killed like Mori did."

He touched her hand, and for a while they simply stood there, looking at each other.

Finally she said, "When we're on the road I'll tell you all

about what happened. And I want to read what Mori wrote about Arcadia. But there's still—"

"Iole."

She nodded, narrowing her lips.

"There's nothing we can do, is there?" His expression was harder again. "We're helpless."

"If we leave Sicily and the police hear about it . . . if they stop looking for us, and word of that gets through to the clans, do you think they'll withdraw from Isola Luna?"

"Maybe."

That wasn't good enough. Of course it wasn't. But what alternative did they have?

"Those forged passports and tickets," she said. "Can we get at them?"

"All Quattrini knew was that I'd had them prepared. They were in a safe-deposit box at a bank in Syracuse for a few days, but they're not there any longer. I got them out of the city. Now they're hidden in an abandoned farmhouse. I can't imagine anyone finding them there."

A bird called above them in the night.

Alessandro looked up at the darkness.

A second bird answered the first, and a third screeched in the treetops farther down the slope.

"Is that them?" she whispered.

"Aliza's screams must have brought them here." He spun around, and his eyes followed a movement above the trees. "They'll arrive anytime now."

They ran.

FLORINDA'S FEAR

THEY TOOK THE FOOTPATH that Rosa had come up, found a road, and followed it to a small parking lot. Beyond that rose the first houses of Ragusa Ibla.

The angry screeching of birds came down the mountainside. Even down here in the valley it was alarmingly loud.

"They've found Aliza." Alessandro took the duffel bag from Rosa and put it over his shoulder as they ran. There was not much in it, but without it she felt faster and more agile.

They sprinted down an alley, then up a broad flight of steps. Three taxis stood in the yellowish light cast by a street lamp. They were all empty. Rosa's hands were shaking far too much for her to venture to break into one of them. And she had no tools with her.

A man emerged from the entrance of a small bar, eating a piece of white bread with grilled vegetables. He munched for a moment, swallowed, and asked, "Want a taxi?"

They nodded.

"Mind if I finish this first?"

"Not if we can wait in your car," said Alessandro. Rosa suppressed an impulse to look up at the sky again.

The driver stopped for a moment, looked past them at the alley with the steps, and frowned. "Okay," he said, unlocking the doors with his remote control, and waving to them. "Won't be a moment."

A few minutes later they were on their way out of Ibla, driving into the modern city center of Ragusa. The taxi turned into a circular courtyard full of scaffolding covered with ads and posters for concerts. Palm trees rustled in the wind. The station was on the other side, a modest, two-story building. The hands of a clock on the roof showed that it was just after ten thirty in the evening.

"If you hurry—" began the driver, as he brought the car to a halt.

"Thanks." Alessandro gave him money. Rosa was already getting out.

She had the feeling that she ought to crouch down as she ran. But if the Harpies had been following them, they hadn't shown themselves. There were only a few people outside the station; most of them must have just arrived and were hurrying to get out of there. It was not an inviting area.

"Quick!" Alessandro took her hand. After a last glance at the night sky, they entered the station concourse. Rosa felt a little safer with a roof over her head, but that feeling disappeared when she saw the pigeons pecking around for food on the floor of the concourse—and all of them raised their heads at the same time and looked at her and Alessandro.

Rosa nearly stumbled as they ran past the creatures. She remembered Florinda's inexplicable fear of birds. And the burnt nests in the basin of the fountain outside the Palazzo Alcantara.

"It's leaving any minute," called Alessandro.

Out on the first platform, a conductor was already raising his whistle to his mouth.

They ran through the glass doors and onto the platform. The conductor had his back to them. Out of breath, they reached the train and flung themselves into the nearest car. As Alessandro closed the door behind them, the whistle blew. A second door closed somewhere farther along the train, which began to move.

Without a word, they hurried past empty compartments, until Rosa said, "This one is as good as any."

Alessandro looked pale as they dropped into seats on opposite sides of the window. Her eyes went from him to his reflection in the pane, then focused on the lights of the station going past.

Dozens of pigeons were sitting on struts under the roof over the platform. Some were hunched in the shadows, others in the pale illumination of the station lighting.

They were all staring at the train.

They all looked back at Rosa.

Had he told the truth about Aliza's death?

Rosa gazed out into the darkness, at the silhouettes of hilltops, gray trees, deserted roads running across the tracks. The night was a black screen on which the light in the compartment projected their faces, two ghostly masks. They were bone tired, but still full of energy after escaping from Ragusa.

Had he told the truth?

Maybe she ought to forget, once and for all, that he had already lied to her twice. First on Isola Luna, soon after her arrival in Sicily, then again when he took out the contract for the assassination of Michele. The first was all in the past; they had hardly known each other at the time, and she had forgiven him for that long ago. With the second lie, he had wanted to protect her, and it wouldn't have infuriated Rosa half as much if she hadn't learned the truth from Avvocato Trevini.

And now the death of Aliza. It probably *had* happened as he said. Aliza had attacked him, he had defended himself. So why couldn't she simply believe him? Why did she doubt his honesty? She knew the answer, even if she didn't want to admit it: He had changed. Ever since Fundling's supposed death, maybe longer than that, an insidious transformation had been taking place in him.

He had what he had fought for, revenge on Cesare and his place as head of his clan. They had been as happy together as circumstances allowed. Now, though, he was becoming more obsessed by the hour. Did he feel his pride was injured? Were all the vengeful instincts that he had only just overcome sur-facing again?

They had both been humiliated by their families, only it didn't mean much to her—not after everything she had already experienced. He, however, was fighting with himself and his circumstances, and that robbed him of his smile and the light in his eyes. His expression was as dark as his mood, and the blackness outside the window had found its way into his heart.

Distractedly, she looked at their reflections in the pane, and thought how much simpler it would have been if they had been able to talk it over. Let the reflections do it for them— grappling with questions and explanations, all the inevitable talking at cross-purposes.

"Well?" he asked suddenly.

She was holding the crumpled pages from Mori's book. Soon after the train left, she had begun reading the chapter, and she'd only just finished it.

"He found out a lot about the dynasties," she said. "A lot of it is superficial, but mostly he wrote down stuff that no one is really supposed to know apart from the Arcadians themselves. No wonder Cesare and your father raised the alarm."

"What did he write, then?" Alessandro stretched, and tried to stifle a yawn.

She leafed through the pages. "He began by summing up the familiar myths. About Arcadia being an island kingdom back in the days of classical antiquity, and King Lycaon falling out with Zeus when he served him human flesh to eat. Angry, Zeus cursed Lycaon and all his people. They became shape-shifters, half human, half animal, blah, blah, blah . . . In fact, the old story more or less as we know it."

A train going in the other direction thundered past them, and for a moment their car shook as if it were about to jump off the tracks.

"What's more interesting is that Mori obviously heard the same story that Trevini told me: how Lycaon was toppled from his throne by one of the most powerful families in Arcadia.

However, Mori doesn't seem to have known that it was the family of Lamias, at least he doesn't say a word about that. He claims that after the fall of Lycaon there was a civil war lasting decades, with the troublemakers—my ancestors—on one side, and the Panthera on the other. Your family obviously had it in for us for a long time."

"Then that would be why the Hungry Man originally made the Carnevares his closest confidants. Until his arrest, that is. The Panthera and the Lamias became enemies when your lot overthrew Lycaon." He shrugged his shoulders. "But I assume it wasn't about Lycaon personally but a matter of who represents the next king, you or us."

"Mori says that finally peace was made—although not until the kingdom had been devastated by war and half the population wiped out. By then Lycaon was long dead. The Lamias probably assassinated him right at the start of their rebellion. Decades, maybe even centuries passed, before both sides finally signed a new peace treaty in the holiest shrine of Arcadia."

"What kind of a shrine?"

"Doesn't say anything about that here. At least—"

They were interrupted when the door of their compartment was pushed abruptly open. Alessandro was already getting to his feet when the conductor said, "Good evening. Tickets, please."

Alessandro relaxed slightly and took the wallet out of the duffel bag. "We still have to buy them. Two tickets to Syracuse, please."

The gray-haired man gestured with his old-fashioned ticket punch. "I don't have any change on me. I'll stop by again on my way back, okay?"

"We won't run away from you," said Rosa wearily.

The conductor left the compartment, closing the sliding door. Shoulders stooped, he set off down the empty carriage.

"Did he recognize us?" she asked.

"Didn't look like it."

She closed her eyes for a moment and let herself lean against the narrow back of the seat.

Alessandro leaned down and kissed her. "I'm sorry," he said, "that you've been dragged into all this."

"It was my own decision to stay in Sicily." She put her hand on the nape of his neck and gave him another, much longer kiss. His lips were dry and cracked, but they were the only lips she ever wanted to kiss.

Finally he dropped back into his seat, ran his fingers through his hair, and linked his hands behind his head. "And what happened then? After they had made peace?"

"That was all. Mori goes in for a little speculation about what may have become of the Arcadians. Their descendants, he says, could have gone on existing in secret, and might show their true face again someday. Which is basically pretty much what the Hungry Man is planning now. Except that Mori is only making assumptions." She put the pages she had torn out of the book back in the duffel bag, with a pang of guilt for having ruined the bookseller's valuable copy for so little that was new to them—that's if he didn't have a whole crate of copies in his cellar.

The landscape outside had become rougher and rockier several miles back. Again and again, steep slopes blocked their view. The scenery was at first lost under wild bushes, then bleak and gray in the light falling out of the train windows.

Once there was a clattering noise that went on for some time, and was unlike the sound of the train passing along the tracks. As if a helicopter had flown overhead.

"I don't like this," she said.

"You mean the conductor?"

She stood up. "If he alerts the police, they'll be waiting for us at the next station." With a single stride, she was at the door, opened it, and looked cautiously both ways.

The corridor beside the compartments seemed to her darker than when they had boarded the train. As if the light had been dimmed.

"Let's get out of here," she said, and was about to turn around, but he was already beside her, carrying the bag.

"Right or left?"

"The conductor went left."

They turned right and hurried down the corridor to the door into the next car. At the narrow junction between them, the noise of the wheels on the rails was deafening. The concertina-like connecting walls were quivering like the inside of a human organ.

They entered a small area with a locked toilet cubicle, and then a large, undivided carriage with rows of hard plastic seats, all empty except for two at the far end. Two heads rocked slightly back and forth there, as if on spikes. When one of the two passengers rose, Rosa saw to her relief that it was a little old woman wearing a broad-brimmed hat. She came toward them, supporting herself on the backs of the seats to compensate for the jolting of the train. Rosa wondered whether to tell her that the toilet was out of order, but then let her pass in silence.

The man in the seat next to the woman's was younger, maybe her son. He looked up and unabashedly inspected Rosa in her tight black dress. She was glad when they left the carriage and entered the next one, also undivided. There were more passengers in here, six or seven.

"Let me go first." Alessandro pushed past her.

She followed him along the aisle down the center of the rows of seats. Most of the passengers were dozing, except for two young women who broke off their conversation when Alessandro and Rosa passed them.

The next carriage was the last in the train and had no rows of seats, only metal stools that folded down along the walls. A few crates and large cartons stood at the far end, with a guard in uniform sitting beside them. He looked up from a newspaper and called, "Didn't you see the notice on the door? No entry for passengers."

Alessandro murmured an apology to avoid unnecessary trouble and was the first back in the carriage they had only just walked through.

"There isn't any notice on the door," whispered Rosa.

The two young women glanced up again. In the neon

lighting, their faces looked as pale as the rocks outside the windows.

The train was leaving a narrow track between high slopes. Once again, a landscape of silhouettes rolled past like a darkened stage set.

"We're slowing down," said Rosa.

A moment later everything was pitch dark outside as the train thundered into a tunnel.

They had almost reached the door back to the next carriage when a violent jolt threw them off their feet. Rosa was just in time to grab the back of a row of seats, and fell on two empty ones. Alessandro stumbled over, landed on all fours, and was on his legs again at once. Brakes screeched. Passengers uttered cries of alarm.

She struggled up. "Was that the emergency brake?"

"We've stopped, at any rate."

The carriages came to a standstill in the middle of the tunnel under the mountain.

Farther forward, someone called something that Rosa couldn't make out. Then there was a scream.

All the lights went out.

IN THE TUNNEL

THE CARRIAGE WAS PLUNGED in darkness. The last thing Rosa saw was one of the young women jumping up from her seat. Then she heard swift footsteps coming closer along the central aisle.

"Alessandro! Here comes—"

She broke off when she realized that he and the young woman were about to collide. Rosa was on the verge of shifting shape, but then she heard Alessandro speaking soothingly.

"It's all right. Nothing for you to be frightened of. The lights will come on again in a moment."

In between his words, she heard the whimpering of the young woman, who was weeping with fear. Her companion, behind them in the carriage, called to her.

"Go back to your friend," said Alessandro. "This will soon be over."

But of course it wouldn't. It had hardly begun.

Once again, someone screamed heartrendingly farther forward in the train, and soon there were more shouts. It couldn't be just because of the darkness.

The young woman's sobbing moved away behind them. Rosa heard her speeding up, then a stumble, followed by a male voice cursing. On the way back to her seat, she must have collided with another of the passengers.

"Alessandro?"

His hand felt for hers. "We have to get out of here."

"Shape-shift?"

"If the lights come on again, and the others see a panther and a snake, panic really *will* break out."

The shouting from the front was coming closer, rolling toward them.

"It's them, isn't it?" she said. "Malandras."

"Yes, I think so."

She moved back to him in the aisle but met first with the duffel bag, which he was still holding tightly, and then with Alessandro himself. The young woman had obviously reached her fellow traveler, because a voice was speaking reassuringly to her, while she went on whimpering. The man let forth a torrent of curses. Someone asked what they should do now. No one answered.

"Come on." Alessandro took Rosa's hand and led her to the connecting door. There would be an emergency exit to the tracks in the space between the carriages.

The sliding door opened, and at once the smell of burnt plastic engulfed them. Maybe as a result of the violent braking.

The screams from the front cars were much louder here, and alarmingly close. Rosa heard Alessandro rattling at the lever to work the emergency exit.

"Bolted down."

The sliding door behind them was still open; the voices in

the carriage sounded more and more agitated. Suddenly the young woman's tears turned to shrieks.

"My God!" bellowed the man. "Keep your mouth—"

A moist, tearing sound silenced him. Then there was a rustling that Rosa knew only too well. Feathers sweeping over something.

"They're here," she whispered. One of the Harpies must have been sitting in the carriage in human form. Rosa remembered the door that she had heard closing just after they boarded the train themselves.

Now all the passengers in the carriage were shouting at the same time, five or six voices. Several of the travelers seemed to have fallen over one another as they tried to leave their rows of seats. A sharp hiss came out of the darkness, followed by the shrill screech of a bird. A short, strong gust of wind blew past. The rustling sound of beating wings caused even more chaos among the passengers, with screams of panic from the injured and dying.

Rosa followed Alessandro forward through the next sliding door. No one but the old lady and her younger companion had been sitting in this carriage before. There was nothing to be heard in the vicinity, only the screeching voices of the Harpies in the car behind them.

Alessandro held Rosa close. "Shift shape and stay under the seats."

"How about you?"

"There must be an emergency hammer for the windows somewhere. If I find it, I can break a pane. We have to get out of this damn train." She heard his clothes rustle, and then the display of his cell phone suddenly bathed their immediate surroundings in bluish-white twilight. For the first time since the lights had gone out, she could see his face again. There was a silvery gleam in his eyes.

"We'll find it sooner if we work together," she said, shaking her head. Looking around her, she was relieved to see that the sliding door had automatically closed. That wouldn't stop the Harpies, but it muffled the screams from the other car.

"Where are the old woman and the man with her?" asked Alessandro.

She swiftly looked around her. "Never mind that. Let's find the hammer."

"It ought to be hanging somewhere on the wall between windows. But it's been some time since I traveled by train." As they ran down the central aisle, with the light of the phone display ahead of them, Rosa looked out for anything else that could break a window. But there was nothing.

"Over there." Alessandro pointed to an empty hook on the wall. "It's been removed."

Her eyes wandered farther forward, but so far as she could see in the dim light, there was the only hook. On the front wall beside the next sliding door, someone had sprayed a slogan in garish colors: SAVE WILD LIFE NOW.

The door was half ajar and sounds came through from the darkness: screams and wails, the trampling of feet, doors being opened, all of it drowned out by the screeching of many birds.

Rosa looked around again. Then the sliding door at the other end of the carriage opened. Something broad and massive pushed its way in. The opening was too small for the creature; even with its wings folded the Harpy could hardly get through. A hooked yellow beak shimmered in its face, and its round eyes gleamed.

"Get down!" shouted a voice, this time from the other direction, coming through the half-open door to the carriage in front.

Rosa reacted faster than Alessandro. As he was still turning to see what was coming their way, she seized him by the arm and pulled him down with her between two rows of seats.

In rapid succession, muzzle flashes flared. Several shots whistled over their heads. For two or three seconds Rosa was almost deafened; she saw the flashes, but heard nothing except a dull thud as the gun was fired again and again. An acrid smell spread through the air.

When she cautiously looked up, the Harpy was hanging with wings outspread over the seats at the end of the aisle, head dangling down. The shift back to human shape was already beginning. The wings receded into the body, which lost its hold on the seats and fell to the floor between the rows.

"Come on, get up!" the voice that had spoken before told her, and only now did Rosa realize that it came from the old woman. When they got to their feet, Rosa was almost a head taller. The woman was very thin, almost bony, and now she wasn't wearing a hat. Her sparse hair was short, and poorly cut.

Alessandro's cell phone lay on one of the seats, illuminating the woman's face from below. "Come with me," she ordered, pointing the way into the carriage ahead of them with an automatic pistol.

"There are several of them." Alessandro was keeping between the woman and Rosa, just in case.

More shots rang out. Something large was flung at the door backward, crashed into the frame, and lost pale feathers that drifted into the carriage like a cloud. The Harpy let out a screech as it swiftly managed to turn its body, thrusting it through the doorway with all its might.

The old woman pressed the trigger. Her shot went into the shallow brow of the bird, killing the creature on the spot. Even as the bird of prey became a woman with blond hair, the man who had been sitting beside the old woman earlier appeared out of the darkness behind her. He, too, was holding a silvery automatic.

"We'd hoped to get you two out of the train at the next station," he said. "But the Malandras boarded the train with you. Some of them must have been waiting here in the tunnel, too, or there'd never have been so many."

"Who are you?" Rosa asked the woman.

"We're the ones who will get you out of here if you get moving. And please keep your mouths shut."

Rosa half expected Alessandro to contradict the speaker, but his restraint surprised her.

They joined the woman in the center aisle, clambered over the body of the Harpy, and followed the man into the next carriage. The weeping and wailing of injured passengers could still be heard far behind them. Rosa tried to block it from her mind.

Somewhere or other the electronics switched in with a humming sound, and immediately the emergency lighting came on: sulfur-yellow bulbs set far apart in the ceiling.

The four of them passed through the empty carriage with separate compartments. The man hurried ahead, and the old woman brought up the rear. She moved remarkably fast, as if her frail exterior were only a costume hiding a completely different person—young, fit, and highly experienced at what she was doing.

That thought occupied Rosa's mind until they entered the next large, undivided carriage. This one smelled so strongly of blood that she stopped, rooted to the spot, even before she saw the bodies. Only when the woman urged her to keep going did she see what the Harpies had done.

Eight passengers had fallen victim to the Malandras. They lay jammed between seats, or with their distorted bodies lying over the backs of the rows. The conductor lay dead on the floor of the central aisle. Window panes, walls, even the ceiling were lavishly splashed with red.

Three Harpies had been wreaking havoc here. They lay, shot dead, among the other bodies, distinguishable from them only by the fact that they were naked. The blood-bath was a taste of what the Hungry Man had in mind for all Arcadians: a return to the customs of their ancestors, killing for killing's sake, to satisfy the hunting instincts of beasts of prey.

"Why this, now?" asked Alessandro, lowering his voice, as three more armed figures appeared. Two of them wore black ski masks, and Rosa had the impression that there was something wrong with the shape of their heads.

"You ask why?" the old woman repeated, scornfully. "Because the Hungry Man is back. Because his followers—and by now that means most of the Arcadians out there, more and more of them every day—are coming out of hiding. No more camouflage, no appearance of humanity. Even the mask of Cosa Nostra isn't enough for them anymore. You two knew that, didn't you? But there's a difference between hearing something and seeing it with your own eyes."

Rosa swung angrily around to face the woman—and realized, at close quarters and in the emergency lighting, that she had been wrong. What she had taken for the folds and wrinkles of old age were something else.

The woman's face was roughened, covered with countless little warts and pustules. The skin of a toad, thought Rosa suddenly, but then she realized what in fact it was: the skin of a human being fixed at an early stage of metamorphosis. Changing into a reptile. The tiny raised bumps on it were not warts, but the first sign of scales that had not fully developed.

The woman was a Lamia.

Or had been before she—

"You're hybrids," said Alessandro.

The woman's voice dripped with sarcasm. "Naturally we apologize for our unattractive appearance."

"What's your name?" asked Rosa.

"Mirella."

"Alcantara?"

The woman smiled. "Not all Lamias are Alcantaras. You're not as unique as you think."

By now Rosa had heard quite enough from her, but she bit back any retort, and followed the hybrids, holding her breath through the carriage full of corpses. They had to climb over the dead conductor. Their shoes left reddish-brown tracks on any part of the floor that was not yet covered in blood.

In the narrow junction with the next carriage, one of the outside doors had been wrenched open by force. She and Alessandro jumped out into the tunnel, breathing in deeply. The stink inside the train wafted out with them, clinging to their hair and their clothing.

A narrow path ran between the wall of the tunnel and the train. Light shone down on them. When Rosa looked up, she saw figures who, although they appeared human, were crawling over the vaulted ceiling of the tunnel on all fours, lighting up the scene with handheld flashlights.

Mirella, her companion, and two other men took Rosa and Alessandro between them, and urged them on. There was a lot of noise at the end of the tunnel. Rosa exchanged a glance with Alessandro. She was ready to shift shape at once if he showed any sign of doing the same. But he looked as baffled as she did.

"Come on, keep going!" The hybrid made them walk on. "We don't have all night."

They all sped up, the flashlight-holders under the roof

running headlong like strange beetles. Another figure jumped out of the carriage in front. The engineer was probably dead, and this hybrid must have switched on the emergency power supply.

"What about the injured passengers?" asked Alessandro.

"As soon as we're on our way, we'll call the police and the ambulance." Mirella sounded as if she didn't want to go into such questions in detail. "There'll be no signal for the passengers' cell phones here in the mountain, so no one will know what happened yet."

"There are people in there losing a lot of blood," said Rosa indignantly.

The woman glanced at her impatiently. "Then we don't want to waste any more time talking."

The end of the tunnel lay a hundred and fifty yards ahead. There, too, lights were moving around. The loud sound of rotors penetrated the stone roof. At least one helicopter had landed outside, maybe several.

The train was behind them, and now Rosa saw that hybrids were also running along the other side of the tracks. Their distorted shadows scurried along the tunnel wall. Yet more masks, yet more wrong dimensions under long coats and Windbreakers. One of the hybrids ran on hands and feet, but had an assault rifle strapped to his back.

Rosa still couldn't estimate Mirella's age, but she assumed that contrary to first impressions, the hybrid was not over forty. She had no eyelids. Her movements showed that she was used to physical strain.

"What do you want with us?" asked Rosa.

Mirella licked her lips with a forked tongue. A man beside Rosa pulled his ski mask off. His face was so hairy that his eyes could hardly be seen, raven black amid his dark fur. He had a slight hump, and looked as if he would drop down at any moment and run like a dog.

"You're expected," said Mirella.

This whole operation, all the equipment, plus a helicopter or two—it must have cost huge sums of money. A few hybrids working on their own could hardly have gone to such expense.

Alessandro looked at the helicopters. "TABULA?"

The man with the furry face bared his craggy teeth in a gesture of hatred, showing the jaws of a predator.

Rosa shook her head. "Thanassis," she whispered, reaching for Alessandro's hand as they ran. "I think they're taking us to the *Stabat Mater.*"

THE *STABAT MATER*

"WHAT DO YOU KNOW about the ship?" asked Mirella, shouting above the noise of the helicopter engines.

Rosa looked away from the window and the pastel colors of dawn breaking over the open Mediterranean. Alessandro was still holding her hand, and had been for hours. His calm appearance was deceptive; he was tense, and seemed determined. A burning, cat-like glint kept appearing in his eyes.

"Not much," she told the hybrid. "The *Stabat Mater* was the flagship of Evangelos Thanassis's fleet of cruise ships. He's a Greek shipowner, one of the richest men in the world, probably has a hand in hundreds of other businesses. He withdrew from public life years ago, and most people don't even know whether he's still alive."

She could guess at a smile on Mirella's pock-marked face. "Not bad for someone who's notable mainly for her lack of interest in such matters for seventeen years of her life."

Piqued, Rosa scrutinized the woman. "Maybe *I* ought to be asking the questions. You seem to be very well informed."

"About you? Only the bare essentials." She's lying, thought Rosa. The hybrid could probably have listed more details about both her and Alessandro than she could herself.

"Why a ship?" asked Alessandro. "Why doesn't Thanassis

live on an island? Or in a villa behind electric fences?"

"He lived like that for long enough," said Mirella, "and he's left it behind. Freedom isn't *knowing* that you can do or not do what you like. Freedom means actually *doing* it. Evangelos Thanassis has loved the sea all his life—and in the end it became his refuge."

"And yours?" Rosa looked from Mirella to the other hybrids on board the chopper, seven men and women who had taken part in the attack on the Harpies. The rest were flying in a second helicopter a hundred yards behind them.

Mirella nodded. Her thin hair clung to her scalp, which made the places where the wrinkled skin on her head showed even more conspicuous.

There were four rows of seats in the helicopter, divided by an aisle down the center. Alessandro was sitting by the window, with Rosa beside him. Mirella sat on the other side of the aisle, next to a man whose face was human, but who had gill slits in his throat, bluish flaps of skin that could be seen above the upturned collar of his jacket. So that was how the people working for Thanassis had managed to salvage the statues from the seabed without diving equipment.

The man with the furry face, half Hunding, half human, was crouching on the floor between the rows of seats. Obviously his naturally stooped attitude made normal sitting uncomfortable for him. He was surreptitiously casting brief glances at Rosa.

The hybrids in the back rows of seats wore billowing shirts with hoods over their heads. Rosa avoided turning to look at them. Those were the figures who had been crawling along the roof of the tunnel. With every movement they made, rough scraping and clicking sounds could be heard under their clothing. Parts of them had hard shells.

One of them said something to Mirella now and then, in a language that Rosa didn't know. Even the hybrid asked him several times to repeat himself before she could answer him. The man next to him communicated only in whistling and humming sounds.

The pilot's voice came over the loudspeaker, telling them that they were about to come in over the *Stabat Mater.*

Alessandro leaned close to her ear. "Whatever happens, I'll look after you."

"Ditto."

He managed a grin that, for a moment, made him appear as boyish as at their first meeting. She wanted to kiss him, but felt the glances of the hybrids resting on them, and made do with a firm squeeze of his hand.

They flew in a slight arc, and saw the gigantic white ocean vessel at an angle below them.

Rosa had read up on the vast ship after it snapped up the statues from under their noses. The *Stabat Mater* was one of the largest ships sailing the seas, built to take four thousand passengers. Her white hull was more than a thousand feet long, almost five times the size of a Boeing 747. A dozen decks loomed over the surface of the water. As they came in closer, she saw several open-air swimming pools and superstructures with a futuristic look to them.

In the middle of the top deck, a huge light-shaft yawned open under a glass roof, allowing a glance down into the ship. It was like the interior of a shopping mall several floors deep, surrounded by glass balustrades. Plants grew at the bottom of the shaft, once, perhaps, a little park at the heart of the *Stabat Mater*, now a rampant jungle.

In contrast to ordinary cruise ships, there were no sun loungers anywhere on board, no bars, no pavilions. The empty upper deck was about as cozy as an aircraft carrier, a wide empty space with a handful of figures lost on it, looking up at the helicopters.

"How many of you live on this ship?" asked Rosa.

"A few hundred," said Mirella tersely.

Alessandro looked inquiringly at Rosa, but she only shrugged her shoulders and said nothing until the helicopter came down on one of the marked landing pads.

They were led from the platform down a flight of steps, white like everything here, but grimier than it had seemed from above. Dust, water, and salt had accumulated in nooks and crannies. The steps themselves were dirty. Looking more closely, Rosa saw the prints of bare feet with abnormally long toes.

The stairway ended on another platform, several yards above what had once been the sun deck. A tall young woman stood alone at the ship's rail, with her back turned to them, looking out at the Mediterranean. Her hair, black as a raven's wing, was piled up at the back of her head and secured with long pins. She wore a tightly tied, red velvet basque bodice, and a wide, black hooped skirt under it. The hem of the skirt was trimmed with lace and fell to the floor.

Rosa recognized her by her clothing even before she turned around to them. The skirt rotated, and the lace border rustled over the steel deck.

"Danai," Rosa whispered to Alessandro, without taking her eyes off the young woman. "Thanassis's daughter."

Mirella, who had accompanied them along with the dog-man and the two hybrids in hooded shirts, nodded to the woman. Then she and the men took several steps back. Rosa and Alessandro stayed where they were.

"Hello," said Danai Thanassis, almost shyly. She might have been in her midtwenties; she had high cheekbones, a small mouth painted blood-red with lipstick, and ears that lay close to her head. Her most striking feature, however, was her eyes, very pretty and unnaturally large. There had been something ethereal about her when Rosa first saw her, dancing in the Dream Room nightclub in New York. And even now, without music, dry ice, and black light, she looked somehow unearthly. Alessandro seemed to feel it, too. He was staring at her as if hypnotized.

"I'm Danai." She linked her fingers on the stiff curve of her hooped skirt. "Welcome aboard the *Stabat Mater*." Putting her head slightly on one side, she scrutinized Rosa. "I know you."

"I don't think so."

"Oh yes, I'm sure I do."

Rosa stroked back untidy strands of blond hair from the

corner of her mouth. With her hair pinned up, Danai, in contrast, posed so perfectly in front of the panoramic view of the Mediterranean that she might have been part of a wall mural.

"Your people helped us," said Alessandro. "Thank you."

Danai's delicate smile widened.

Rosa took a step forward, leaving only an arm's length between her and the Greek girl. The dog-man growled behind her. "Listen," she said, "we didn't really want to come on this expedition. So tell us what we're doing here."

"My father would like to talk to you." Her gaze rested on Alessandro. "Both of you. He has a proposition for you."

"What kind of proposition?"

"He'll tell you that himself. I'm only the welcome committee."

"And I already feel at home."

Danai beamed. "That's nice."

Alessandro touched Rosa's arm. "Let's hear what he has to say."

She stared at him. "You really are curious about this damn ship!"

"Aren't you?"

Not in the least, she was going to say, but Danai circled them with a hovering movement and got her response in first. "I'll show you around a little if you like."

One of the men opened a double door in the interior of the ship, just wide enough for Danai's hooped skirt. As she went ahead of them, her upper body remained perfectly still; she seemed to be gliding along like a clockwork doll on wheels.

At the same time, something moved beneath her skirt, kicking against the fabric all around the inside of its hem. It gradually dawned on Rosa what that movement reminded her of. Spider's legs.

"She's an Arachnid," Alessandro whispered to her. "At least, half an Arachnid."

He took her hand as they entered the interior of the *Stabat Mater*. An animal stench wafted up from the depths of the ship, a mixture of monkey house and dog kennel.

Danai went down a corridor lined with doors beyond which, according to the inscriptions on them, there had once been seminar rooms. The wooden panels were scratched, and in other places claws had scraped the paint off the walls. The carpet, too, was dirty and threadbare.

The corridor widened out, ending in a foyer with four silver elevator doors and access to a stairway.

"We'll have to go down to Deck Four," said Danai. "My father recently moved there."

Alessandro was about to press the button of one of the elevators, but like a flash Danai was beside him, snatching his hand away from it.

"Better not," she said. "The elevators are out of order now, and the shafts are inhabited. It's better if what's in them doesn't pick up your scent."

Only now did Rosa see that one of the elevator doors bulged out, as if something had beaten against it from the inside. Danai moved over to a flight of stairs with scratched brass banisters. Everything here looked dilapidated, and much of it intentionally damaged.

Sounds came up from the depths of the stairway. Roaring and squealing, mingled with human voices. Somewhere in the midst of this chaos, someone was singing an operatic aria.

Rosa shook her head. "Why, for heaven's sake, do you want us to go down there?"

Danai gave her a challenging smile. "Do you want to find out more about your family? And TABULA?"

The dog-man let out a short, harsh bark. In the background, the exoskeleton shell-cases of the insect hybrids rattled under their hooded shirts.

"Come on," said Alessandro.

She reluctantly started down the stairs with him. "Didn't you have to read *Animal Farm* in school?"

"The one with the talking pig in it?"

"That was *Babe*."

Danai laughed softly. "Or *Lord of the Flies*."

"I liked *The Island of Dr. Moreau*," said Mirella. "Particularly the ending."

Beyond the wall, something began going berserk in the elevator shaft.

HYBRIDS

THEY REACHED THE BOTTOM of the stairs and turned into a corridor teeming with hybrids. Many of them were standing around in passages, as if to lure the unwary into their cabins and devour them there. Others trotted around with their heads bowed, seeming not to know what to do with themselves. When a quarrel broke out close to them, Mirella let out a whistle and signaled to the dog-man. He flung himself between the combatants, throwing one of them against the wall and the other through an open doorway.

"Thanassis," he hissed, in such a threatening tone that it gave even Rosa goose bumps.

The brawlers, and several others too, looked nervously around, saw Danai, lowered their heads respectfully, and waited like that until the group had passed.

"I'm sorry," said Danai, "that you have to see this part of the ship first. There are others."

"Are they all better?" asked Rosa.

"No. A couple of the decks have been sealed off. Anyone who gets in there doesn't come out again. It's better that way for everyone."

The comings and goings in these corridors were a strange sight. A number of the hybrids wore clothes that disguised them, while others openly displayed their deformities. Most of them were more human than animal, but not all. There were big cats who went on all fours, but had no fur; foxes with forelegs ending in hands; a bear with a human face.

"Over there," said Alessandro. "Harpies."

Rosa saw three children with naked torsos. Behind them, they had wings without feathers dragging uselessly along the floor. The wings resembled wrecked umbrellas: bony spokes with pink flaps of skin stretched between them.

"Suicides are a problem," Danai admitted. "Not all of them here can come to terms with their fate."

Ahead of them, a little girl in a grubby jogging suit was doing gymnastic exercises in the corridor. She turned a cartwheel, landed crouching in front of Danai, and licked her outstretched hand with a dog's pink tongue. Mirella let the child do as she liked for a moment, and only when Danai gave her a sign did she push her aside. The little girl growled at Alessandro as he passed her.

At the end of the corridor they came to a steel bulkhead. Danai unlocked it with a number code. Before opening it to the passage beyond, she gave Rosa and Alessandro a smile. "It gets prettier now."

They entered a wood-paneled hall with old-fashioned chandeliers, and candles standing on neatly laid tables. There was a glass wall with a view into the broad light-shaft that they had seen from the helicopter, and of the green jungle at the heart of the *Stabat Mater*. A Plexiglas balustrade ran around the outside of the huge pane.

"There's going to be a dinner for the first-class passengers here this evening," Danai explained, as they passed the empty tables.

Next they walked down corridors with solidly made saloons opening off them. Hybrids sat in armchairs or on sofas, reading, playing Scrabble and backgammon, or talking quietly. A good-looking man in a suit was in conversation with a leopard woman. He turned his profile to them, and as they passed he looked around at them. The left side of his face was that of a moray eel.

Not all the hybrids, however, were ugly or grotesque. Many were covered with fine, silky down; others had brightly colored plumage instead of hair on their heads. A young man was sitting at a grand piano, playing a sonata so melancholy that it went to Rosa's heart. His face was covered with scales shimmering in all colors of the rainbow.

Once again they reached an elevator, this time with wood-paneled doors. Danai used a key to activate it. "This one is safe," she said, when she saw Alessandro wrinkling his brow.

At every deck they passed during the ride down, the background noises outside the elevator door changed. Once they heard terrible roaring, then the sound of an orchestral rehearsal, finally a voice reciting a poem. Only when the elevator came to a halt did silence reign again.

"Here we are," said Danai.

Mirella tensed her body. The two shell-plated hybrids had not made a sound for a long time. The smell of sweat spread through the elevator.

They entered a corridor with gray metal walls. There was a pungent smell of mixed disinfectant and the odors of long sickness in the air. Mirella's disfigured skin looked grayer than ever. Her two companions hunched their heads farther down between their shoulders.

Two guards stood in front of a door. They reminded Rosa of Danai's bodyguards in the Dream Room: bald-headed lunks with headsets and black overalls. No visible sign that they were hybrids.

Apologizing to her guests, Danai went through the door and signed to Mirella to go with her. "Wait here," she told Rosa and Alessandro. "We won't be long."

Before the door closed, Rosa caught a glimpse of the room inside. White walls, glass-fronted cupboards, machines with flashing lights. The impression of a figure on a bed.

The insect hybrids were standing in front of the opposite wall of the corridor. They and the guards at the door never took their eyes off one another. No one spoke.

Danai's soft, girlish voice could be heard beyond the door, and then Mirella's sharper tones. Rosa could catch only scraps of the conversation. The hybrid was reporting on the incidents in the railroad tunnel.

A little later, Mirella came back into the corridor and beck-oned to them. "He'll see you now." She stayed outside while Rosa and Alessandro entered the room.

Someone had tried to equip the sickroom as luxuriously as possible, but that merely emphasized the fact that this was no place where you would take up residence voluntarily.

Danai was standing beside the bed, her hoop skirt pressed against its frame so that she could be as close to the man on the pillows as possible. She was holding his hand, while a nurse sat in front of a row of touch screens, obviously programming infusions. A long cat's tail hung down under the skirt of her white uniform, the end of it dangling a hand's breadth above the floor.

Whole bundles of tubes led from bags of fluids to the bed, and disappeared under the covers.

The old man scrutinized the two young people. His alert gaze was in stark contrast to the rest of his appearance. The white coverlet was drawn high up on his chest, his bony limbs stood out in sharp outline under it. He did not seem to be an Arachnid like his daughter.

Without speaking to the visitors, he signaled to the nurse. She left the computers and turned back the coverlet. Rosa instinctively held her breath, but when she did breathe in again, she could smell only chemicals.

"I am not a hybrid," he said, in perfect Italian. "Isn't that what you were wondering?"

"You certainly owe us some explanations," said Alessandro, "but that one's not high on the list."

Thanassis gave him a benevolent smile. The old man looked as if he had undergone all kinds of cosmetic surgery many years ago, and the effect of those operations had long since reversed itself. He had wrinkles in the wrong places, there were visible scars just below his hairline, signs that his skin had been tightened and fallen in again. Maybe he had once set great store by his appearance, but that was over now. Just as life on board the *Stabat Mater* had also lapsed into disorder.

"I've heard about you two." He signed to the nurse, and she covered him up again. Danai, motionless, was holding his hand. "In fact, it is difficult *not* to hear about you these days."

"Not by our choosing," said Rosa.

"Are you aware that the police now doubt whether you were guilty of the judge's death? Of course they're still looking for you, but there are forensic experts whose opinion is that Quattrini was killed by an animal. There's talk of traces of DNA that's definitely nonhuman, quite apart from the nature of the wounds inflicted."

They exchanged a glance. For the moment, that made no difference to their situation.

"But never mind that," said Thanassis. "Today I find talking more of a strain than I like, so let's not waste time. Ask me your questions."

"Why did you have us brought here?"

"First, I was curious about you. And secondly, I need your help."

Rosa laughed quietly. "*Our* help?"

"In a certain way, yes." A fit of coughing interrupted him. One of the countless instruments beside the bed beeped harder, but then calmed down again. "The Arcadian dynasties are in a state of flux. Much is happening that is not good, but significant. The Hungry Man left prison days ago and is back in Sicily. The Harpies would have handed you over to him if you hadn't killed them. We know what happened. But the death of the two Malandra sisters complicated matters, both for you and for him. He is an old man, like me, and his experience with young Arcadians is long in the past. Back then there was no resistance to his decisions, no one openly opposed them. He underestimated you when he set the sisters on you. However, it is extremely reassuring that he made his first serious mistake so soon after seizing power again."

"Are the clans really all behind him?" asked Alessandro.

"A great many of them are. It was easier for them to reject the Hungry Man when he was still behind bars. But now that he is back, *capo* after *capo* is ready to pay him homage. Some who refused have died unpleasant deaths in the last two days. The search for you two isn't all that he has on his mind just now. He aims to renew his old power on a comprehensive scale, and he is exerting his influence to that end, far beyond Sicily itself."

Rosa glanced at Danai, who never once took her eyes off her father. Her chest rose and fell slightly, in a rhythmical movement that looked strange above that monster of a dress.

"I've never understood," said Rosa, "why everything is supposed to have been so much better in the old days. What exactly was better? I'm an Arcadian, but the mere idea of eating human flesh . . . I mean, I'm a *vegetarian*!"

With a smile, Thanassis looked from her to Alessandro. "And how about you, as one of the Panthera? What do you feel about the idea of hunting humans and tearing them to pieces?"

Alessandro said nothing for a moment, avoiding Rosa's eyes. Then he shook his head. "It's not about nourishment. It's about showing who's stronger."

"But that's not an instinct known only to animals," said Thanassis. "Didn't you yourself do your utmost to become *capo* of the Carnevares?"

"And one of the richest men in the world blames me for that?"

"I'm not blaming you. I dreamed for years of controlling shipping in the seas all over the world. And for a while I did. You don't have to be an Arcadian to have ambitious aims. But the Hungry Man is not concerned with wealth, he wants to subjugate an entire species. There's blindness and maybe insanity in that. But above all a desire for retribution. It was human beings who put him behind bars thirty years ago, and he wants humans to pay for it. However, revenge is a petty and narrow-minded motive. It brings only a moment's satisfaction, like eating a piece of chocolate. Anticipation often makes one happier than the act itself. Did you feel happy when you killed Cesare Carnevare? Or was there only the sense of a great void after you had done it?"

Rosa took Alessandro's hand. His fingers were cold.

"The Hungry Man knows how fleeting that moment of happiness is," said Thanassis. "That's why he is simply extending his desire for retribution to the entire human race. He hopes for a triumph lasting years, decades, and he's ready to stake everything on getting it."

Alessandro looked as if he were about to object, but Rosa

stopped him. "He's telling the truth," she whispered. "I've met the Hungry Man. I've—" She had been going to add, *I've looked into his eyes*, but that wasn't so. In all the time she had spent talking to him, she had not once seen his face. Yet all the same, she thought that what Thanassis said was true.

"You mean he thinks humanity as a whole should pay for betraying him?" asked Alessandro.

"Exactly right." Thanassis signed to the nurse again. She touched a screen, and at once two fluids mingled in one of the containers to drip through a tube into the old man's body. He closed his eyes and took a deep breath. "There's only one problem. Human beings are no longer lambs who'll let themselves be led to the slaughter. That may have been different in the age of classical antiquity, when no one thought it unusual for people to fall victim to a werewolf or a giant snake. But today? How long will it be before all the nations of the world are up in arms against anyone who seems even remotely like an Arcadian? The dynasties now face the threat of extermination. Give humanity a reason to be afraid, and it will try to eradicate that reason root and branch. At the moment human beings fear epidemic sickness or terrorism. But if the dynasties drop their masks they'll provide a perfect target, and you will see Arcadians burnt at the stake again."

A warning signal sounded as his heartbeat speeded up. His daughter reassuringly caressed the back of his hand, which was freckled with age spots.

"Danai and all the others like her will be the first to be crushed between the opposing forces," he went on. "What we've built up here, a refuge for all who are different, won't withstand them for long. At the moment we can stay in hiding because no one is looking for us. But if it comes to open war between Arcadians and the human race, then people will start to take an interest in us again, and find us. In fact I am afraid they will find us very quickly."

"What are you planning?" asked Alessandro.

"Arcadians are to blame for the fact that hybrids like my daughter must live like outcasts. And even worse, because some of the dynasties work in secret with TABULA, more hybrids are still being produced in their experimental stations. Only a few of the passengers on board this ship were born naturally as hybrids, or became hybrids by some whim of fate—far more of them were bred by TABULA. We liberated some of them, while others managed to escape and made their own way to us. But those are only tiny moments of success. Not until there are no Arcadian dynasties left will TABULA also lose its justification for existence."

Did he know that Rosa's grandmother had handed Arcadians over to TABULA? And that her father, who she had thought dead for years, was working for that secret organization under the name Apollonio? In a flash, she saw images before her eyes again, the video images of her rape by Tano and Michele. Saw her father standing beside those two and telling them what to do.

Alessandro stepped impatiently from foot to foot. "Then you want to oppose the Hungry Man and the dynasties in order to destroy TABULA at the same time?"

"I want to do them all the harm I can," agreed Thanassis. "Can I really destroy them? Maybe in the long term, but it won't be done overnight. It's possible to kill the Hungry Man. But TABULA is a many-headed monster. I can try to deprive it of nourishment and hope that will be the end of it. And that may be enough, who knows?"

"You said you need our help," Rosa interrupted. "What did you mean by that?"

Thanassis looked up at his daughter, who slowly shook her head. "You don't know? Are you clueless about your importance to the Hungry Man?"

There was a menacing vibration in Alessandro's voice. "What importance?"

"Does it have to do with the statues?" asked Rosa. "We saw them. We went diving there ourselves to find them. And then your people came along and snapped them up from under our noses."

Thanassis smiled. "Very possible."

"What did you mean about our importance?" asked Alessandro again, and this time the note in his voice made Danai put her left hand out to an alarm button beside the bed.

Thanassis was unimpressed. "Has no one really ever told you about the downfall of Arcadia and what brought it on?"

"Lamias overthrew King Lycaon," said Rosa. "But that was thousands of years ago. What does it matter today?"

"The Lamias overthrew him to raise themselves to be rulers of Arcadia," said Thanassis, with an exhausted nod, "while the Panthera did their utmost to oppose them. Your ancestors waged a bitter war with one another after the rebellion against Lycaon. The Panthera were on his side, and still are. That's why the Carnevares were the first to declare their support for the Hungry Man when he claimed to be the reincarnation of Lycaon—not just a descendant, but the King of Arcadia in person."

"But in the end he held us responsible for his arrest," Alessandro objected. "He thinks my family are traitors."

"So," said the old man, "*did* they betray him?"

"No," said Rosa. "It was my grandmother who handed him over to the state prosecutor's office. Costanza Alcantara. She and Salvatore Pantaleone, who then succeeded him as *capo dei capi*."

Thanassis pricked up his ears. "Costanza?"

"You knew her?"

"Your grandmother was a powerful woman. I met her a few times at various official occasions. It's possible that one of my companies did business with her."

Something in his tone of voice roused her suspicion. He was holding things back, fobbing her off with fragments.

But just as she was about to demand that he explain himself, he said, "It's high time for you two to learn more about what happened in Arcadia. About your ancestors. And about the concordat."

THE ANGER OF THE GODS

"LYCAON WAS A CRUEL monarch, worse than even the worst of the Roman emperors," said Thanassis, as more medication was pumped into his body through the tubes. "He was a tyrant of the most atrocious kind, and when the Lamias finally overthrew him I imagine no one was particularly sorry. It's said that Lycaon was cut into four quarters, and his remains were thrown into the sea off all the coasts of Arcadia. Although I think it more likely that someone simply smashed his skull in, and his corpse ended up on the nearest bonfire.

"But whatever happened, Lycaon was dead and the Lamias claimed the throne for themselves. However, the Panthera had always been his allies, and their power was closely bound up with his. It was clear to them that they would lose their privileges once Lycaon's enemies had taken leadership by force. So they accused the Lamias of high treason, claimed his estate as their own, and declared themselves his legitimate heirs. What had begun as a kind of quarrel over the inheritance soon became wildfire devastating the whole of Arcadia. It led to a terrible civil war that went on for decades. It was almost the end of Arcadia. Towns, villages, even the most remote parts of the countryside were laid to waste, their inhabitants butchered.

"In the end neither side won; the victor was common sense. It was generally acknowledged that if the bloodshed went on, nothing and no one would be left. The survivors of the war, we are told, turned to the gods and begged them to settle the conflict. Good advice from on high was not long in coming.

"First, the gods ordered the Arcadians to work together to build a monumental tomb in honor of the dead Lycaon. The task was intended to unite the warring groups. And it seems to have worked, since once the mausoleum was built, the next step followed. It was decided that the Lamias and the Panthera, the leaders of the two sides in the war, were to share in ruling the kingdom. There was not to be a single king, but a tribunal consisting of members of both dynasties. They would work together to rebuild the ruined cities and lead the kingdom of Arcadia to new prosperity.

"The gods made one condition in giving their aid and goodwill: A child was never to be born of the union of a Lamia and a Panthera. The families were to rule side by side, but never merge into a single dynasty. So much power could have led them to question the authority of the gods themselves—not such an outlandish notion if you look at the history of Rome or ancient Egypt.

"To seal this pact, a great festival was announced, with a ceremony to prove that the enemies were now united. It was performed at the mausoleum of Lycaon that had just been built, the cornerstone of the new Arcadia.

"Those were cruel times, when life meant little, and treaties were written in blood. It was decided that only human sacrifice would carry enough weight to go down in history as a symbol of the pact between the dynasties. A highborn daughter of the Lamias and a son of the Panthera were married on the steps of the mausoleum—only to be sacrificed directly after the wedding, to show everyone what such a union would lead to. The Lamia was forced to kill first her bridegroom and then herself. In that way, both clans demonstrated their unconditional will to serve the rise of Arcadia."

Thanassis stopped, drew in air with a labored rattle, and for a while hardly seemed able to go on. But after a pause, he began again. "Well, the people of that time liked to watch high drama. On the other hand, if they had all simply signed a treaty, who knows whether anyone would remember it today? A spectacle involving bloodshed has always been the most impressive way to ensure that your reputation survives the passing ages. Otherwise, who would still remember Herod? Or Nero and Caligula?"

Rosa's eyes met Alessandro's. "She had to kill him first, then herself?"

"The story isn't over yet," said Thanassis, after Danai had held a glass of water to his lips while he slowly drank it down. "The ceremony was performed, and the Arcadians who had survived the civil war were witnesses to the conclusion of a historic pact between the Panthera and the Lamias—the concordat. The last victims of the struggle for the throne, the unfortunate couple, were buried with due solemnity, and the work of reconstruction began.

"In the following decades the kingdom recovered: the

Arcadians got their old self-confidence back and began making plans for expansion. They were not yet strong enough for open war against the naval powers of the Mediterranean of that time—above all Greece—so they decided on another approach. Spies were sent out, merchants, diplomats, even soldiers who joined the Greek army. The Arcadians set about undermining the state. They held high positions and diverted wealth for their own purposes and for their people at home.

"Increasingly, the Arcadians were becoming the puppetmasters of Greek politics. Outwardly, there might be nothing to see, but secretly they pulled the strings by means of advice, bribery, and intimidation. Arcadia grew richer, and its cities flourished again, even more magnificent than in the time of Lycaon. The concordat, the pact between the two dynasties, brought prosperity to the ruling class and a certain amount of security to the common people, who no longer needed to fear either poverty or war.

"We don't know exactly how long this happy state of affairs continued. Much of what I'm telling you is based on myth and legend. There is no official history—or if there was, it has remained undiscovered to this day. Actual dates are also unknown, but we can assume that the double rule of the Lamias and the Panthera lasted for at least one to two hundred years. Only then was there a development of the kind that has ruined so many nations.

"The Arcadians became arrogant. Triumph followed triumph, wealth flowed from the Greek colonies to the island, everything they touched seemed to succeed. Then the dynasties decided that it was time to erect a memorial to the fame and progress of Arcadia. The mausoleum of Lycaon had shown that Arcadian architects were capable of great things, and the Arcadian people were ready to carry out such a task. But now there was to be a work of architecture the likes of which had never been seen before. Not a tomb, not a Tower of Babel, certainly not a temple to the gods—but a bridge that would join Arcadia to the mainland. A bridge over which Arcadian genius would flow out of the island, and the gold of other nations into it."

All this time Rosa had hardly moved, only shifting her weight from one foot to the other. Now, however, she could not refrain from taking a few restless steps around the room.

"This bridge," she said, "the island and the mainland . . . Arcadia was never Atlantis, or any other island that sank into the sea. Arcadia was Sicily."

"Sicily is a part of it," agreed Thanassis. "What's left of Arcadia."

Alessandro linked his hands behind his head. "And that bridge was to cross the Strait of Messina? By the same route that the Dallamanos surveyed a few years ago in order to build a *new* bridge there? The bridge the government in Rome decided on?"

"Exactly."

Rosa was chewing a strand of her hair, while it all finally clicked in her mind. "But the statues in the sea, the ruins around them . . . does that mean that the Arcadians really did build their bridge? And the statues are the remains of it?"

"The bridge was built," said Thanassis. "It stretched for I don't know how many kilometers across the open sea. The coastline was different then, and the island was larger, but all the same it had to cross a vast length. They had chosen not the shortest route but the one where the waters were shallowest. Gigantic piles were set up thirty or forty meters below the surface, and whole generations lived and died while the building work approached completion, very slowly but steadily.

"If the Arcadians had contented themselves with that, who knows, maybe they would not have brought such disaster on their kingdom. But they felt secure, almighty, and they had had statues of panthers and snakes set up all along the bridge, countless numbers of them, as well as temples where travelers were expected to make sacrifices before images of the two ruling dynasties."

In her mind's eye, Rosa saw the underwater stone statues. "And when they did that, they offended the gods."

"Well, naturally there were still no official links between Lamias and Panthera, no marriages, certainly no children. They stuck to that, and came down heavily on anyone who threatened to change the laws. However, the dynasties forgot the real reason for that one, which was originally meant to prevent the Lamias and Panthera from elevating themselves to the status of gods."

"But those are all just legends," said Alessandro. "I mean, gods who come down from Olympus and force their laws on human beings don't really—"

"And how about your own shape-shifting ability?"

Thanassis interrupted him. "Do you have any explanation for it that *excludes* the influence of the gods?"

"What happened then?" asked Rosa.

"The gods were angry with the Arcadians—at least, that's what the *legend* says," said Thanassis, glancing sideways at Alessandro. "The bridge was completed, and the people celebrated on the shores of the island and the bridge itself. The Lamias and Panthera saw themselves at the height of their power."

"And the gods put an end to it," whispered Rosa.

"There was an earthquake," Alessandro contradicted her. "The Strait of Messina is one of the most notorious parts of the world for seismic activity. The seabed is never at rest, it's always shifting somewhere. Gods have nothing to do with it."

"Who knows, maybe it really was just an earthquake," said Thanassis. "The few traditional accounts that have come down to us say that the gods moved invisibly among the rejoicing people, watching the spectacle with resentment. Finally, when the festivities reached their climax, they let loose the forces of the sea. The seabed rose and broke apart, the incoming tide flooded the shore, as well as whole stretches of the coastline and some of the island's largest cities. That was when Sicily got its present shape. The bridge disappeared into crevices and ravines at the bottom of the sea, and with every earthquake that has plagued the area ever since, another part of the truth was lost. With a few exceptions. One of those earthquakes, perhaps the great quake of 1908, made something emerge, literally washed it up from the abyss."

"Our statues," said Rosa. "Or yours."

"They must have been enclosed in a space in the rock down there, or it's hardly likely that so many would have been found. It's as if a few of the old Arcadians themselves had risen from the dead."

"But there must have been survivors," said Alessandro, "or we wouldn't be here."

"Naturally. Arcadian merchants, diplomats, and scholars were traveling in all parts of the known world at the time. A great many of them would surely have come home to join in the triumph of the bridge-builders, but by no means all. And even the catastrophe itself did not affect the entire population. Some inhabitants of inland areas surely remained alive. Many may have mingled with the other Mediterranean nations in the coming years, while others could have gone farther afield, to Asia, Africa, to the north. Most of them must have found a new home in Greece and its colonies and slowly began to reach new positions of influence there. That is why the Arcadian dynasties exist to this day, but in secret, behind masks."

"I'd like to see the statues," said Rosa. "They're here on board, aren't they?"

Thanassis turned his head on the pillow toward his daughter, and grimaced when one of the tubes came under strain. At once the nurse was beside him. "Danai," he said, "be good enough to show our guests the finds."

"Are you sure?"

"I think they deserve it."

The hybrid rocked uncomfortably in the middle of her

hooped skirt, as if on a black cushion, and then nodded.

"My voice needs a chance to recover." He looked at Rosa again. "But we haven't reached the end of the story yet. There's more that you ought to know."

"You still haven't told us what you expect from us," said Alessandro.

"Don't worry, I'm not about to run away from you."

Danai glided past the two of them to the door. She gave Alessandro a smile, but ignored Rosa.

"Follow me."

SNAKE AND PANTHER

"THIS DECK USED TO be for the cars," said Danai, as they entered the gigantic hold of the *Stabat Mater*.

Yellow markings could still be seen in many places on the floor: parking places laid out like anatomical sketches of backbones and ribs. Dozens of neon tubes illuminated the deck; there were no portholes to the outside world, and if Rosa's sense of direction did not deceive her, they were below the surface of the sea.

It smelled like a building site, like earth, damp rock, and mortar. A large part of the floor of the hold was covered with broken stones. The sight would have brought tears to the eyes of any archaeologist. Chunks of stone of every size and in every condition were piled up together like refuse, in spite of the damage it did them.

Rosa counted ten mountains of rubble as high as houses, five on each side of the deck, and among them many smaller piles, as well as countless single pieces, the remains of arches and reliefs, and again and again columns, many broken into segments, other intact like fossilized mammoth trees.

Bulldozers with encrusted scoops stood alone near the main bulwark at the end of the hall, along with vans and a forklift. Wheelbarrows and tools for an army of workers were fixed to the walls. There was not a soul in sight.

Danai had dismissed Mirella and the others, and had brought Rosa and Alessandro here on her own, down steel stairways and along abandoned corridors, where the noises from the upper decks—shrill voices, roaring—could be heard now and then.

Rosa looked around her critically. "Doesn't look like there was much expertise at work here."

Alessandro went over to a fragment of masonry on which the remains of a relief could be seen, showing a scene with humans and animals. He ran his fingers around the outline of a stylized lion. "Is all this Arcadian?"

"Every stone of it."

"But this isn't a storehouse," said Rosa, glancing at the heaps of rubble.

Danai smiled. "No."

"Why are you collecting all this stuff?"

"To sink it far out to sea. The *Stabat Mater* travels between Europe and North America several times a year, and throws all this overboard in the deepest part of the Atlantic Ocean. It disappears a couple of kilometers down there, never to be seen again."

"You retrieve it from the sea only to throw it back again?"

Danai laughed, a peal of laughter clear as a bell. "Very little of it comes out of the sea, except maybe in the coastal areas. A great deal had been taken inland. We buy it from the farmers on whose land it was discovered. We often get there before the museums and universities move in."

"But why?" asked Alessandro.

"We're erasing Arcadia from human memory. Covering all the tracks, including many pieces that are generally considered Greek. We have our own experts and contacts; the Thanassis Foundation is one of the most generously funded archaeological institutes anywhere in Europe. And before anyone can draw the correct conclusions, we get rid of the evidence. You might say that we're retroactively destroying Arcadia. Robbing it of its history. The descendants of the old Arcadians aren't the problem. They are mortal and will disappear of their own accord some time or other—but those stones can tell their story thousands of years later. And that's what we're preventing."

Rosa looked around her. "Show us the statues."

The delicate lace at the hem of Danai's skirt rustled as it passed through gray stone dust, as she led them between the heaps of rubble to the far side of the hold. And there they lay, most of them on their sides, carelessly thrown down on top of one another and broken. There had been twelve statues, seven of them almost intact. Now they were all badly damaged.

Each statue showed the snake and the panther in the same pose. The big cat stood on his hind legs, and the reptile was coiled around his body. They were looking into each other's eyes. What at first glance appeared to be a fight was in reality an embrace. Judging by all that Thanassis had told them, that position must have been a provocation, the greatest imaginable challenge to the gods.

"Oh, fuck," whispered Rosa.

Alessandro looked at her inquiringly.

"I just thought of the Greek gods as living beings. That's totally crazy."

"Is it?" asked Danai. "Would we go to such trouble and expense if it were all just fantasy?"

"Why ask me?" Rosa snapped. "You're Daddy's little princess, not me." Alessandro shot her a warning glance, but she was not to be stopped in her tracks. "You drag us into this floating freak show, you come up with a few tales about the old days, and you're trying to tell us that it would be a good idea for all Arcadians to be dead—including the two of us, right?" She faced Danai and tried not to think of the part of the young woman that was hidden under the black velvet skirt. "There's more than that behind it. And if you want us to trust you, it would be a good idea if you finally told us the whole truth."

Danai looked past Rosa and smiled at Alessandro. "We're glad to have you as our guests. In fact, very glad."

To her annoyance, Rosa had to stand on tiptoe in order to break the eye contact between them. "By the way, he *hates* spiders."

"Then it's a good thing I'm not one."

"Arachnida can be all kinds of creatures," said Alessandro. "Including crayfish and crabs."

"And scorpions." Behind Danai's back, something pushed out from under the wide skirt, a huge, drop-shaped spike made of horn and bony plates. It reared up in a wide arc around the hem of the skirt, its fist-size tip swaying back and forth.

Rosa wrinkled her nose scornfully, and Danai's features

slipped. She bared her teeth, and her eyes went black, as if ink were spraying out of her pupils. A rattling sound came through her lips, one that no human larynx could produce. But the metamorphosis went no farther. Danai remained a grotesque cross between woman and animal.

Rosa showed her own snake's fangs, and hissed menacingly. She did not shift shape entirely; only her face was covered with scaly skin for a few seconds.

Then she said softly, "Oh, forget it," took a step back, and turned toward the statues without taking any more notice of Danai. It made her sad to see this wanton destruction of the embrace that had united snake and panther in the darkness for thousands of years.

"It's not right to just throw all this away," she said quietly.

She sensed Danai coming up behind her. The lace at the hem of the skirt touched her calves, but she didn't turn around. Instead, she crouched down. Her fingers gently stroked a panther's stony face.

"What's the alternative?" asked Danai calmly. "Telling the world the truth? Is everyone to know what you are? What Alessandro is? Do you think you can count on tolerance if it all becomes common knowledge?"

Rosa shook her head. Alessandro crouched down beside her, putting an arm around her. "This is only stone," he said. "It doesn't mean anything. Only a few old chunks of rock on which someone or other carved faces."

"Our faces."

Then he kissed her, a long and tender kiss, and it didn't

matter that Danai was standing there, watching them without a word. Rosa stroked Alessandro's unruly hair from his eyes, couldn't suppress a grin, and pulled him up with her from their crouching position.

Almost reluctantly, she turned back to Danai. "Why did your father give up everything to rescue a few hundred hybrids?" At last she put what she had been wondering all this time into words. "There's something that won't let him rest."

Alessandro, too, looked at the hybrid. "Is it TABULA?"

Danai slowly sank to the ground in front of the piles of rubble from the broken statues. It seemed as if her upper body was suddenly too heavy for the black masses of velvet. "It probably doesn't matter whether you hear this from him or me," she said. "He and TABULA . . . yes, there is indeed a connection."

"Another foundation that he generously supports?" asked Rosa sharply.

"His first wife, who wasn't my mother, was an Arcadian. Over fifty years ago, soon after the wedding, she became a hybrid. She shifted shape, as she had done so many times before, but for some reason she couldn't complete the metamorphosis. She couldn't return entirely to human form either. I've seen photos of her before the wedding. She was such a beautiful woman—a Hunding, a swift, slender hunting hound. But in the end she was neither one nor the other. She hid away in one of my father's villas, and never showed herself outside it again."

Rosa watched Alessandro out of the corner of her eye. His

own mother, Gaia, had not been an Arcadian, but she, too, had gone into voluntary exile alone on Isola Luna. There was sorrow and maybe sympathy in his eyes.

"My father stood by her," said Danai. "He promised her that he would find a cure, even if it cost him his entire fortune. He consulted the best doctors, the most highly esteemed scientists, but his wife refused to see a single one of them. She wouldn't have anyone setting eyes on her in that condition. For a long time my father respected her wishes, but when she became severely depressed he had to do something. He anesthetized her and had several doctors come to examine her. None of them could suggest anything. They wanted to take her away with them and investigate her in their institutes like some kind of laboratory rat. At that, my father sent them all packing. When his wife came back to consciousness, she realized what he had done. She felt that he had deceived her and, even worse, humiliated her."

"No wonder," said Rosa.

"Of course he was very sorry, but she wouldn't listen to him. Then he knew that he wasn't going to get any further by ordinary means. He had to try another, more dangerous way."

"He must have loved her very much," said Alessandro.

Rosa groaned. "Yes, but he abused her trust."

"*Because* he loved her."

That's no excuse, she was going to say. But then she thought that maybe she wouldn't like what he might reply: that love justified anything, even deceit. On that point their convictions were poles apart.

"In his search for a solution, after many years my father finally came upon a group of men who were experimenting with ancient alchemical formulas, writings from the Middle Ages. These people claimed that they knew how to transform one . . . *substance* into another. They were already calling themselves TABULA at the time, but they were a very small, unimportant outfit, with no money, only a few crazy ideas. In a half hearted way, some of them had written studies of human beings undergoing transformation into animals, not because they knew about the Arcadians, but because there's a lot about it in alchemy. And of course they also knew the historical records of werewolves, bear-men, fox-spirits, all the old legends that originated a few thousand years ago in Arcadia."

She sounded sad now, as if she herself wished for nothing so much as to be able to move freely among other people. Rosa remembered Danai's bizarre appearance in New York, when she had tried exactly that: to be like other girls at any price, do what they did, create an impression of normality. Except that in fact there had been nothing normal about the dance she performed in the Dream Room, and people had stared as if she might be all kinds of things, but certainly not one of them.

"After my father had made contact with TABULA, he got to know a young scientist there, a man called—"

"Eduard Sigismondis," whispered Rosa.

"Do you know him?"

"Only his name. We know he belongs to TABULA." Strictly speaking, that was something of an exaggeration. In fact she had only the information that Eva had gathered for her, no evidence. But the name had simply been on the tip of her tongue, as if waiting for a gap in Danai's account into which it fitted.

"Sigismondis made my father all kinds of promises," Danai went on. "As a matter of fact, he had been experimenting for some time with crossbreeding humans and animals, not because of some kind of alchemical nonsense, like the others, but out of scientific curiosity. Sigismondis had joined TABULA because up to a certain point the interests of its members coincided with his own. But my father says he was never really like them. Alchemy and all that stuff meant nothing to him. My father trusted him because Sigismondis promised him nothing short of a miracle." There was a sharp undertone in Danai's voice. "No, said Sigismondis, of course he did not have to see the woman with his own eyes in order to concoct a cure for her, since there were plenty of other crossbreeds available for that, weren't there? The world was positively teeming with them, he said, you just had to know where to look. With a little financial support, it would be no problem to capture some of them and carry out certain tests." She fell silent for a moment, and then said, more calmly and softly, "My father agreed. He gave Sigismondis everything he asked for. A laboratory was set up, then a second, a whole troop of talented and unscrupulous assistants was hired, anything that Sigismondis wanted. They all worked for him under the seal of absolute secrecy, and if anyone threatened to talk, Sigismondis was not squeamish in his methods of dealing with that person."

Danai rose and glided on the black tip of her scorpion's tail several yards past the mountain of broken statues. Then she turned around. She seemed to be looking straight through Rosa and Alessandro.

"Sigismondis told my father that he could reverse the metamorphosis only if he had first created a cross between human and animal himself. He had to understand the process in order to make it work in the opposite direction. So he began creating hybrids of his own by means of operations and insemination."

"The first artificial inseminations were at the end of the 1970s," said Alessandro.

"The first that were successful and known to the public," replied Danai. "But they had been taking place earlier; there were trials years before that. And I didn't say that all the inseminations were *artificial*."

For a couple of seconds, Rosa closed her eyes, fighting off a sense of nausea.

"And of course he experimented with Arcadians as well," said Danai. "Heaven only knows how he came to know so much about them. Very likely the other members of TABULA, all those alchemists and esotericists and weirdos, found out and told him. It doesn't make any difference now. At first they may have been volunteers who let him examine them in return for money, but the more extreme his experiments were, the more difficult it was to find suitable subjects. He'd probably been having people abducted earlier for his first experiments, but now it was open season for him to hunt Arcadians. The kidnappings, the specter of TABULA so feared by the Arcadian dynasties, the rumors about secret laboratories and experiments—all that started then."

Alessandro was furious. "And your father knew all this?"

"Thanassis was the sponsor in the background," said Rosa, angrily. "The generous patron. Who cared about a few Arcadians who'd mysteriously disappeared, if it meant that his wife got better?"

Danai's gestures and facial expressions suggested that she couldn't choose between rage and tears. "She never did get better. Sigismondis deceived my father. There was no cure, and he had never seriously been looking for one. All that he did come up with was a kind of side product of hybrid blood, and even that he found by pure chance—a serum that kept an Arcadian in his or her shape for a few minutes, either in human or animal form. Sigismondis's assistants used it during their experiments, to ensure that their victims couldn't change shape under their knives and in their radiation chambers and breeding stations. It must have come in very useful to them, but it wasn't a great success, and it certainly wasn't what their experiments were aiming for. Only later did it become important."

"They began marketing it," concluded Rosa. So at last *that* made sense. For the first time she was on a trail that might explain the part played by her grandmother. And also what had become of her father.

"Forty years ago my father's wife killed herself," said Danai. "Overnight, he found himself facing a gigantic pile of ruins. TABULA had committed terrible crimes with his money and on his instructions, indeed was still committing them, and at last he realized that for almost a decade Sigismondis had been pulling the wool over his eyes. At first my father threatened to make the whole thing public, but of course he knew what would happen to him and his fortune then. So he withdrew into the background, broke his connections to TABULA, put a stop to all payments to the organization, and hoped that would be enough to starve Sigismondis out."

Rosa's mouth twisted. "You mean he was too cowardly to go public. Because it would have cost him his shipping empire. Because he'd have been put in prison, never to come out again. Do you really think he wanted you to tell us *that*?"

"Yes, I do," replied Danai, with spirit. "We discussed it at length before you came on board. He is offering to be absolutely straightforward with you."

"In exchange for what?" Alessandro snapped. "What does he expect us to do?"

"Listen to the rest of the story first." Danai took a deep breath, cut Rosa's objection short with a gesture, and went on. "What my father didn't guess was that for some time Sigismondis had no longer been dependent on his money. Meanwhile, he and his assistants had set up a flourishing business. The serum they gained from hybrid blood was a blessing for Arcadians. For the first time, there was a way to hold a metamorphosis back. And during the quarrels of the dynasties with one another, during the great Mafia wars of the seventies and eighties, the serum was a weapon of incalculable value for the clans. So TABULA began selling the stuff, through middlemen, to the dynasties, who were ready to pay a fortune for it. It all became a vicious circle: TABULA abducts Arcadians, breeds hybrids, manufactures the serum from their blood, and sells it back to the Arcadians—even those whose own family members have been abducted."

In her short time at the head of the Alcantara clan, Rosa had heard of many crimes, but this was the worst of all. "The furs," she said. "Were they part of the bargain as well?"

Danai nodded. "TABULA is still selling the coats of murdered Arcadians to collectors all over the world, humans included, in the United States, Japan, all over Europe. Certain circles in Russia—even Arcadians, as far as we know—will pay more for them than for the best sables. Strictly speaking, TABULA is no longer a secret scientific society, but a criminal organization like your own. And don't look at me like that—they are *not* unlike you whether you want to admit it or not. The clever business ideas with which Sigismondis financed his experiments after my father pulled out of TABULA has become a secret monopoly. It sells the serum, the furs, and other substances, too. In Japan there are billionaires who swear by the effects of powdered Arcadian bones, supposed to increase potency—"

"Yes," said Rosa. "We get the idea. And in order to put a stop to TABULA's trade, your father wants to eradicate all Arcadians." She added, with biting sarcasm, "Because he's already been so successful in turning off the money supply to TABULA."

All emotion drained from Danai's face. The excitement she'd worked up during her long account was gone in a heartbeat.

"That's the plan," she said wearily. "And unfortunately it won't work without you two."

THE CONCORDAT

DANAI LED ROSA AND Alessandro up a series of metal stairways and back into the daylight. On the way, she told them about her mother.

"She was rescued from a TABULA laboratory during one of the first liberation raids. She was an Arcadian, but not a hybrid, abducted from some coastal resort in Croatia. Obviously they were going to artificially inseminate her to get her pregnant with God knows what." She stopped for a moment as they passed another steel bulkhead on their way up. "Even the creatures in these elevator shafts had human mothers, although no one would think so now. TABULA made them what they are."

"But why are you a hybrid?" asked Rosa.

"They'd probably given my mother all kinds of drugs before she was freed from the lab. Her arms were covered with the marks of injections, my father says, and she was hooked up to a drip when the experimental station was raided. Presumably her blood already contained everything necessary to create hybrids. At the time my father didn't yet know much about what Sigismondis and his people were up to. He'd seen some of the results, that was all. With every lab that he and his men destroyed, they gained new knowledge. Maybe it wouldn't have made any difference if he'd known what they had injected my mother with. He fell in love with her, and I guess she did with him. I was born as a hybrid, but they did all they could to give me a normal childhood. If you can call places like this normal."

"Have you always lived here?" asked Alessandro.

"Oh no, the *Stabat Mater* is much younger than me. She was converted to her present form only eight or ten years ago. My father has many houses, islands, and ships. . . . I spent time sometimes in one place, sometimes in another. It depended how long I could bear it somewhere."

Rosa pricked up her ears. "How long you could bear it?"

"I have . . . attacks," replied Danai hesitantly. "Sometimes I'm not feeling well. And then I'm . . . difficult. I was always angry that the Arcadians never accepted us. They ought to have taken us in. Instead, hybrids have nearly always been outcasts, until they fell into the hands of TABULA, committed suicide, or in these last few years ended up here with us. I can understand that people see me as a freak. But the Arcadians at least ought to recognize what we are and how much most of us have suffered. Don't get me wrong, I know that I'm relatively well off. I'm privileged, my father is a rich man who has always done everything in his power for me. Yet I always wanted to be like you, able to stand up for what I am, not live hidden away in a"—she hesitated—"in a damn floating zoo."

Before either of them could reply, they passed a bulkhead and came out into the open air. Ahead of them lay a wide deck, and a little way off a swimming pool. It was covered with a sheet of black plastic. Beyond the ship's rail, the

Mediterranean glittered inky blue and turquoise. The sky was cloudless, with not even streaks of condensation to be seen.

They followed Danai and saw something moving near a superstructure on deck. Evangelos Thanassis was being pushed out of a transport lift in his sickbed by his bodyguards. Not far from the rail, he waved to them. The bed was stabilized, stands with containers of infusions anchored at the head of it.

Danai led them past the swimming pool, and Rosa realized that she had been wrong. There was no black plastic cover over the pool. The water itself was pitch black, and something moved in it. Outlines were gliding along under the surface, winding around one another like huge eels. Once Rosa saw parts of a shimmering fish, and then something that was almost a human face.

They left the pool and its inhabitants behind, and reached Thanassis's sickbed. It stood with its long side aligned to the rail, so that he could look out to see past the bars of the frame. Danai leaned down and whispered something to him. Thanassis slowly nodded.

"There's something I'd like to ask," said Rosa. "Your people took our cell phones away during the flight. But there's someone I urgently have to speak to."

"We do all we can to be as invisible as possible. A phone call that could be traced back here—"

Alessandro spoke up. "We're not your prisoners. You can't simply—"

"Can't I?" Thanassis sharply interrupted him. "I can tell you exactly what you are, you and your girlfriend. You're wanted criminal suspects. The police are looking for you.

Your own families set the Malandras on you. And I'm pretty sure that TABULA would also like to exchange a few words with you. At the moment you are guests on board *my* ship, and I would advise you not to adopt that tone, young man."

Alessandro laid a hand on the balustrade and closed his fist around the steel rail.

"We shouldn't be here at all. Your stories of gods and sunken bridges, and all these creatures here on board—none of it has anything to do with what I am or what Rosa is. Arcadia fell thousands of years ago, and it doesn't interest me why—"

"Arcadia is about to fall for the second time," said Thanassis. "And *that* ought to interest you."

Rosa's angry glances were for Thanassis and Alessandro alike. "All I want is to make a phone call, okay?"

Thanassis turned to her, but before he could say anything Danai came between them. She spoke to her father vigorously in Greek.

Finally, if reluctantly, the old man nodded. Danai gave Rosa a shy smile, touched her hand, and led her a little way along the rail. Alessandro was about to follow them, but Rosa gestured to him to stay behind.

"Here," said Danai, handing her a smartphone.

Rosa nodded gratefully, and called Iole's cell phone number. Danai moved a little way off, but stayed within earshot.

A metallic female voice answered. "This is the mailbox of—" Rosa was about to break the connection when Iole's recorded voice came in. "Rosa, everything's okay." She gave the time of day, less than two hours ago. "I'm fine. Signora

Falchi is complaining a lot, but she'll survive. And Cristina can't keep her hands off all the old papers down here. I'll try to update this every two hours and—" The recording broke off; the voice mail setup did not leave her more time.

"Everything all right?" asked Danai.

"I hope so." Rosa handed her the phone back. As Danai took it, Rosa touched her wrist. "Thanks. That was really nice of you."

Danai looked almost moved. She smiled briefly, and led the way back to the others.

"Well?" asked Alessandro, sounding anxious.

"She was fine two hours ago, at least."

The worry lines didn't disappear from his forehead, but he breathed a sigh of relief.

Thanassis spoke up again. "Now that that's cleared up, I suggest that we—"

"Who is Apollonio?" asked Rosa.

"What?"

"You're the first person I've met who knows anything about TABULA. That's why I'm asking you: Who is Apollonio?"

Bewildered, Thanassis looked from her to Danai, then back to Rosa. "I don't know anyone by that name. TABULA has changed during the last couple of decades. We learn less and less information about it."

Danai came to his aid. "We're more or less sure that Sigismondis stopped playing a leading part some time ago. He must be over eighty now. The structure of leadership in the organization has changed, and we think Sigismondis fell victim to a coup in its ranks. If there is an Apollonio in TABULA, he could be anyone, from a mere assistant to Sigismondis's successor."

"Don't try telling me you know where TABULA has its secret labs, but you don't know any names. That's nonsense!"

"Of course we know names, but by no means all of them."

"Apollonio did deals on behalf of my grandmother, selling the furs. He was probably the supplier who sold Tano Carnevare the serum. He must be some kind of middleman, the link between TABULA and the Arcadians."

"There are several of those." Thanassis waved the subject away. "We picked up two or three of them, years ago. But they're always quickly replaced."

"What happened to those you picked up?"

"We killed them," replied Danai, dispassionately. "What else?"

"We're fighting a war," said Thanassis. "You ought to have grasped that by now. And neither of the two sides is particularly considerate of the other."

"Three," remarked Alessandro.

"Hmm?"

"There are three sides. You, the Arcadians, and TABULA."

Rosa wondered for a moment whether to say more about her father. But she was a prisoner on board the *Stabat Mater*, whatever Thanassis claimed, and she felt no need to tell him and his daughter such intimate details. The memory of her rape lay deep inside her like a sealed package. She wasn't going to take it out again and open it up before everyone's eyes.

Yet the question of why Apollonio had tried crossing a Lamia with one of the Panthera outside a laboratory tormented her. She tried with all her might to look at it soberly, with almost medical detachment. But the pain came back at once, the humiliation, the feeling of being helpless under Tano Carnevare's naked body, lying there drugged, with her eyes open and wide awake.

She realized only a moment later that Thanassis had been going on with his account for some time, and had to force herself to listen to him.

". . . no doubt at all that the Hungry Man will make himself leader of all the Arcadians again," he was saying. "There have always been those in the dynasties who look back at the past. Conservatives, if you like. They don't want progress; for them, it's a synonym for the game of hide-and-seek that they hate playing in front of the world. They brought all their influence to bear on the government in Rome to get him freed. Now he's back in order to rise—symbolically—to the throne of Arcadia again."

"Which you intend to prevent *how?*" asked Rosa.

"We have informers inside the dynasties. Spies. So we know that the Hungry Man is going to give a sign. He plans to shore up his bid for power by means of a ritual, and he is looking back at tradition in order to divert attention from his weaknesses. Exactly as the rulers of ancient Rome did, or the Fascists in Europe in the twentieth century. He is making use of the same tasteless methods as all other dictators. As *capo dei capi*, he learned how insecure subjects want to be ruled. Furthermore, he had influential supporters and followers, and he has to live up to their expectations. He intends the ritual of his return to burn itself into the memory of one and all."

Rosa moved very close to Alessandro by the parapet, until their arms were touching. She leaned against the cool ship's rail. A sea breeze behind her blew through her hair, swirling it over her shoulders.

"He's not going to make the same mistake Lycaon once did," said Thanassis. "Instead of making the most powerful dynasties his enemies, thus risking another coup, he's including them in his plans. He wants the Lamias and the Panthera on his side from the start, and the way it looks, he's already achieved that. The murder plot against the judge, the hunt for you two, they're all part of the plan."

"I spoke to him in prison," said Rosa. "He wanted Alessandro and me to go over to him."

"When was this?"

"A few weeks ago?"

"And you refused?"

"He'd set hit men on Alessandro. He thought the Carnevares were responsible for the thirty years he spent behind bars. I had to promise him something to get him to go back on his order to kill Alessandro. I had to promise that someday I would do him a favor."

Thanassis and his daughter exchanged a glance. "Did he say what kind of favor?"

Rosa shook her head. "He didn't keep his side of the bargain anyway, or the Harpies wouldn't have attacked us. So I owe him nothing now."

"The Harpies were meant to catch us, not kill us," said Alessandro. "Only after we . . . after I killed Saffira and Aliza did the Malandras strike back. The attack in the railroad tunnel must have been entirely their own affair."

"I think so, too," said Thanassis. "The Hungry Man has been making use of the dissatisfaction between the Alcantaras and Carnevares and brought them over to his side, anyone who isn't happy to take orders from a couple of teenagers any longer." He said that with a smug smile. "And now I'm sure you want to know what he is planning for you two."

"Dramatic pauses for effect don't exactly enlighten us," said Rosa.

Thanassis laughed, a noisy rattle of laughter, almost choked, and earned a reproving glance from his nurse. "You're right, forgive me," he said hoarsely to Rosa. "The Hungry Man wants power over the dynasties, and to get it he needs the support of all the important clans, more particularly the Lamias and Panthera. He wants to unite the rivals of the past, and prevent another act of betrayal. With that in mind, he is trying to reactivate the ancient alliance made when the dynasties signed the peace treaty after the civil war. He wants a new concordat under his control, as a symbol of the return of old Arcadia."

"The ceremony at the mausoleum of Lycaon," said Alessandro, putting into words what Rosa had suspected herself for some time. "He plans to perform it again."

Thanassis nodded thoughtfully. "They will marry you to each other. And then they will force you, Rosa, to kill Alessandro—and directly after that to kill yourself. Your sacrifice is to seal the new concordat in blood."

BAIT

IN HER MIND'S EYE, Rosa saw a wedding cake of several tiers, a dream of a cake filled with whipped cream and buttercream. On it stood two figures dressed in black and white. The bride was holding a kitchen knife and hysterically stabbing the bridegroom with it.

If you reduced the Hungry Man's plan to its essentials, there was something absurdly comic about it.

However, she was alone in seeing it that way. Even Danai looked shocked when Rosa abruptly burst out laughing. She laughed so hard that she could hardly catch her breath. She couldn't restrain herself, particularly when she thought about how she hated buttercream and how whipped cream gave her a rash.

Alessandro kept his eye on her, said nothing, and waited until she had calmed down. He knew her so well. She reached up and kissed him. His lips tasted salty.

"Well," said Evangelos Thanassis, "that was an interesting assessment of the situation."

"But how crazy can you get?" exclaimed Rosa. "Is that the bastard's idea of leading the Sicilian Mafia?"

"The Mafia is obsessed with blood rites," replied the old man. "If anyone can be impressed by such things, it's Cosa Nostra."

"But the thought of anyone taking it seriously . . . It's total garbage!"

"You'd better take it seriously," remarked Danai. "After all, you're going to play the leading lady."

Alessandro put an arm around her. "Assuming that he can get his hands on her. And me. Which is not going to happen."

"And here we come to a difficult point." Thanassis signed to his nurse, who at once did something to one of his infusion bags. "Lycaon's tomb," he said, as he visibly relaxed. "We don't know where it is."

"And what, exactly, is the problem with that?" asked Alessandro.

"I thought you'd understood. He wants to repeat a ceremony thousands of years old as precisely as possible. He wants to revive the ritual. It's meant to be the completion of a cycle that would then begin again from that point. He's not interested in supernatural hocus-pocus or silly prophesies. The whole thing is a show! The effect of a conjuring trick is greatly increased by the spectacular element of its staging. A theatrical magician could simply make a rabbit disappear out of a hat, but instead—"

"He'll make the Eiffel Tower disappear," said Rosa. "Or the Statue of Liberty."

Thanassis nodded. "That's why the Hungry Man can't conduct the ritual in some conference room or palazzo. If he really wants to impress the dynasties—and that is the *only* point of it—he has to conjure up the spirit of the past, consistent in every detail. It must be at the same place where the first concordat was sealed."

"We think," Danai added, "that he already knows where that place is. He's found the site of the mausoleum of Lycaon."

"If Sicily really is the former Arcadia," said Alessandro, "then his tomb must be somewhere on the island, right?"

"Yes," agreed Danai. "From all the information we've been able to gather, preparations for the ceremony are now in full swing. All the important representatives of the dynasties will learn where they are expected to go just before it begins. Nowhere in Sicily is more than a few hours' journey from any other point. The Hungry Man has issued instructions to them all to be at the ready. The time will soon come. Now he needs only the two most important guests of all."

Suspiciously, Rosa bent her head. "Why are you telling us all this?"

"I am going to eliminate the Hungry Man and all those associated with him." Thanassis sounded as objective as if he were planning the hostile takeover of a rival firm. "As soon as they assemble to usher in the new era, we shall strike."

"Assuming you find out the location of the mausoleum in time," said Rosa.

"And this is where you two come in."

"Forget it."

"Only the *capi* of the clans and their closest confidants will be present at the ceremony. None of our informants are among them. We've tried to find substitutes, but there aren't any. No one willing to work with us will be there."

"That's your bad luck," said Alessandro.

"We *need* you," said Thanassis. "We could outfit you with radar tracking devices. Then you'd lead us straight to them, to

another way to locate the tomb. If we knew where Mori's archives are, and we could evaluate them—"

His daughter interrupted him. "Even *if* we find them, it would take us days to get even a rough idea of what's there. You don't leaf through several crates full of papers in a couple of minutes."

"Without us, the Hungry Man can't throw his party," said Rosa. "As long as we're here, there's no time limit for us, either."

Alessandro's glance told her that he wasn't happy with what she was trying to do. He probably would have rather brought the discussion to an end and refused to go further into the plans that Thanassis had made. And until two minutes ago, Rosa had seen things exactly the same way.

Now, however, she told Thanassis, "I think I know where the Carnevares hid Mori's documents."

Alessandro stared at her, in concern rather than surprise. Danai and the old man were waiting impatiently for her to go on.

Rosa kept perfectly calm. The snake was with her, and for the first time she felt that its proximity was reassuring. Its cold-blooded nature came back, the sense of being able to control a situation. Ultimately, it was like stealing things—except that she wasn't stealing wallets from other people now, she was stealing their attention.

"We can show you the way there," she said. "But in return, you have to do something for us."

"And that is?" asked Thanassis.

"I want you to rescue someone."

STORMING THE BUNKER

EVENING TWILIGHT FELL AROUND Isola Luna in hues of gloomy purple. The cone of the volcano rose black against the horizon, as if a scrap had been torn out of the panorama of the last of the daylight, revealing the darkness behind it.

The *Stabat Mater* was approaching the island from the east. She came in over the sea with the dark showing no lights, with engines throttled, a steel monster on a furtive voyage.

Rosa stood at the large window on the bridge, letting her eyes wander over a row of monitors. Indistinct images flashed across them. They came from cameras operated by a detachment of hybrids preparing down below for the assault on the island. Mirella was a member of that troop, and so was the dog-man. Metallic voices all talked at once; final orders were issued. There was frequent loud crackling as someone adjusted a microphone, or knocked into it while setting up the equipment.

The crew on the bridge didn't seem bothered by this background noise. Presumably raids to rescue hybrids from the secret TABULA laboratories followed a similar pattern. All these men and women might well have taken part in such operations before.

At a top speed of twenty-five knots—less than fifteen miles

per hour—it had taken the *Stabat Mater* over half a day to reach Isola Luna, which lay off the north coast of Sicily, an isolated chunk of lava rock with only two buildings on it.

One of them was the villa Alessandro's mother used to go to for solitude. It stood on a small plateau near the top of the slope, a higgledy-piggledy flat-roofed building with white-washed walls and many large windows. It had been built in the 1970s and had the psychedelic aura of an artist's home— an impression reinforced by Gaia's eccentric furnishings.

The second building was the old World War II bunker not far from the landing platform on the north shore of the island, a colossus of gray concrete. From the outside, no one would guess how far it extended back inside the rock. Iole and the two women had been hiding there for several days now, assuming that the Alcantara and Carnevare men who had come to attack the island hadn't found them there in the last few hours.

"Look at that," said Danai.

A satellite picture of the island came up on the largest screen at the center of the wall of monitors. It was white on black, like an old photographic negative. Tall structures showed up as gray shading. The outlines flickered, as if made of lightning flashes. In addition, there were several red dots, concentrated on two parts of the island in particular.

Almost playfully, Danai was manipulating a kind of joystick that regulated sections of the screen. Alessandro stood between her and Rosa, his arms folded, a worry line between his eyes. In the background, the crew on the bridge were busy with technical equipment.

Thanassis had returned to his sickroom quarters. Orders up here came from the captain, a lean man of around sixty. He did not wear a uniform, only a white shirt and dark pants. His manner was authoritarian, and his glance seemed to say: I've seen enough of the world not to let a few hundred human and animal crossbreeds bother me.

No doubt the truth was more complicated. There was likely an unusual story behind every one of these men and women on the *Stabat Mater*, and they were not all hybrids; there were normal human beings among them. Rosa felt curiously close to them. They were all outcasts.

"How many are there?" Alessandro asked, as Danai enlarged the section of the picture shown on the screen. The joystick zoomed in on the northeast part of the island. The red dots dissolved into glowing orange and yellow sparks.

"Five in and outside the villa," said Danai, "and another four outside the bunker to the north. Five more are patrolling the island. That's to say, they're not actually moving at all most of the time, probably sitting on a rock somewhere or sleeping. They don't seem to expect any more problems." She smiled with satisfaction. Absorbed in her task, she had lost much of her ethereal appearance. "No helicopter anywhere in sight; they've probably called it back. But there are two speedboats at the landing stage, and we've found a third in a bay on the southern shore of the island."

The beach. That was where Rosa had first set foot on Isola Luna with Alessandro last October.

"The boats themselves seem to have been abandoned."

"Three boats for just fourteen men?" asked Alessandro.

"Those are only the men we can see. These thermal imaging systems aren't particularly precise. Someone might point that out to the Americans the next time they go blowing some nest of terrorists sky-high. In reality, a whole series of factors can impair pictures taken at such a distance."

"How about the bunker?" asked Rosa. "We can't see anyone under the rock, right?"

Danai shook her head. "No, your three friends won't be visible unless someone drags them out into the open. They almost certainly haven't been found yet, or they'd have been brought out."

There was another alternative, but she didn't voice it. Maybe all three were dead. Corpses generated no warmth, and they would have been as invisible as rocks on the screen.

"What's that?" Rosa pointed to two marks outside the entrance of the bunker, standing out like dense drops from the white outline of the building. They were darker than the other marks, and they also seemed to take up more space.

"Oh," said Danai.

Rosa and Alessandro exchanged an anxious glance.

"Arachnida," said the hybrid. "That's not good. People like to station them on impassable terrain, especially in darkness."

Rosa's short fingernails dug into the palms of her hands. "Meaning that they're large, fast, and they can see in the dark?"

"I'm afraid so."

"And they've just come out of the bunker," said Alessandro. "So they're looking for something. Or someone. They know that Iole and the others are hiding down there."

Rosa imagined the girl being hunted by man-size scorpions and giant spiders down the dark corridors of the bunker.

"What are they waiting for?" She pointed to the trembling pictures being transmitted from the helmet cameras of the assault detachment to the other monitors.

"We're almost close enough," said the captain from behind her. "Then the boats will put out. Only a few minutes to go now."

Danai let go of the joystick and turned to Rosa. "And you're sure that Mori's papers are in that bunker?"

"Absolutely," she said, lying through her teeth.

"This is not just a trick to get us to set your friends free?"

"They've found mountains of documents down here." That, at least, was the truth; Iole had mentioned it more than once. "Could be that the Carnevares stored all kinds of stuff there, any number of papers that they wanted to clear away but not destroy."

Alessandro came to her aid. "I knew nothing at all about it until Iole came upon the papers. Whatever they are, Cesare and my father were very keen to keep them secret. Over the last few months I've found out everything about my family's business deals. There are hardly any gaps. But all the same, no one ever said anything about archives in the bunker. I don't know what else they can be, if not Mori's papers."

There was still a trace of suspicion left in Danai's eyes.

Rosa found it difficult to understand her opaque character. Sometimes she was the abstracted, other-worldly creature from the Dream Room, at others she was her father's determined right-hand woman.

"Here we go," said the captain.

Danai looked back at the screens. The satellite image with the dots of heat was at the center, with the helmet camera pictures filmed by the hybrids arranged around it in a rectangle.

"Captain?" asked Alessandro.

"Yes?"

"Please tell your people that there's a dog down there, and we'd like them to make sure nothing happens to him."

"A Hunding?"

"A mongrel," said Rosa. "His name is Sarcasmo."

A smile flitted over Danai's features. "I like mongrels."

Ten minutes later they heard the first shot.

Rosa stared at the wall of monitors and wondered exactly what she was looking at. Unsteady pictures from the night-vision camera, reminiscent of a glance into a washing machine tossing clothes around. Coded numbers and letters that meant nothing to her. Distorted voices, whispered progress reports, then heavy breathing again. Now and then animal sounds, yowls and growling. The moist smacking of the muzzles of beasts of prey.

Once she saw one of the insect hybrids, a swift outline chasing across the courtyard of the villa. She had already given up trying to work out which hybrid was transmitting pictures to which monitor. The best she could do was identify Mirella's voice now and then.

More shots rang out, a total barrage. The pictures on two monitors froze, one soon followed by the other. The hybrids wearing them had collapsed and no longer moved.

Most of the pictures flickered in front of Rosa like a series of images showing interference. If she looked at any one of the monitors for too long, her sense of vertigo was almost overpowering. If she switched too quickly from one to another, to gather all the information she could, she also felt ill. All the same, there was something she found fascinating about the fading, pixelated filming.

Now and then her conscience pricked her, because what was going on didn't move her more strongly—humans and hybrids were dying on the island, but for some reason that and all its logical implications never quite penetrated. It was like wartime pictures on TV, taken by cameras mounted on remote-controlled drones or warheads on rockets. You knew that the clouds of dust and smoke onscreen meant the death of human beings, but ultimately it didn't affect you.

If it hadn't been for the certainty that the skirmish on the island was for the lives of Iole, Cristina di Santis, and Raffaela Falchi, she would probably have wandered off at her leisure to the coffee machine out in the corridor to make herself an espresso. And *that* frightened her almost more than anything she saw on the wall of monitors.

Alessandro still had his arm around her, and she thought she could feel his skin moving under his shirt. Panther fur appeared as fine down under the fabric and disappeared again. Unlike her, he seemed to wish he could join in the fighting. She had inherited the cool, distant attitude of the snake, he the hot-blooded instincts of the panther.

One of the monitors showed something indistinct, distorted, but it was large and had many legs. One hybrid ventured close, and, for several seconds, rigid with fright, directed its camera on something that looked like a string of black beads—the wreath of eyes above a spider's face. Then the Arachnid's jaws seized the hybrid. From a second monitor, showing film taken from the viewpoint of another hybrid, you could get an idea of what was happening to the poor creature. Finally everything dissolved in a white inferno of pixels. Uninterrupted muzzle flashes were superimposed on all the pictures. When the shots died away, a naked man was lying motionless among the remains of the hybrid that had been torn to pieces. Breathlessly, Mirella gasped out her report of a death.

Soon after that came the final confrontation with the occupiers of the island. It was not the quivering images that told the viewers what was going on at the scene, but indefinable noise that turned out to be the breaking of large glass panes. Several hybrids had met with resistance inside the villa.

The defenders did not hold out for long. When the windows broke, and hybrids streamed into the villa, the men in the building were overrun. Shots were still whipping through the air, and Rosa feared that the prisoners were being executed. She tried to find some feeling in herself that went beyond superficial horror and moral condemnation—but then she recalled that these men had spent days on end hunting for a girl of fifteen who had to hide from them in a cold, dark bunker. And yet the disturbing certainty remained that all this fitted her image of the secure life on board the *Stabat Mater* only conditionally. More and more, she was realizing that Evangelos Thanassis was as uncompromising as his enemies in his methods.

After all the shots had died away, the cameras worn by the dead were switched off, numbers of casualties had been announced, and yet the talk was of victory, Rosa asked, "How about Iole?"

Danai, who had just finished a low-voiced conversation with the captain, counted the points of heat on the screen. "Your friends won't come out of the bunker. They're probably not sure exactly what's been going on up above."

"Someone had better go down and talk to them," said the captain. "Someone they trust."

Alessandro nodded. "I'll go."

"We'll go," said Rosa.

Then, with a crackle, Mirella's voice came over the loudspeakers. "There's one of the other side missing," she reported. "One of the Arachnida has disappeared inside the bunker."

ARACHNID

Rosa lowered the megaphone, suppressing a sigh. Since she and the others had entered the bunker, she had called out several warnings through the darkness to Iole and the two women. Even after she stopped, her voice still echoed back from the concrete walls of the underground complex, dying away as a whisper deep in the rock.

"Are you sure that the Arachnid is down here?" she asked Mirella, who was walking to Rosa's left with a submachine gun leveled at the ready. The wiry hybrid wore a close-fitting black jumpsuit. Anyone who didn't look at her pock-marked face, where the structure of scales had only half developed, could have taken her and Rosa for the same age.

"If he'd escaped among the rocks, the thermal-imaging camera would probably have picked him up." Mirella didn't look at Rosa as she spoke; her eyes remained forward the whole time. "I don't know how long he's been searching for your friends down here, but we can be more or less certain that he knows his way around better than we do."

Rosa had no idea how large the bunker was. Until a few months ago, the concrete building above ground, through which the passageway to the underground complex was built, had been the enclosure where the Carnevares kept their beasts of prey. Cesare had let lions, tigers, and other big cats roam free on the island before Alessandro put an end to it. The wild animals had been captured and given to zoos on the mainland. Since then, the cages in the enclosure had been empty, but the smell of the big cats still filled the entire building. Even here, a floor lower down, it had settled into the shafts.

"Iole!" she called through the megaphone again. "If you can hear me—lock yourselves in somewhere, and don't come out until I say so. There's an Arachnid hiding in the bunker. Wait until we've found him."

"If we drive him into a corner, he'll attack," said Mirella. "So stay very close to me."

Ahead of them went three armed hybrids, one of them the Hunding. Behind those three came five more men at different stages of metamorphosis. One of the insect hybrids was running along under the roof on all fours. Curved bony spurs with points as sharp as a knife on the palms of his hands and the soles of his feet gave him a secure grip on the porous concrete surface.

Farther forward, even ahead of the Hunding and his two companions, Alessandro was prowling through the darkness in his panther form. He saw in the dark better than any of the others with his cat eyes, and his black coat made him a shadow. Now and then he was caught in one of the flickering beams from a flashlight, but he was out of it again at once.

The group was moving down a long corridor with open doorways on both sides. Beyond the doorways, they saw rooms with rusty camp beds, folding chairs, and metal lockers.

The complex was supposed to have been empty for over sixty years. But the farther in they went, the more Rosa doubted whether the Carnevares had left such a place unused. For decades, Alessandro's family had charged a fee for disposing of the victims of the other clans, and this bunker was ideal for that purpose. If there were really no corpses here, that was probably because the space had been used to store something else. Something that would not be polluted by the stench of decomposition. Rosa's conviction that Iole had discovered Leonardo Mori's archives grew with every untouched room they passed, every dusty storeroom.

"He could have scurried away anywhere," said Mirella after they had passed yet another.

The Hunding muttered impatiently to himself. Under the roof of the corridor, the insect hybrid made clicking noises that sounded like crazy giggling. Rosa never looked straight up at him, but she was aware of him clinging upside down there. Whenever she caught a glimpse of him out of the corner of her eye, a cold shiver ran down her spine.

They reached the end of the main corridor and were at the top of the steps down to the second underground floor. Alessandro must have run down them silently on his cat's paws already. Her concern for him almost persuaded her to shift shape herself, particularly as her reptilian vision would register sources of heat that other eyes couldn't see. However, she would then have lost her voice, and with it the opportunity to warn Iole and the two women of danger.

The handheld lights cut bright paths through the stone

dust in the air. They climbed down the steps in a bewildering confusion of intersecting beams. The insect hybrid brought up the rear. Rosa heard him first scraping the wall as he climbed down it, and then behind her on the steps.

They entered a corridor with broad pipes running along the left wall, and among them skeins of tubes and supply cables. The hybrids shone the beams of their lights on this tangle, but they would have had to climb along the back of it to make sure no one was hiding there. The insect hybrid did just that: He slipped in between two pipes, and scurried on invisibly behind forests of cables and rusty wiring.

Mirella pointed to the megaphone. Rosa repeated her message. Once again, the only answer was the echo of her own voice.

Ahead of them in the dark, something hissed.

"Alessandro?"

The sound came again.

Mirella raised her gun, and the others held their pistols and machine guns at the ready. Behind the pipes and cables, the insect hybrid let out something that sounded like the distorted chirping of a cricket.

A sharp meow, then pattering and rustling.

Rosa's voice sounded as if she had swallowed dust. "Alessandro, for heaven's sake!"

"Quiet!" Mirella snapped at her.

Furiously, Rosa spun around to face her, but something in the Lamia hybrid's grim expression stopped her in her tracks. Mirella's lips silently formed two words.

He's here.

The panther's hiss was repeated, full of anger this time. A heavy body came down on something hard and resistant, and claws scraped over stone.

Beams of light groped frantically around. An outline shot out of the dark, guns were raised, and someone fired—but Mirella had swiftly struck the weapon aside, so that the bullets ricocheted off the walls. The leaping figure was Alessandro, and he seemed to be hunting something that Rosa couldn't see.

Several voices cursed at the same time. Once again, Rosa heard pattering on the roof above her. A split second later she realized that the insect hybrid was still behind the pipes, and could not possibly be above her head at the same time. She looked up, saw a body with angular limbs, and was still flinging herself to one side when the Arachnid landed in the middle of the group.

Rosa hit the ground, rolled under the pipes, and just escaped the attack. Instantly, the creature turned against the hybrids. Rosa had never seen such an unequal fight. The Arachnid killed three of them with well-aimed blows from his hooked claws in the first few seconds. Throats and bellies were slit open before a single shot was heard, but in this cramped space the hybrids couldn't fire at the Arachnid without hitting their own men.

Mirella was caught by one of the creature's eight legs, flung against the Hunding, and disappeared in the dark. Rosa had not been able to see how severely injured she was. She herself was on the point of shifting to snake form; she could already feel the cold creeping from her chest into all her limbs, a defense mechanism that her body initiated involuntarily. But as a reptile her chances against the Arachnid were as poor as if she stayed in human shape.

Two more hybrids fell victim to the beast. Then a majestic roar sounded. Alessandro shot forward with a mighty leap, landed on the Arachnid's hairy back, dug his claws into it, and sank his teeth deep into the spider's body. The beast began to rage, but Rosa still couldn't see anything clearly, only a twitching scene of chaos with too many legs, visible in the beams of the few flashlights still in use.

Once again someone opened fire. Rosa shouted in the direction of the noise, fearing that Alessandro might be hit. But then she saw that the marksman, an injured hybrid, was now lying under the Arachnid and pumping several bullets into the creature's underbelly.

At the same time, Mirella reappeared. And as Alessandro moved out of danger with another leap, while Rosa fought off her own metamorphosis, and two hybrids staggered out of the line of fire, Mirella stood with legs wide apart and fired three rounds at close range into the ugly body of the injured Arachnid.

Rosa stayed where she was until it was over. When the shots died away, the creature's distorted, ruined legs changed shape, and seconds later a man lay there, face down in his own blood, in as bad a state as his victims.

Thick smoke filled the corridor. Alessandro stepped out

of it, in human shape again, naked and, so far as she could see, uninjured. The blood on him didn't seem to be his own, and he was walking upright without any visible wounds. He was about to bend down to her, but she was already sliding out from under the pipes on the wall and almost slipped as she stood up, clung to him, and quickly embraced him. Then they both bent over the lifeless hybrids on the floor, searching for a pulse, any sign of breathing, listening in vain for groans or whispers. Mirella, the Hunding, and the others crouched down as well, while someone called for paramedics over the radio.

The stench in the corridor was barely tolerable. An acrid mixture of gunpowder, blood, and wounds settled in their lungs and eyes. No one spoke more than necessary. Mirella gave orders to separate the injured carefully from the dead. Footsteps and voices were heard from the far end of the corridor, as help approached.

Alessandro took Rosa's hand and led her on, putting a finger on her lips when she tried to protest, and a few yards farther on pointed to a place where the corridor branched. At the end of a passage off to one side, there was an iron door. A very thin line of light was visible under it.

Alessandro nodded when she glanced at him. Rosa looked behind her, but through the haze she could only make out indistinct movements. She heard the voices of the others, saw the insect hybrid emerge from behind the pipes and disappear into the smoke again. They were now about thirty feet away. When Alessandro guided her into the side passage, the voices were suddenly more muffled. She felt calmer with every step she took beside him.

She knocked on the door quietly.

"Iole," she whispered, her lips close to the place where the door closed, "it's us. Rosa and Alessandro. You can open up."

A dog whined on the other side of it. Inaudible voices. And then the snapping of locks, the sound of bolts being pushed back.

Iole's face appeared between the door and the doorway. She was about to shout with delight, but Rosa was faster. Her hand shot out and closed Iole's mouth. At the same time, she pushed her into the room. Alessandro followed them.

"Quiet!" she whispered as she stepped inside. She must be a horrible sight—and Alessandro was even more so, naked and stained scarlet from head to foot.

Sarcasmo raced toward her to welcome her. At the last minute, his nose registered the smell of fresh blood, and he swerved away from Rosa and rushed at Alessandro, licking him frantically.

"Traitor," murmured Rosa.

Iole flung her arms around her, while Alessandro closed the door behind them. As he turned around again, he found himself looking down the barrel of a gun that was probably as old as the bunker itself. Cristina di Santis was aiming it at his face, while Raffaela Falchi, Iole's private tutor, was pointing a meat knife at him with trembling hands.

Rosa cautiously pushed Iole away from her, feeling thankful that the girl kept her mouth shut. However, Iole seemed to have realized what was going on already. In any normal situation, Iole saw its slightly crazy side first, as if she went through life with a magnifying glass that enlarged only the oddities and curiosities for her benefit. At a moment like this, however, she was the first to understand the true state of affairs. Rosa would have liked to give her another hug for that alone.

But first she had to make sure that Cristina di Santis didn't shoot Alessandro. Or that Signora Falchi didn't thrust the steak knife into his chest.

"Listen," she said quickly, although she rejoiced inwardly as soon as she looked at brave, grubby, pretty Iole. "The good news is that the men who've been keeping you holed up down here are dead. The bad news is that we don't know exactly what to think of the people who killed them."

Signora Falchi was about to say something, but Cristina got in first. With the same grim expression she'd had when she tricked Avvocato Trevini back in the Hotel Jonio, she reached her arm out sideways and placed her hand over the tutor's mouth. Signora Falchi seemed as if she wanted to protest, but the dark looks on the faces of the others deterred her.

"Go on," said Cristina. She lowered the gun and pushed Signora Falchi's knife down with its barrel.

Rosa nodded gratefully to the young attorney. "They'll be here any minute, so I have to keep this short. You've found something down here, haven't you? Iole, you told me about papers, some kind of archive."

Iole grinned broadly. Her short hair was untidy and gray with dust after her days in the bunker. She had rings of dirt under her eyes, and like the others didn't smell very good. "Over there," she said, pointing to a wooden table behind which several banana boxes full of file folders, loose-leaf binders, and papers were stacked. A whole pile of others, a good half a yard high, lay on the table. A candle flickered beside them.

"You know what that is, Rosa?" asked Cristina, turning to Rosa. They had been on a first-name basis since she joined them on Isola Luna. It didn't mean that they were bosom buddies, but at least they felt mutual respect for each other. Recently they had been able to spend several hours in the same house without going for each other's throats.

A voice called out from the corridor. It wouldn't be long now before it occurred to someone—probably Mirella—that Rosa and Alessandro had disappeared.

"Did all this belong to a man named Leonardo Mori?" asked Rosa. "Is his name there anywhere, on a folder or—"

"Those are typescripts of his tape recordings," Cristina interrupted her. "He asked a whole series of people a great many odd questions. They call him by his name several times. Signor Mori."

Alessandro hadn't said a word yet, probably because he knew how little time they had. Rosa saw the excitement in his eyes. She, too, felt new hope, because it was Cristina who had read these papers. Cristina, who had a photographic memory, and was able to recollect every detail, however tiny.

"It's about the Arcadian dynasties," said Signora Falchi, joining the conversation. She had been in the Palazzo

Alcantara when the Hungry Man's Hundinga mercenaries attacked it, and knew the secret of the shape-shifters. In spite of that, however, it was a surprise to hear her mention the dynasties so matter of factly.

"The others know about everything I've read," said Cristina, with a challenging look at Alessandro. "After all, we had to talk about something down here."

The voices in the corridor were louder now. Were they calling their names?

"This is very important," said Rosa hastily, "and whatever happens, the answer must be kept strictly between us. If anyone asks you later, you just looked at a few of the papers, but you didn't understand much, okay?"

Iole smiled. "Acting stupid isn't difficult when everyone's always thought you were mentally challenged."

"Did you find out anything about a shrine?" asked Rosa. "Information about an ancient tomb, a kind of a mausoleum of—"

"The tomb of Lycaon," said Cristina.

"King Lycaon," added Iole.

Alessandro broke his silence. "Is there anything about its location? Did Mori find out where the tomb was built?"

Cristina nodded. "Yes, he went there."

Now footsteps could be heard, coming closer. Mirella called to them. She must have seen the candlelight under the door. Sarcasmo growled quietly.

"Where is it?" whispered Rosa. "Where is the damn tomb?"

"In Sicily."

"More precisely?"

Sarcasmo began to bark.

"In a valley," said Cristina, "near a village called Giuliana."

Rosa's heart missed a beat.

"Shit," murmured Alessandro.

The iron door flew open into the room and crashed against the wall.

THE SHRINE

ROSA COULDN'T GET ENOUGH of the feel of hot water on her skin. Even after the last of the dirt and blood had disappeared down the drain, she let the shower run for a long time. The steaming heat on her body was wonderful, but she still didn't feel entirely clean.

She had used up half a bottle of shower gel. The water had been running for twenty minutes. But her bruises and red marks couldn't be washed away. Was she getting compulsive about washing? No sooner was she rid of her old neuroses than she developed new ones. What the hell, she thought, as she let herself sink to her knees in the jet of water and turn into the snake.

Her body lost its human shape as the skin roughened. All the outward features she didn't like about herself—her thin legs, sharp bones, small breasts—simply ceased to exist. Her hair turned to strands of skin and tissue, fell around her shoulders and head, and merged with her amber-colored scaly body. Her tongue became forked, shot out of flat reptilian jaws. Her vision also changed; her surroundings were bathed in brightness as clear as glass.

Finally she lay in the shower as a snake, stretching and coiling in the water, and she couldn't remember when she had last felt so good.

After a while the water ran cooler; the boiler at the villa had reached its limit. Rosa changed back and found that she had a new skin, free of bruises and cuts.

When she got out of the shower, Alessandro was standing in front of her. She wondered how long he had been there, watching.

"There's a word for what you're doing," she said with an embarrassed smile as she reached for a bath towel and rubbed her hair. For the first time in days she could bear her own smell again; not even the artificially floral perfume of the shampoo bothered her.

Alessandro's own hair was wet; he had showered in another bathroom in the villa. As she dried herself off, she admired the well-proportioned build of his body; he wore nothing except for a towel knotted around his waist. Her robe hung on a hook beside the door behind him.

The bathroom was on the second floor of the villa. Its exterior glass wall reached smoothly from the ceiling to the floor. A few yards lower down, the gray slope of lava rock, creviced and precipitous, fell away to the sea. Although the glass was slightly clouded with condensation, the morning sunlight bathed all the faucets, fittings, and mirrors in gold. Like Alessandro's skin.

"I didn't want to wait any longer," he said.

Amused, she raised an eyebrow. "Now? Here?"

"I didn't mean that," he replied, smiling. "We have to talk about Giuliana."

"Giuliana no longer exists." She went on drying her long

hair. "The valley disappeared under a lake when a dam was built. Cesare and your father did all the work on it."

She hadn't been in Sicily long when her sister, Zoe, took her there. From the dam wall, they had looked at the depths below, to where a lake had swallowed up a whole village—and allegedly its inhabitants as well. It was said that the Carnevares had been given the contract to build the dam, even though no one had any use for the water or the energy that it produced. The project had brought millions upon millions into the clan's bank accounts. According to official sources, the inhabitants of Giuliana, who had protested against the clearance of their village, had been resettled in Calabria. Yet there were persistent rumors that the Carnevares had silenced them and sunk them into the lake created by the dam, along with their houses.

Alessandro was aware that Rosa knew the story of the villagers' murders, but he had dismissed the whole thing as a modern legend.

"If Lycaon's tomb does exist," said Rosa, "or even a single stone is left of it, then it's all buried deep in that lake. I'm gradually starting to understand what made Cesare tick. He was a bastard, but he was also an enemy of the Hungry Man. And whatever really happened in Giuliana—the reason for building the dam was obviously not so much the money your clan made out of it as trying to stop the Hungry Man's attempt to seize power for a second time."

He was leaning against one of the marble sinks. In the mirror, she could see his muscular back and had to tear her gaze away in order to look into his eyes. She liked those even better, the only green thing in the sterile room.

"Up to that point maybe it all makes sense," he said. "Cesare and my father turned the valley into a lake to make sure that the site of the tomb was inaccessible forever. But there was one thing they didn't take into account."

She put the towel down and examined her long hair in the mirror. It looked like an exploded bale of hay. "And that was?"

"The possibility of an upheaval within the clan. Enabling the Hungry Man to gain influence over the Carnevares."

"How long would it take," she asked, "to get a lake like that to run dry again? A year? Two years?"

"Four months."

"Only four months?" She shrugged. "Still, that gives us at least four months to think something up—"

"Four months ago, one of my *capodecini* came to me and told me how bad the whole Giuliana story was for the image of our firms. You and I talked about it, too, but you didn't believe me when I said the people really had been resettled."

"Are you saying that—"

"I wanted to find out what really happened. Maybe I'd even have done it myself, sooner or later, without anyone else bringing my attention to it. I didn't need a permit. The land on both sides of the river belongs to my family."

"Wouldn't a few phone calls to Calabria have been enough?"

"It was also a matter of ending all the talk. I wanted people to be able to see, with their own eyes, that there's nothing but abandoned houses down in that lake." He hesitated for a moment. "*If* there is nothing but abandoned houses there."

"So the whole lake has been drained now?"

He nodded. "I haven't thought about it for a couple of weeks, but the water ought to be out of it by now. I've looked at the construction paperwork from when the dam was built, all the applications and permits. Not a word about any archaeological finds or excavations. If there was anything there, then no one recognized it for what it really was. Maybe only a few stones, some kind of rubble that no one thought important."

"And you think the Hungry Man is behind it? Through his middleman, he gave you the idea of draining the gravesite?"

"Could be possible. But I wanted to know whether my father was a bigger bastard than I even thought." He looked down. "Whether he and Cesare were mass murderers."

"Is that why you never told me about it?"

"First I wanted to know whether there were any bodies down there or not."

She groaned. "We're both chasing the shadows of our dead fathers. And as if there wasn't enough shit in our lives anyway . . ." She went up to him and caressed his cheek. "If Thanassis and Danai find out that the tomb is in that valley, and the lake has been drained, they're going to insist that we turn ourselves over right away."

He took her hand and kissed each fingertip separately. "We have to get out of here before they've studied Mori's papers. We still have an advantage—we know more than they do. Or were you really planning to go along with this game of theirs?"

She shook her head with a bitter smile. "But the stupid part is that more than likely they know that very well."

"They're having the villa watched," he said. "But we'll get out of here."

"And then what? This is an island, and they have one hell of a large ship."

He buried one hand in the damp hair at the nape of her neck and drew her close. Their lips touched.

There was a knock on the door—once, twice—and suddenly Cristina di Santis was standing in the room.

"Sorry," she said, seeing the two of them in the steam from the shower. She looked at the floor, moving backward to the door. But wasn't she sneaking a surreptitious glance at Alessandro?

"Why does everyone just come wandering in when I'm in the bathroom?" asked Rosa.

Cristina straightened up and put her hands on her hips. Now she was looking openly. "You didn't lock the door."

"So?"

"That's what doors have locks for."

"It's a *bathroom*," said Rosa. "A place where you do private things. Bathroom things."

"So I see."

Alessandro cleared his throat. "I'll just go and get dressed, then."

"Good idea," said Cristina, and when they both stared at her she added, "I have to speak to Rosa. Alone. That's why."

Alessandro gave Rosa a kiss and whispered, "Hurry up. We'll be off. I'll think of something."

Before she could reply, he had passed Cristina, who by chance was standing in the doorway so that her breasts brushed against his bare chest as he left. If Rosa had been one of the Panthera, her claws would have shot out on the spot. But she didn't even have poison fangs. Lamias were useless.

"What do you want?" she asked when Alessandro had closed the door and she was alone with Cristina.

"Can you put something on?"

Rosa pointed to the bathrobe hanging behind Cristina. "Do you by any chance want *me* to have to squeeze past you too?"

The attorney took a step to the side, but Rosa shook her head. "Okay." The things she had taken from her wardrobe before showering lay on the second sink. Black jeans, black top, a close-fitting black leather frock coat. She would hate to lose that if she had to shift shape somewhere and leave these clothes behind.

As Rosa slipped into her underwear. Cristina took a deep breath. "Those archives down in the bunker . . . there's something else you ought to know."

"But not Alessandro?"

"That's for you to decide. First and foremost, it concerns you."

Rosa did up the jeans and put her thin arms through the armholes of the shirt. All of a sudden she didn't know why in the world she had laid out a leather jacket in a tropically hot bathroom. "Come on, let's go next door."

Cristina followed her into one of the bedrooms. The villa still had the same bizarre seventies-style furniture that Alessandro's mother had liked so much. The bed was made of transparent lucite, like clear Saran wrap.

Rosa closed the door. "Sit down."

Cristina stayed on her feet. "The papers down there weren't complete. The file folders are numbered, and a lot are missing. About half, I'd say. Any idea where the rest could be?"

Rosa thought of Fundling, who had taken up residence in the Hotel Paradiso, tracking down his murdered parents. It was possible that he had found part of the documentation somewhere else and taken it to a safe place.

"No idea at all."

Cristina took something out of her pocket. "This is from a folder with your family's name on it. I hid it before the hybrids packed everything up and took it on board the ship." At this very moment, Danai and some of the hybrids closest to her would be combing through the material for references to Lycaon's tomb.

Cristina handed her a photograph, with the yellowed back of it facing up. For a moment they both held it, before Cristina finally let go. Rosa wasn't sure whether she really wanted to see the photo. For the first time there was sympathy in Cristina's eyes. That worried Rosa more than her air of mystery.

Finally she took the photo, but she didn't turn it over. "What is it?"

"That video," began Cristina, "the one that Trevini sent you—"

"That *you* sent me on Trevini's behalf," Rosa corrected her.

"That man was in it—not Tano Carnevare, the other man. Apollonio."

"My father."

"I compared some of the pictures. The likeness is really startling."

Rosa's fingers began to tremble as they held the photo. "Cristina, the man *was* my father! My own father stood there while Tano was raping me. He gave him the *contract* to do it!"

"Possibly."

She didn't like this conversation at all, but that wasn't entirely Cristina's fault. Slowly, she turned the photograph over.

It showed a metal bedframe in front of a white wall, maybe in a hospital. A woman in her midthirties with long, blond hair was lying on it. A woman who resembled Rosa herself much more than she liked—her grandmother, Costanza Alcantara. She recognized her at once from photographs and the oil painting that had gone up in flames with the palazzo.

Beside the bed stood a man with his hair cut short, wearing nickel-framed glasses. He was tall and burly, with broad cheekbones and a flat nose. He wore a white medical coat, and he had a clipboard in his hand.

Costanza looked weary and exhausted, but a smile hovered around the corners of her mouth. In a surprising way, it veiled the cruelty she had been capable of.

There were two babies in her arms.

"Read what it says underneath," said Cristina. "That must

be Leonardo Mori's handwriting. At least, it's all over the place in his papers."

C. Alcantara. Forward slash. *E. Sigismondis.* Forward slash. *Campofelice di Fitalia.* And after it a date that she knew.

"Campofelice di Fitalia is a small town in the west of Sicily," explained Cristina, while Rosa was still unable to utter a sound. "It's near Corleone. It's a little bit of a no-man's-land out there."

Rosa stared at the picture a little longer, then looked up at Cristina. "You think they're twins?"

"That would be possible, wouldn't it?"

"They're babies. All tiny babies look alike."

"But she's holding them both in her arms. And the date is your father's birthday. What mother has herself photographed, just after giving birth, holding her own baby and someone else's?" She reached out a hand and tapped the paper with a fingertip. Sometimes she was more like a teacher than Signora Falchi herself. "Don't lie to yourself, Rosa."

"Fuck."

Cristina raised both hands in a gesture of resignation. "I thought you'd be pleased."

"Pleased? I'd only just come to terms with finding out that my father's the biggest bastard in the world. That I hate him worse than anyone, even worse than Tano and Michele. And now there's someone who looks just like him? Someone I don't know, who might not have any problem about arranging for his brother's daughter to be raped?"

Cristina nodded. When she continued speaking, she

sounded dismayed. "If I'd known that you wouldn't—"

"No," Rosa said quickly. "No, I'm sorry. I . . . of course I'm pleased. Kind of. It's just that I thought I was finally sure about something, even if I didn't like it. Something that was simply true, no ifs, ands, or buts."

Cristina smiled. "You have Alessandro to be certain about."

Their glances locked and held in a silent struggle for conviction.

Then Rosa looked back at the photograph. "Why is Sigismondis with her? I know he got her to supply those furs, but this . . . did he bring my father *into the world*?"

"Seems like it." Cristina took a step back, as if to give Rosa more room to face the truth. "I checked the internet just now. At that time there wasn't any hospital in Campofelice. Wherever that bed stood, it wasn't in a normal hospital."

Rosa couldn't take her eyes off the picture of the two tiny baby faces. "Does that mean they were born in a TABULA laboratory?"

A SEA OF SHARDS

ALESSANDRO WAS STANDING ON the terrace of the villa, on a carpet of sparkling shards of glass, looking out over the sea.

Rosa wore steel-toed shoes, one of the pairs she had left at the villa. The broken glass from the terrace window crunched under their soles. All the bodies had been taken away; the hybrids had probably taken their own dead with them and thrown the others into some hole in the rock.

Alessandro wore washed-out jeans and a close-fitting black shirt. In the days before Fundling's funeral, they had spent a great deal of time together on Isola Luna, so some of his clothes were in the dressing room. His sneakers were gray and well-worn, bearing the traces of their climbs together on the slopes of lava rock.

It was still early in the morning. Neither of them had really had enough sleep, but Rosa felt more dazed than tired. Sleep wouldn't help much with that.

She went to stand beside him by the walled parapet. The sun, still low in the sky, made the crevices of the volcanic slope look bottomless. On the horizon, another island rose from the blue sea, a gray triangle like the fin of a shark. To their left, two hundred yards from the coast, the *Stabat Mater* lay at anchor in deep water. Several of the hybrids' boats were moored down by the shore. Guards were patrolling in front of the villa, on the pier outside the bunker, and at other places on the island. But from here there were only two that were visible, tiny figures among the rocks farther down the slope.

"I'm not letting them hand you over," he said.

"Hand us over," she corrected him.

"They should have injected us with the serum. If we shift shape, they'll never get hold of us."

She gave him a doubtful look. "And how about Iole and the others? Never mind what hole in the rock we crawl into, Thanassis only has to threaten to do them harm, and they have us where they want us."

"We have to get away from here. At once." He looked darkly over at the *Stabat Mater*. From a distance, it was impossible to guess what was going on in the interior of the steel giant. "As soon as they find out about Giuliana, they'll hold us to our side of the bargain. They've done their part."

"It was only the documents they wanted, not Iole," Rosa halfheartedly contradicted him. She knew she was splitting hairs.

"We'll never get at the two speedboats by the pier," he said. "But the satellite picture showed that the third is down in the sandy bay. I didn't see them take it back to the *Stabat Mater*. It's probably still on the beach."

Surreptitiously, she pushed the photograph to him across the parapet, keeping one finger on a corner so that the sea breeze didn't blow it away.

He read the handwritten notes at the bottom and looked

blankly at Rosa. "From Mori's archives?"

She nodded and quietly told him what she had learned from Cristina. Her voice trembled a little, though she tried to be as objective as possible. Finally, she said, "I have to go there. Maybe someone will still remember something. If there's paperwork, documentation of any kind—"

"How long ago was this? Around forty years?"

"I know. But if there's even the tiniest chance that Apollonio isn't my father, how can I do anything else? I can't hate my father all my life for something that may have been done by someone else who looks exactly like him. Don't you understand that?"

"I don't want you to nurture a false hope, that's all. The hills between Campofelice di Fitalia and Corleone are a wilderness, nothing but abandoned farms and deserted herdsmen's villages. The district was once called the Mafia graveyard, because the Corleone clan buried their victims there."

"I thought that was what the Carnevares did?"

"Not for the Corleonese. We never had much to do with those pigs." After pausing briefly for breath, he added, "At least, not as far as I know."

She put the photo away, then took his hands and drew him toward her. They held each other close in front of the shining panorama of the Mediterranean. The sun bathed them in its warmth; the wind smelled of salt and the pleasures of a vacation. Only the broken glass underfoot reminded them of what had happened here.

At last she looked into his eyes again. "You really are afraid, aren't you?"

"What do you mean?"

"Afraid of what we might yet find out. About your father, my father, everything that happened in the past. Afraid that most of what we've always believed was only a deception."

He searched for words. "I've always known what my family does. There was never a particular moment when I suddenly saw through it all, or at least not as far as our business went. It was always taken for granted. Other fathers were mechanics or teachers, mine was a member of Cosa Nostra. There was no mysterious silence at the supper table, no concealed glances and whispers. Business was business, regardless of whether it was legal or dealt in drugs, money laundering, or arms. I always thought there were no secrets. Even when I heard about the Arcadians and what we are, I still believed I'd been initiated into everything." He stopped and closed his eyes for a few seconds, then said, "But now I feel as if I were walking through a house I've known from my childhood—except that there are strange rooms behind all the doors. Rooms that I never in my life went into."

"And that you don't want to go into." She knew exactly how he felt. Everything was fine as long as they agreed on what really mattered.

He kissed her again, smiled, and gave her another kiss. That Morse code was so typical of Alessandro—something only she knew about him—that for a moment she actually felt a little weak at the knees. She had to laugh. It was so silly, and at the same time so wonderful.

"What are you laughing at?" he asked.

"Only myself."

She laid her cheek against his chest, closed her eyes, and listened to the roar of the sea down below, the wind rushing through the crevices of the volcanic rock, his heartbeat or her own, she wasn't sure whether there was still any difference. At that moment, the same heart kept them both alive.

Down on the shore, the engine of a boat revved up. Rosa was ready to think it was Danai, who had found what she was looking for and was coming to the island to take them away. But the boat went over from Isola Luna to the ship, with a crew of two hybrids, tiny dots in the cockpit.

"And now there are only six," said Alessandro. "I went up to the roof and counted them. Four around the villa, two at the pier. Maybe some in the bay. I can't tell from here."

"Do you think they know the way down there? The path through the rocks?"

"I'd guess not. They didn't have time to scout out the whole place. And on the satellite pictures they couldn't possibly make out the steps down among the rocks. It was all gray on gray."

"How about Iole and the others?" she asked.

"They come too."

"Of course they come too. But do we tell them how dangerous it is? They're of no value to Thanassis. And if the hybrids come hunting us, they could be killed."

"You think he'd go that far?"

"You know him by now. Thanassis has no scruples when it comes to getting what he wants. He must hate TABULA and the Hungry Man like poison. The minute he knows the location of the tomb, it won't make any difference whether we help him voluntarily or he forces us to do it. He'll only have to hand us over to make sure the chiefs of the clans all assemble at the same place." She glanced at the *Stabat Mater* standing out to sea. "I wish I knew what he plans to do then. Do you think he's going to turn up with his private army?"

"Those pictures taken from the air come from military satellites," said Alessandro. "Just like the photos of the statues being salvaged that we saw aboard the *Colony*. These people have links with the army, sources in the supervision control centers of the secret service, how would we know exactly what? But Thanassis is one of the richest men in the world. He must have the best contacts imaginable."

She started to sigh and repressed it. "Almost all the satellite pictures on which the *Stabat Mater* could have been seen had been deleted. You think that if he has enough influence to get something like that done—"

"Then he may also have access to other things. Remote-controlled rockets. Armed military drones. All the modern means of waging war at the touch of a button."

"Meaning that he could blow them all sky-high. While watching in comfort on board the *Stabat Mater*."

"And the irony is that our own firms probably supplied him with the material. Or at least the access codes."

"All the same, he needs us as decoys. Without us, there won't be any ceremony." This time she made up her mind without hesitation. "We'll cut and run. Right now."

"Talk to the others. But go carefully. We can do without an attorney who always knows best, or that tutor nagging us."

"They'll keep their mouths shut when it matters."

"We'll meet in the passage to the generator house. In ten minutes?"

She nodded, gave him a last kiss, and hurried back over the sea of sparkling broken glass.

THE PARTING

A NARROW CONCRETE CORRIDOR with a tiled floor. On the ceiling were round lights, and there was a fire extinguisher in a niche in the wall. The musty air had a strong smell of chlorine. The technological controls for the swimming pool were through a side door.

Alessandro walked ahead. His hair had taken on a tinge of black. Rosa followed him, holding hands with Iole. She in turn had the dog's leash wrapped tightly around her right wrist, and Sarcasmo stayed obediently beside her. She was all in black, which was unusual when she was so fond of white.

Cristina and Signora Falchi brought up the rear. They both wore jeans and dark T-shirts. The washed-out logo of a band was displayed on the tutor's, encircled by stylized flames. Iole hadn't been able to stop grinning since they all met up in the cellar; neither she nor Rosa had ever seen Raffaela Falchi in a getup like that.

Motion detectors switched on the lights as Alessandro approached them. Only at the end of the corridor was there still darkness.

"Not far now," he whispered. "The generator house is about fifty meters south of the villa, level with it on the mountain."

"Why aren't the generators in the cellar?" asked Rosa.

"They're gasoline-driven. The tank ought to be still full. My mother wouldn't have all that in the house, so it was stored separately." Gaia Carnevare had already feared for her life years before she died, and she hadn't wanted to make things easier than necessary for her murderers.

As they passed the last motion detector, the lights came on, and the end of the corridor was visible ahead. Just before reaching it, Alessandro stood still for a moment, listening for any voices on the other side of the door.

Cristina, who had tied her black hair back in a ponytail, looked tense. Beside her, the tutor was white as a sheet, but Rosa hadn't forgotten Raffaela Falchi's determination as she kept the Hundinga under fire when they attacked the palazzo. She could be relied on in a serious situation.

Alessandro opened the door slightly and peered cautiously through it, then signed to the others. The coast was clear.

The two emergency generators and the huge white plastic tank almost filled the entire space. Iole kept Sarcasmo on an even shorter leash; the dog didn't seem to like the smell of gasoline. He was restless, but he didn't utter a sound.

The way out of the generator house wasn't guarded, either. As the group stepped out of the small, square building into the open, two seagulls flew up, screeching. The group hoped that they wouldn't arouse suspicion. From now on the five of them would converse only by signs.

To everyone's surprise, the tutor brought a small pistol out of her fanny pack and took the safety catch off. Mirella had told them to hand over all weapons, and Rosa had told her, truthfully, that no guns were kept in the villa. But she really should have guessed that, after Signora Falchi's feats back at the palazzo, she would be the one to have a pistol hidden in her baggage. Alessandro, however, cast disapproving glances at the gun and its owner.

Ducking low, they set off southward through the rocks. Alessandro led them through crevices and hollows between craggy gray stones and down the slope. There were no man-made paths here, no flights of steps or other tracks. If anyone sprained an ankle on the porous rock, their flight would be finished. Alessandro had told them over and over before they set off, until after a while Cristina exploded. He obviously thought all women were total idiots, she said, too stupid to put one foot in front of another. He had looked at Rosa for support, but Rosa had only grinned and shrugged.

Sarcasmo found the climb down through the rocks easier than the rest of them. Running, jumping, protecting Iole—that was all it took to make the dog happy.

Rosa kept her ears strained to pick up any sign that their flight had been seen. A siren on board the *Stabat Mater*, the howl of the speedboats by the pier, shouts and roaring from the hybrid guards. So far, however, there was nothing to suggest that anyone was pursuing them.

They had to force themselves to go on watching their feet, instead of looking back over their shoulders every few seconds. At any rate, there was no one there but the tutor with her pistol. If Signora Falchi stumbled and fired a shot by accident, maybe hitting Iole in the back—no, she couldn't think about it. Go on. Don't keep looking on the dark side.

After ten minutes they reached a set of steps carved into the rock. Rosa recognized the place. The stairs went around several bends, steeper and steeper as they made progress. Before every bend, Alessandro raised a hand to stop them. Then he went a couple of steps on his own, to make sure that no one was lying in wait or coming toward them.

The staircase ended on a tiny plateau surrounded on three sides by rock. Beyond the other side, which had no security barrier, an abyss yawned, and the sea raged five yards below. Rosa liked this place; it had been a favorite of Alessandro's mother. Gaia often used to come here to paint.

Alessandro led them through crevices down to the water, and then along a rocky shore. The waves broke on mounds of seaweed encrusted with mussel shells. Finally, they crept through a gap in a rampart, and then on down over a few more carved steps.

Ahead of them lay a white, sandy beach, the bay on the southern coast of Isola Luna.

The speedboat that had brought some of the attackers to the island was anchored a stone's throw away from the shore: a pitch-black arrowhead shape, with a chromium rail. Rosa knew very little about such craft, but hoped it was as fast as it looked.

An inconspicuous inflatable dinghy had been beached on the fine sand. The men must have gone the last few yards to the shore in it.

Iole murmured, "They shoot people, but they're afraid of getting their feet wet."

"Or maybe of getting their guns wet," commented Signora Falchi, waving her pistol in the air until Alessandro threatened to take it away from her.

They cautiously stepped out of the cover of the now petrified slope of lava rock and on to the broad beach. It had been artificially created years ago, when the island passed into the hands of the Carnevares. It lay in a crescent shape at the foot of the gray rock walls.

Rosa kept her eyes on the top of the cliffs above them. Why was no one guarding the speedboat?

They had covered almost half the distance down to the shore when Alessandro shouted, "Run!"

He quickly shifted to his panther shape. It was the first time Cristina had seen it happen; she stood there as if paralyzed.

At the other end of the beach, several hybrids stormed out from between the rocks. One of them went on all fours, but looked more like a human being than the Panthera hybrid running erect beside him, whose torso seemed to consist entirely of muscles covered with spotted leopard fur. His face was neither human nor animal, a distorted mask under which the skull had changed, but the skin of the face had not caught up with it. There were several openings through which bones and rows of teeth showed.

At first sight the other two were almost men, although one stooped like a hunchback, while the other's stiff hips twisted his whole body first one way, then the other, with every step he took. He would have seemed the least dangerous of the four if he hadn't been holding their only semiautomatic. The other three carried pistols, at least one of them loaded with tracer ammunition, for at that moment a shot was fired into the air, and exploded high above them in a ball of glowing white light.

Rosa pulled Iole along the beach with her. Sarcasmo overtook them and ran ahead on his leash, although not toward the boat but in the direction of the four hybrids.

"Let him go!" shouted Rosa, but Iole shook her head.

"Never."

She hauled the dog around. He barked a protest, but obeyed. Cristina and the tutor were beside them; they all reached the water at the same time. Without stopping to use the inflatable dinghy, they rushed out into the breakers, making straight for the speedboat lying at anchor. They would have only a few yards to swim.

"Go on!" Rosa shouted at Iole. "Whatever you do, don't stop!"

Then she let go of the girl's hand, stood where she was, and looked around her at the guards racing up—and at Alessandro who, leaping for the hybrids at that moment with his panther body at full stretch, collided with the hybrid holding the semiautomatic and dug his fangs into the creature's throat.

The leopard-man roared and sprang at Alessandro with a movement that was not entirely animal, but not human either. He was too late to save his companion's life, but he tore Alessandro away from the dying hybrid. As he bit into the panther's side, the whole scene unfolded in front of Rosa's eyes as if in slow motion.

With a scream of fury, she raced forward. Behind her, Iole called her name, and then she heard the two women as well. She could only hope they wouldn't stop, but would somehow make it to the speedboat.

She took hardly any notice of the two hybrids coming toward her with their swerving, clumsy gait. She had eyes only for Alessandro and his opponent, who both landed on the ground, sending sand rising into the air.

Another warning shot was fired over the beach.

She ran on, trying to skirt around the two armed hybrids, whose main goal must surely be to keep the fugitives away from the speedboat. Except that they obviously had other orders, and knew that Rosa and Alessandro were the only two who mattered.

Halfway toward him, the hybrids cut across her path. She realized, a second too late, that she would never get past them in human form. One was now standing with legs apart, pistol in both hands, taking aim at her. The other called out something, a final warning, but it was drowned out by the sound of the shot.

Would a transformation also cure broken bones? But the bullet hit not her but the hybrid with the gun. It tore him off his feet and sent him toppling into the sand. His companion looked angrily from Rosa to the water, and now she, too, turned that way.

Raffaela Falchi was standing among the breakers, holding

her gun in both hands. She fired for the second time. The shot missed the hybrid in front of Rosa, but made him duck, as if he seriously thought that would help him to avoid a bullet. It was a reflex, but it gave Rosa precious time. As she saw, out of the corner of her eye, that Iole and Cristina were heaving Sarcasmo on board the speedboat, and Signora Falchi was lowering her gun, she threw herself against the hybrid and pushed him back. She had not yet fully shifted to her snake form, but her fangs came out of her distorted mouth like needles and punctured the man's throat at his carotid artery. He stayed down on the ground, screaming, while she got to her feet again with a leap and ran to Alessandro and the leopard hybrid.

More figures appeared behind them both, standing out against the dark rocks. Yet more emerged from a crevice, spilling out on to the beach, some swift and light-footed, others so heavy that they sank into the soft ground underfoot up to their muscular calves. They must have been patrolling along the lava cliffs above when they saw the struggle on the sand.

A blow from Alessandro's panther claw tore the scarred openings on the leopard-man's face farther open. The pain made him incautious when, after a moment to get his breath back, he went for Alessandro again. Alessandro, however, dove away from the attack and dug his claws into his adversary's back. There was a terrible crack as the hybrid's backbone snapped. Roaring, the creature sank into the sand. The panther stood over him, and before the other hybrids came up, or Rosa could reach the two of them, he dug his teeth into his opponent's side.

"Watch out!" cried Rosa.

The next attackers were not so reckless as to tackle Alessandro directly. Instead, two of them threw a net over him. A third was carrying a metal rod with a horseshoe-shaped end, and when he touched the raging panther with it, electric shocks ran through the supple big cat's body, making him collapse.

Rosa shouted Alessandro's name as he turned back into human shape under the net. For a second, she was sure that he was dying, that the shift back had brought on his death. But then he reared up, ignored the hybrids surrounding him, and looked past them straight at Rosa.

"Get out of here!" he cried. "Don't . . . come any closer."

She was less than fifteen yards now from the hybrids who had left the main pack and were running toward her. It was her last chance to turn back, but she couldn't leave him lying there alone with these creatures. She took two or three more steps as her forked tongue passed over her lips, licking off her victim's blood.

"Run!" shouted Alessandro, as the device administering the electric shocks approached his bare skin again. Rosa was sure that she also heard him call out something else, although the roar of the hybrids almost drowned it out, and she couldn't see him any longer.

"Go to the hospital!" he cried in a strained voice, and then something that sounded like *find*.

She completed the change into her snake form and coiled her way swiftly out of reach of the hybrids' claws. At the same time, however, more shots were fired over the beach, maybe from the tutor's pistol, maybe from the hybrids' guns. Rosa glided over the sand, eluding feet and paws, and then, at last, she realized that she could no longer reach Alessandro.

There were too many of them. And if there was one thing that would have sealed his fate, it was her own capture. They were valuable to the Hungry Man only as a couple.

She couldn't see him anymore; she could no longer hear anything, she only felt the sand grating under her scaly skin as she changed direction and made for the breakers. The hybrids followed, trying again and again to grab hold of her, but she escaped them with her winding movement, swept two off their feet with her tail, severed the Achilles tendon of another with her teeth, and suddenly felt the water spraying around her.

Roaring noise surrounded her as she shot into the waves, and soon she was hidden from her pursuers. She needed air, but she stayed below the surface for the time being, feeling as if the sea were her natural element.

A yard and a half below the surface, she shifted back to human form, lost her sense of direction for a moment, then found her way back into a horizontal position and began to swim, almost blinded by salt water, but strongly enough to make progress. She couldn't think, couldn't think of *him*, because all her senses were bent on survival.

The roaring sound around her was louder now. As she surfaced, she drew air into her lungs in panic. She vaguely saw something blurred in front of her, something tall and black, not ten yards away.

Raffaela Falchi was kneeling above the silvery ladder leading from the rail of the speedboat down into the water. Iole joined her, but the tutor made her go back. Meanwhile, Cristina had started the motor. The propeller of the speedboat was swirling up foaming water.

Rosa looked over her shoulder, saw the outlines of the hybrids against the white sand, turned around, and swam on. The tutor had seen her now, called her name, and waved the pistol in one hand.

Suddenly, even before she realized that she had reached the boat, Rosa was holding the bottom rung of the ladder. With a desperate effort, she hauled herself upward.

Someone seized her wrist. Moments later, Signora Falchi pulled her up on board, away from the rail, while the motor howled, the hull reared up, and the speedboat shot forward out of the bay and into the open sea.

Rosa faintly saw Iole's face and heard her voice, and at the same time the tutor's voice and the excited panting of the dog. She turned over on her side, lay there, and looked back at the shore. Salt water was stinging her eyes, or maybe tears, but she could see again with pitiless clarity.

The hybrids in the breakers were staring at the speedboat as it raced away. There were even more of them at the foot of the cliffs. They were carrying a motionless body that no longer put up any defense, no longer called to her, was being carried away like something with no will of its own, no strength left. No life.

INCONSOLABLE

FOR THE FIRST TIME in days, he wasn't near her. She couldn't see him, couldn't hear him, couldn't touch him whenever she wanted.

The others were with her, Iole and the two women, but they might have been vague shapes behind a wall of opaque glass. Their voices hardly came through to her, existing outside her narrow world of fear and rage and grief.

Everything around her was in black and white; nothing seemed to have color anymore, not the sky or the sea. Wrapped in a blanket, she huddled on a seat in the stern of the speedboat, her hair tangled by the wind, her skin pale as death, her breath rattling in her throat. She didn't speak, and if the others said anything she didn't listen.

Sarcasmo nudged her with his doggy nose a couple of times. She patted him mechanically, and wished it was panther fur under her fingers. But he wasn't giving up; he stood on his hind legs, put his forepaws on her shoulders, and licked her face. She hardly noticed.

"We've lost them," Rosa heard Iole saying, her voice muffled and far away. They must have been followed. It was a slight relief to know that there was no one coming after them now, because it also protected him. It was so absurd—their separation meant that he was safe. If the hybrids had captured both of them, they would probably be on their way to the Hungry Man by now.

But the memory of his last glances at her, his voice shouting, was like a noose constricting her throat, slowly throttling her a little more with every mile between them.

Cristina was now steering the boat toward the north coast of Sicily, but the movement required to look forward would cost Rosa too much strength, and didn't seem worth the trouble. They would arrive some time or other. Something or other would happen. She didn't care about that.

Then, however, the sound of the motor changed, the airflow was weaker. She heard curses and firm footsteps. Suddenly, someone was standing in front of her. And the palm of a hand slapped her face so hard that her head tilted to one side.

She opened her mouth and hissed like a reptile.

Cristina di Santis glared furiously at her. "Pull yourself together, for heaven's sake!"

Without exerting herself at all, Rosa felt her fangs growing.

"And don't you dare turn into a snake!"

Another hiss, although she had merely meant to tell Cristina what she could do with her good advice. She tried again, and once more nothing but the snake's hiss came out. She gave up, pulled the blanket closer around her, and laid her face on her knees.

"What do I have to do?" Cristina shouted at her. "Slap your face again? We only just got away with our lives. And we need you. The Alcantaras have houses everywhere, and many of them are empty. Try to think about that, will you? Somewhere we can hide will surely occur to you."

Signora Falchi appeared beside the young attorney and laid a hand on her arm. "Leave her in peace."

"No! They're not going to hurt a hair of Alessandro's head anyway. And wallowing in self-pity won't help him or us. I lost almost my whole family in the past, shot or burnt alive. And I never once sat like that, blaming the bloody world for it."

Rosa raised her head. "No, you screwed an old man in a wheelchair instead. But it wasn't the *world* that made you do that."

Cristina turned to stone, one hand half raised as if she really was about to slap Rosa a second time.

A nasty, malicious pleasure in this game stirred in Rosa. Her teeth returned to human shape, her tongue was a human tongue again. This took her mind off things. It did her good. "You flattered Trevini, and then you enjoyed breaking his neck. No, worse, you watched while other people did it for you. First me, then the Hungry Man." She stared Cristina in the eye. "I may have lost something just now. Call it courage or self-control or my wonderful cheerfulness. But you? You lost all decency, every trace of honor. You left your honesty behind at the door of Trevini's goddamn hotel. It was *only* about you, your loss, your bloody feelings. And you stand there and read me a lecture about self-pity and egotism?" She smiled up at her from below. "Go fuck yourself, Cristina."

For a moment the attorney didn't seem to know what to do. Her expression was fixed and empty. She just stood there, withstanding Rosa's venomous looks, not saying a word.

"Have you two quite finished?" asked Iole.

Still not a word. They both kept silent.

Iole shook her head. "Oh, you crazy, stupid, bloody silly cows."

Raffaela Falchi nodded, as if Iole had expressed her own ideas exactly.

Rosa sensed her own heartbeat, like an echo of the slap that had brought her out of her lethargy. Now she was looking through Cristina, but in truth it wasn't about Cristina at all.

Finally Cristina turned around and walked away. The next moment, the sound of the motor was louder again, the airflow increased, and they were racing south.

"Shit," whispered Rosa.

Iole nodded.

Signora Falchi looked out to sea.

"She saved us," said Iole. "Neither of us could have steered this thing."

Looking at it objectively, the situation was better than a few hours ago when they had *all* been prisoners, not just one of them. Only that hadn't hurt her so damn badly.

She stood up, pulled the blanket around her, and climbed up to the cockpit.

She wasn't going to apologize to Cristina.

She was going to thank her.

IN THE END IT wasn't Rosa but the tutor who helped find them somewhere to go. The Alcantara clan had real estate all over Sicily, but Rosa knew what only a few of their properties were like. Did she own any buildings on the north coast where they could take refuge? She hadn't the faintest idea.

"This place is a former church," Raffaela Falchi had said, but she didn't seem entirely comfortable with the idea. In fact she came out with the details only when land was in sight, and they had to make a decision. "It's in a tiny village right by the sea. Almost no one lives there these days, now that everyone uses the expressway and hardly anyone still drives along the coastal road. The village is just about deserted, so the church was on the market cheap."

"And who lives there?" asked Iole.

"My ex-boyfriend."

Iole stared at the logo surrounded by flames on Raffaela's T-shirt. "The musician?"

Her tutor nodded.

Cristina, standing on the cockpit steps, looked down at them. "I wouldn't trust my life to *my* ex-boyfriend. Why would we trust yours?"

"Lorenzo won't give us away!"

Cristina grinned. "Do I detect lingering tender feelings?"

Rosa was standing by the rail, still wrapped in the blanket because there had been no clothes on board for her to wear. She had stared out to sea while the others were discussing where to go, but now she turned around. "I have to get to Campofelice di Fitalia as fast as I can."

Iole bowed her head. "And what about Alessandro?"

"When they took him, he called something to me. About a hospital. And that I'd find him there. Or he'd find me."

"Romantics, the whole lot of you," groaned Cristina.

This time Rosa stayed calm. "If he can get away from them somehow, that's where he'll go."

"What makes you think he *might* be able to get away from them?"

Signora Falchi got her answer in first. "Hope," she said, in a tone of deep conviction. It was about the only time she'd ever taken Rosa's side.

Iole stared at her, then at Rosa, and finally she smiled.

Cristina's mouth twisted. "Well, first you need clothes. Unless you're planning to hitch a ride to get there. You'll have better chances of that the way you are."

"Maybe Lorenzo will lend us his car," said the tutor.

"And will he hand his last savings over to you as well?"

"He's a good person," she said indignantly. "And a Christian."

Cristina rolled her eyes heavenward.

"Wow," whispered Rosa.

"I thought he played rock music," said Iole.

"Christian rock music. To biblical texts. Well, he used to, anyway."

Rosa saw Iole's smile. The girl had probably guessed all along that her tutor couldn't have a really cool boyfriend.

"Is there a map in this boat?" asked Signora Falchi with sudden vigor.

Resigned, Cristina nodded.

"Then I'll show you where it is, and we can pull up close to shore. I'll fix everything else."

"With your inimitable charm?"

The tutor gave her an embarrassed smile.

"And in that getup?"

"That's his band." She indicated the flame-ringed logo over her breast, and then added, more quietly, "Well, former band."

For the first time, Rosa went to the trouble of deciphering the ornate lettering. *Sinners & Winners.*

"*So* eighties," said Cristina.

SINNERS

THE WIND BLEW DUST and dried *macchia* debris over the empty main road. The dozen or so houses on each side of it were abandoned, doors and windows boarded up from outside. Someone had sprayed most of the boards with graffiti. At some point, one of the buildings had caught fire. The roof truss was exposed; the charred remains of rafters stuck out above the walls like black fangs.

At the end of the road, not far from the precipitous coastline, stood a small church, a plain, sand-colored structure with a squat little belfry on the roof above the porch. The tutor told them that in the 1970s a hippie commune had lived here—you couldn't miss the floral ornamentation painted on the porch—before its members fled from their midlife crises and menopause. The last couple to leave, however, had been able to show a contract of sale, and Lorenzo had acquired the structure from them.

"You mean they desecrated it, right?" said Cristina tartly. "I mean, hippies! Orgies in front of the baptismal font. Junkies taking trips in the sacristy. Hash cookies instead of wafers for the Host."

Raffaela Falchi wrinkled her nose as she led them away from the path they had been following up from a small, stony beach and along the cliffs. Wrapped in her blanket, Rosa felt like one of the apostles on pilgrimage herself.

An ancient VW minibus stood beside the church. Pale blue, but no floral motifs by way of decoration. It wouldn't take her a minute to break into the old thing.

As they got closer, she saw bars over the church windows. Its double doors also looked massive. That should have made her uneasy, but indifference still held her firmly in its grip.

"It's full of expensive studio equipment," said the tutor. "That's why there's so much security on the building."

Iole, her cheeks red, inspected the faded paintings in the porch. "I like flowers."

"Lorenzo hates them."

Sarcasmo barked at the door. The tutor gently moved him aside and pressed the button of an intercom. It was some time before a voice spoke.

"Yes?"

"It's me. Raffaela."

Silence.

"Well, this is a good start," commented Cristina.

Still no answer.

"Lorenzo?"

"What do you want?"

Cristina jerked her thumb upward. Iole giggled. Rosa watched the gulls flying over the sea.

"I've brought visitors with me," said the tutor.

Iole whispered, "Want to bet he hates visitors?"

"Who are they?"

"Friends of mine." Signora Falchi cleared her throat. "Fans."

Sarcasmo lifted a leg and pissed on the wall.

"I need to pee, too," said Iole.

"I don't like visitors. You know that."

Raffaela Falchi furrowed her brow. "And how about all that famous love for your fellow man?"

Locks snapped on the other side of the door, and then it swung open. A man with dreadlocks down to his elbows stood outlined in the light, in jeans, old sneakers, and a dark red shirt with its sleeves rolled up. The smell of marijuana wafted out.

"Incense," said Iole, pleased.

Sarcasmo wagged his tail wildly, pushed past the man, and set out on a tour of inspection inside the house.

"Hey," grumbled Lorenzo, but Rosa could tell immediately that he liked dogs a lot better than his fellow men.

The tutor put her hands behind his neck and kissed him on both cheeks. Then, rather hesitantly and briefly, on the mouth. He looked surprised, but didn't object.

Lorenzo was more attractive than Rosa had expected. He tossed his dreadlocks back over his shoulder with a movement of his head, and stepped aside. "Are you hungry? Thirsty? There's beer."

Raffaela cast the others a proud glance. *Mine*, her smile signaled.

Cristina, one of the most beautiful women Rosa knew, seemed to be enjoying provoking the tutor. With a swing of her hips that might have shaken even the church walls to their foundations, she walked past Lorenzo, gave him a cool smile, and said, "I'd just *love* a beer. Thanks."

Rosa nodded to him without a word, and followed Cristina inside. His eyes rested on her only for a moment, as if naked women wrapped in blankets turned up at his door every day. He scrutinized Iole with more curiosity, then turned back to his ex-girlfriend.

"Fans?" he asked doubtfully.

"They love music."

Cristina looked around. "Especially Christian music."

"Does your group throw Bibles off the stage at the audience?" asked Iole. "I saw that once, on TV."

He shook his head. "A long time ago. And there's no group anymore. I compose alone and sell my albums online."

They were in the main nave of the former church. If it hadn't been for the columns and the altar at one end, you might have thought the tall room was an untidy but very chic loft. There was a sleeping area with a crumpled futon in one corner; in another a couple of armchairs and a large bean-bag, which Iole instantly claimed for herself. The heart of the room, however, was a fortress of synthesizers, monitors, and mixing desks, with endless rows of regulators and a great many tangled cables.

At last Rosa saw the fresco on the right-hand wall, partly hidden by the massive stone columns. Several spotlights were turned on it.

"May I look?" she asked.

With a wave of his hand, he invited her to examine the huge wall-painting more closely.

It was the kind of thing she had seen in countless churches: the temptation of Eve in paradise, depicted in several scenes in front of the same background, a naively painted, candy-colored Garden of Eden. But Rosa's eyes were drawn not to the flourishing vegetation, or the figure of Eve with her nakedness chastely concealed. She was staring at the snake, a glittering golden monster twice as large as the woman holding the apple.

Lorenzo pointed to a refrigerator. "Help yourselves." Then he went up to Rosa, standing under the arcade of the aisle. Her interest in the fresco seemed to impress him more than Cristina's ass.

"That's why I compose music," he said.

"That's why?"

"To keep the enemy within bounds."

She nodded understandingly. "The serpent."

"Satan."

For a moment there was silence, until his ex-girlfriend appeared beside them and pressed a bundle of clothing into Rosa's arms, with a pair of pale canvas shoes. "These were in the wardrobe. Maybe something will fit."

"All yours, Signora Falchi?" Rosa looked at her doubtfully, because she and the tutor were nowhere near the same size.

"Only some of it," said Lorenzo.

The tutor ignored him, and told Rosa, "Call me Raffaela. It's about time we used first names. I don't even know if I'm still employed by the Alcantaras or not."

"I'm Rosa." She took the clothes. "I'm afraid my access to the bank accounts is blocked right now. So as for your salary—"

"Forget it."

Rosa tried to smile. "Thanks, anyway. Thanks for not leaving Iole in the lurch."

"She deserves to have us look after her."

They both glanced at the girl, who had made herself comfortable on the beanbag and was petting Sarcasmo. Rosa hadn't told her about Fundling yet, and decided to bring her up to date as soon as possible. Iole had a right to know the truth. Fundling had saved both their lives at the Gibellina monument, and she had spent as much time at his bedside as Rosa.

"Do you believe in God?" asked Lorenzo abruptly.

"I've never had any reason to."

He looked her up and down. "Something bad has happened to you."

"I lost my clothes. So?"

"Something else, too. Before that."

Raffaela cleared her throat. "Lorenzo sometimes gets inspirations. It comes from the stuff he smokes."

He took no notice of her. "We turn to God when we're in a bad way. Sometimes he will help us."

She cast a surreptitious glance at the snake on the wall. "Not me."

"Maybe you haven't prayed to him about it hard enough. Or not with your whole heart."

"Would it help if I bought your CDs?"

"Help you to find God?"

"Help me to get you to drop the subject." She smiled. "You mean well, I know. But it's not his help I need. Only yours."

Cristina opened a can of beer. Foam spilled out and splashed to the floor. She swore.

Rosa pointed to a side door. "Bathroom?"

Lorenzo nodded.

A little later she came back. The shoes fit, but the white T-shirt was loose around her narrow shoulders. The jeans were also too large, but they would do. She had rolled up the legs at the hem a couple of times, and threaded a belt that she had found in the bathroom through the loops at the waist. The big metal buckle was shaped like a fish.

Lorenzo and Raffaela were standing by the kitchen counter in a side aisle of the church, quarreling.

"Rosa." Iole waved to her across the room.

Rosa went past Lorenzo's studio equipment. Sarcasmo saw her, and wagged his tail.

"I think he's not missing Fundling quite so much now," said the girl.

"Mmm-hmm."

"I'm so glad we managed to bring him with us. Away from the island, I mean. He doesn't like to be alone in the villa."

"You know all about that."

"Exactly."

"I have to talk to you," said Rosa.

Iole lowered her voice and gave her a conspiratorial look. "You want to get away from here. Without us."

"That's not what I meant." Iole was always a puzzle to her, surprising her again and again. "It's about Fundling. He . . . he isn't dead. I think."

The corners of Iole's mouth moved, but no smile came. "Like your father?"

"Alessandro and I"—even mentioning his name hurt—"we found out a few things. About Fundling. And the judge. Probably the accident and Fundling's death was only a trick so that he could disappear."

"But why would he have to do that?"

"Fear of the clans." She herself didn't believe what she was saying. Of course Fundling had had good reason to get himself to safety, away from the revenge of Cosa Nostra. But that couldn't be the whole story. What had he been doing in that hotel? What exactly was he looking for?

Deafening electronic feedback boomed from the big loudspeakers in the middle of the church. "Sorry," called Cristina, who had sat down with several cans of beer at one of the mixing desks, and was playing around with the knobs.

Lorenzo, muttering in annoyance, hurried up to keep her away from his expensive equipment.

"Does she have to get drunk now of all times?" murmured Rosa.

Iole smiled. "She's seen a lot of pretty sick stuff these last few hours."

Rosa's eyes went back to the huge serpent in the fresco. "Human beings turning into animals?"

Iole leaned forward on the beanbag and hugged Rosa. "*I'd*

like to be like you. But I'd rather be like Sarcasmo even more. All soft and fluffy."

Rosa hugged her back. Iole had many remarkable talents, and one of the greatest was her ability simply to speak the truth at the most complicated moments, thereby reducing the world to manageable dimensions.

The girl let go of her and looked critically at Rosa's clothes. "You can't go out like that." She took her own black T-shirt off over her head. "Here. That white thing doesn't suit you."

Rosa had to smile. Then she exchanged her top for Iole's, which fit her perfectly.

With the baggy white shirt flapping around her, Iole looked like the cartoon character Casper the Friendly Ghost. "When are you going to take off?"

"As soon as I can," said Rosa.

"You should have something to eat first."

"Yes, Mom."

"I bet this guy has a gun somewhere. Did you see how heavily secured this whole place is? He's afraid of people breaking in. Bet you anything he has a shooting-iron somewhere."

"Don't try talking like a Mafioso."

"You want to meet Alessandro. And if he doesn't turn up you'll try to find him. I know you. If you do that, you'll need all the help you can get."

"I'm not taking you with me, no matter what."

"I know." Iole slid off the beanbag and wandered over to the sleeping corner. "Keep his attention away from me," she whispered to Rosa.

It was too late to stop her quietly. But Lorenzo still had his hands full keeping Cristina away from his synthesizers. When she pressed another button, otherworldly New Age music boomed out of the loudspeakers.

Rosa quickly went past them, watching Iole out of the corner of her eye while the girl approached the bed, as if for no real reason.

"Sounds great," she told Lorenzo. "Is that one of yours?"

He nodded grouchily and snatched up Cristina's beer can before she could spill the contents over the sensitive regulators.

"Oops," said Cristina.

"I thought you composed rock music. And I thought you were a singer." Rosa stationed herself in front of him so that he would have to look away from Iole and the sleeping corner to speak to her.

"Can you help Raffaela make coffee?" he asked Cristina, annoyed.

"But I want beer."

"There's more in the refrigerator." Obviously he didn't mind anything as long as she stayed away from his technical equipment. Gulping the beer down, he drained her can.

"Good idea." Cristina stood up.

In the background, Iole was feeling around under Lorenzo's pillows, obviously not finding anything. Next she turned her attention to a wooden crate that he used as a bedside table.

While Cristina wandered over to the coffee machine, the refrigerator, and Raffaela, Lorenzo dropped into the swivel chair at the mixing desk so that no one else could sit there.

Iole had cleared all sorts of things off the crate and opened it carefully.

"I wanted to apologize," said Rosa, claiming Lorenzo's attention for herself. "For what I said just now. You're being so kind to us, I mean, helping us although we're total strangers. And I couldn't think of anything better to do than insult your beliefs." She knew she was behaving badly—and she enjoyed it. "God may not mean much to me," she blathered on, "but all the same, I ought to show more respect for what you think. It's nice when someone thinks something is so important that he'll give his whole life to it."

Iole glanced over to them, her brow furrowed. There was no gun in the crate. Rosa dared not signal to her to move away from there. Instead, she chattered on. "And honestly, your music is great. I think it's so . . . soothing."

He raised his left eyebrow. "That's what the people at iTunes said, too."

"I'm sure it's good music to pray to." Oh, for goodness' sake! This was going to arouse his suspicions.

"My music *is* the way I pray," he said with deep conviction. "I talk to God through it."

On the other side of the church, Iole raised an arm in triumph. She was holding a black automatic that she had found in a basket of dirty laundry. A pair of crumpled boxers hung over the barrel.

"And there are CDs of it?" asked Rosa.

"Twenty-four."

"Wow. You must be so famous. We just drop in here, like groupies, and you stay so . . . so amazingly cool."

The last time she had made an idiot of herself with this kind of trick, she had ended up being hunted through Central Park by a pack of Panthera and was nearly torn to pieces. Other people learned from their mistakes.

A touch of doubt flitted over Lorenzo's face.

"Hey," she said quickly. "I have an idea."

"You do?"

"Why don't you play us something?" When she saw Raffaela and Cristina busy with a large pan of spaghetti, she added, "After we've eaten. How about it?"

Iole had concealed the pistol under her ghost costume, and was hastily tidying up the chaos she had created.

Lorenzo leaned back in his chair. "I'll have to smoke something first."

"Of course."

Before she could do anything to stop him, he gave the chair a push and swiveled around in a circle.

She held her breath. Bit her lower lip. Waited for the inevitable moment when he caught sight of Iole.

But when the chair had completed its circle, and he was facing her again, his eyes were closed and his head thrown far back. "I have to say," he told her, "you really do inspire me."

"I do?"

"When you were looking at the fresco just now, there was kind of a force field between you and the picture. Like it was something that speaks only to you."

Iole stole back to her beanbag and the panting Sarcasmo. With her thumb and forefinger, she gave Rosa an okay sign.

"I really feel like I could play a little piece when we've eaten." Lorenzo opened his eyes again, but Rosa was no longer standing in front of him. He tipped the chair forward and looked around for her, irritated.

She waved to him, halfway to Raffaela and Cristina. "I'd better see if I can help."

Lorenzo nodded, stunned.

When she reached the two women, the tutor said, with a dark look at Cristina, "She's drunk."

Rosa was prepared to deal with a hundred tipsy female attorneys, as long as she never had to talk about prayers and inspiration again.

"Only a teeny little bit," babbled Cristina, groping around for the refrigerator door.

THE TEMPTATION

SHE WAITED UNTIL AFTER they had eaten—mountains of spaghetti with tomato sauce and garlic—before deciding it was time to put her plan into action.

While Lorenzo had another quarrel with Raffaela, she took a thick Windbreaker from a pile of clothes near the porch and squeezed out of the barely open door. The jacket was heavier on the right side than the left. A little while before, Iole had inconspicuously slipped the pistol into its pocket.

The sun was low on the horizon; it would soon set. The roar of the sea at the foot of the cliffs, and the howling of the brisk wind, drowned out all other sounds. The expressway ran only a few miles south of the village. When it was built, it had struck the little place a deadly blow, but the traffic noise went in the opposite direction.

The abandoned village street lay ahead of Rosa. She took a deep breath and then swiftly skirted the front of the church. Pebbles crunched under her feet. She almost expected the bell on the roof to ring, sounding the alarm and terrifying her. It had to be rung by hand; inside the church, Rosa had seen the thick bell rope dangling from an opening in the ceiling.

She turned the corner and stopped dead.

The VW minibus had disappeared.

Its tires had left deep ruts in the grass. They led to the sacristy, which had a garage with an old-fashioned double door beside it. A chain lay around the handles of the two sides of the door, secured with a padlock. Lorenzo must have driven the vehicle in there while she was changing in the bathroom.

Shivering, she pulled the jacket closer around her body and approached the door. The chain was wound several times around the handles, the padlock firmly in place. From inside, she would be able to smash through the decaying wood with the VW, but it was impossible with her bare hands. She went along the side of the garage and to the back. There was no window, no gap that she could have wriggled through in her snake form. There had to be a door between the garage and the sacristy. That meant she would have to go back into the church.

Once more, she went to the door and rattled it. Not a chance. The chains were much too solid.

"I knew it the minute you turned up," said Lorenzo, behind her.

She spun around. There he stood without the others, both hands in the pockets of his jeans. A gust of wind blew into his long dreadlocks, moving them like the plastic strips of the curtains that Sicilians liked so much.

"You were naked under that blanket," he went on, "but you didn't seem the least bit disturbed. Not even ashamed. You just looked determined, as if you weren't going to let anything or anyone stop you."

"If you're so sure of that, then please open this door." Her hand went to the gun in her jacket pocket, but she didn't take it out yet.

He shook his head. "This is my car."

"You'll get it back."

"What are you planning to do?"

"None of your business."

"You were about to steal my car. Now you expect me to lend it to you. And you're not even saying where you want to drive it?"

"It's better if you don't know."

She tensed slightly as he came closer, but his casual stroll didn't seem threatening.

He stopped three paces away from her. "What happened, Rosa Alcantara?"

He knew who she was.

"I watch the news," he said. "Your photo is everywhere. Yours and your boyfriend's. Is he hiding out here somewhere? Did you think it would be easier for you to take me for a ride without him?"

"He isn't here. I need your car to go and meet him." And she hoped she was right. Alessandro *must* be there. Although she could guess how poor his chances of escaping from the *Stabat Mater* were.

She drew the gun and aimed it at him.

He didn't seem in the least surprised. "Did the girl look to see if it was loaded?" He smiled, but it was a sad smile. "Because *you* didn't, as I noticed."

"Why don't we find out?"

"Are you really going to shoot me? For a VW minibus forty years old that hasn't gone farther than the nearest supermarket for ages? How long do you think it would last?"

She was feeling even colder, in spite of the jacket. The sun touched the land to the west. The falling twilight was fiery red. The rough grass, the church wall, Lorenzo's eyes—they all looked suffused with blood.

"Do you have the key on you?" she asked.

"Maybe."

"Raffaela still likes you a lot. She'd be angry with me for shooting you in the leg."

"If you do shoot. And if there's a bullet in it."

She stepped to one side and waved him over to the door. "Open the padlock."

He stood there with that idiotic New Age expression, as if he were about to press some esoteric pamphlet on her.

"Lorenzo," she said softly. "Please."

"I've called the police."

"You're lying."

"Not a bit."

"Why, for heaven's sake?"

"I was waiting to see what you'd do. I wouldn't have called them if you hadn't gone off with the gun. We don't even know each other, I have nothing against you. But if you really have murdered someone, I don't want you going around the island with my pistol."

"It's got nothing at all to do with you."

"The gun's registered in my name. Perfectly legal. But

suppose you shoot someone down with it, who do you think will get their ass kicked?"

How long ago had he called? And how long would it take the police cars to get here? Were they coming from Palermo? Cefalù? One of the smaller towns? Or were they bringing the whole anti-Mafia squad into the hunt for her?

Festa wouldn't want to miss putting the handcuffs on her himself. Nor would Stefania Moranelli. Rosa should have stapled her eyelids together when she had the chance.

"For the last time." The cold filled her whole upper body now; the skin on the backs of her hands was tingling. "Open that door."

He looked back over his shoulder at the corner of the church. None of the others appeared there. Iole at least must have realized that he had followed Rosa.

"You locked them in," she said.

"They're not stupid. Sooner or later they'll find the only barred window that can be opened from inside. But I didn't think this would take that long. If you're as innocent as some say on the internet, then turn yourself in to the police."

"We didn't kill the judge. She was almost . . ."—she hesitated—"a friend." Kind of. A little like a friend.

"A lot of people say you're Mafia."

"Unlock this damn garage."

"Jesus will save you, too."

That was the last straw. She pulled the trigger. The shot whistled over the plateau.

The hole in the ground beside his foot was large enough to fit a football.

A dangerous hiss left Rosa's lips. "That's enough." Her anger drowned out even her relief at finding that Iole had indeed thought to check for ammunition. What a sweetheart.

Lorenzo hadn't moved from the spot, but even in the poor light she saw how pale he had turned. Any red on his face he owed to the setting sun.

"This is crap," he said quietly.

She pointed to the padlock. "Go on."

His eyes slowly widened.

"The key."

His lips opened slightly, as if he were about to speak, but not a sound came out.

She moistened the corners of her mouth with her tongue, and could feel that it had forked. Her scalp itched, a sign that it was changing. Her eyes had probably already become slits.

Couldn't he just have been a guitar-playing druggie? Without all that stuff about Satan and Jesus and salvation?

"What are you?" he asked hoarsely.

"The reason why you want to take off that chain."

His mouth formed two syllables, but once again his voice failed him.

Then she put the pistol to the padlock and turned her face aside. It worked in films, but in real life it would probably tear her arm off. She could only hope that she'd have a new one after her next metamorphosis.

She fired.

Something struck her. At first she thought it was the ricochet. Then it dawned on her that Lorenzo had hit her on the head as hard as he could.

She fell to her knees and saw that the lock had broken to pieces. The chain looked like a silver snake.

He hit her again.

This time she avoided him, sank with her shoulder against the garage door, turned around, and aimed.

"Try that again," she challenged him in a brittle voice. She couldn't shift shape, not now. All this was costing her way too much time.

He stared, astonished, into the barrel of the pistol. His expression had nothing to do with the gun, only with the scaly strands of skin surrounding her face instead of hair. The double fork of her tongue. Her snake's eyes.

"I promise you," she whispered, "I'll blow your face off." Suitably satanic, she thought—and effective. He took a step back, and seemed to be wondering whether to run for it. But he probably wouldn't put it past her to shoot him in the back.

With difficulty, she hauled herself up by the door. There was a rustling around her ears as the strands of snake skin turned back into blond hair.

"Another two steps back," she said with a slight lisp, but her voice was already more human. A Hunding would have growled; one of the Panthera would have snarled. She lisped. Typical.

With her free hand, she pulled the chain away from the door handles. It fell to the ground with a clink.

Lorenzo didn't say a word. The sight of her had deprived a rock musician of speech. Someone ought to have told her *that* when she was fourteen.

She was just about to pull one side of the door open when she saw the headlights at the end of the village street. Two cars. No, three. They were driving with their brights. The light passed over the deserted ruins of houses by the roadside.

The vehicles raced up at high speed. None of them had a blue light on the roof. Three black Mercedes. Not patrol cars.

"Is that some kind of special squad?" asked Lorenzo.

She recognized the registration numbers. The same abbreviation three times. "No."

He looked from the oncoming cars back at her. She was entirely human again now.

"Carnevares," she said.

MASSACRE

THE CHURCH DOOR CRASHED shut behind them.

Even before Lorenzo could lock it, Iole went for him with a guitar. He tried to avoid the blow, but she hit him on the shoulder and pushed him to the floor.

"You asshole!" she said angrily, as she stood menacingly over him with the instrument.

He put out a hand to ward her off. "*She* was going to steal *my* car. Why does everyone seem to think there's nothing wrong with that?"

Rosa turned the key in the lock and threw it to Cristina, who caught it with surprising expertise. "Leave him alone," she told Iole. "He's right."

"He locked us in."

"We have other problems right now." Quickly she told them about the arrival of the Carnevares. She had hardly finished before several car doors slammed outside.

Lorenzo stood up without taking his eyes off Iole. She was still holding the guitar aloft, as if just waiting for a reason to bring it down on him again.

He turned to Raffaela, pointing at Rosa. "What kind of a creature is she? What have you brought into my house?"

Iole got her word in before her tutor. "Rosa is not a

creature!" With that, the guitar started coming down again, but this time Rosa caught it in midair. Swiftly and skillfully. Snake reflexes.

"Let it rest now," she told Iole. "The Carnevares will kill us all if they get in here."

Cristina stayed cooler than anyone. "How many ways are there into this church?"

"The windows are all barred." Lorenzo's voice was still unsteady. He had just met the devil in person. "There are only two doors. The one on the porch, and one from the sacristy into the garage, but it has an iron bolt over it. No one will get in there in a hurry."

Rosa looked up at the small windows, each three yards above the floor. They were more like loopholes than church windows. No one could possibly get in through them.

The sacristy windows were another matter. It would take a little while to remove the gratings over them, but they were on the first floor and more easily accessible.

"They don't have much time left." She urged the others away from the porch. "They could have only found out this quickly that I was here from the police. Probably from the same informant in the anti-Mafia unit who has the judge on his conscience. So they're certainly not the only people on the way here. The police ought to turn up soon, too."

Raffaela shot Lorenzo a furious glance. "You're such an idiot!"

He still didn't look as if he knew whether he was on the right side. The black cars outside the church had obviously not inspired confidence in him.

Rosa took the pistol out of her jacket pocket again. "Do you have any more of these?"

He shook his head.

"Lorenzo," said Raffaela forcefully, "if you do—"

"No, damn it!" he shouted. "I don't have any other guns."

Iole was holding the guitar in both hands like a battle-ax. Rosa drew her closer. "You stay with me. No matter what happens."

Cristina frowned. "Where are they? They ought to have been here long ago."

As if they had needed only that cue, there was a vigorous knocking at the door. Like someone hammering on it with the butt of a pistol.

"We want Rosa Alcantara," called a muffled male voice through the wood. "We're not interested in the rest of you. If you hand her over, no one will be hurt."

"Sounds okay to me," said Lorenzo.

Raffaela hit him. Rosa was starting to see what had gone wrong between the two of them.

He cursed, then stepped out of range of her and moved his lips soundlessly.

"Piss off!" called Iole to the Carnevares outside.

"Nice of you," said Rosa quietly, "but that guitar won't do you any good if they get in here."

Thoughtfully, Cristina looked from the porch to Rosa. "Suppose it wasn't an informant? You said this man Thanassis has access to satellite pictures. Couldn't he have seen where we came ashore? It would be simpler for him to set the clans on you than send his own people here."

That sounded logical—and probably meant that the hybrids would deliver Alessandro to the Hungry Man even without her, as long as they were sure that the clans would capture Rosa themselves. "That would suggest," she said, thinking out loud, "that the guys out there have no idea the police are also on their way here."

Cristina nodded.

Rosa looked all around the church, in search of a way out. The three cars were probably occupied by a team of twelve. Some of them would certainly be prowling around the building in the shape of big cats.

"Can we barricade ourselves in here until the police arrive?" asked Raffaela.

Iole shook her head. "They'd arrest Rosa, and she'd never get to—" She interrupted herself, glancing suspiciously at the musician. "She'd never get to Alessandro."

Lorenzo leaned against a loudspeaker as tall as he was. "But the rest of us would probably survive."

"And who says the guys out there won't simply shoot the cops down?" Once again, Cristina was calm personified.

The knocking on the door came again. "Two minutes to go," called the man outside. "After that we're coming in."

Rosa's eye fell on the bell rope beside the porch. "Does that still work?"

Lorenzo nodded.

She went over to the rope, picked it up in both hands, and

tugged at it with all her might. High above her in the little belfry on the front gable of the church roof, the bell tolled. First quietly and irregularly, then with a stronger, louder sound.

"What's the point of that?" inquired Lorenzo.

"I suppose there's no way up there from inside?" she asked. The belfry was too small to have a flight of steps going up to it, and served only as housing for the big bronze bell.

"If anyone has to get at the thing, it can only be done from outside with a fireman's ladder," he said.

She let go of the rope. "We have to find out what they're doing."

A siren sounded far away, probably at the other end of the village.

"Here comes the damn cavalry," said Lorenzo happily.

A little later, blue lights flashed behind the clouded window panes. Then shots rang out.

"Here we go," whispered Rosa.

She shifted into snake shape within seconds, slipped out of her clothes, and grasped the bell rope in her teeth as hard as she could. She had never tried anything like this before, but it was their only chance of getting some idea of the situation outside the church.

With crazy speed, she coiled her reptilian body around the rope and climbed up. It was much easier than she had expected. Very soon she reached the vaulted roof of the church, six or seven yards above ground level. Here the rope disappeared into a rectangular shaft, just large enough for her to get through. She wound her way onward and upward, through cobwebs and clouds of dust, and soon reached the bell. It hung in a small chamber with open rounded arches facing all four points of the compass. The floor was covered with bird droppings and feathers. When she shifted back into human form, she could feel both under the soles of her bare feet.

In the red glow of sunset, she straightened up just enough to be able to look down over a stone parapet into the courtyard of the church. Twelve or maybe fifteen yards below her, shadowy figures were locked in a fierce exchange of gunfire.

The new arrivals had not driven up in patrol cars but in two BMWs, one black and one silver. Rosa had been followed by them both more than once in the last few months. They were from the vehicle fleet of Quattrini's anti-Mafia unit. The dark BMW was usually driven by Antonio Festa.

The dead judge's assistant, his colleague Stefania, and three other officers of the Special Commission had sought shelter behind the cars and were firing their automatics at the Carnevare clan's hit men. The latter crouched behind three Mercedes, which they had drawn up in a semicircle outside the church.

But Rosa also saw the Panthera to one side of the skirmish, where the bushes and rocks cast deep shadows. From above, she made out two lions prowling toward the police officers in a wide arc from the west while a panther, a leopard, and a gigantic creature that might be a Bengal tiger were approaching the four men and one woman from the east.

She shouted a warning to Festa and Stefania, but her voice was drowned out by the staccato exchange of gunfire. All the cars had already been affected, the windows shot out, under-carriage perforated. One of the Carnevares was hit, and the next moment so was a police officer.

She shifted shape, made her way over the parapet, let herself drop to the slope of the church roof, and glided down to the gutter along the west wall. She followed it without entrusting her full weight to the crumbling metal gutter, to the point where the sacristy met the wall.

It was three yards down to the roof of the garage annex, but her supple serpentine body sprang back so softly that she hardly felt the impact. She slid down a drainpipe to the coarse stones outside the church.

The shots were deafening, and smoke drifted over the plateau. Rosa stayed close to the wall, and out of the corner of her eye saw two big cats behind the bushes looking for a way through to come up behind the police officers.

Keeping close to the ground between the stones and the grass, she was all but invisible. When she reached the cover of the building, she saw the backs of five men who had taken cover behind the Carnevare car. Two more Mafiosi had been hit, and were lying on the ground. One was still alive, pressing a bloodstained hand to his throat. The others were firing in sequence, trying to divert the attention of Festa, Stefania, and the other officers from the Panthera stealing up behind them.

None of them noticed the snake gliding past them and under one of the cars. From this vantage point, Rosa could also see the two BMWs behind a wall of smoke. Muzzle flashes flared, while the police themselves remained shadowy silhouettes.

She had broken into cars in New York to go joyriding through Brooklyn. Those had been rickety old things, as decrepit as the apartment buildings in Crown Heights. There had never been a brand-new Mercedes like this one among them. In the dim light, she searched the underside of the car for cables and pipes. Covers and trimming protected the sensitive technological devices, but there were still plenty of openings to the engine compartment through which she could push her snake's head. Tough plastic and layers of rubber offered resistance to her teeth, but she had soon bitten through several cables. The nauseating taste of oil and gasoline coated her tongue, but as long as she didn't swallow any, it wouldn't hurt her.

She was almost deaf from the sound of bullets striking the vehicles when she cautiously slid along over the ground to the next car. Here, too, she bit through electric cables and piping. She could only hope that some of the really important connections were among them.

When she moved on to the third car she was almost discovered. One of the Carnevares taking cover behind the wing noticed her; when she looked up their eyes met. His eyes were those of a cat, although his body and features were human. In alarm, he opened his mouth, straightened up slightly—and was hit by a bullet that blew his skull to pieces from the eyebrows up.

Rosa pulled her snake's body under the car. From here she

could guess at the other big cats from vague movements over the ground, heading for the place where the police were taking cover behind the swathes of powder smoke.

Rosa set about sabotaging the third vehicle as well. When she moved back into the open, the ends of cables were dangling from the engine like creepers torn loose from their supports.

Once again, one of the Mafiosi cried out and collapsed. When she looked back, she saw him lying on his side. His dead eyes, wide open, stared out from under the car as if he had seen Rosa as he drew his last breath.

There were about fifteen yards of open ground between the Carnevare cars and the two police vehicles. Heading straight across that distance was too dangerous. She had to try to approach from the side.

Her sense of time was letting her down. It felt like an eternity before she finally reached the silver BMW. The two cars were parked at an angle to each other, forming a broad V-shaped opening out on the facade of the church and the Carnevares. Stefania Moranelli, Antonio Festa, and the two other surviving police officers were crouching behind them, firing in rapid sequence.

Rosa had just coiled her whole body under one of the cars when she saw the Panthera stealing up out of the milky smoke, approaching their human prey from behind. None of the officers had yet noticed the five big cats.

She could warn them only if she shifted back to human form. The BMW was low-slung, but even in her human shape she was slender enough to fit under it. However, it was an effort to initiate the metamorphosis in such a cramped space.

"Stefania," she shouted. "Behind you!"

She could see only the policewoman's legs, but from the jerk that ran through Stefania, Rosa saw that she had heard her.

"They're coming up from behind!"

Stefania flung herself around and instantly opened fire on the big cats. Her first bullet hit a lion and killed him. The others were racing up toward the four police officers—and Rosa, who had returned to snake form. She could no longer see what was going on, she only heard screams, shots, and the roars of predators.

While the humans and the Panthera clashed only an arm's length away from her, she randomly bit through the first leads she saw.

She had really intended to put the last car out of action as well. She thought better of that when she moved on from the first BMW to under the second, and saw one of the police officers pumping bullets into the tiger. Then the policeman's feet disappeared from her field of vision, and she realized that he was retreating into the car.

The panther swept up. With one long leap, he chased into the vehicle after the man. Rosa could feel the heavy impact as the car rocked. Another shot, then a roar of torment, and the bloodthirsty snarling and snapping of the big cat. One leg dangled, twitching, in the gap between the ground and the vehicle; the man's shoe was torn away, his foot twisted.

Blood trickled from his leg.

Rosa looked back at the church, where the Carnevares in human form were still crouching behind their cars, leaving the massacre of the police officers to the big cats.

When she turned around again, she was no longer the only one to have taken refuge under a car. While she lay in snake form underneath the black BMW, Stefania, bleeding and exhausted, had crawled under the silver car beside it. One of the Panthera was about to follow, but without further ado the policewoman took aim at his skull and pulled the trigger. The big cat went limp, and his metamorphosis into human shape set in at once. The corpse was far more massive than Stefania, and was squeezed tightly between the car and the ground, which meant that he shielded her from the eyes of the other Panthera.

At least one of the officers was still alive. Rosa heard him firing, then saw him for a second—before he was buried under the Panthera.

That was the moment that she used. At high speed, she wound her way out from under the car, and in through the back door of the BMW beside the dead police officer's motionless leg. The panther had inflicted severe injuries on him before rejoining the other Panthera. Rosa had to glide through sticky blood, but all she felt was wild elation. It frightened her, but at the same time she welcomed it.

After she had her entire reptilian body on the backseat beside the dead man, she looked around. No one was following her; the Panthera hadn't noticed her yet. In animal form, they were far too busy tearing apart the body of the last police officer.

This time her change back to human form hurt. Too many metamorphoses in too short a time, leading to the sense of strain and the adrenaline surges coursing through her body. Even as she returned to human shape, her eyes fell on the dead man's face. It was Antonio Festa. She felt nothing, no pity, no anger, certainly no triumph. She had little time left to think at all. The windows of the car were soiled, but all the same, anyone looking into it from outside could see a naked blond girl who had apparently materialized out of nowhere on the backseat.

Working frantically, she set about pushing Festa's body out of the car. It was easier than she had feared to move him over the wet leather upholstery, and a little later his head hit the ground. Rosa risked one last look at the three Panthera busy with the other corpse. Stefania couldn't be seen from here. With luck, she would still be lying under the second car, which offered the best cover at the moment.

Impossible to close the car door quietly. With a jerk, Rosa slammed it shut. She didn't even have to look to be sure that the Panthera had noticed.

She hastily squeezed between the seats to reach the driver's seat in front. Festa's blood was all over her, and her fingers felt as if they had been dipped in syrup. The key was in the ignition. The police officers had come under fire from the Carnevares so abruptly on their arrival that no one had thought of taking it out.

She activated the automatic lock, and the doors locked all around her.

With a crash, the leopard landed on the hood of the car in front of her. Dark red blood dripped from his muzzle, and there was bloodlust in his eyes as he stared through the windshield at Rosa. His skull was less than a yard from her face, but the glass was still between them.

The lion appeared at the side window beside her, let out a roar, and struck the door with his paw.

Rosa instinctively flinched away, throwing herself half over the passenger seat. She opened the glove compartment, hoping to find pepper spray or a truncheon.

A sturdy flare gun lay there among chocolate bars and crumpled paper. Rosa opened it, and found a single cartridge in the barrel. As she was about to snap the gun shut again, a bullet struck the side window at the back of the BMW. It had been hit several times already, and this time the shot almost wrenched the glass out of the frame.

Rosa could have shot one of the Panthera, turning his head into a fireball, but then she would have used up all her ammunition. As the leopard's paws struck the windshield, and the lion worked on the driver's door—where was the panther?—she threw herself across the passenger seat again, opened the door just a crack, took brief aim, and pulled the trigger.

The tracer bullet raced above the ground in a low trajectory. Rosa closed the door again and looked through the window at the Carnevares' cars in front of the church entrance The men behind them were on their feet, one of them laughing contemptuously.

But she hadn't been firing at any of them. A few sparks were enough to set the grass under their vehicles on fire. She had bitten through the connections supplying the engine with fuel, and for some minutes now the tanks had been pouring out their contents on the ground. The Carnevares would have caught the scent of the gasoline long ago if they hadn't been so intoxicated by the smell of blood in the air.

The next moment, a wall of fire rose in front of the church, and a wave of flames shot out of it.

Three explosions at almost the same time. The vehicles were torn apart by the blast, their parts flung away, while the men fell back against the church, human torches. One of them stayed standing, six feet tall, sticking to the masonry of the wall, where he burned like a bonfire.

The lion was no longer at the driver's door. The leopard had been flung off the hood of the BMW, but was already struggling to his feet. Rosa turned the key in the ignition and roared the engine.

Something banged into the passenger window. Stefania was hammering with her fist on it, barely recognizable under a mask of blood and dirt.

Rosa reached over and opened the door. The policewoman slipped in, her breath rattling in her throat, and slammed the door shut. "Drive!"

The lion collided with the driver's side window again. Rosa stepped on the gas. The leopard was lying on his side in front of the hood. She rammed him, and felt the wheels drive over him.

The burning corpse was still there against the facade as

Rosa stopped the car outside the church porch. The two halves of the door had been forced in, and parts of the wood were crackling as the fire caught.

She pushed the driver's door open, shouting, "Iole! Where are you all? Come out, quick!"

A black shape shot out of the church and into the open air, leaped across her, and landed on Stefania's lap. Thinking that yet another wild beast was attacking, Stefania yelled, pushed Sarcasmo off against the dashboard, and then saw her mistake. The dog withdrew into the floor in front of her seat. He was too large for it really, but he seemed to feel safer in a confined space.

Cristina and Raffaela were the next to run out of the church. The tutor flung the back door of the car open, and slid in over the slippery leather. Cristina stood outside for a moment calling to Iole, then hauled her along with her as the girl finally appeared. Cursing, she steered Iole in between herself and Raffaela on the backseat. Iole had picked up Rosa's crumpled clothes and brought them.

"Lorenzo?" asked Rosa.

"Barricaded himself in," replied Raffaela. "All on his own in the sacristy."

Iole shouted a warning. Two big cats, lion and panther, came leaping through the flames toward the car and flung themselves against it. Cristina slammed the door.

Rosa stepped hard on the gas, and the BMW shot forward.

The Panthera followed them for some way along the village street before finally giving up. Looking in the rearview mirror, Rosa saw them standing in front of the wall of flame on their hind legs, shifting back into human shape.

The three women in the backseat were all talking at once, but Rosa wasn't listening. The air whistled through bullet holes in the windows. Stefania, beside her, stared out into the darkness without a word.

Rosa understood. Silence was salutary. Silence was exactly what they needed now.

Soon the others fell silent as well, and there was only the purring of the engine and the rushing of the wind outside to fill the car.

They drove fast in the direction of the expressway, deeper into the night.

GRAVEYARD COUNTRY

At the first rest area Rosa stopped the car to put on the clothes that Iole had brought for her. Iole handed the bundle forward. As Rosa took it, she could feel that there was something hidden in it. Lorenzo's pistol.

It wasn't difficult to conceal the gun to the left of her seat. Stefania was looking fixedly through the dirty window at the nocturnal landscape along the expressway. It was as if she were trying to block everything around her out of her mind: maybe so that she could think, maybe in a state of apathy.

Rosa was about to start the engine again when Stefania put her hand on the door handle beside her. "I'm getting out." On the floor at her feet, Sarcasmo woke up and yawned.

"What, here?" asked Rosa doubtfully. The rest area was nothing but an asphalt surface with a few garbage cans crammed full. The expressway ran along one side of it, a terraced field along the other. Their car was the only one anywhere in sight. "There isn't even an emergency phone here."

"I'm not about to set my colleagues on you." As she spoke, Stefania seemed to be looking at her reflection in the splintered wing mirror. "I told them about you two, about the metamorphoses. They wanted me to take a break, that's the way they put it. And get some psychotherapy. This operation was kind of my last chance to show I'm still responsible for my actions. And I got that chance only because Antonio spoke up for me." She abruptly turned her head, and looked directly at Rosa. Her eyes were a ghostly white in the middle of her black and red mask of blood. "What am I going to tell them this time? The truth again?"

"You'll have to think something up. There's a pile of dead bodies outside the church, and half of them are naked. Even if they dismiss Lorenzo as a deranged junkie, someone or other—"

"I was unconscious when it all began. A glancing shot, something like that. I have plenty of injuries to prove it. You dragged me into the car and threw me out here."

"Well, thanks a million," Iole commented.

Stefania let herself drop back into the seat for a moment, exhausted. "I admit it doesn't sound like an abduction. If that still makes any difference."

Rosa shook her head. "No one's going to find out what happened this evening. The clans will make sure it's all swept under the carpet before the media get wind of it. Or if not the clans, then the politicians in Rome who got the Hungry Man out of prison. I'll bet you the investigations are discontinued by midday tomorrow, at the very latest."

From the backseat, Cristina agreed with her. "People turning into animals—that doesn't sound good in a press release. They'll do all they can to keep any journalists from finding out."

Rosa touched Stefania's hand. "Look after yourself. They're

not squeamish when they think someone might tell people the wrong things. And by *they* I don't mean Cosa Nostra."

The policewoman swung both legs out of the car, but sat where she was and took a deep breath. "Well, the air's much better out here."

Inside the car, it stank like a slaughterhouse. Festa's blood had dried on the seats and their bodies some time ago. If they came to a roadblock, they'd be taken for a gang of serial killers.

What they needed was another car. And water to wash in. Clean clothes. But most of all, Rosa was wondering how, and how soon, she could shake off the others.

Stefania looked at her once again. "Whatever you're planning, Rosa, it can't end well."

"I'm doing my best."

"Sure," said the policewoman. "Of course I know you are." With those words she got out of the car, hesitated again, and closed the door without another word. She walked slowly away toward a solitary bench at the side of the rest area.

Sarcasmo jumped up on the seat she had just vacated and sniffed at a bloodstain.

"She'll give us away," said Raffaela.

"No," said Rosa. "I don't think so."

She started the engine, glanced at the lonely figure on the wide parking area, and then drove on.

Turning her head, Iole glanced out of the rear window. Rosa, too, thought she saw something in the rearview mirror, a faint flash in the dark, just as she turned the car onto the expressway.

"Did she have a gun?" whispered Iole.

In silence, Rosa stepped on the gas and didn't look back.

Three quarters of an hour later, a sign told them that they were on the outskirts of Bagheria.

"I have friends there," said Raffaela. Those were the first words she had spoken since they left Stefania behind. "I can call them. They'll help us."

"Good," said Rosa. "Then you three can get out here."

Iole shook her head. "Forget it."

Neither of the others protested. Cristina gazed out the window in silence. She had long ago accepted the fact that Rosa didn't want any of them with her as she continued her journey. When Iole looked indignantly from one to the other of them, the tutor laid a hand on her thigh.

"This is Rosa's business, not ours." It sounded honest, not like an excuse to clear out as soon as possible.

Iole shook her head vigorously. "I want to go too."

After a few hundred yards, Rosa left the expressway.

"Don't drive into the town," said Raffaela. "Bagheria will be full of police. Drop us off somewhere here. My friends can come and collect us."

Rosa took the BMW into the parking lot of a McDonald's and drove to the far side of it, where the glow of the streetlamps was lost in the darkness. Beyond a low wall lay a stretch of urban wasteland, and two hundred yards away there were ugly apartment blocks with lights in rows of windows.

Iole didn't want to get out, but Cristina and the tutor gently pushed her into the open air. It helped that Sarcasmo had taken the lead, full of enthusiasm, and was now waiting for her with his tongue hanging out, panting happily.

Rosa was left on her own in the shot-up, bloodstained car. She felt very much alone, even before Cristina closed the door behind her.

Iole tore herself away from the two women and opened the passenger door. However, she didn't jump in, as Rosa had feared she might, but leaned into the car and gave her a long, sad look.

"You will come back, won't you?"

Rosa nodded, a lump in her throat.

"Promise?"

She nodded again.

"You're lying," said Iole quietly.

She tried a faint smile. "Wish me luck."

"I wish you both luck." Iole swallowed, but no tears flowed from her glassy eyes. "See you."

When she closed the door from outside, another crack ran through the perforated glass of the window.

Rosa left the three of them and the dog behind, and did not rejoin the expressway, but let the GPS guide her along a country road going south. After the first few miles, she placed the pistol on the passenger seat beside her.

"Now turn right," the metallic voice instructed her.

Rosa was grateful for any company.

At just after eleven, she was following winding minor roads leading from the 121 up into bleak, mountainous country. In the village of Mezzojuso she left the BMW in an unlit parking lot at the foot of several palm trees whose leaves rustled with a ghostly sound in the dark. Without much difficulty, she stole an ancient silver Honda with the passenger door unlocked. In this vehicle she drove the last few miles back to Campofelice di Fitalia.

The hills rose as black outlines against a clear, starry sky. In the beam of the headlights, she saw that the area around the town was not as dismal as she had thought. There were a few vineyards, some green cultivated land, and low copses of trees. The wilderness must lie farther to the west, that area between Campofelice and Corleone that Alessandro had called the graveyard of the Mafia. Rosa had heard of it before: lonely, windswept peaks of rock, bare slopes, and hidden valleys where a few decades ago the Corleonese clan had buried hundreds of victims.

By night, Campofelice di Fitalia did not look very inviting. She doubted whether more than a thousand people lived there. Yet she passed several coffee bars still open at this hour. She couldn't go into one in her present state, but she had to find out somehow whether there had once been a hospital here. And if so, whether anyone who had worked in it still lived in Campofelice.

But it was nearly midnight, and she realized that she wouldn't find anyone by driving aimlessly along the streets. Instead, she left the town, parked the Honda in the shelter of some rocks, and followed a footpath with a few signs pointing the way to a small spring. Like every other such spring in

Sicily, it seemed that it was credited with healing powers.

She washed herself as well as she could in the narrow channel of water. She soaked the black T-shirt, wrung it out, and put it back on still wet. She wasn't going to get the stains out of the jeans, so she spared herself the trouble of trying. As she stumbled through the dark landscape back to the car, the slaughterhouse smell still followed her.

She spent the night in the Honda, the pistol jammed between the seat and the emergency brake.

She was awoken in the morning by a radiant blue sky and the tinkling of goat bells. Exhausted as she was, she would probably have slept on until evening if a herd of goats hadn't made itself comfortable around the car. She had turned off the only paved road anywhere around, and was now a little ways along a dirt path.

The bleating of the animals was loud enough to wake the dead, not to mention the dozens of little bells that were ringing. When she looked around, she saw a weather-beaten old man. He was sitting in the grass a little way from the herd, an antiquated herdsman's crook in one hand, a cigarette in the other. He stared at her without a word. Maybe he had been staring at her for ages already.

She rolled the window down. "Excuse me," she called, "are you from this area?"

"Do I look like I'm on vacation here?" His rasping voice made him seem even older.

"I'm looking for a hospital."

"What hospital?"

"It may not be a real hospital, something more like a first-aid station."

"Not here, there isn't."

The disappointment in her face must have been visible even across the distance between them.

"There's a doctor down in the village," he went on. "A girl, kind of a young thing from Palermo. Says I badly need massage. What would my wife have said to that, God rest her soul? Massage at the expense of the state. Like those high-up fellows in Rome, eh?" He gave a bleating laugh. "Young folk these days get funny ideas. No wonder the bloody TV programs are so bad."

"No wonder," she agreed, not that she could see any conclusive connection. "Well, it could be something like a clinic. A place where scientists work."

"Doing research and that?"

Her tongue felt as furred as a goat's ear. "Yes, exactly."

"There's an old weather station."

"Hmm, probably not that."

"And then of course there's the base."

"What base?"

He got up from his place in the grass and came over. "Where the Resistance hid away in the war, back in the forties. We kids swapped stuff with them for cigarettes. Full cartridges that we'd collected. Found a landmine once, blew half Salvo Pini's leg off. He never touched another cigarette, never again. Died of cancer all the same. Cancer of the ass. Didn't come from smoking, that's for sure."

"And this base—"

"After the war the army did exercises on the land there. They built the fences a good bit higher. Barbed wire, electric fences, all that stuff. That's what the commies like. Barbed wire and walls."

She instinctively thought of autopsy tables with silvery surfaces, shining operating instruments. She thought of long rows of cages, with live experimental subjects shut up inside them.

"All that's empty these days," said the goatherd. "It's been a while since the last transports went down the old road."

"How long a while?" She didn't like the smell of the goats much better than the smell of the blood on her jeans. "I mean, when did they close up shop at this base?"

"Oh, thirty, forty years back. No big deal, none of us had much to do with them. They even flew in their own goat's milk after they built a landing strip out there."

"And now?"

"Like I said. All deserted. A few buildings were blown up in the early nineties, after that crap over in Corleone got so hot it finally boiled over. Luciano Liggio, Totò Riina, Bernardo Provenzano . . . all those men of honor from Corleone, well, I guess you know about that. Felt for a long time like the police wanted to dig up the whole province, looking for bodies and folks shot in the neck and all that. If you ask me, people shouldn't disturb the peace of the dead. At least, they were in the base too, blew part of it sky-high, and then after a while things got quiet again. Not much left to be seen there now."

"Have you ever been there?"

"Not after that. The ground's poisoned, they said. On account of all the maneuvers and the stuff they tested. Sheep and goats that graze the damn grass will get sick and die, folks say. You can't sell the milk from here these days, and if any of it gets out of these parts they'll close your whole herd down. Could be that a few of the kids go in and out of the place, to drink and have a scuffle. But most of them get out of here the moment they can tell a road from their playpen. There's hardly no work here, there's no cinema no more either."

A nanny goat chewing at her leisure looked Rosa in the eye, as if she knew exactly why she had all these questions.

"Can you describe the way to this place to me?" she asked the old man.

"All they show on TV is crap." He rose and made his way through the herd of goats. She quickly thrust the pistol a little deeper into the space beside her seat, but left her hand close to the butt.

"Seen you somewhere before," he said as he stopped outside the open window.

And I thought you hated TV, she was tempted to retort, about to start the car.

"You look like that actress in the sixties," he decided.

Most. Certainly. Not.

"Oh no, not an actress. A model, she was. Twiggy. Not much flesh on her bones."

"Is it *this* way?" she asked, pointing straight ahead.

"There's only two ways," he said. "Forward or backward. You better go forward, signorina, follow this track. It's eight or nine kilometers, maybe ten. Then you'll see part of the old fence. From there on the land's all poisoned, that's what they say. Not good for the milk, that's what they say."

"You mean along this trail through the fields?"

He nodded. "Eight or nine kilometers, maybe ten, like I said," he repeated, as if he were running out of words.

She turned the key in the ignition. The goats surged apart in a movement like a breaking wave.

He still kept his eyes on Rosa. "Wasn't you looking for a hospital?"

She pressed her lips together and waited impatiently for the last animals to get out of the way.

"On account of the blood?" he asked, putting out his hand to touch her face. She must have overlooked something, maybe at her hairline.

A goat let out a high-pitched bleat. The path ahead of the Honda was clear. Rosa stepped on the gas.

She reached the trail and headed for the empty hills, the steep rocks, and deserted valleys. She drove on into the graveyard country of the Mafia.

THE BASE

AFTER SIX MILES OVER bare hilltops, and through a valley recently devastated by a steppe fire, the trail led to a high plateau enclosed by hills and strange rock formations that might have come from another planet. Battered warning signs—BEWARE! MILITARY EXERCISES!—hung on posts stuck in the ground at an angle. Some of the notices had been peppered with bullet holes.

Far ahead, at the center of the plateau, a few low-built huts stood in a cluster around a craggy hilltop. All around, there were a handful of remains of larger buildings, distorted steel cages, masonry rubble, and concrete walls. The ruins were evidently a leftover product of the complex that the goatherd had mentioned had been blown up. It was natural enough to assume that the Corleonese had used the terrain as storage for drugs or a place to make them. But Rosa thought otherwise. The attention aroused by the raids—a couple of explosions, a few well-placed rumors about infected land to keep herdsmen away—all that fit only too well into the picture she had formed of TABULA and its methods.

At the moment, however, she wasn't interested in the past. All she wanted was Alessandro. Alessandro and a lot of answers.

As she jolted up the track to the plateau in a cloud of dust, passing a ruined guardhouse and iron gratings in the ground, she thought it had been naive of her to assume he might have made it to this bleak place. It had taken her almost two days to get here from the island, and she hadn't had to escape from the *Stabat Mater* first. Had she been harboring false hopes? She felt a sudden wave of despair, and her hands began to shake on the wheel.

She passed a row of concrete and steel posts. Local farmers had probably stolen the barbed wire once slung between them, or the Mafiosi of Corleone might have used it in their strongholds in the city. A few twisted spirals stuck up from the ground like the bones of half-buried animals. Ragged plastic film hung on some of them, wafted across the plains by the wind over the years.

There were still a few yards to go when she passed the first buildings that had been blown up. They seemed to be former large sheds for housing vehicles and military equipment. All that was left of them were concrete slabs on the ground, partly buried under the remains of fallen walls and distorted iron girders.

The trail was asphalt now, but the surface was crumbling so badly that she was jolted about in the car as much as she had been on the dirt path through the fields. A flock of birds crossed the sky and disappeared behind the buildings. At this distance she couldn't assess their size. She hoped they were only crows.

At last the trail went uphill, past another ruined guardhouse.

Dust and wind had worked the mortar out of the masonry; the doorframes and windows in the low-built structures were bleached by the pitiless sun. A few panes were broken, but most were still intact. There were six or seven of these buildings, all on a single floor and built close together. There was nothing to suggest that any of them were still in use.

The trail led around a bend to a small square between the huts. Rosa abruptly hit the brakes. The tires swirled up yet more dust. It clouded her view through the windshield.

At the side of this square, in narrow alleyways between the buildings, were two vehicles. One looked like an old army jeep: mud-colored, rusty, and with clouded windows. The other was a modern BMW cross-country vehicle: black, slightly dusty, but no dirtier than Rosa's Honda.

She reversed a little way and parked the car in the shelter of a building. Maybe it would be best to shift her shape and explore the terrain in snake form. On the other hand, then she would have had to do without the pistol and she didn't want that.

Once again she looked around carefully, and then climbed out. With the gun at the ready, she approached the two vehicles. The army jeep didn't seem to have been moved for years and was just as dirty inside as outside. Dust had gotten in through every crack and lay thick on the seats and the rest of the interior. After a moment's hesitation, Rosa tried the door handle. Not locked. She reached under the wheel and pulled out the ignition lead with a jerk.

Then she skirted the building to reach the BMW in the alleyway on the other side. She could have taken the shorter way across the square but she wanted to try getting a look inside. She cautiously approached the first window and scratched the encrusted dust off the glass with her fingertip. The room seemed to be empty. Bare walls, no furniture.

Still cautious, she approached the black BMW along the alleyway between buildings. The front of the car was turned in her direction. Holding the pistol in both hands, arms outstretched, she aimed at the driver's side. She still couldn't see whether there was anyone in the vehicle.

Another five yards. Then three. She expected to hear the engine roar at any moment and see the BMW move forward. She couldn't have swerved out of its way in the narrow passage. Her gun was still aimed at the windshield; she thought she could see the outline of the headrest. At least there was no one at the wheel.

The door was closed. Cigarettes and a half-empty pack of chewing gum lay on the passenger seat.

She moved away from the vehicle and stepped out into the square. She looked hard at all the buildings, all the windows, all the alleys between the fronts of the buildings. No one there. All quiet. She was alone.

Once again she glanced back at the BMW and saw tire tracks. So it couldn't have been standing here very long. And now she also saw footprints leading away from the driver's door and toward one of the huts.

She followed them slowly, still holding the gun in both hands. The footprints were much larger than her own. The hope that Alessandro might, after all, have escaped the hybrids flitted through her mind.

The tracks led up three wooden steps to a small platform in front of the entrance. Unlike the other buildings, this one stood on a stone base. The door was closed, but not locked. Beyond it lay a small front room, full of a brownish twilight that forced its way through the dirty windowpanes. Two old folding chairs covered with dust leaned against one wall.

Rosa went into the hut and moved slowly to a second door. A sign hung on it: ENTRY FOR AUTHORIZED PERSONNEL ONLY.

She slowly pressed the handle down, holding the gun very close to her body so that no one could strike it out of her hand. At the same time she prepared to shift her shape.

It was as if this building were inside another one, much larger than it appeared from outside. At first sight, the room behind this second door looked too tall, but there was a reason for that. The hut had been built in front of an opening into the rock, the way down to an underground bunker complex.

A hall with high concrete walls opened out ahead of her. At the front end there was a broad gate with grating over it, a freight elevator large enough to take a vehicle or a trailer. Beside it was a steel door on which the faded symbol for a flight of steps could be seen.

Rosa's heart hammered as she crossed the hall. Nothing that could be used as cover. She didn't see any cameras. The elevator stood ready beyond the grating, so she figured that the driver of the BMW had probably used the steps. There was another way out, a ramp for heavy vehicles to her right, but the roll shutter at the end of the slope was pulled down.

Taking a deep breath, she opened the door to the stairway. A gray concrete shaft. Neon lighting, almost every other bulb out. Rosa listened hard, went to the banister railing, and looked carefully down.

Three floors, maybe four. Iole would have enjoyed exploring this place. Rosa, however, felt her heart racing and had to fight down the chill rising inside her, fearing she might not be able to hold back her metamorphosis.

After the third step, she took her shoes off. Now her footsteps were almost silent. The palm of her hand on the butt of the pistol was wet with sweat. What she was doing was lunacy; she didn't even know whether the sickroom from the photograph of her grandmother with the two babies really was taken in this complex.

She cautiously passed two landings on the stairs. On both, there were niches in the walls for firefighting equipment. The metal doors in front of them had been broken open, and several yards of one of the hosepipes lay unrolled on the floor. She was more intrigued by the empty hooks on the back walls of the niches. Outlines in the dust told her that two long-handled axes had hung there. Neither was still in its place.

She suppressed nightmarish images of a figure with an ax in each hand coming up the stairs in total silence. With her lips pressed together, Rosa leaned on the wall and closed her eyes for a few seconds. *Pull yourself together. Concentrate.* When she opened her eyes again, sweat was running down her forehead.

Her throat constricted, she kept climbing down until she

reached the end of the stairs. There was another steel door here, unlocked like the others. A stench assaulted her nostrils when she slowly opened it.

Beyond lay a hall similar to the one on the first floor. The freight elevator ended at a grating with loops of cables dangling behind it like huge cobwebs.

There was a steel door in the left-hand wall of the corridor, with a smaller door set into it. Both were locked.

The cages stood directly opposite her, on the other side of the hall. Several rows, reaching all the way up to the ceiling, like book-lined walls in a library. Many consisted of bars, others of sturdy wire netting. Their floors and covers were made of wood or plastic.

She counted ten rows of cages, side by side, with aisles between them wide enough to take a forklift truck. How far they went back in the neon lighting she couldn't be sure. However, it seemed certain that the hall stretching that way was far larger than its counterpart on the first floor.

An uncanny silence filled the space. Not a sign of life. The fear that each cage might contain a dead Arcadian, mummified or decomposed, clawed its way into her gut. Nausea rose in her, and a sour taste turned her throat.

Very slowly, she moved out into the hall. As she did so, she kept her eye not only on the aisles between the rows of cages, but on the steel door to the left as well. The pistol no longer gave her a sense of security. It was only a heavy lump in her hand, useless against the lifeless silence in this concrete dungeon.

The cages were empty, the barred doors in front of them

unfastened. The occupants had probably all been taken away in haste. But why not in their cages? She could think of only one answer to that, and it was a dreadful one. They had all been killed.

With great caution, she slipped into one of the aisles. She could see through the gratings into the next aisle, but hardly any farther. Many of the neon tubes under the ceiling no longer worked. Others were flickering frantically. More than once she thought she saw movements out of the corner of her eye, but when she swung around, holding the gun ready, it was only the twitching shadows of the cage.

The row—at least forty yards long, maybe as much as fifty—consisted of thousands of these cages. Even if they had not all been occupied at the same time, the chaotic sound of animal cries and human voices whimpering, with the stench of excrement, sweat, and vomit, must have been horrific. Even the lingering smell was still hard to bear.

The video that Cesare Carnevare had shown her last October, in an attempt to intimidate her, could have been filmed here. Here, or in some similar place where TABULA extracted the serum from hybrid blood. Thanassis had spoken of his people rescuing hybrids from many laboratories. Maybe there were places like this all around the Mediterranean, perhaps even all over the world.

Except that here, all of it must have been given up long ago, and the place left to itself. Rosa had to fight the impulse to turn back at once. She had come here to find out more about her father's birth—and to see Alessandro again. But she couldn't, she mustn't think of him just now; it took her great determination not to let the thought of him distract her.

There must be a labor ward, somewhere in this complex, for delivering hybrids. But had they really been born here in this bunker? Or in one of the huts? Maybe in one of the buildings that had been blown up.

She heard something, and stopped. Listened.

Footsteps.

Whoever it was wasn't stealing surreptitiously along, more like a leisurely walk. Somewhere in this huge hall, someone was moving around without bothering to keep quiet. Someone who thought he was alone down here. Or who felt so much in control that he didn't have to conceal his presence.

She leaned back against a cage and strained her eyes to see in the flickering twilight. The sounds came from the left, and then next moment from the right. Once she thought for sure someone was behind her, but when she turned there was no one. The neon tubes crackled quietly.

The steps were coming closer. Not in this aisle, but in another one nearby. She crouched down, making herself as small as she could. Propped her elbows on her thighs, and held the gun upright in front of her face. And waited.

The hoarse sound of a throat being cleared, then a cough.

Five yards ahead of her, someone stepped out of the wall of cages like a ghost. There had to be an aisle crossing those between the cages in the opposite direction, and from where she was she hadn't been able to see it.

A figure dressed in white.

It disappeared as quickly as it had appeared, crossing the aisle without noticing Rosa.

The footsteps sounded heavy and labored. The figure was slightly stooped.

Rosa slowly straightened up and moved forward on tiptoe. She reached the cross aisle. Just wide enough for two people side by side.

With the pistol raised, she turned the corner.

No one.

Her jaw was clenched. She stood upright, legs apart, as if she knew what she was doing, clutching the pistol in both hands like someone who often went around armed like that.

The cough again. The footsteps.

Then the man in the white coat. He must have turned off into the next aisle but changed his mind, and was now coming back. Like a ghost, he made straight for Rosa.

And took no notice of her.

"Stop where you are," she said.

He came closer, still ignoring her. Looked at a block of paper that he was carrying on a clipboard. As he walked along, he wrote something on it.

"I said stop right where you are!" This time she spoke more sharply, but her tone bordered on panic. She couldn't let herself show any fear.

He glanced up, looked at her and at the same time right through her, shook his head, and went on past her. She had to move aside to keep him from bumping into her, but it was not aggressive, not even carelessness. He simply didn't see her.

She raised the muzzle of the pistol behind him, aiming at his broad back, the gray-haired head. He was tall and looked strong, in spite of his advanced age.

"Professor Sigismondis!" she said, as he moved away. "Stay where you are."

This time he surprised her, doing as she said. But he did not turn around, only let the hands holding the clipboard and his pencil drop.

"You knew my grandmother," she said. "Costanza Alcantara."

His ragged breathing stopped short, as if he couldn't think and breathe at the same time. Then he sighed softly.

"Costanza," he whispered.

"She was here, with you. You brought her children into the world." Rosa was standing ten feet from him, the arm holding the gun outstretched, aiming it between his shoulder blades. His coat was dirty and gray, with threads hanging loose at the hem.

He slowly turned toward her.

STUFFED ANIMALS

BUSHY EYEBROWS, HIGH CHEEKBONES. A flat nose like a boxer's. If Rosa hadn't known anything about Sigismondis, she might have taken him for all kinds of things, but not a scientist who had nearly won the Nobel Prize. He must once have been over six feet tall, and even now that his back was crooked and his shoulders slumped, he towered a head above Rosa.

A smile raised the corners of his mouth, as if they were hanging on fishhooks. "Costanza," he whispered again.

Except that this time he was staring at her. And he obviously thought he recognized her.

"I'm Rosa Alcantara," she said, looking over the butt of the pistol. "Costanza's granddaughter."

He slowly nodded.

"You also knew my father. He was born here, wasn't he? Davide Alcantara."

His smile disappeared; his face was expressionless. Now he was only an old man again. A *demented* old man. But she didn't want to acknowledge that, not now that she finally had him before her—the monster who had been the head of TABULA all those years.

But Eduard Sigismondis must have exhausted his stocks of evil long ago. Given all that she knew, he had drawn on them deeply over the decades. No wonder he seemed hollow now.

She took care to keep the pistol steady. Aimed at his heart, then at his face. Finally at his chest again.

"Davide," he said quietly. "Costanza's son."

"Davide was my father." Or perhaps, she thought, *is* my father. *If* he was still alive and was the man on the video who contracted her rape, the man whose fault it was that she got pregnant and had her child, Nathaniel, aborted.

"Davide," he said once more. "And Apollonio."

Mr. Apollonio, Michele Carnevare had said to her father. Or was it her uncle?

"Who *is* Apollonio?" Her voice shook. She was all the more determined to make someone pay for it. Even if it was this confused old man.

"They were brothers," said Sigismondis. "Davide and Apollonio were twins. Costanza's twins."

"Why didn't anyone ever mention him? What happened to Apollonio?"

Sigismondis put his head on one side, inspected her, then smiled again. "Costanza was a beautiful woman. So are you."

"I am not Costanza."

There was something mysterious about his smile as he turned and walked away, despite the gun aimed at him.

"Stop!" she snapped at him.

He took no notice.

She went after him, caught up, put out her hand to hold him back. But he was much taller than she was, and she wasn't sure how demented he really was. He might seem harmless, but she didn't know how he reacted to being touched. She could have shot him, but then she'd have no chance of getting answers to her questions.

"Where is my father?" she asked, as she followed him farther between the rows of cages in the underground hall. "What became of Davide?"

He did not reply.

"And Apollonio?"

Only silence. The crackling of the neon lights sounded like insects caught behind glass.

They reached the end of the row of cages. Sigismondis turned left and went along the back wall of the hall, gray concrete with old memos hanging here and there. What to do in the case of a fire. Ways of escape shown on a diagram of the bunker. Once even a board with blurred chalk lettering on it, the ghosts of words that had long ago lost their meaning.

Yellowish light fell through an open doorway that led into another hall, much smaller, but still of considerable length. Maybe this had once been a cafeteria, as the long tables from one side of the room to the other suggested. There were no chairs or benches now. Not far from the entrance, Rosa saw an unmade bed and an open cupboard with dozens of white coats spilling out of it. Large quantities of mugs that had held dried soups were stacked on the floor; all you had to do was add hot water. It looked as if after drinking the soup Sigismondis had simply thrown the empty mugs into a corner, where they formed a tall, stinking heap.

On the long tables stood hundreds of stuffed animals. In

pairs, two of each species.

The air smelled like straw and mothballs. There had been some hunting trophies in the Palazzo Alcantara, fox and beaver, even a young wolf. They had smelled the same; you needed only to get close to them to pick up the odor. But here the whole room stank of it.

In passing, Sigismondis put his notepad down on one of the tables and took a full syringe out of a metal dish. Rosa stiffened, but he made no move to attack her. Instead, he began walking down the row of stuffed animals, injecting a few drops into each. After five pairs of animals the syringe was empty, but the next one lay ready. Sigismondis went on down the row with it.

He worked with great care, going from animal to animal, inserting the needle with precision. As he did so, he slowly walked away from Rosa, who was standing near the doorway and who suddenly no longer knew what she really wanted.

The stuffed animals were not Arcadians. She saw martens, polecats, foxes and hares, as well as hawks, owls, and crows. None of the creatures was larger than it would be in nature. After metamorphosis, Arcadians seldom deviated much from their human dimensions. That was why the Harpies had been so murderously large, the Hundinga so strong. But these animals could never have been the captives from the cages.

Sigismondis's experimental subjects had been exchanged for these. And the old man never noticed that he was not injecting drugs into live bodies but rather into stuffing made of straw or synthetic material.

"What are you doing?" she asked.

"Looking after them."

Sigismondis was now more than ten yards away from her. She started to follow him at a distance. The creatures' glass eyes watched her.

You don't belong here, they seemed to want to say. *Leave us in peace. Leave him in peace.*

"How long have you been doing it?"

"A very long time."

"Did you look after Costanza, too? And her sons?" She still found it difficult to speak of them in the plural. Sons. Twins. Davide and Apollonio.

Was her father really not responsible for what had happened to her in New York? Had the man in the video been her *uncle*?

"Look after," repeated Sigismondis thoughtfully, injecting another dead animal.

"Are you alone down here?"

"No. I am never alone. They are all with me."

She would have liked to rob him of that illusion out of vengeance because she wanted him to suffer. But she knew it wouldn't make any difference what she said. He had been living in a world of his own for a long time now.

She slowly followed him, watching every movement he made. If he approached her with a syringe, she would shoot. He might be old and sick, but somewhere in him the monster he had been still lurked. The monster who had abducted Arcadians and made them into hybrids. The monster who was also responsible for everything that had been done to her.

"What happened back then?" she asked, without much hope of an explanation. "What did Costanza have to do with TABULA? And what did my father have to do with the organization?"

He went on working in silence. She was on the verge of snatching the animals off the table in front of him. But she dared not get too close to him.

"What became of my father? He wasn't in his casket in the family vault. I saw that for myself." It was making her more and more aggressive to be ignored like this. Or maybe he simply kept forgetting that she was here at all.

He reached the end of a long line of tables, went around to the other side, and moved back in the opposite direction. Pick up a syringe, ten injections, put the syringe down again. Pick up the next one, ten injections, and so on.

She quickened her pace and slowly caught up. Her forefinger was shaking on the trigger.

"Where is he?" she asked. There were only a couple of yards between them now. "Where is Davide Alcantara?"

Sigismondis stopped, without looking at her. "Davide?"

"What happened to him? I was told he died. Was that the truth?"

He repeated the name again, as if now he understood who she was talking about. Slowly, he turned around to her.

"He's here."

She aimed at his forehead. Her hand was shaking; her whole arm was shaking up to her shoulder.

"Here?" she whispered.

Then she saw the figure who had silently appeared in the doorway.

"Hello, Rosa," said the man.

TWINS

SHE SWUNG THE GUN around and took aim.

"I didn't mean to startle you." He stepped out of the shadow of the doorframe into the neon lighting, but he was too far away for her to make out every detail. Yet she recognized him, even after fourteen years. It was something in his appearance, in the sound of his voice.

Cats can't be tamed, a voice from the past echoed in her head. She had been four at the time. Surprising that she remembered it so clearly. But it was one of the last things he had said to her. *Cats can't be tamed*. And: *It will hurt you.*

"Stay where you are," she told him. "Don't move from that spot."

With a nod, he obeyed. He was wearing a floppy white coat, the kind of thing that scientists put over their clothes when they entered a laboratory. She knew that from movies. All of this was like a movie. The stupid thing was, it was her own story.

"You're furious with me," he said gently. "It's been a long time. I can understand that." Only now did she realize that he was speaking English to her—and she to him.

"Are you . . . him?" Wonderful! She was stammering like an idiot.

His smile looked mild, even at this distance. "You wouldn't believe me, I imagine. But Sigismondis? He's not in any state to think up lies these days."

She glanced at the old man, still doing his rounds and injecting the stuffed animals. Once again he seemed to have lost all interest in Rosa.

"You're my father?" she asked the man in the doorway.

"The chances are fifty-fifty, right? And so are the chances of you killing the wrong man if you pull that trigger."

"You didn't answer my fucking question!" she shouted.

"I'm Davide Alcantara. And yes, I'm your father. Gemma would tell you so, too, if she were here."

"If she were here *she* would shoot you."

He avoided meeting her eyes. "There was no other option. I had to go. She'd never have understood."

"Never have understood what?"

He pointed to the way out of the hall. "Come with me. I'll show you something."

"I've seen those cages. And a video of them when they were still full of Arcadians. The two of you belong to TABULA. You're mass murderers."

"No," he said calmly, pointing to Sigismondis. "Only him."

"What about Apollonio?"

"My twin brother."

"I know that. And I also know about his little deal with Tano and Michele Carnevare."

From a distance, he hardly seemed to have changed. He looked very much a southern Italian, with black hair, skin tanned brown, and dark eyes.

He still didn't move from his spot. He didn't seem afraid that she might shoot him. "What Tano and Michele did was appalling. But it has nothing to do with me."

"Michele filmed it all. I've seen the recording. I know exactly who was there."

"Apollonio wasn't in his right mind." Why did he smile when he said that? He knew about all of it, and now he was *smiling*? "That's why I killed him."

"You—"

"Killed him. Right after I heard what he had done to you. He deserved it." Now she realized that his smile was not cheerful, but cold as ice. The kind you would smile thinking about your worst enemy before shooting him in the kneecaps.

She slowly followed Sigismondis along the tables toward the door. She kept her eye on both of them, although neither man seemed like he was going to attack her. Sigismondis was much too busy injecting the corpses of his animals, while the man who said he was her father just stood there, looking at her.

"Show me your hands," she demanded.

He did. They were empty.

"Turn around. I want to see your back."

He obeyed that order, too. No hidden weapons. The white coat had no belt or pockets.

He sighed. "Doesn't sound like there's going to be a big hug for our reunion."

"I was four when you deserted us," she said. "That's

fourteen years ago. Without any good-byes, without a word to Zoe and me. Mom is heartbroken about it to this day. What did you expect? We'd fall into each other's arms and I'd tell you how great it is that you just happen to have stumbled back into my life? Not, by the way, because that's what you *wanted*, but because I *found* you. Here in this dump."

"You sound like your mother."

And for the first time, she was proud of it. At last she realized how very much she loved Gemma. All the anger she had felt toward her mother for years was really for him.

"I've behaved like a bastard," he said. "But are you going to shoot me for that?"

"Give me one good reason why I shouldn't," she replied.

"You're right. I didn't go looking for you. Meeting again today has nothing to do with paternal feelings—it would be a farce to put on that kind of show for you. We're here together because you turned up at this place, where, by the way, you have no business being. *That's* the truth. But as you are indeed here, I can also show you something. And explain a few things, if you would like that. Maybe it would keep you from pumping your dad full of lead."

Considering that he had never had much to do with Cosa Nostra in the past and had steered clear of his family's businesses, the Mafia slang flowed easily from his lips today.

"I'll go ahead," he offered, "and you can follow. With your gun at the ready, for all I care. Only do me a favor and don't trip. That would make this occasion a rather short family reunion."

"Where are we going?"

He put a conspiratorial finger to his lips, nodding in the direction of the old scientist. "To the *real* laboratory," he said quietly. She almost expected a familiar wink, but he didn't overdo it to that degree.

She glanced at Sigismondis, who was carrying on with his injections at the next row of tables while muttering quietly to himself, and paying them no more attention.

"What's the matter with him?" she asked.

"He's been in this state for years. He eats, he sleeps, he works. Or at least, that's what he thinks."

"And you've been looking after him?"

"Not because I've taken him into my heart, believe me. But should I have let him starve? Or shot him?" He pointed to her pistol. "I don't have your expertise with these things."

"It's not by choice."

"No," he replied seriously. "I know."

Only the width of a table still separated them, less than a yard and a half. At close range, she recognized the little lines around his eyes. His lips were rough and cracked, possibly the result of the air-conditioning in the bunker.

"You really do have a lot of explaining to do," she said, but she did not lower the pistol.

"I guess I do."

"So why not here?"

"Because you have to see what I'm doing in this place before you can understand *why* I'm doing it. What's more, I'm never quite sure how much he really understands. Sometimes he says surprising things, then he goes back to being as helpless as a baby."

She made a face. "Do you change his diapers?"

"It hasn't reached that point yet. But you're welcome to move in with us and make yourself useful." His tone bewildered her. Caustic but at the same time familiar, as if they had never parted.

"You go ahead," she said.

He gave her another brief smile, then turned around and went out into the huge hall.

"Slowly."

"If I was planning to run away, I'd hardly have come here to you and our confused friend, would I?"

He was walking along by the side wall now, next to the outer row of cages, back to the front area with the freight elevator and the stairway. Rosa glanced over her shoulder, to reassure herself that Sigismondis was making no move to follow them. She didn't like knowing that he was behind her back, but she had to deal with that.

"Is there anyone else down here?"

"No, no one."

His arms swung at every step, and the material of his white coat rustled. She walked about three yards behind him, watching the shadows of the gratings on the cages pass over him. "My mother worked with TABULA," he began. "Costanza never had anything in mind but her own gain. I'm sure Gemma has told you about her. In that case, you probably have a good impression of what she was like. A Lamia through and through."

Curiously enough, this last comment affected her more than she wanted to admit. He hadn't said it about her, he was speaking of his mother, but it annoyed her to hear him lumping all Lamias in together.

"Costanza was a monster," he went on, "but all the same, there was someone at least as bad as she was, if not worse. *Her* mother. She was well over forty when she brought Costanza and her twin sister, Catriona, into the world, and she nearly died at their birth. The clan would have been left almost without a leader, the business would all have been managed by *capodecini*, by men—unimaginable for a Lamia family. Many of them weren't too happy when your great-grandmother came back after a few weeks. For her part, she had informed herself in detail about those who had been counting on her death, and she wasn't squeamish when it came to avenging herself. She had nineteen men murdered in a single night—men who, she thought, wanted to divide her power between them. She was right about some; others were innocent. When it came to Costanza's right to lead the clan, that made no difference. She didn't want to run the risk of men determining the history of the Alcantaras again."

"What does that have to—"

"Everything," he interrupted her. "It has *everything* to do with the present situation. And if you want to try to understand what drove Costanza, then you must know the background. So let's fast-forward thirty-five years. By now Costanza and Catriona are grown women, but their mother is also still alive, and in her early eighties she still won't allow anyone but herself to direct the Alcantara affairs. She is sick, maybe already slightly confused, but she can't let go of her power, or bring herself to name one of her daughters as her successor.

"Catriona can live with that; she hasn't inherited her mother's ambition. Costanza, on the other hand, is consumed by hatred for the old woman, who doesn't trust her to lead the clan. Sigismondis, still in the early stages of his research into the Arcadians at the time, gets wind of the existence of a Lamia who is making no secret of her dissatisfaction. And he sees that this is his chance to get insider knowledge about the structure of the Arcadian dynasties. He makes contact with her, promises her God knows what, maybe impresses her with his knowledge or his vision . . . Well, however exactly he manages it, Costanza begins supplying him with information about some of the dynasties. Of course, only those who are not well-disposed to the Alcantaras, enemies who are also waiting for the old woman to make a mistake so that they can finally get their hands on the family's businesses. In that way, Costanza succeeds in eliminating several of the worst adversaries of the Alcantara clan—she simply ensures that those Arcadians are the first to be abducted by TABULA and to end up on Sigismondis's dissecting table.

"The old woman doesn't guess anything about that, but she is gradually coming to realize that she doesn't have long to live. And at last she decides to make one of the two twin sisters her successor in her own lifetime. But neither Costanza nor Catriona has children, in spite of various love affairs, and the old woman begins to worry about the continuation of her bloodline. She commits herself to making whichever of them first brings a daughter into the world her successor, remembering only too well how the late birth of her twins almost cost her her life, and the clan its female leadership, and she does not want such a thing to happen again, not at any price.

"Costanza and Catriona, although they are twins, do not get on very well. Catriona is the happy-go-lucky one, men dangling at her fingertips. Costanza thinks her sister might get pregnant just to spite her. She herself has tried in vain, in the past, to have a child, and she fears she might be infertile. And who do you think she remembers in that situation? Who maybe even owes her a few favors?"

"Dr. Frankenstein," said Rosa.

He looked over his shoulder as they approached the end of the rows of cages. "You've inherited her subtle sense of humor as well as her good looks."

"Go to hell."

Laughing quietly, he gazed ahead of him again. "The trump card up her sleeve is indeed Sigismondis, *the* authority on the subject of genetic research. And she makes a deal with him. Sigismondis has been experimenting for a long time with methods that we would call artificial insemination today— even with cloning. Though at the time those terms were not in wide use. All this happened a few years before the birth of the first official test-tube baby. And Sigismondis's practices were entirely different from those used today for fertilization in vitro. He was always obsessed with old formulas and experiments, the precepts of alchemy, and everything that had a reputation for being forbidden and mysterious. There's been a secret society known as TABULA since time immemorial, but before Sigismondis came upon it and shook the whole thing up it consisted of a few old fools drinking tea together in dusty libraries. He made TABULA what it is today."

"You say that as if it were something for him to be proud of."

"Depends on how you look at it. You yourself have had a shot at leading a criminal organization—he built one up with his own hands! But never mind what the two of us think, Costanza saw him as a tool she could use to gain power over the Alcantaras. And considering all she had already done for him, and the prospect of what she might yet do, he was ready and willing to help her."

"But surely she would never have put herself in danger as a guinea pig for scientific research."

"She thought he would simply make it possible for her to get pregnant. He, however, had something else in mind, something that he naturally preferred to keep secret from her. But here you have to know something else. Have you heard the story of the concordat?"

"I've heard of the civil war between the Lamias and the Panthera long ago in old Arcadia. And about their peace treaty."

"And you've also heard that Lamias and Panthera were forbidden to have children together?"

"To prevent two strong families from merging into a single invincible clan, yes."

He stopped at the end of the row of cages. "Allegedly that

was what the gods commanded. You may call it garbage, but as a rule there's a kernel of truth in such stories. It's easy to understand that the pact kept the power in Arcadia evenly balanced, as a kind of coalition with an equal division of labor. But that was not the only reason why Panthera and Lamias were right to keep their hands off each other."

As hard as she tried, she could no longer blot the thought of Alessandro out of her mind. Suddenly she felt so queasy that she was afraid she might have been trapped into taking some kind of poison.

"There's a biological reason for the fact that Lamias and Panthera don't suit one another," he said. "It has to do with their children."

She clutched the pistol, thought of Nathaniel, and then of Alessandro again. She had been forcibly brought together with Tano, one of the Panthera. She had been a guinea pig herself, her rape nothing but an experiment. All at once she was terrified of what he might say next.

He went over to the tall steel door in the side wall, only a few yards from the stairway and the freight elevator. The smaller door set into it was open just a crack.

"You weren't the first it's been tried with," he said, turning to look at her with a dark expression. "The first Lamia—or at least the first we know—to be crossed with one of the Panthera was Costanza. Except that she didn't know anything about it. The good professor knew the old legends; he was obsessed by the myths of Arcadia. And he wanted to find out whether there was any factual reason for the ban on unions between Lamias and Panthera. Myths can often be a disguise for the truth. People blamed the gods for everything that they couldn't understand. Or used them as a pretext for banning such things. Almost certainly there *were* unions between the two dynasties in times of classical antiquity, but the children born of them were . . . different. And above all weak."

"Weak?" she asked quietly.

"Sickly at birth, but that wasn't the worst of it. For some reason, the genes of the two species don't suit each other; newborn babies from their mating almost never grew up in those days. Today, however, there are ways of keeping such weak babies alive and raising them. And that is what Sigismondis did. For him, the birth of Costanza's twins was a scientific triumph. Without her knowledge, he impregnated her with semen from one of the Panthera. The fact that my brother and I had only barely survived our first few days confirmed his hypothesis. The concordat anticipates natural selection. Instead of bringing into the world children who would soon die anyway, Lamias and Panthera were forbidden to produce them at all. They were kept apart, maybe for fear that any surviving sons and daughters could poison the bloodlines of all the dynasties."

Rosa was still aiming the pistol at him, and had no intention of lowering it. At the same time, she was starting to feel childish, because he knew as well as she did that she wouldn't pull the trigger.

"So Costanza was mated with one of the Panthera against her will," she said. "And the twins, you two, were living proof that it was not the gods who had forbidden such unions but the dynasties themselves? Is *that* what Sigismondis wanted to show?"

"Among other things, yes. The facts behind the old legends interested him. Of course he didn't tell Costanza anything about it; she was angry enough with him already. She had wanted a daughter, or even two, but not even Sigismondis could influence that. He may have liked the idea of playing the part of a god, but he was still a long way from being a real one." That appeared to amuse him, but when he went on he seemed to be entirely serious again. "Her sons' weak condition after their birth was, as I said, due to only *one* defect. The second showed itself only much later." He looked almost a little sympathetic. "You're wondering what that means for you and that Carnevare boy, am I right?"

She had indeed been thinking about that, but above all she wanted to know what it meant for herself. So her unknown grandfather, the father of Costanza's children, had been one of the Panthera. Meaning that a certain amount of Panthera blood flowed in her own veins. And the *defect* he was talking about affected her, too.

"Don't let that worry you," he said. Obviously it was easy enough to tell, from looking at her, what was on her mind. "It has to do with the shape-shifting. And you seem to have no problems at all with that, from what I hear."

Were they broadcasting it on the eight o'clock news? How on earth had he heard about her shape-shifting in this hole in the ground?

"It was heart trouble," he said, "with both my brother and me. If we shifted shape, the heart stopped. Just like that. Not strong enough for the metamorphosis. The heart stops. R.I.P." He struck one hand with the fist of the other. "That's all."

So far, her own heart had always gone along with the shape-shifting. But who could guarantee it would stay that way?

"What happened to Costanza, then?" She had hated her grandmother without really having known her—and now she almost felt sorry for her, because TABULA had treated Costanza as shamefully as they had treated her, too.

You're running away from the ghost of Costanza, Trevini had said to her once. That was all over. She would face her inheritance. And she wanted to hear everything, the whole story.

"She brought us into the world," he said, "and then she went home to place herself at the head of the clan once and for all, without consideration for anyone or anything else whatsoever. That's why the first thing she did was to shoot her mother."

Rosa's aunt Florinda had also died of a gunshot wound.

"And then she murdered her sister."

Zoe, too, had been killed. Zoe, who had really been destined to succeed Florinda.

"So that made Costanza the head of the clan." He smiled. "And who does that remind you of?"

FATHER AND DAUGHTER

"How much of all this did Evangelos Thanassis know?" asked Rosa. "He was financing Sigismondis, after all."

The man who might be her father was still standing in front of the steel door, as if suddenly reluctant to reveal the last piece of the research-station puzzle. It was only a few steps from here to the stairs and the way up to the surface. Rosa could have run away from the truth. But she didn't even consider it.

"Thanassis had no idea," he said. "Sigismondis exploited him, just as he exploited Costanza, but the two of them knew nothing about each other. If there was one thing he couldn't allow himself, it was to make enemies of those two, at least not at the beginning of his work. Later, after TABULA was well established and earning millions from the sales of the hybrid serums, it wouldn't have made any difference. By that time, he had long ago built up such a network of supporters, sympathizers, and those who benefited from his work that even a man like Evangelos Thanassis could no longer have been a serious danger to him."

"Until his friends themselves threw him out." She was gradually getting the hang of all these entanglements.

"He realized, too late, that he had made a pact with the

devil. You don't do business with such people without sur-
rendering some of your power to them. Sigismondis had built
up TABULA so that he could pursue his experiments at his
leisure. The serum trade was meant only to finance his work.
However, his partners didn't see it the same way, and before
he knew it they wanted to share in the profits. Naturally they
couldn't care less about an old man doing research in an abandoned bunker somewhere. They forced him to withdraw
from TABULA—and in return they left him with this complex and a modest amount of financial support, and made
sure that the place was well and truly forgotten. They did it
by using all the methods at their disposal: rumormongers,
the army, even the Corleone clan. This isolation was all the
reward Sigismondis got for everything he had built up."

She pointed to the door behind him. "What's behind that?"

"The laboratories and the former hospital wing. You want
to see them, do you?"

Rosa nodded, although she wasn't sure that she did. She
was wasting time. What she really wanted was Alessandro.
And she was starting to believe that she wasn't going to find
him here.

Davide pushed the door open and climbed over the ankle-
high steel threshold. More neon lighting, this time in a long
corridor with concrete walls. There were several rooms on
both sides of it. At the end of the hall was an opaque glass
double door.

Rosa followed him down the corridor, past the first room, a
medical laboratory with microscopes, centrifuges, incubators,

and refrigerators, and other equipment she couldn't identify. All the doors on the left side were closed; those on the right side wide open. In the next room several clunky computer monitors stood, out of use with one exception. An orange row of figures glowed on a black background on its screen. Beside it was a modern laptop on which filmed images with captions running underneath them shimmered; it looked like a news bulletin. He must have been sitting here when she entered the bunker.

"Why did no one ever mention Apollonio?" she asked. "None of my entire family has ever said a word about him, not even Florinda."

"Florinda was born a few years later. I don't think her conception was intentional. By then Costanza had probably given up hope of a daughter of her own. Later, she initiated Florinda only into the bare essentials about the family. She knew nothing about Apollonio, and very little about the Alcantaras' links to TABULA."

"But Apollonio was her brother!"

"Apollonio never lived with the Alcantaras. Sigismondis claimed him for himself directly after the birth, and Costanza, who had wanted a girl anyway, didn't care what became of him. She took one baby home with her and left the other here. She didn't even name him; Sigismondis did that. In the Arcadian myths it was the god Apollo who, with the help of Hermes, brought peace to the kingdom. To Sigismondis, on the other hand, Apollonio was the symbol of hope for new scientific discoveries, new knowledge."

"You mean Apollonio was a kind of lab rat?"

"To begin with, anyway. Apollonio grew up here at the institute under constant observation, every fiber of his body scientifically investigated, his every step, every word, every mood recorded. After a while Sigismondis may have seen him as a kind of foster son, but that didn't keep him from studying the boy day and night. For the first few years he wasn't allowed to leave the complex. Later he went out only under supervision for short excursions in the light of day."

She was very far from feeling sorry for Apollonio, yet the idea of the little boy kept down here year in, year out, having needles stuck into him, being measured, weighed, x-rayed touched her heart.

"And Costanza never took any interest in him?"

"Not the slightest. She simply expunged him from her memory like afterbirth left behind in the hospital. Sixteen years passed before she was reminded of him again."

"What happened?"

"Apollonio was a teenager. He was curious about the outside world, and he rebelled. By that time he was free to move about down here in the Institute, and one day he came upon the documents recording his birth. Until that point he hadn't known that he had a twin brother who had grown up in the Alcantara family, had total freedom, and enjoyed every imaginable luxury. Costanza was not a loving mother, but she had made sure that Florinda and I lacked for nothing. Among other things, the files of the institute contained press clippings about the Alcantaras, mentioning the appearance of

Costanza with her son and daughter, who was the younger of her children, at social occasions. You can probably imagine it for yourself. Sigismondis was always a dedicated collector and archivist, and his documentation on the Alcantaras was comprehensive."

"So Apollonio got out of here and set off to see the Alcantaras, right?" She would probably have done the very same thing.

"We were seventeen at that time. Apollonio got into the grounds of the Palazzo Alcantara and caught up with me on the way to the garages."

"And you'd known nothing about his existence before?"

He shook his head. "All of a sudden we were facing each other, almost mirror images, but one in expensive clothes, all spruced up, the other unkempt after his flight from the institute and several days living rough. Yet there could be no doubt about it. We could have been looking at our own reflections. It was far more than just the similarity. The only problem was that he dealt with the meeting far better than I did. He was prepared for it; he'd been working on it for weeks. While I was taken entirely by surprise. And then something happened that, properly speaking, was impossible. In the midst of all this emotional turmoil I began shifting shape."

"But male Alcantaras—"

"Can't in fact shift shape. Or never grow to an age when they'll try it. However, Apollonio and I were half Panthera— and that made it complicated. For one thing, we had not, like the other male Alcantaras, died soon after birth, and for another we definitely had the ability to shift. That was the first time it had shown itself in me, maybe because of the excitement, the surprise, I don't know exactly. My body changed shape—and in the process my heart stopped."

"The defect," she whispered in a dismissive tone designed only to divert his attention from her own uneasiness.

"I survived. Costanza and a couple of other people appeared, and they somehow managed to revive me. The meeting with my brother had very nearly killed me. Costanza was beside herself with fury, on the verge of striking Apollonio dead. But he managed to get away again, and fled back here. It was the only safe place he knew, and in his confusion and rage—and yes, his hatred for the Alcantaras—he decided to stay here, to accept his role as Sigismondis's foster son and become something like his student. Within a few years he went from being an experimental subject to acting as Sigismondis's right-hand man, not just in his work at the institute but also, after a while, in the sale of the serum. While the professor hid away in his laboratory, devoting himself entirely to research, Apollonio took over more and more of the business side. He traveled the world on behalf of TABULA, made contact with the Arcadian dynasties in Europe, America, and Asia, supplied them with the hybrid serum—and also, in the case of a few privileged collectors, with the furs of Arcadians who had been killed in the course of laboratory experiments. Here he had to deal with Costanza again, whether she liked it or not. She had to accept the fact that she was doing business with him, even long after she had stopped giving Sigismondis information. Apollonio demanded exorbitant prices for the furs and the serum, but she seems to have come to terms with that—maybe, after all, some remnant of conscience stirred in her."

Rosa's blood was boiling. "TABULA abducted thousands of Arcadians, murdered them or made hybrids of them, but Costanza and the others were still *doing business* with Apollonio and Sigismondis?"

He shrugged his shoulders. "The idea of morality has never figured much into our family history."

She felt like she needed a long, hot shower to wash all the filth away.

"In the end the others, who were pulling the strings, left Sigismondis powerless," he said. "And no one wanted any more to do with Apollonio, who was thought to be his son. He could either leave, burning all his bridges behind him, or stay down here with his foster father and continue to work as his assistant. He chose the second option. And what else would he have done? Most of the money had been handed over to TABULA, and he had no friends or anyone else to turn to. As for his family, he hated them with all his heart, me—his brother—as much as Costanza."

They stopped at the double door of opaque glass. A pungent medicinal smell hung in the air. Somewhere on the other side of the corridor, electronic devices were beeping.

"After Apollonio heard of Costanza's death, he decided to get in touch with me again. But I wasn't in Sicily any longer. I had moved to New York with your mother, Zoe, and you. I assume Gemma's told you how that happened."

She slowly nodded, not sure whether she wanted to hear his version of events as well. However, she didn't say so; she was afraid of taking his attention off more important matters.

"Apollonio turned to Trevini, claiming that Costanza hadn't paid him for some of the furs before her death. He knew very well that alarm bells would then start ringing for Trevini, and he would get in touch with me. If Costanza's link to TABULA became known, there would have been disastrous repercussions for all the Alcantaras, including you and Zoe. The other dynasties would have avenged themselves on us, so we had no choice but to try silencing Apollonio. Trevini kept the threat on ice for a time by paying him, and at the same time I set out for Italy to meet my brother."

"You wanted to kill him."

"I wanted to find out what he was going to do. And he made no secret of that: He wanted a large part of the Alcantara fortune handed over to him. In return he would keep his mouth shut, and as a gesture of goodwill compensate Florinda with a suitable sum of money. You can imagine what I said to that. To cut it short, we quarreled. We fought. He won."

"As simple as that?"

He laughed bitterly, placed the palm of one hand against the opaque glass, but did not push the door open yet. "He locked me up down here. He didn't kill me, that would have been too easy. He wanted me to go through what he had experienced himself."

"You mean you've been here all this time? For *fourteen years*?"

He turned around to her. Now there was such honesty in his eyes, such deep sorrow, that she almost softened. "Believe me, I know what it is to be buried alive in this place."

"What about Florinda?" she asked. "She told Mom that you'd died of a heart attack on a plane."

"Florinda told lies from the moment she opened her mouth."

"That sounds like you're blaming her for—"

"Did she so much as lift a finger to find me?" he retorted. "She could think of nothing better to do than have me declared dead, and bury a casket full of bricks in the family vault."

He cast a final disapproving glance at her pistol, and then pushed the double doors open. The pungent smell surrounded her at once with such intensity that it took her breath away for seconds on end.

"Come along," he told her. "This way."

She lowered the gun, but kept the safety catch off.

Another hall opened out before them, higher than the corridor and the rooms along it. The sounds of obscure instruments came from all directions, technology that was probably decades old, but was still working like a perpetuum mobile.

This was where Sigismondis and Apollonio had stored the subjects of their experiments, taken them apart—tall shelves stacked with cylindrical glass jars where specimens floated, pale, bloated, some of them disintegrating, or cut into slices. Very few of them could still be recognized as what they had once been. These were body parts of hybrids and Arcadians, clumps of muscle, blistered organs, bizarre formations of fibrous flesh and venous systems. Pupils of eyes, earlobes, jawbones, joints, skullcaps, and spiky bones. Every fragment was preserved in a solution, most of them distorted by the curves of their jars.

Rosa opened her mouth and then shut it again. Took a few awkward steps past him into the hall, and stared at all these remains, an archive of Arcadian body parts.

A passage ran down the middle, with narrow aisles branching off it between the shelves to the right and the left. Rosa could see only the front compartments, with the vague outlines of the other rows behind them.

"Why all this?" she finally managed to say, turning around.

He was gone.

Alarmed, she leaped backward, swinging the pistol around.

She hadn't heard him moving away, but now she saw him some way off, standing by a heavy steel partition in the side wall of the hall. She was instinctively reminded of the entrance to the cold storage in the Palazzo Alcantara.

"Can't you stop waving that thing about?" He pointed to the gun. "You're so easily frightened, you'll pull the trigger without wanting to."

"Don't think *you* know what I want," she snapped. "You don't know anything at all about me."

"I know you want to see Apollonio."

She asked more quietly, "Is he in there?"

He placed both hands on the crank to open the cold storage. "Of course he is."

The door swung open. A wave of bitter cold surged out toward Rosa.

"You go first," she ordered.

"Do you really think I want to shut you in?"

"It wouldn't be anything new down here."

He sighed, obviously upset by her continued suspicion, and then went past the partition. She followed him into the cold, staying a few steps behind.

The cold storage was a long tunnel with ugly neon lighting, and plastic shelves on the white-tiled walls. Stacked on the shelves were transparent plastic bags. Ice crystals had formed inside, as if what lay inside had been breathing to the last. That was nonsense, as she knew, yet for a moment she saw it all before her: hundreds of pulsating plastic bags in the compartments, walls of twitching life under ice-pale plastic.

"Rosa."

The bags lay still. Everything in this cold storage was frozen stiff. Nothing moved on the shelves.

"Are you coming?" He pointed to a curtain of vertical plastic slats dividing the back part of the room from the front of it.

He struck the frozen curtain hard to loosen it. There was a crunch as the layer of ice on it gave way. He pushed the plastic aside with both arms, and opened a way through for Rosa.

She gripped the pistol more tightly, and hesitated.

Behind the clouds of white vapor from his breath, his expression was concerned. "You'd rather not?"

Maybe it was a mistake to entrust herself to him. It was possible that all this was wrong, the worst of stupid ideas.

Stooping slightly, she stepped past him through the curtain. He let her go two steps in, then followed her and stood beside her.

"Are you sure you want this?" he asked, with more

sympathy than she had expected.

"Yes."

She was still in nothing but jeans and a T-shirt, and was freezing to the bone. Better get this behind her quickly.

There were no shelves in the back part of the cold storage, only five stretchers on small rubber rollers, the kind used in hospitals. Four of them were empty.

On the front stretcher, only a few steps from the slatted curtain, lay a body covered with a sheet of black plastic up to the throat. She went closer to look at the face.

His features had fallen in; his skin was almost white. There was a hole no bigger than the opening of a pencil sharpener in his forehead. Not a drop of blood; perhaps it had been wiped away before he was deep-frozen.

It was no surprise that he looked like the man beside her, yet it was a shock all the same. The triangle around his lips formed by the two lines running from his nostrils to the corners of his mouth looked shadowy, as if part of his face had sunk inward.

Her glance went up to the bullet hole in the forehead. "You did that?" she asked calmly.

"Yes."

"When?"

"When he came back here"—he hesitated briefly—"from New York. A good year ago. Sigismondis was not a particularly careful prison guard, and with every passing year of his dementia he became more forgetful. One day my chance came, and I used it. Once I was free I lay in wait for him down here in the bunker."

She put her hand out to the head of the dead man. Hard and cold as a block of ice. Slowly, she leaned over him so that she could look at his face from in front. Her hand touched the sheet of black plastic over his chest. Its folds were frozen almost rigid. All the same, she grasped it, felt the material give under pressure, and held it yet more firmly.

"No." His fingers on her shoulder, touching it very gently. "That's enough. Do you believe me now?"

"I still don't understand," she said, her breath coming out as vapor. "Why the rape? After all, Sigismondis had every means of crossing Lamias with Panthera artificially down here."

He didn't seem to think this the right moment to talk about that subject, but he answered her question anyway, perhaps to show that he respected her feelings. "For a long time he considered the ban on mating the two species purely rational, from the medical point of view. But finally he wondered whether the traditional myth might not, after all, be true. You've seen what he's like—he didn't lose his mind overnight. All of a sudden it was no longer a case of investigating his theory of the biological origin of a myth—now he wanted evidence of the existence of the gods!"

"By doing all he could to break their commandments?" she asked in a toneless voice, frozen almost as rigid as the dead man.

"He thought he could challenge them by bringing a Lamia and a member of the Panthera together in the natural way, not in a test tube. And in addition, two Arcadians of high standing in the succession of their clans: Tano and you. You were to be impregnated by Tano—and that would show how the gods reacted to it. *If* they reacted to it. If they even exist at all."

An idea stirred in her mind. Someone else had tried to get such evidence, but in a different way. In the search for the invisible being who had caused all those historical disasters. The gaps in the crowd. She had a feeling that the circle was about to close—but something was still missing. A last piece of the puzzle.

Once again she clenched her fist around the frozen folds of the plastic sheet, as firmly as if to dig her hand into the dead man's rib cage and pluck out his ice-cold heart.

"Never mind what you do now," he said, "it won't change anything."

She nodded, very slowly. Then she let him lead her a little way toward the curtain. She was walking backward, without taking her eyes off the body.

"Come away from here." He spoke to her as if she was a child. His child. "This place is too cold. Apollonio is dead. And we are together again. Together you and I can—" With a jerk, she tore herself away and hurried back to the dead man. This time she took the sheet of plastic by its upper edge. It was like removing a board nailed into place from the body, but she tried it anyway with just one hand, pulling as hard as she could.

"Don't do that!"

The frozen covering had taken on the contours of the body,

like a mold for a gelatin dessert. Tiny cracks formed in the layer of ice, and then the black plastic sheet gave way.

And Rosa saw what was underneath it.

"Rosa . . ." He was standing behind her again.

She spun around to him and looked into his eyes. And found a silent request there, nothing bad, just exhaustion and a plea.

Fingers shaking, she raised her left hand and touched his cheek, let her fingers wander to the back of his neck, drew him toward her. Her head hurt, with sharp pains on all sides.

"You want evidence of the existence of God?" she whispered.

Then she shot him in the stomach.

NATHANIEL

HE SCREAMED AND HOWLED, but she closed her ears to him.

As he writhed on the floor, she looked back at the dead man on the stretcher. There was a rough incision on the left-hand side of his chest. Someone had removed his heart and closed the body up again without going to much trouble about it. Under the white skin, she could see where parts of the ribs had been taken out. The incision had not been properly stitched; the edges were merely stapled together.

Rosa touched the place with great tenderness. He no longer felt like someone who had once lived, laughed, and loved her. But she knew who he was. Davide Alcantara, her father.

She carefully picked up the sheet of black plastic and spread it over him again, trying to cover his face as well, but the material was too rigid for that.

Apollonio was lying doubled up on the white tiles, one leg bent at a sharp angle while he kicked out with the other in convulsive spasms. He was pressing both hands to the wound. Rosa had heard that few things hurt as much as a shot to the stomach, and she saw, with satisfaction, that this was true. He was still screaming his head off, and she watched him from above for a while, then stepped over him and crouched down in front of him. He tried reaching for her with one blood-stained hand, but not to hit her. It was only a gesture, a plea for help.

"How long?" she asked calmly.

Little bubbles of blood were bursting at the corners of his mouth.

"How long have you had him on ice down here? All fourteen years?" Once again she pushed his hand away. "You exchanged his body for the bricks, didn't you? When was that? On the evening of his funeral? On the day itself?"

Her bullet must have caught all kinds of organs that were well supplied with blood. In between screams, he could manage only tortured breathing, no words.

"You shouldn't have mentioned the bricks," she said, in a tone of mild reproof. "I didn't realize it right away. I only thought, there's something wrong here. Something didn't happen the way he claims. Clear as day, don't you agree? Whatever really happened fourteen years ago, *you* couldn't have known about the bricks. Unless you'd put them in the casket yourself."

Threads of bright red saliva were dropping from his mouth. "He . . . he could have been . . . been the solution."

"You shot him in the head to make me think it looked genuine," she commented. "When did you do that? When I arrived here in my car? I assume you have cameras up there. And then you thought you could act out a touching scene of a father taking his long-lost daughter in his arms. You didn't get your hands on the Alcantara fortune fourteen years ago, but you worked out that now it would be really easy. Father and daughter return to lead the clan together. They didn't want me on my own—and I can't really blame them for that—but they'd have accepted you. Costanza's son, formerly believed dead, now running the show. No more games of hide-and-seek, no false identities—and with all your insider knowledge about TABULA, they'd have willingly laid the Alcantara fortune at your feet. And I'd have been your trump card. If I accepted you as Davide, they certainly would."

He grimaced with pain and his screams had turned to groans, but his eyes showed her that he could hear what she was saying.

"The bad news is that it was all for nothing. You couldn't have known, down here in your bunker, but there have been a few changes. For several days the Hungry Man has been back in Sicily, and right now I'm anything but reliable life insurance."

Did he understand what she meant? It made no difference, although it gave her a certain satisfaction to make his inevitable failure clear. Physical pain wasn't enough. Not for him.

"That heart attack on the plane," she went on. "Was that when you saw each other again?"

He opened his mouth, tried to form words, but only spat blood.

"It was just like when you were still boys, wasn't it? You met, you got him to shift shape. But his heart wouldn't stand the strain. You knew that would kill him."

"No," he gasped. "It wasn't . . . like that."

"How, then?"

A wave of pain shook his body. He stretched, and then doubled up again.

400

Without pity, she put the barrel of the pistol to his wound, close to his twitching fingers. "I want to know the truth. Now."

He screamed.

She withdrew the gun. "Well?"

"I didn't . . . mean to kill him. Not at first . . . we wanted to investigate him . . . to find the . . . the defect . . . why metamorphosis would kill us . . . him as well as me. But then he died on the plane . . . *before* we met again."

"Of natural causes?"

A faint nod.

"So then you stole the body to investigate it? To turn that at least to your advantage?"

"I went to see Florinda and . . . gave her an ultimatum. She . . . laughed at me and threw me out. 'Go to the other clans and tell them about TABULA,' she said. 'You'll see what they do to you then.' And she was right, it was only . . . an empty threat. But I took Davide's body away. . . . Florinda *gave* it to me. She knew there were only bricks in the casket because we—she and I together—we put them in there and . . ."

Maybe she should have guessed that. But it changed nothing. "Florinda is dead, and so are you." She stood up. "Did you find it?"

"What . . . ?"

"The remedy. For your heart."

At that, his face distorted in a grin of malice. "You're *scared*, little Rosa. Scared stiff the same thing may happen to you some day . . . like Davide, that coward. Ran away from responsibility . . . went off to New York . . . and then, later, again . . . so scared of meeting me that it finished off his heart . . ."

She aimed the gun at his face. He had shot her father's body in the forehead. What kept her from doing the same to him? A little shocked, she realized that she was enjoying this. The power she had over him. The same power that he had wielded when he stood beside her and Tano in that New York apartment.

You're not being paid to have a good time.

It would have been so easy to pull the trigger. Pay him back for everything, do away with him once and for all.

Slowly, she lowered the gun again. He would die anyway, he had already lost large quantities of blood. The prints left by her feet were deep red, and already freezing to ice.

She turned away and pushed the slats of the curtain aside.

"Rosa . . . !"

She went through it, and past the shelves with the frozen clear plastic bags.

"Don't leave me here!"

With firm footsteps, she left the cold storage, closing the heavy steel door behind her. Her eyes fell on a display beside the entrance. Ten degrees below zero. Pressing a button, she lowered the temperature to twenty degrees below. Then she activated the locking mechanism, and heard the bolts shoot into place.

She walked through the hall in a daze. When she was passing the room with the monitors that opened off the corridor, she noticed something. Glancing down the passage at the great hall—no sign of Sigismondis—she entered the computer room and went straight to the old-fashioned screen with the rows of orange lettering. The news bulletin was still running on the laptop beside it. A wheeled chair stood in front of it.

She felt dizzy as she sat down and skimmed the words on the older of the two monitors. They were names in alphabetical order. After each there was a date from the last four decades. Then came combinations of signs; she couldn't make anything of them. Possibly the places on the shelves where the remains of the person were stored.

The computer had no mouse. She scrolled down the screen for a while, using the arrow keys, shaken by the vast numbers of men and women listed in this catalog. The surnames beginning with *A* alone occupied three full screens.

Instead of continuing to search manually, she typed her father's name into a field at the top of the monitor. His entry appeared a few seconds later.

Davide Alcantara. Followed by a date fourteen years ago. The day of his death as told to her by her mother had been just under a week earlier, so the date on the screen must be for the arrival of his body at the station here. It was followed by the same kind of jumbled figures and letters as the other entries. She was sure now that they indicated the place in the archive hall where a container with his heart in it would be found. Or what was left of his heart, after Sigismondis and Apollonio had finished their investigations.

She stared at the display on the screen for some time, until her attention was distracted by a news picture on the laptop. Wobbly images filmed through the window of a helicopter flying over a gray sea, with a pillar of smoke on the horizon. Then the picture switched to a woman reporter with a microphone in her hand, trying to shout in competition with the noise of the rotors. The sound on the laptop was switched off. Rosa didn't understand what it was about. Never mind.

She looked back at her father's catalog entry. Hesitantly, her fingertips hovered over the keyboard, and then she deleted his first name from the search window. Now it said only *Alcantara*. Once again she pressed Enter.

Eight names came up. Davide first, then a couple of others that meant nothing to her. Their dates were several decades back. Probably family members who Costanza disliked, so she had handed them over to TABULA.

The last name on the list was her own.

Eyes closed, she leaned back in the chair. What Apollonio had said just now ran through her mind, distorted like a defective soundtrack: He had returned from New York *a good year ago*. The date after her name matched that span of time.

Her rape was farther in the past, sixteen months ago. Had he stayed in New York for several months until he returned to Sicily? Or had he flown to the States again later?

She would never in her life forget what had happened *a good year ago*, exactly one day before the date next to her name.

When she jumped up, the chair rolled back with a clatter. She looked at the numbers and letters once more, then she ran out into the corridor and through the opaque glass door, into the archive hall. She glimpsed the locked cold storage room out of the corner of her eye, ran on, and concentrated on the markings of the shelves. Each was numbered, and the compartments on them meticulously identified by letters.

The one she was searching for was in the back part of the hall. She turned into the narrow aisle and, holding her breath, looked for the right place. Tears were streaming down her face, and her vision was blurred—it passed over dozens of glass jars, with strange eyes staring back at her from some of them.

At last she stopped in front of one container, at shoulder height and in the third compartment.

With shaking hands, she took it off the shelf. It was cylindrical, with a screw top, and no larger than a jam jar. She hugged it to her chest, fell to her knees, and bent her upper body over it, because she had a feeling that she had to protect it with her life.

She stayed kneeling like that for a long time, maybe an hour. At some point in that space of time Apollonio must have died behind the steel door, drained of blood and frozen rigid, but she hardly wasted a moment's thought on him.

The jar was no longer cold against her body, and she felt her heart beating against it, first at high speed, then more and more steadily and calmly.

At last she rose to her feet, left the pistol behind in the laboratory, climbed up through the echoing stairway, and carried Nathaniel out into the light of day.

SINKING THE SHIP

ON THE FAR SIDE of the huts, Rosa climbed to the rocky top of the hill. A rock formation as high as a house stood there, a structure of fissured limestone with crevices and furrows running through it. She made her way along one of the deep indentations up to the highest point and reached a small plateau. Soil had accumulated in many hollows there, and weeds and grass, even clover, grew where there was protection from the wind.

With the help of a flat stone, she dug a hole no broader than her fist, but twice as deep. Then she opened the lid of the glass jar, ignoring the pungent smell of the chemicals in it, let the clear liquid run away, and with infinite care lifted out the tiny thing that lay inside. She placed it gently on the bottom of the grave she had dug, placed a cloverleaf on it, and slowly covered it with dirt. She placed the stone on top.

Once again she knelt, not moving, head bowed, while tears ran down her chin and moistened the soil. The liquid had drained away, she smelled the grass and the damp earth, felt the wind blowing over the hilltop and through her hair, and she thought this was a moment of closure that she could live with.

When she stood up, she did so in the certainty that he

would rest in peace here, because it was one of those special places at the ends of the earth where no one ever came. She knew two of them already.

With one last look at the grave, she set off to climb down. Once again she followed the indentation in the rock until she reached the first huts on the base. Maybe she ought to set fire to the place, destroying the underground complex forever. But she didn't know where to begin, or whether it was worth the trouble.

Deep in thought, she went down the alley between the huts, past the new cross-country vehicle that Apollonio had parked there. She had not closed any doors behind her when she left the underground complex with Nathaniel. Why bother? There were no keys around, and the doors couldn't be bolted. But when she came out into the small square, she wished she had thought of some way to secure them.

Sigismondis was there, looking at her, and holding a stuffed fox in his arms.

Tangled strands of white hair fell to his shoulders. Half the buttons were missing from his dirty lab coat, and syringes stuck out of its pockets. He was supporting himself on an ax with a long handle painted red, acting as a walking stick. Her imagination conjured up the rhythmic clatter it must have made as he climbed up step by step, as if the echo of those sounds was only now coming up to them.

First Pantaleone. Then Trevini. Now him. Three old men who had influenced Rosa's life. Two of them were dead, and she knew now that the dying wasn't over yet.

Suddenly Sigismondis smiled and let go of the handle of the ax. Then he stroked the coat of the fox in his arms and whispered something to the stuffed animal. He reminded Rosa of all the odd old people she used to see as a child when she fed the pigeons in the park, men and women who talked to birds and animals because their links with the rest of mankind had been broken.

Was there anything left to say? The sight of him filled her with vague sorrow, and that was worse than rage. She could manage anger, she had lived with it so long, it had so often been what drove her—but melancholy caught her off guard.

Sigismondis patted the fox's head, then crouched down and put it carefully on the ground. *Off you go.* His lips soundlessly framed the words. He gently gave it a little nudge. When the animal didn't move the old man patted the fur on its chest and whispered, "You're free now, little one."

He straightened up and reached for the ax.

Rosa heard a metallic sound to her right, in the next alley between the huts. She knew what it was, although from here she couldn't see whoever it was who had just loaded a gun.

"No," she said quietly, and repeated it in a louder voice.

Sigismondis ignored her. Supported by the wooden handle of the ax, he took a step forward, toward Rosa, and raised the ax a little way from the ground, using it to support himself.

"He's not going to—" she called, not sure why she was trying to protect him.

The gunshot tore the words from her lips.

The old man's head jerked backward, thrown that way by

the force of the impact. For an endless second he stood there as if frozen in midmovement, with his skull sticking out behind at the wrong angle. Then he fell on his back in the dust and lay there beside the fox. Its dark glass eyes stared at him, while the syringes fell out of his pockets, and finally the ax also fell, as if in slow motion.

A slim figure not much taller than Rosa, and wearing a dark leather jacket, emerged between the buildings. In the sunlight, the skin of her face looked like coarse sandpaper.

"Mirella?" whispered Rosa.

The hybrid went over to the body of the old man and kicked him in the side. He did not move. Satisfied, she stood over him and watched a dark puddle forming around his head.

Rosa heard something rustling behind her, in the alleyway behind the car. She was about to turn around, shifting shape at the same time, when she felt a sharp pain between her shoulder blades. She staggered as she turned and fell to the ground, hoping that she would turn into the snake anyway, but at the same time she sensed that that wasn't going to happen. Her vision blurred. She put a shaking hand over her shoulder to feel for whatever had struck her. Something was certainly there, but she couldn't get at it.

Danai Thanassis clambered up on the BMW from behind and sat on its roof, like a spider the size of a human being. Her hooped skirt had slipped, and Rosa thought she caught a glimpse of the brown, horny scorpion's legs that the Arachnid hid under it. She was holding a heavy pistol in one hand.

Was she smiling? Rosa was too dazed to be sure.

"Where's Alessandro?" It was only a croak, and no one answered her. "What have you—"

Her head slumped powerlessly to the ground. She saw the blue sky above her, then a face coming into her field of vision from behind.

"She's still awake," said Mirella.

Danai replied, saying something that Rosa didn't understand.

The color blue was gradually superimposed on the features of the hybrids. Rosa opened her mouth. No sound came out.

Where is he? she thought vaguely.

Where is

Where

A jolt awoke her. Her head jerked up, fell back, and painfully struck something hard.

The earsplitting grinding and droning were drowned out by a metallic drumming. Flickering twilight surrounded her, sometimes bright, then gloomy again.

She was lying on the floor of a small van. Daylight fell in a strobe effect through the gaps in a tarpaulin fastened over it.

Her arms and legs were bound, not only at the joints but to each other and her body. She was lying on her back, right beside a wheel. Small pebbles thrown up by the tires hit the metal housing of the wheel arch, causing the infernal noise. The van was driving over rough terrain, bumping through potholes. Her body felt as if it had been beaten, but that could be just because she had been jolted around, heaven knew for how long.

Cautiously, she raised her head, looked down at herself and then aside.

And there he lay. Warmth exploded in her breast. She felt as if she might go up in flames.

"Alessandro!"

Like her, he had a plastic cord wrapped tightly around him. There was sand in his dark hair. He, too, lay on his back. His eyes were closed, his face strained.

"Alessandro?"

He moved, but only because of the jolts underneath him as the van shook on the bumpy road.

She desperately tried to get closer to him. She had to bend her arm in the cords tying her up and spread her fingers to reach his hand. It was like an electric current when their fingertips finally touched.

"He's out like a light," said a female voice above the noise. "He has a triple dose of anesthetic in his blood, as well as a large amount of serum. He was rather difficult, lashing out as long as he could, and after a while I'd had enough of it."

Only now did Rosa register the fact that there was a broad opening between where they were and the driver's cab. She was lying with her feet pointing the way they were going. Danai, her beautiful doll-like face reddened by stress, was looking at her over the back of the seat. With all those legs, she couldn't sit on it comfortably.

The hybrid was holding up something with a distant

resemblance to a dart. She must have shot one like it from her pistol into Rosa's back. "A combination of an anesthetic and TABULA serum," she said, picking up a syringe in her other hand. "Until we reach our journey's end you'll both be getting a dose of it every fifteen minutes. I'm afraid you have quite a severe reaction to the injection on your lower leg. It's probably itching badly."

Rosa could feel it, but she had other problems.

"Don't look at me like that," said the hybrid. "He's only unconscious. It would be a shame to lose him."

Rosa's fingers were still on his, and the warmth inside her was as strong as ever. It had nothing to do with shape-shifting. Only with him. Ultimately everything had to do with him: What she said, what she thought, what she felt. Even her hatred of Danai came more from her fear for him than for herself.

"How did you find me?" she asked hoarsely.

Danai pointed to the sky and an invisible satellite, then she picked up a laptop from the seat beside her. "We never lost sight of you. The boat, the church, your visit to the experimental station. We were with you the whole time."

"Where are we headed?"

"Can't you guess?"

"You're really going to hand us over to him?" exclaimed Rosa. "To the Hungry Man? Maybe you can kill him, but with all the dynasties you'll never—"

Danai interrupted her. "You can leave that to me."

Rosa raised her head again and tried to see who else was

in the van. Danai was alone on the backseat, but Mirella sat at the wheel.

"Are you two going to get rid of him on your own?" Rosa cast Danai a furious glance. "What a great plan!"

"You don't understand."

"He won't—"

"For God's sake, Rosa!" Danai interrupted her, and the stress marks were a brighter red than ever. "No one has any intention of killing the Hungry Man."

Rosa closed her mouth and stared at her.

"It would never have worked," said the hybrid. "My father was an embittered old man who didn't understand that there's no way we could win. He always did see everything in black and white; we were the good ones, the Arcadians and TABULA the bad ones. Think about it for a moment, and you'll agree that it was downright ridiculous."

"Your father . . . *was*?" asked Rosa.

Danai avoided her eyes, hesitated briefly, then turned away and looked at the windshield.

"What happened?" Rosa braced herself against her bonds in vain. "Come on, tell me."

Fingers clasped hers. Cool fingers. His fingers. She almost bit her tongue, she was so relieved.

"They're dead," he whispered, barely audible through all the noise.

"How are you?" she asked quietly, while she felt a sensation like a rubber ball bouncing up and down inside her.

"They blew up the ship," he whispered, still not fully

conscious, almost as if he were talking in his sleep. "Danai and Mirella . . . they blew the *Stabat Mater* sky-high."

Rosa's glance went from him to the head of the young woman on the backseat, and the piled dark hair from which some strands had come loose and were falling to her shoulders. She didn't seem to have noticed yet that Alessandro was coming back to his senses.

The news bulletin. The helicopter flying over the sea. The black smoke on the horizon.

"The ship." Alessandro groaned. Only now did he open his eyes. His lids were fluttering, but the green under them glowed. "They set off explosives to sink it . . . they must have been planning it for a long time. The ship was mined from stem to stern."

"But that makes no sense." Rosa could hardly hear her own voice above the infernal noise on the payload area of the van. "Danai was—"

"Danai is a traitor." His voice was getting a little stronger. "She got in touch with the Hungry Man . . . he's promised to take her in, make her a full member of the dynasties. Who knows what else . . . no more games of hide-and-seek, no running away, no more secret war against TABULA. She didn't want to live the life of an outcast. Her father didn't understand that. She saw herself as an Arcadian, while he was only a man."

Rosa's eyes wandered from him to Danai and back again. "He trusted her," she whispered.

But couldn't she have guessed it? She had seen Danai in

New York, in Michele Carnevare's club. *Anyone who comes to the Dream Room sees things you don't see anywhere else,* he had said. The eyes of predators in the shadows of a private box. Transformations after midnight. Danai went to the Arcadians willingly; she felt at home with them. She wanted to be like them.

"She and Mirella took me off the ship in secret last night," he said, "after they'd found the location of Lycaon's tomb in Mori's papers. They needed something to get the Hungry Man to take them seriously. They wanted to impress him with what they knew. And then, at a safe distance, they set off the explosives by remote control. I saw it, Rosa . . . the explosions on all the decks, the fire . . . burning hybrids jumping overboard. A few of the amphibians may have survived, but the rest . . ."

She wanted to clutch his hand in her fingers, but she couldn't get close enough. She was being jolted violently about again. Only their eyes lingered on each other.

She wanted to kiss him so badly.

She had never wasted a thought on what it would be like to be on the way to her own wedding.

Now she knew.

A ROYAL TOMB

THE VAN WAS SPEEDING downhill around sharp turns. The light in the cracks of the tarpaulin had turned red; evening was coming. A strong gust of wind struck the side of the van, making the tarpaulin billow in as the vehicle lurched along the road.

They stopped once, briefly. Mirella spoke to someone outside the window. The tarpaulin was opened a little way; a man looked in, nodded, and let them go on.

The sharp turns were followed by a long stretch of straight road. The surface had been better for some time, and they were now driving over level asphalt. It was only the wind that gave Mirella trouble, and she had to steer sharply against the gusts several times.

Even before the hybrid brought the van to a halt, Rosa knew where they were. Mirella got out, went around to the back, and opened the tarpaulin. Although the sun was setting, Rosa was dazzled by the brightness after the dim light in the back of the van. There were several figures standing behind Mirella.

Danai's hooped skirt rustled as she pushed herself off the backseat and out into the open. A few minutes ago she had given them more injections in the lower leg. The itch was becoming a painful stinging and burning.

"Get them out," someone said.

Men in expensive suits climbed up into the back of the van and unloaded Rosa and Alessandro like packages. They were laid down on warm asphalt; the sun had been shining on it not so long ago. Now it was half a fiery globe above rising ground, bathing the sky in streaks of violet and red.

There were parapets to the right and left of the two-lane road. Beyond them lay the abyss where the lake had been, and mountains could be seen again only very far away. The wind blew keenly through the wire netting between the struts, pressing the men's suits close to their bodies.

The Giuliana dam.

The road was a gray concrete bridge on the dam wall, more than a hundred and fifty yards above the valley floor. The van had stopped in the middle of this bridge. It was at least three hundred yards in both directions to the end of it, much too far for running away—even if their legs had not been tightly bound for hours on end. As it was, they'd probably find it difficult to stay on their feet.

Rosa had assumed that they would be taken straight to the ruins of the village. The water dammed up in the lake had been drained, Alessandro had said. If the tomb of Lycaon was really here, as Mori's papers seemed to show, then it must be exposed now. She was expecting some kind of archaic vault, pillared chambers with dusty reliefs on the walls. According to legend, the tomb was an architectural work of breathtaking size, and it had taken the labor of a whole nation decades to build it. As Rosa imagined it, whatever was left of it must rival the tombs of the pharaohs in the Valley of the Kings, and the jungle pyramids of the Mayans.

Rosa could see that Alessandro had to struggle against the aftereffects of unconsciousness. She felt the same, even though the anesthetic had worn off. Maybe it was the sheer amount of the hybrid serum that Danai had injected into them.

The men had laid her down on her side. When she tried to loosen her tight bonds, Danai stepped into her field of vision.

"Stop that." Thanassis's daughter seemed nervous.

"You're trembling," said Rosa. "A poor performance for a murderess of your caliber."

Danai did not reply. Instead, Mirella's foot landed in Rosa's side. The kick took her breath away for several moments as she gasped for air like someone drowning.

There was a wolf-like growl, and then quiet words in a tone that brooked no dissent. "Get away from her, snake!"

"Do as he says, Mirella," Danai told the hybrid.

Even doubled up and in pain all over her upper body, Rosa felt some satisfaction as Mirella hastily took a couple of steps back.

The man who had spoken was behind her, somewhere near the van, and now she heard his footsteps on the road. But she was lying with her face to Alessandro and would never willingly have turned away from him.

His eyes narrowed as he looked over her and up at the newcomer. Hatred blazed in his glance.

"The serum?" asked the voice behind her.

Danai, whose wide skirt was blown close to her circle of angular legs by the wind, sketched a bow. "I've been giving it to them every fifteen minutes, the last time just now. They can't change shape."

"Undo their bonds except for their hands. And then stand them on their feet. This is unworthy of them."

Rosa had recognized the voice at once, although it now sounded clearer, and was no longer distorted by the intercom in prison. She had not been able to see his face there; a pane of mirrored glass had separated them.

The men rolled her and Alessandro over. Someone cut the cords tying them up and then pulled the cords out from under their bodies. The bonds around their hands stayed, but their legs were free. The cord had bitten deep into her skin.

One of the men pulled Rosa to her feet, and just as she had expected, her knees gave way again at once. She could feel nothing from her hips down; even the tingling was gone. Like the sting of the injections in her lower leg.

The man who had put her on her feet was holding her under the armpits from behind, as if she were a puppet. Two men grabbed Alessandro, who stared at them grimly, as if he would go for their throats with nothing but his teeth. She was turned around, and now stood beside him.

The sunset behind their backs bathed everything in fiery red; the sunglasses of the men and women assembled on the road, their faces, gleaming with expectation, even the men's black suits and the expensive skirt suits worn by the women looked as if they had been dipped in blood. There were forty or fifty of them. Rosa knew many by sight, among them two of her distant cousins from Milan—undoubtedly they were the ones who had pulled the strings of the plot against her. Rosa thought it only appropriate that she couldn't even remember their names. They were sisters, granddaughters of Costanza's cousin. And Lamias, of course.

The Hungry Man was not standing directly behind her, as she had thought until now, but some way off. More evidence of the power of his voice. There was something incantatory, intoxicating about it, and now that she could see him she understood why some of the Arcadians took him for the real Lycaon, not the cunning, manipulative imitator that he really was.

"Welcome." He stepped out of the shadow of the van and came slowly toward Alessandro and Rosa. "I regret that you have been mistreated." There was a pale glint in his eyes, the look of a wolf at night; he glanced at Mirella, who was standing a little way to one side, and she shrank nervously. Danai moved a step away from her ally, as if afraid that the stigma might rub off on her.

The Hungry Man—whose real name was not forgotten, although it had been of no importance for a long time—had scarcely changed since the only photograph of him had been taken. At that time he had looked like a cross between Jesus of Nazareth and the leader of a student revolt. He still wore his hair down to his shoulders, and his full beard was neatly trimmed. He had already gone gray at the temples in the photograph, taken at the time of his arrest thirty years ago.

She would have thought he was in his late forties rather than almost seventy. It was as if his prison cell had preserved his body.

She had expected a raving madman, a kind of high priest in flowing robes. She had been very much mistaken, which showed that the reality of the Arcadian dynasties was still alien to her.

He wore a black pinstriped suit, a white shirt with a silk tie, and a knee-length coat. If it hadn't been for the long hair, he might have been mistaken for a businessman about to launch into a PowerPoint presentation.

He gave Rosa an almost courteous smile. Then he went to Alessandro, who reared up in the grip of his guards and bared his teeth.

"So you are young Carnevare. We have not had the pleasure of meeting before."

"Correct," said Alessandro. "We have a lot to catch up on." And with that, he thrust his head forward with all his might, trying to tear free from the men and snapping at his adversary's throat, like a predator who had forgotten that he was imprisoned in a human body.

For a moment the Hungry Man was taken by surprise and had to step back. He was in no serious danger, but it could not have escaped anyone's notice that the attack had caught him unawares.

Rosa ought to have feared for Alessandro, but she felt only pride, and her own readiness to die with him.

Mirella, standing a few yards away, let out a serpentine hiss at Alessandro. Rosa thought the hybrid had never looked so reptilian before, with her pocked skin in the red light of sunset, the blazing fury in her eyes, and the tension in her body.

The growl of a very old, very angry wolf came from the throat of the Hungry Man. He spun around, and even as he moved forward his features altered. His head changed shape in the blink of an eye, while his body remained human, as if he did not want to ruin his suit.

Maybe Mirella saw him coming, but if so it was the last thing she ever saw. His jaws snapped and severed her neck with a single bite. A jet of blood splattered him while the hybrid was still standing upright. His hands seized her upper arms and flung her against the parapet with great force. She fell back, lifeless, and disappeared into the depths below. The abyss swallowed up even the sound of her impact on the valley floor.

The Hungry Man turned around and was instantly human again. His mouth was smeared with blood, even more so his white shirt, but he ignored both, smiled again, and went over to Danai. She seemed uneasy beneath his gaze, and her legs moved up and down under her hooped skirt.

"She was no part of our agreement," the Hungry Man told her, very calm again, very matter-of-fact.

"I needed her help," began Danai in a small voice, "but I'm sorry if—"

"Hush," he said softly, licked the blood from his lips, and gently touched Danai's cheek with his fingertips. "You are one of us now, Danai Thanassis. Go over to your new brothers and sisters."

He made an inviting gesture in the direction of a group of men and women standing on the edge of the crowd, outsiders even among their own kind. Representatives of the Arachnida dynasty.

Hesitantly, Danai stepped forward. She seemed to be expecting an attack from the Hungry Man with every move she made. But he let her pass and watched until she had reached the Arachnida. She would certainly not have expected her acceptance into the clan to be so unceremonious and unwelcoming. If this was her reward for betraying the hybrids, it might be dawning on her that the deal had not been as good as she had hoped. The others looked at her with dislike, particularly for her hooped skirt. But before they could express their disapproval, the Hungry Man set them straight.

"Danai Thanassis is one of you now," he said sharply, "and you will treat her like a true daughter of your clan."

The oldest Arachnid, a white-haired, spindly, thin old man with a high forehead and tiny eyes, bowed to the Hungry Man, then went up to Danai, took her hand as if he had just invited her to dance with him, and offered her a place at his side. Some of the other Arachnida flinched away, but their clan leader let out a hiss that sounded like spitting, not like words or animal noises.

Rosa fought against the grip of the man guarding her. She was getting some feeling back in her limbs, but she couldn't even contemplate running away, particularly as she could see roadblocks at both ends of the bridge over the dam. They had just passed one of them in the van. The parked cars of the *capi* also stood there.

"You're all falling for a farce," cried Alessandro, in a voice loud enough for everyone to hear. "A dusty old ritual that means nothing today. It's not going to bring old Arcadia back. This is the twenty-first century. Our families have had enough to do maintaining the influence of Cosa Nostra for the last hundred years. And now you want to revive something that ended thousands of years ago?"

His words were carefully chosen and meant as much for the heads of the clans as for the Hungry Man. All eyes were turned to him, and he seemed to know that this would be his only chance to address them all. One of the men holding him made a move as if to silence him, but the Hungry Man shook his head.

"Alessandro Carnevare is a highborn member of the Panthera," he said. Mirella's blood gleamed like war paint on his face. "Let him speak openly."

Alessandro shook off his guards. Swaying slightly, but staying on his feet through his own efforts, he stood with his back to the two men, who themselves were *capi* of two clans from Trapani. There were no mere henchmen at this place; everyone who had been invited to the renewal of the concordat either held a leading position, or was a close relative of the head of a family.

Now Alessandro seemed to be intentionally looking past the Hungry Man, as if he stood before the others as their equal, not someone who needed permission to speak. "We have all fought to maintain the values of Cosa Nostra and the honor of our one great family," he cried. "It is what rules our lives, our everyday occupations—all that means something to us—and not a handful of legends from a time of which we know nothing. Cosa Nostra has always distinguished itself by keeping up appearances to outsiders. That's what has made our families strong, that's why organizations all over the world envy us. Are you going to risk all this? And for what? What do you want to be in the future—men and women with large fortunes and the prospect of adding to them even more? Or a pack of wild beasts who sooner or later will be hunted down and killed? Our ancestors were burnt at the stake, crucified, tortured in the dungeons of the Inquisition. Is that what you want back? Sicily, Italy, Europe—they are no longer lands held by assorted barbarians as they were in the days of the real Lycaon." Here he looked at the Hungry Man again and added, "The *only* Lycaon."

Then, turning to the heads of the families again, he went on. "In those days it was easy for the Arcadians to hide behind popular superstition. Those like us were feared, and other people didn't have the courage to strike back with all their might. But now? If we behave like brute beasts again, how long will it be before there are attempts to eliminate us all? You all know how hard the law is coming down on our business deals. We've survived because we had something to offer our adversaries. Bribery and conspiracy have kept Cosa Nostra going. You've all brought your influence to bear on members of the government; you've invited judges and public prosecutors to your villas to keep them on your side. But business deals like that, however illegal, are not the same as mass murder. Do you really want to hunt like predators again, tearing ordinary humans to pieces? How are you going to keep that secret? And how are you going to make friends of our enemies? They may let you buy their silence as long as it's all about real estate, or arms deals, or drugs. But they'll turn on you if you hunt down their children outside their schools and shed blood in the streets. How are you going to pacify them then? With a chunk of raw meat on their plates?"

Some uneasiness was aroused in the assembled ranks of the Arcadians, but no one was saying anything against the Hungry Man yet, let alone rejecting his proposals.

The old Arachnid beside who Danai, looking lost and uncertain of herself, was still standing, slowly shook his head. "Fine words, my boy. But only words, that's all. Arcadia didn't fall because our ancestors were afraid of bureaucrats. Arcadia was the victim of megalomania on the part of the Panthera and the Lamias—and because they tried to outdo each other."

He earned disapproval for that from the Carnevare and Alcantara camps—all those who had handed Rosa and Alessandro over to die.

The Arachnid made a dismissive gesture. "In the old days, anyway, the Arcadians brought peace, and that's why we're here. To renew our alliance and show the Hungry Man our respect. The new Arcadia will combine the best of both epochs, the determination of Lycaon and the power of the united dynasties. And so I say, the sacrifice goes forward. If Cosa Nostra is going to survive, it must draw on the power of

Arcadia. All will come full circle for a new beginning."

"And you say that *I* speak empty words?" Alessandro glared belligerently at him. He had finally overcome the side effects of the anesthetic. "Haven't you understood anything?"

Attacking them head-on like that was a mistake. Rosa knew it, and so certainly did he. The Hungry Man's smile showed that this was the moment he had been waiting for. He had never met Alessandro, but he must have heard of him. Of his skill with words—and his weakness, which was to press on too fast and overshoot his target.

Alessandro was not to be deterred. "You want to renew the concordat beside Lycaon's tomb. But instead we're standing up here. Nothing from those ancient times still exists, not even a heap of stones. Arcadia has fallen to dust." He was playing a game of Russian roulette, and it could go wrong. But they had nothing left to lose.

The Hungry Man signaled to the guards behind Rosa and Alessandro and, before they could resist, syringes plunged into their arms again. Then the reincarnated Lycaon went up to the parapet and beckoned them over to him.

"Come with me."

Rosa and Alessandro exchanged a glance, then followed him. Their guards stayed close behind, but did not touch them again.

The rail over the parapet was cold when Rosa placed both hands on it. She felt dizzy, perhaps because of the overdose of serum. Looking down into the abyss made it even worse.

They were a hundred and fifty yards above the rock of the valley floor. Rosa had been here once before, with Zoe, almost five months ago. Then, the glittering surface of the lake had stretched away beneath them to the steep mountain slopes. Today, there was only a channel of water trickling along a winding path through a desert of dark stone. The sun had now disappeared behind the crest of the hills. Darkness seemed to rise from the crevices in the rock.

The ruins of the village of Giuliana lay at the foot of the huge wall of the dam. It crouched in the shadow of that concrete wall, a collection of low-built houses. A few roofs had fallen in under the pressure of the water, but many were still intact. Roads and paths could be made out, and a few metal skeletons of tractors and other agricultural machinery that had been left behind. From up here it all looked pitch-black, as if the whole valley were covered with tar. A smell like dead fish wafted up from the abyss.

"My father drowned this valley so that no one could misuse the tomb for the purposes of a new concordat," said Alessandro quietly, as if proving that not all the baron did had been bad. Rosa felt for the parapet with her hand.

The Hungry Man looked away from the derelict buildings in the valley and glanced sideways at them. "Is that what you really think? That he and Cesare built the dam for that purpose?" He sounded almost pitying.

Alessandro took his tone of voice as condescension. "What other reason would they have had?"

Rosa had to lean a little way out over the abyss to look past Alessandro at the Hungry Man.

"You're right about one thing," said the new leader of the dynasties. "The ruins of ancient Arcadia have fallen into dust.

Lycaon's mausoleum, in its time the greatest work of architecture in the kingdom, perhaps in the whole world, who knows? Lycaon's tomb is only a memory. But memories can be refreshed. Even the greatest architecture can be rebuilt on the ruins of the past. And if you are going to erect something so large, then it must be done in public these days. That's why it was necessary to make it seem like the monument was something else. Just as large, just as massive as before. A monument to the honor of fallen Arcadia, but one that only those who know the secret will recognize for what it is."

Alessandro's eyes narrowed. "That's a lie."

"You thought that dam was built to hide Giuliana from me? Until recently I thought so too. But the truth is that your father and Cesare built it with an eye toward seizing power for themselves someday. This dam is an altar. The altar on which the sacrifice sealing the new concordat will be made. It's a stage. A masquerade, like everything behind which the inheritance of Arcadia has had to hide too long. At this place, in this valley, the old Arcadians built the tomb of their king, and Leonardo Mori rediscovered it. He did it for me, but your father and his advisers had him murdered and took part of the results of his research for themselves. And they built a second shrine, to unite the dynasties there one day."

The Hungry Man stepped back from the parapet. Rosa did not turn to him, but when he spoke she could hear that he was smiling.

"That day has come," he said, "and with it the king of you all."

THE CEREMONY

T𝚆ILIGHT WAS RISING TO the top of the dam. Night would fall entirely in an hour's time, but the abyss was already filling with darkness.

On the asphalt of the bridge, a semicircle of lights had been turned on: phosphorus lamps casting their icy white illumination over the road. The representatives of the dynasties were waiting outside the semicircle. The van had been moved and parked fifty yards away, at the side of the roadway beside a square, block-shaped concrete structure, an entrance allowing technicians who would never service this dam now to climb down to it.

At the center of the semicircle of lights and figures, not far from the parapet, Rosa and Alessandro stood facing each other, their hands still bound. The Hungry Man was performing their marriage ceremony.

Just before it began they had been given another injection, in the upper arm again. Rosa's shoulder was now stinging almost as much as her leg. Danai, who was responsible for the inflammation, had disappeared among the other Arachnida. The men and women were standing a little way outside the lights. Their faces were lit from below and looked pale as bleached bone above their black clothing. Many were twitching as if they had to fight off the urge to shift shape.

Two guards each stood behind Rosa and Alessandro, with full syringes and pistols with the safety catches off. Rosa had given up resisting for now. Alessandro had made one last attempt before the ceremony began, but the superior strength of his opponents had made it useless. As long as they couldn't shift shape, their chances were zero.

However, there was one thing that Rosa could still do. She was saving her strength for the moment when she would be ordered to kill Alessandro. They might threaten her, but what threat could you use on someone facing certain death? They could add to the pain she suffered, but she would bear that. Not for the world would she do anything to hurt him. Ever.

While the Hungry Man was reciting something that might be an old traditional poem or just a few lines that he had thought up in prison, her eyes were firmly fixed on Alessandro's. Wait, choose the right moment. It hadn't come yet. They were still only standing there, bride and bridegroom, while the Hungry Man's sermon washed over them.

Fear rose within Rosa. Sometimes she missed a heartbeat and could hardly breathe because her throat felt so tight. But she hid that as well as she could, and suppressed any trembling.

"There's something I have to say to you," she whispered.

There was a smile in his eyes, as if to say: *Well, this is our best chance.*

The Hungry Man went on talking. Rosa wasn't listening; it was only a meaningless rushing of syllables in the background.

She tried to find the right words, but there weren't any. She could only say as she felt, even if it sounded clumsy or silly. What she did *not* say was: *I love you*. He'd known that for a long time.

Instead, she whispered, "We did everything that mattered right. From the very first moment."

He nodded. "Yes, every time."

"It was right for you to speak to me on the flight. And give me the book, *Aesop's Fables*. It was right for us to drive to the end of the world, and for you to tell me it wasn't really an end because the world goes on beyond it, on the other side of the abyss. It was right for us to dive together in the Strait of Messina and look for the statues. And for you to teach me to listen to the animals in that zoo near Etna. All of it, all of it was right."

Their surroundings might have been blotted out: the Hungry Man's voice, their armed guards, the silhouettes of the other Arcadians.

Their hands were bound in front of them. Rosa put out her arms, and he his, and they linked their fingers together as if this were their own very private ceremony, a moment that existed only for the two of them.

A last red glow lay over the rugged outlines of the mountains. The moon was shining brightly in the sky. In its light, the Hungry Man produced a silver blade from under his coat and raised it in the air. It was more of a large scalpel than a sacrificial dagger.

A distant humming sound was heard, as if a generator had

been switched on in the depths of the dam.

The Hungry Man gave a sign to the guards, and two of them stepped forward. Rosa was expecting the prick of another needle, but it did not come. Instead, she felt the muzzle of a pistol held to her back.

"If you think—" she began, but the Hungry Man signaled to her to keep quiet. She obeyed only because the expression on his face had changed. He looked uneasy.

Alessandro took a deep breath and tensed his upper body. There was murmuring among the Arcadians outside the semicircle of lights, a whispering that the Hungry Man silenced with a gesture. Everyone was now staring at something going on behind Rosa.

She slowly turned her head, and when no one stopped her, turned around and looked in the same direction as everyone else. For a moment the muzzle of the pistol was withdrawn, but in the next moment she felt it again, in her side this time.

Something was happening at the end of the wall of the dam, near the roadblock. A few scraps of words were blown toward them, and the sound of an engine.

The assembled Arcadians were asking questions now, a collective *what's-going-on*, murmured so softly that the words could not be made out, only the tone of voice. There was alarm in some of that whispering; in other Arcadians a hunting instinct seemed to be aroused. An acrid animal odor wafted over the asphalt of the road.

Rosa could still see nothing clearly, what with the dazzlingly bright lamps, and the Arcadians blocking her view.

A cell phone rang. And then another.

At the same time the humming noise was heard again, and this time it went on, a constant undertone in the background.

The ringtones stopped when the phone calls were answered. Rosa heard agitated whispering, quickly drowned out by the swelling sound of approaching engines.

"They've surrendered the roadblocks," called someone outside the semicircle of lights.

The Hungry Man moved to the edge of it. "Surrendered them?"

Rosa's guard pressed the pistol even more firmly into the tender spot below her ribs. But she was under such strain anyway that she wouldn't have felt even the pain from the stab of a knife.

"What does this mean?" asked the Hungry Man, with a calm that sounded more dangerous than any outburst of fury. "What's the matter with the men posted there?"

"They've abandoned the barriers," replied someone. "At both ends of the dam."

Rosa looked around at Alessandro and whispered, "If it was the police we'd have heard shooting, wouldn't we?"

Frowning, he nodded. The man threatening him with his gun gave him a push. Alessandro took a step forward, which brought him closer to Rosa.

"They're saying people from the media have turned up," said one of the Arcadians who had answered a phone call.

"That's impossible," cried another. "No one knew—"

"This means treachery," said someone. "But which of us—"

And then they were all talking at once, until the Hungry Man ordered silence in a sharp voice. "Treachery is a possibility," he said. "But there's a way to deal with it. What are a few journalists? Tell the guards to kill them."

"It's not as simple as that," said the old Arachnid, the first to summon up the courage to object. "A great deal has changed in the last few decades, as we've all had to learn. The death of journalists would attract more attention than one murdered judge. The media network—"

"I don't want to hear any more of this nonsense," the Hungry Man interrupted him. "Shoot them."

Rosa was watching her guard out of the corner of her eye. His glance went from the Hungry Man to the solitary vehicle driving toward them over the dam. It was a small white car, seeming lost on the long, empty road. That was not what a special anti-Mafia commando unit looked like.

The engine noise came closer, too, filling the valley from the north. A helicopter flying through the dark without lights.

Someone let out a shrill screech. Looking around, Rosa saw a woman shifting shape. Her dress and coat tore into strips of black fabric. In the bright light of the phosphorous lamps, she became a bird the size of a human being, rose from the ground, and soared into the air, her plumage rustling. A second Harpy beside her looked at the Hungry Man with trepidation, and then she too shifted her shape. At first Rosa thought they were going to attack the helicopter together, but they both turned east, followed the course of the dam for a while, and then flew away toward the mountains.

Several of the others were moving about restlessly, but the

Hungry Man was not to be intimidated. He had first become *capo dei capi* at a time when few in Sicily dared to oppose the power of the Mafia. A handful of journalists were not going to scare him.

He put the knife away and walked up to a man who Rosa recognized as a member of Alessandro's family. "Your gun," he said.

Alessandro's Panthera cousin took out a pistol and handed it to him.

"No one move," said the Hungry Man, as he loaded the gun and put it in his coat pocket.

The small white car braked and rolled slowly up to the semicircle of Arcadians. Rosa saw burning eyes and bared teeth, but no more metamorphoses.

Five more vehicles followed the car at a considerable distance, two of them minibuses with the logos of TV stations on their sides. When Rosa looked back, past Alessandro, she saw that floodlights had appeared at the other end of the dam. The guards would have engaged in a gunfight with the police, but the idea of seeing their own faces on TV in connection with a Mafia assembly would strike panic into them. Most of them had probably shifted into animal shape and run away.

The Lamias, Rosa's distant cousins, left their positions behind the lights and moved back to the parapet. In snake form they had a better chance than anyone, apart from the Harpies, of disappearing unnoticed.

Several Arcadians stepped aside as the white car stopped. The Hungry Man looked at it, both hands in his coat pockets.

The sound of the helicopter was very close now, but while its lights remained switched off it couldn't be made out in the dark. It had to be flying very low over the valley floor.

The driver's door of the little car swung open. A pair of sneakers appeared between the door and the ground, followed by the rubber ends of two crutches.

"They'll take him apart," said Alessandro.

Are you two from the media as well? the hotel receptionist had asked. *There's been a lot of coming and going.*

Fundling's head came into view above the side window as he stood up, leaning on his crutches. He had come by himself. Slowly, he went around the car door and approached. He still looked lanky and a little awkward, as Rosa had thought when she first met him. He wore a stained old T-shirt and jeans too large for him. His wild dark hair had grown back since the doctors had removed the bullet from his skull.

When they met, he had seemed to Rosa rather strange—today she was convinced that he had lost it. Never mind what offer from the media had gotten him on his own feet again, he couldn't survive this intact. The Hungry Man might not have all his old influence as head of the Arcadian dynasties back yet, but the fact that he had succeeded in assembling the *capi* of all the clans in this place left little doubt that he was extremely powerful.

Aside from having a pistol in his coat pocket.

Fundling's eyes rested on Rosa and Alessandro. He gave them a fleeting smile. Then he turned to the assembled clan leaders.

"I am the son of Leonardo Mori," he said in a voice loud enough to be heard above the invisible helicopter. "A few of you know me"—he nodded to the Carnevare delegation—"and some of you know what part my father played in all that's been going on here. It was he who found the site of Lycaon's tomb. If not for him you wouldn't be here today."

The Hungry Man took a couple of steps toward Fundling, and then they both stopped, only an arm's length apart. "Your father was a man of great merit, boy. That's the only reason you're still alive. Call off your friends and get out of here. Nothing catastrophic has happened yet."

Fundling indicated Rosa and Alessandro. "I'll be taking these two with me."

"I do not," said his adversary with a smile, "think that you will."

The obvious superiority of the Hungry Man was rubbing off on some of his loyal followers. First a handful, then more and more of them came past the phosphorus lamps and approached Fundling. In their dark clothes and long coats, they still looked like bank managers.

"Listen to me!" Fundling raised one hand, and the vehicles coming closer from both sides of the dam stopped. "I know what you're planning to do. I'm here to appeal to your common sense." He spoke better than he used to; he was more articulate and self-confident. Maybe the wound had straightened out something inside his head. "When the Carnevares killed my father, not all his papers fell into their hands. He had long ago evaluated the information in some of them, and his conclusions were hidden in a safe place." Fundling never took his eyes off the Hungry Man, although he was speaking to everyone present. "I've read most of them. And basically it comes down to something very simple: If you carry on with this ceremony, if you seal a new concordat with a wedding and a sacrifice, then you're all as good as dead."

A murmur of mockery ran through the ranks of the Arcadians.

"And that's what you have to say to us?" asked the Hungry Man. "You say we'd better do as you ask, because otherwise we'll . . . what? We'll all perish?"

Fundling did not move a muscle. "Yes, that's right."

"The one who won't survive this evening is you, my boy."

"Arcadia has already fallen once," replied Fundling. "And you'll fall yourselves if you don't stop stomping the will of the gods underfoot."

"The *gods*?" cried the head of the Arachnida. "We are not fools, young Mori. If you hope to intimidate us with tales of gods and spirits and—let me guess—the gaps in the crowd, you have a mammoth task ahead of you. I knew your father. I know what occupied his mind."

Fundling owed the fact that the Arcadians had not killed him by this time solely to the teams of journalists who were now on the bridge. No one here could say how many telephoto lenses were turned on the assembly, and none of the Arcadians now dared to show their true nature. However, their patience was visibly running out. Fundling was walking on thin ice.

"My father realized who the invisible beings are, and who

sent them. I don't need to try frightening you. *They* will do that very ably for themselves."

"That's enough!" cried a Hunding.

"Let's silence him," one of Rosa's cousins agreed, letting out a venomous hiss.

Several Arcadians took a few steps forward, passing Rosa, Alessandro, and the men guarding them. All at once the two of them were behind the agitated men and women. When Rosa sensed that the attention of the others was not on her anymore, she was able to take a deep breath again.

"You don't believe me?" asked Fundling, without retreating a fraction of an inch. "You really intend to deny the existence of the powers that destroyed the ancient bridge and brought down the kingdom of Arcadia?"

The Hungry Man let out a quiet laugh. It sounded almost pitying.

The corners of Fundling's mouth lifted. Then he said, very slowly, "And yet they have been present today, walking here among you."

Even Rosa could feel the ripple of cold that ran through the crowd. A kind of collective shudder from all the Arcadians that spread to her as well.

The Hungry Man opened his mouth to answer.

What he was going to say was lost in an infernal roar of noise.

For a moment Rosa thought that Fundling's prophecy was in fact being fulfilled. That the dam beneath them was breaking up, like the old bridge over the Strait of Messina in the distant past. That it was all really true.

The helicopter was rising from the depths below to the level of the parapet on the far side of the dam wall. Blazing searchlights flared on in the darkness, bathing the scene in artificial daylight. The stormy wind of the rotors caught them all, made the Arcadians' coat tails dance, blew in their hair and clothing, and flung the Lamias back from the parapet into the road.

For several long seconds, everyone was dazzled.

RUINS

THE HUNGRY MAN THREW back his head. Not even the noise from the helicopter could drown the wolf's howl that came from his throat.

The Arcadians scattered to escape the pitiless light. A cameraman sat in the open side door of the helicopter, taking pictures of the crowd. The chopper was hovering only a few yards away from the parapet, a little way above the road. The searchlights were attached to the fuselage of the helicopter, a whole battery of high-performance lamps flooding the asphalt with light over a large area.

This far out on the dam, there was nowhere to hide. Only the van in which Rosa and Alessandro had been transported offered any protection from the eyes of the cameras. A handful of men and women hurried toward it, many with their arms raised to their faces in a helpless attempt not to be recognized. By midday tomorrow at the latest, these pictures and their names would be on YouTube for anyone to see.

An army unit couldn't have spread such panic among them. Arrests were made every day, and highly paid attorneys had their clients freed pending trial within a few hours. Once, TV reports had been as fleeting as those arrests, but now they ran on the internet for all eternity. Live pictures exposed even the most powerful, destroying their reputations. It wasn't the prospect of arrest that deterred a *capo*—the warrant was hardly worth the paper it was written on—but no other Mafioso would ever work with someone who let himself be filmed at secret meetings.

This evening, however, far more was at stake. Fundling had undertaken to reveal something more sensational than the criminal machinations of wealthy businessmen. The cameramen and journalists would have been satisfied with that alone; what they now saw, however, must have far exceeded their expectations.

When the Hungry Man let out his howl, and the first Arcadians fled to the van, Danai and the Arachnida were in the beam of the searchlights. As their *capo* told her to keep calm, the stormy wind of the rotor blades blew under her wide-skirted dress. Its hem rose in the air, and the telephoto lens zoomed in on something more spectacular than criminals in flight from bad publicity.

The hybrid's insect legs shimmered in the searchlights, segmented monstrosities roused from their rigidity to frantic life. Danai scurried left, scurried right, but the camera followed her. The hybrid howled, not as much of an animal howl as the Hungry Man's, but the desperate weeping of a young woman who saw no way out of her predicament. She tried in panic to smooth the skirt down over her scorpion legs with her slender white hands, but the wind kept lifting it again.

The men guarding Rosa and Alessandro were not sure how to deal with the new situation. The Hungry Man was about to throw himself on Fundling and was taking no notice of his prisoners. The guards, however, were *capi* like everyone else here, and neither of them was ready to run any risks. They hesitated, exchanging glances. And Alessandro acted.

Moving with the speed of a cat, he rammed one of them in the larynx with his elbow. A shot rang out as the Mafioso collapsed, but it missed its mark. Alessandro hammered his bound fists into the man's side. His second guard came storming up from behind, as well as one of the two who had been guarding Rosa. Alessandro raced for the parapet, as if he were going to swing himself over it. His real goal, however, was to distract the men from Rosa.

Her last guard swung his pistol around to aim at Alessandro. That gave her a chance to hit him on the nape of his neck with her bound hands. The blow made him stumble forward, groaning. One of his legs gave way as if he were about to curtsey, and Rosa used the moment to kick him as hard as she could right between the shoulder blades. He slumped to the ground, tried to turn over, but she was there with him, stamping her heels down on his wrist with all her might. This time his bones broke and the gun skittered away from him. Rosa leaped out of his reach, grabbed the pistol, and aimed it, in one swift movement, at one of the two men trying to seize Alessandro.

Her bullet hit the man's shoulder, flung him against the parapet, and set off his metamorphosis at the same time. He must have been related to Alessandro, for in the next moment he was a lion, stumbling because of his injury, getting entangled in the remains of his clothes, and hesitating just a split second too long. Rosa's second shot killed him.

Her other guard was also about to draw his gun, but Alessandro leaped at him as if he were in panther and not human form, flinging him against the rail of the parapet with all his weight. The man's eyes widened as he saw his fate coming, then he tipped over the rail and backward at an almost leisurely pace. As he fell, he became something else, but Rosa saw only his human outline dissolving as he disappeared over the edge.

Alessandro ran to her, past his fellow Panthera, who was now a human corpse lying on the asphalt. There was utter chaos all around them.

Danai was still running around frantically, but she could not elude the light and the camera lens; both followed her pitilessly. The other Arachnida had hurried to the parapet, and now Rosa realized what they were planning to do.

While the cameraman in the helicopter concentrated on Danai, all four became gigantic spiders. Scraps of fabric stretched between their long legs and tore as they started moving. Some were hairy while others had smooth, armored bodies. Even in animal form the old man was gray and dry—a huge daddy longlegs.

The four came racing toward Rosa and Alessandro, but they didn't attack. Instead, they stalked past them and climbed over the rail of the parapet with the spindly movements of large stick puppets. Rosa went to the parapet, both repelled and fascinated, and saw the Arachnida find footholds on the steep concrete wall below. They let themselves run nimbly down the old dam to the depths.

Danai screamed again, furious and deeply insulted to be left behind by her new family. She, too, stormed past Rosa and Alessandro on her scorpion limbs, climbed clumsily over the wire netting between the struts, and felt with her front pairs of legs for irregularities in the concrete. Blind with panic and her injured feelings, she decided to risk it. She hauled herself over the parapet to follow her brothers and sisters.

Rosa held her breath as she watched, and for a few seconds it really did look as if Danai could make it. But then her legs lost contact with the wall, a screeching wail came from her lips, and she fell and hit the ground somewhere in the dark.

While all this was going on, Fundling had retreated. The convoy of press vehicles was approaching fast behind him. The Hungry Man looked from him to his own followers in flight, and the few of them who had stayed at his side. He still had not drawn his gun, probably knowing what would happen if the *capo dei capi*, so recently released from prison, was seen with a pistol in his hand on TV news. Not even his allies in Rome would be able to save him again.

At the same time, it must be clear to him that his plan had failed. Once again he turned his attention to Fundling. From under his coat he took the knife with which Rosa had been supposed to kill Alessandro.

Suddenly there was a small revolver in Fundling's hand. He must have had it on him the whole time. He aimed at the Hungry Man, who howled with rage again, stood there undecided for a moment, and then abruptly swung around.

He saw Rosa and Alessandro coming from his right. To his

left, the cameraman was hovering toward him over the dam.

Then there was no human being standing there, but a black and silver wolf instead. With two or three bounds, the creature raced toward the parapet and the helicopter. If the cameraman saw what was sweeping toward him, over the parapet rail and the abyss below, and straight through the open door in the side of the chopper, he had no time to react.

Rosa, Alessandro, Fundling, and the remaining Arcadians saw the gigantic wolf come down on the cameraman, fling him inside the helicopter, and fall on him. The man screeched as the wolf's jaws bit down, and Rosa saw his legs kick out and then go limp. At the same time, the helicopter flew in a narrow curve and went into a spin.

The chopper turned on its own axis above the road, tipped to one side, righted itself, and narrowly missed the opposite parapet. In the glare of several flashlights and car headlights, it tipped again, its rotor almost passing over the concrete, and went on circling around itself.

Rosa and Alessandro, running to the parapet, saw the helicopter rotate and then sink toward the valley floor and the ruins of Giuliana.

Fundling limped up on his crutches, propped himself on the railing beside them, and cut through the cord binding Rosa's hands with the knife. She pressed a kiss on his stubbly cheek.

"Thank you," she said, knowing it was far too weak an expression for all that she felt. Then she took the blade from him and freed Alessandro.

The helicopter was still whirring through the night like an

intoxicated insect, falling to the rocky ground and the abandoned houses. Many reporters and cameramen were leaning over the parapet rail, some way from the three of them, while the last Arcadians took the opportunity to get away.

Alessandro didn't wait for the impact. He bent down to pick up a gun that had belonged to one of their guards, and put it in the waistband of his jeans. He thanked Fundling with a firm hug, grabbed Rosa's hand, and then the two of them ran.

All the cameras were trained on the inevitable crash down below as they sprinted past the van and reached the square concrete structure at the side of the road. Graffiti had been sprayed clumsily across a metal door and the gray wall.

It didn't surprise Rosa to find that the entrance to the path down the dam showed signs of chiseling—the Hungry Man's followers would have checked the inside of this concrete block before the assembly began.

They hastily slipped in. When Alessandro touched a switch, neon tubes flickered on under the ceiling and lit up an ash-gray stairwell. Rosa slammed the door and wedged the knife under it.

Before they started down the stairs, she drew him to her and looked into his eyes. "You may now kiss the bride."

His lips were firm and dry. She would never have enough of them.

Outside, there was the sound of a muffled crash. At the same time, the sound of the rotor died away.

LYCAON

THE STAIRWELL HAD NO windows, and went on and on. Occasionally, they passed doors to the interior of the structure, but Rosa and Alessandro raced on down without stopping to open any of them. They were breathing faster, and their joints hurt from all the times they had jumped down several steps at once. Rosa had lost all sense of time. The structure of the dam, if it had been a building, would have been about fifty floors high, but the levels were not numbered. After every bend in the stairs came the next, and then another and yet another.

After an eternity they reached the bottom, dizzy and drained of strength. They both had to lean against the wall until the ground under them seemed to have stopped swaying, and they could go on without finding that their feet were searching for the next stair after every step they took.

At the bottom there was only one door, a rectangular one with a metal wheel in the middle of it. Beyond lay an airlock with another steel door at the end of it. The wheel on this one stuck, but between them they managed to move it; the absence of water pressure must have set off its automatic lock days ago. With a grinding sound, the steel door could be pushed open.

Before them lay a concrete platform half covered with sand

and pebbles. Beyond it they saw the bed of the former lake formed by the dam.

They walked out into the darkness. The moon was behind them on the far side of the dam, and a broad strip at the foot of the high concrete wall lay in deep shadow. They would have had to search, half-blind, for the ruins of the village if it hadn't been for the burning helicopter. The outlines of the houses stood out in front of the blazing fire.

More than fifteen minutes had passed since their last injection, but both stayed in human form. Alessandro handed Rosa the pistol. "In case I have to shift shape in a hurry," he said.

She had an objection on the tip of her tongue, but then she took the gun in silence and carried it the rest of the way. Together, they left the platform and set off toward the flames. It was still unclear whether the helicopter had come down in the middle of the village or beyond it.

Once she looked up at the titanic dam wall. The structure seemed to loom over her. Only an optical illusion, but it made her feel more uneasy than ever, and gave her a sense of something staring at her out of the darkness, invisible in deep shadow. Maybe it was the wall itself, a new monument to the first and genuine Hungry Man.

It wasn't far to the village. The part of it that had been too close to the dam and was in the way of the construction had been demolished, but fifteen or twenty houses were still standing. There were no boundaries left between the plots of land, and the roads, too, had disappeared under a layer of dried silt. The mud came up to the lower windows on many facades, like black snowdrifts.

A derelict agricultural machine stood between two ruined houses, a hunched silhouette. Rosa walked faster to leave the large, rusty thing behind. She felt as if the searchlights might come on again at any moment to catch them in their pale beams.

The helicopter had crashed into one of the farmhouses on the way out of the village. It was burning fiercely, but the explosion hadn't been strong enough to bring the last remains of the ruined walls down. The cockpit was in flames; parts of the shattered rotors were scattered around in a circle. There was nothing to be done for the pilot and the cameraman; their bodies were burning in the blaze inside the steel skeleton.

How long before a rescue team arrived? It would take at least an hour to drive here from the nearest hospital, along the winding mountain roads. Even a paramedic in a helicopter would take some time getting to this remote region.

She was watching the flames from a safe distance when Alessandro stiffened, bending slightly forward, eyes narrowed, nose raised.

"He's not in there anymore," he said grimly.

Narrowing her own eyes, Rosa looked at the wreck. "How can you see?"

"I can't, but I can smell him."

She shivered in spite of the heat. All she noticed was burning fuel and melting plastic.

She raised the pistol and looked around. "Which way?"

He waited a moment, picking up the scent, and then

pointed past the flames. "Over there. He's bleeding."

When he cast her an inquiring glance, she nodded. He quickly stripped off his shirt and jeans. Black panther fur meandered over his body, enclosing his limbs even as their shape changed, and he dropped to the ground on all fours. When he set off, his movements were elegant and fluid, and his silky coat shone in the firelight.

She stayed human in order to keep the pistol with them. It was really high time for her to trust her own abilities more, but all the same there was something reassuring about the weight of the weapon. If necessary she could still shift to her snake form quickly.

As she went along she picked up the discarded clothes and took them with her. Alessandro, in panther form, ran ahead, but not too fast for her to stay close to him. In that way they skirted the burning wreck, keeping a good distance from it, and left the ghost village in the direction of the mountain slopes.

They had not gone far, less than a hundred yards, when the panther stopped. He turned to her and nudged her with his nose. It was a signal that she should wait here.

"Forget it," she said, and walked firmly on again. She almost thought she heard him sigh as he caught up with her and then went on ahead again. The firelight hardly reached as far as this, but they had left the shadows of the dam wall behind and were now in the silver light of the moon.

The huge wolf lay on his side in a hollow. Smoke still rose from the places where his fur had burned, one flank and his back. His tail was charred and lay between his hind legs. Splintered bone stuck out of an open break on one forepaw. Blood was running from his muzzle, gleaming as it trickled into the dark dust. He was dying and probably knew that as well as they did.

Rosa stopped three yards from him, raising the pistol. Alessandro prowled around him, getting a hoarse rattle from the wolf's throat by way of response, and returned to Rosa's side. He sat there motionless and watched the wolf on the ground.

"Now what?" she asked quietly.

The panther still did not move, only sat there like a statue. Was he waiting for her to make a decision? She couldn't bring herself to fire the pistol, not while the Hungry Man lay in front of her in the shape of a helpless animal.

Perhaps he guessed that as a wolf he aroused her pity, and that was why he didn't change back. Or perhaps he was simply too weak.

"I can't do it," she whispered to Alessandro, while they watched the singed flank of the wolf rising and falling. She might have said: *I don't want to do it*. But that wasn't exactly right. She couldn't believe that she was feeling sorry for him, of all people. Fuck.

Up on the dam wall, there was a movement in the ranks of the journalists. They had been standing in rows beside the parapet, a chain of lights along its rail. Now Rosa saw a pair of car headlights making its way down the mountain, probably along the old road that used to lead to Giuliana.

"Do you think there are any more of them around?" she

asked, without taking her eyes off the wolf or lowering the pistol. She still felt as if she were being observed.

The panther sketched a movement that might have been a shake of his head.

She herself didn't seriously think that any more Arcadians were close to them. Many had probably escaped from the scene in their cars, others on foot. They had a long walk ahead of them, whether in human or animal form. The first to get away were probably already planning their exile abroad.

The wolf raised his head and tried to look at them. A fresh surge of blood flowed out of his huge jaws, which were stained dark red. Then his head slumped back on the ground.

The headlights were coming closer. Other cars were beginning to move up on the dam wall, but it would be some time before they, too, arrived. Rosa could guess who was driving the car that was just now reaching the valley floor.

The wolf's breathing became more irregular. His trembling died down.

The small white car was not built for a surface like this, but somehow Fundling managed to reach the village. He stopped close to the crashed helicopter and opened the driver's door.

Rosa called to him and waved, although he probably couldn't see her in the dark. However, he heard her, turned the car, and drove in their direction over the bumpy ground. When the headlights caught them, Alessandro was just changing back into human form. He put on his shirt and jeans and slipped into his shoes while Fundling brought the car to a halt.

Rosa pressed the pistol into Alessandro's hand and hurried

over to Fundling, to help him climb out with his crutches. He smiled, stroked her tousled hair, and limped toward Alessandro. They didn't exchange any words, but to Rosa they looked like brothers who understood each other without a lot of talking.

Incomprehensible sounds came from the wolf's throat. He raised his head again, and this time kept it in the air long enough to see Fundling. A growl came from his throat.

The convoy of journalists was winding its way down the slope. The burning helicopter was their only point of reference; they couldn't possibly see what was farther out in the darkness.

"There's something else you must do," said Fundling.

She looked inquiringly at him.

"Make a journey," he said. "And a sacrifice."

She shook her head blankly. The wolf was still growling, although he could barely move now.

Alessandro was aiming the pistol at the wolf. "Because of what you said up there just now?"

"They *are* here." Fundling nodded. "And they're waiting to see what you will do."

"What we—"

"You broke their laws. All the people up on the dam broke their laws."

Rosa stared at Alessandro, and then at Fundling again. "But that's—" She interrupted herself when she realized that they could both feel it as well. Glances trained on them from the darkness. As if other beings were nearby.

"Can you talk to them?" she asked hesitantly.

Fundling shook his head. "They have punished the Arcadians once already, and I think they will do it again. But just as some rituals break their laws"—and he looked up at the wall of the dam—"there are others that can make up for the wrong that was done."

"Wrong?" cried Rosa indignantly. "That bastard forced us into it!" But as she spoke she looked at Alessandro, as if asking forgiveness. How could something that brought them closer together ever really be wrong?

"They've sunk cities in the sea, they've annihilated entire kingdoms," replied Fundling. "Do you think that every single human being who died deserved it? Heaven knows how many children. None of them ever built a bridge, or a temple, or committed any crime. So there must be another reason for them to give you two a chance."

Something was moving around them. As if the darkness were becoming denser in some mysterious way, and even more impenetrable. Then she realized that it had nothing to do with light or dark. The wide-open space of the valley suddenly seemed to have physical weight. There were no words to express it, only sensations that laid themselves on her chest and took her breath away.

The Hungry Man's growling grew louder, and now she recognized that it had never expressed aggression, only panicked terror. He scraped his hind legs in the dirt as if, even in death, he wanted to run away.

Alessandro too seemed to feel the change. He came closer,

putting his arm around Rosa. "What do you mean by a sacrifice?" he asked.

Fundling limped to his car, opened the passenger door, and took something off the seat. Moonlight shone on sharp metal.

"You'll have to move fast."

Then he told them what they had to do.

CRETE

THEY COVERED THE LAST few miles even faster. Alessandro drove the car around hairpin turns without any guardrails, past precipitous drops between bleak rocky slopes. Nothing grew here except for low bushes, and a few trees with their tops lashed by the wind until they bowed, as if now and then one of the gods still went this way to Mount Ida.

Rosa was in the passenger seat, a map of Crete on her lap. The roads and symbols blurred before her eyes. It wasn't hot yet here, so early in the year. All the same, it felt like an oven inside the car.

She had drawn her knees up and braced her feet against the glove compartment. A blue and white electric cooler stood on the rubber mat in front of her feet. Her legs would have fitted into the space, but when her calves touched the plastic of the box she felt a slight vibration that she very much disliked.

Common sense should have told her that the sounds she heard were only the electric cooling system; a cable led from the cooler to the cigarette lighter beside the hand brake. But she had left common sense behind more than forty hours ago, in a dark valley back in Sicily, and nothing, absolutely nothing of what they were doing, could be understood by rational standards.

During the long crossing, five hundred miles across the open Mediterranean, they had gone over it all again and again. They had found no explanations. Yet they both believed that Fundling had told the truth—because they had felt the real presence of something around them in that valley. Something that showed itself only in crowds of human beings, not in that wide, empty void.

Their breakneck drive through the mountains had been the last stage of a race against—what, exactly? Time? Their powers of imagination? Or was it, after all, against the anger of something conjured up by the Hungry Man with their unwilling help?

They had collected cash, new passports, credit cards for secret accounts, and half a dozen secure cell phones from Alessandro's hiding place in Syracuse. Then they had made contact with the captain of the *Gaia*.

Within three hours the yacht had been with them. The authorities had released the ship ages ago; she had been cruising off the Sicilian coast under another name and with forged papers. It was true that the police still wanted to see Rosa and Alessandro, but as witnesses, not murderers, which had considerably decreased the urgency and extent of the search for them. So ultimately Stefania's statement, maybe even Lorenzo's, had helped them after all.

And no danger from their families threatened them now, either. Those who had betrayed Alessandro and caused the upheaval among the Carnevares had disappeared without a trace since their flight from the dam. It was the same with

Rosa's distant cousins and all the others who had taken part in the Hungry Man's ritual. Either they had fled rather than face the TV images of what happened on the dam when they aired the next morning, or else what had been down there in the valley had caught up with them.

A return to being heads of their families was certainly out of the question for both Rosa and Alessandro, at least for now. But those who had remained loyal to Alessandro, like the captain of the *Gaia*, could now move freely again without fearing for their lives. Rosa had had her doubts about the captain, but Alessandro trusted him without reservation. And rightly, as it turned out when the *Gaia* reached the harbor of Heraklion on Crete without any trouble.

From there they had hired a car and driven south, past Thylissos, uninhabited chains of hills, and olive groves that were almost painfully reminiscent of Sicily. They followed a deep ravine into the Ida range, racing along narrow, winding roads toward Anogia. The slopes and valleys became bleaker; gray rock dominated this mountainous world. Sheep and goats crossed the road at their leisure; several times Alessandro had to brake sharply to avoid hitting one. Once the cooler fell over. Rosa cursed fluently, and then, reluctantly, righted it again with her fingertips.

The first sight of the Nida Plateau far up in the mountains, quite close to their destination, was a surprise. In the middle of colorless mountaintops, a fertile plain opened out, with a few herds of cattle grazing on it. Some tracks intersected, looking lost, on the wide expanse of the plateau.

It was getting dark when they reached the end of the

asphalt road outside a dilapidated building, a taverna with its shutters closed. They had met only two cars going the other way in the past hour. The taverna was dark—it was probably open only in the summer—but there was a parking lot outside it, and a notice for hikers pointing the way up a gravel path. There were no people or other vehicles anywhere in sight.

They parked the car and got out. The sound of goat bells came from somewhere far off, and the cry of a bird of prey. Soon after that, a hawk hunting mice flew over them.

Alessandro took the bag with their equipment out of the trunk, and Rosa unplugged the cooler. Its plastic was still vibrating when they set off, with batteries to supply the power now. Rosa shuddered whenever her leg touched the box as they walked.

Only a little later they passed a small chapel near some graves. They left those behind, too, and kept on climbing up. They stopped only once, and looked back. From here they had a fantastic view over the plateau. The last daylight was glowing in shades of carmine streaked with gold above the distant limestone mountains on the other side of Nida.

They could have enjoyed their view of the plain in the evening light, if they hadn't had to cover such a vast distance. They didn't know if anything was following them, and might even be quite close. Rosa wished she were anywhere else, someplace full of people—Times Square, the crowded concourse of Grand Central Station, a football stadium. Crowds made the watchers visible; this wilderness camouflaged them with its void.

After twenty minutes they reached a grotto at the foot of

a gray massif of rock. The Ideon Andron, the Ideon Cave, lay behind an opening in the rock that was much wider than it was high, as if the mountain were gradually weighing the entrance down. The track of an old freight railroad, partly overgrown by weeds, ended at the edge of a steeply falling precipice.

There was no one in sight. No barriers, no one on guard duty. They were alone in front of the great chasm in the rock, Rosa holding the cooler, Alessandro with the bag in which they had two strong flashlights and some other utensils.

Rosa seldom felt awestruck, but she did feel respect and awe at the sight of this place. She was no longer ashamed of believing in something that only recently she would have dismissed as a legend.

Climb down into the cave, Fundling had said. *Only you two, don't take anyone else with you.*

A narrow flight of steps led down the slope inside the entrance. They were carrying their flashlights now, letting the beams wander over the steps and walls of the grotto. Pigeons who had built their nests in the rock fluttered around the roof of the cave.

Decrepit wooden planks, the remains of old excavations, lay on the uneven floor of the grotto. When they stepped on them, the creaking echoed back from the limestone walls. They preferred to make their way over the rocky floor itself.

It's said that Zeus spent his childhood in this cave. Fundling had seen Rosa's skeptical look, but only responded with a smile. *His father, the Titan Kronos, feared that his children might usurp his power. So he ate them alive—all but his youngest son. Zeus was still a baby when his mother hid him from Kronos in the Ideon Cave.*

The Ideon Andron consisted of one large and two smaller caverns, leading into one another. To Rosa, it looked like any other grotto—until Alessandro stopped, turned around, and glanced past her back at the entrance.

"He was right," he whispered. "Can you feel it?"

Not it; *them.* Rosa sensed their presence with as much certainty as if she had heard footsteps or seen moving shadows behind her. In fact she saw and heard nothing; yet all the same she knew that they were no longer alone.

Zeus lived in the grotto for many years, Fundling had said as he drove them out of the Giuliana valley in his car. *His mother gave him guards to protect him, the Curetes. Demons or spirits, who knows which? They were his bodyguards and servants. Later, he often summoned them to carry out tasks for him.*

Myths and legends, of course. But wasn't it the same with her, and every Arcadian who had the power to shift shape? Sigismondis had tried to find a scientific reason for these mysteries. Leonardo Mori had traced them through libraries and old manuscripts. But in the end no one had been able to come up with anything but assumptions, hypotheses—and yet more myths.

Once again she shone her flashlight over the rocky walls. Darkness didn't scare her, because what had entered the grotto with them far outdid any other menace.

The great domed cavern was the most impressive part of

the grotto, tall as the interior of a church. They went through it, and entered one of the chambers opening off to one side. According to Fundling, this had been a temple of Zeus long ago, and his worshippers had celebrated their rites here.

The Lamias were here once before, he had said. *Back when they overthrew Lycaon and killed him.*

She put the cooler down. Where the beam of her flashlight didn't reach, there was impenetrable black. Even the entrance stood out in the darkness only as a patch of gray.

The chamber in the rock was spacious and empty, yet it seemed to Rosa as if it were full to bursting with life. All at once she felt hemmed in, surrounded, as if someone were leaning over her shoulder.

"This should be the right place," said Alessandro.

They stood there, undecidedly, and looked at the cooler, hearing the quiet hum of the refrigeration system.

"Oh, fuck," said Rosa. "What the hell." And she crouched down, put her shaking hands on the catches, and lifted the lid. As she raised it, the thought occurred to her that the smell might have been worse.

"Come on," he said gently. "I'll do the rest."

"Wait." She picked up the other bag and took out some candles, as well as a couple of brass bowls the size of side plates, and divided herbs and aromatics from little paper bags between them. Myrrh, bay, thyme, sage. She arranged the bowls and the candles in a small circle on the floor, and set light to the herbs and the wicks of the candle with matches. The aroma was so strong that it made her eyes stream.

"Okay," she said. "Now."

Alessandro reached into the box, took out what had been lying in it, and laid it in the center of the circle. Up to this point Fundling had told them exactly what to do, every single step of the way.

And then go, he had said. *Go, and don't turn around. No matter what happens, if anything does happen, don't look back.*

They stood, picked up the bag and the box, and watched the smoke rising in the flames of the candles. Already the center of the circle was almost invisible in it.

As they turned and slowly walked away, with their bags, the inexplicable sense of confinement in the cave seemed to give way a little.

Don't turn around.

They left the ancient temple of Zeus and went back through the main cave.

Don't look back.

As they reached the steps on the slope, the way out to the red evening light, they stopped. Rosa breathed deeply and felt the fresh air driving the fumes of the herbs and aromatics out of her lungs.

Alessandro took her hand, and they climbed up together.

They stepped out into the open air. They smiled at each other.

They didn't look back.

ONE DAY

THE SEA WAS THE world, from the beginning to the end.

In the middle of all the blue there was a white dot, the *Gaia* and the foam behind in her wake. The *Gaia*, on course for Portugal.

"Sicily is somewhere over there." Alessandro pointed to starboard over the rolling, white-capped sea.

Rosa nodded over the rail to port. "And Lampedusa over there." Both islands were invisible beyond the horizon. Invisible in their past.

She had looked at charts of the Mediterranean and its coasts in the captain's cabin. Her instincts told her that they would spend a great deal of time out here, that their home was no longer any island, but the sea. The whole wide south.

Iole was waiting for them in Sintra, in her uncle's care at the house of the strange Signora Institoris. Sarcasmo was with her, and Raffaela Falchi. Cristina di Santis had gone underground to appropriate as much as possible of the Alcantara fortune and divert it to Rosa's new accounts. In the current leaderless chaos of the clans, she was not likely to find that difficult.

As for Fundling, he had disappeared again, on the trail of his father and Leonardo's research. They would see him again sometime. He had survived death—he probably had more surprises in store.

"A thousand kilometers to the Straits of Gibraltar," said Alessandro. "And then along the coast for a way."

"Plenty of time."

"There's never enough time."

She smiled. "There is now."

They were sitting on the top deck of the white yacht, on a leather couch, sharing a thin throw. The sky above them was cloudless, the sun shone down, and its warmth let them know that they were closer to the coast of Africa than to Europe.

Rosa's bare legs showed under the hem of the throw. She was sure she would never feel freezing again; she had used up all her ability to shiver. In the cave, and after that on the way back to the light. And he was here to keep her warm.

They had gone the same way that the Lamias had once taken, after overthrowing the king of Arcadia. Had Zeus accepted their sacrifice at that time? How could she be sure, when she didn't know what her ancestors had asked for? If their wish had been for him to lift his curse on all the Arcadians, then it hadn't been granted. For the next generation, too, had been born with the stain of metamorphosis on them, and so on through hundreds of other generations to the present day.

How would they ever know for certain whether they were free of it? Maybe they had been forgiven for taking part in the ritual that the Hungry Man had forced them to share. But how about the law that they broke every day, with every breath they took? If panther and snake were forbidden to love each other, then wasn't everything they did an offense against the law of the gods?

Go fuck yourselves, gods.

"They'll be glad to hear that," said Alessandro, with a smile. She had spoken her thought aloud.

"Then they'll know it comes from the heart."

"I'm sure it was only about the wedding. Nothing else bothers them. So long as we don't set ourselves up as objects of worship in temples, they're not interested in us."

"Suppose Sigismondis was right?"

"Right about what?"

"Suppose the idea really was to keep Lamias and Panthera from having children together? He thought it could be something physical. Something that the gods wanted to prevent."

"Cats with scales on their skin?"

"You know what I mean."

He tightened his arm around her and gave her a long kiss. "Is this the moment you tell me you're pregnant?"

"No!" she cried indignantly.

He grinned. "These things happen."

"Not to me anymore."

"That's not very romantic."

"You weren't buying a pig in a poke."

He was laughing quietly. "I know you so much better than you know yourself."

Now it was her turn to press her lips to his, because

sometimes, just sometimes, he was a little bit right. Not very right. Just a little bit.

She leaned back, threw her head back, and gazed up at the sky. No aircraft in sight. No birds.

"Sometimes," she said, "two people pass each other by, look into each other's eyes for a moment, and all that's left is a wish. A dream of what might have been. And then they move away from each other with every step, and away from all their dreams."

He stroked her hair. "That could have happened to us. Back at the airport in New York. I saw you, but you took no notice of me."

Everything could have turned out differently if he hadn't happened to be sitting behind her on the plane. If the man beside her hadn't called the flight attendant to complain about her. If Alessandro hadn't intervened.

A year before that, they had even been together in the same room, in Greenwich Village, New York. So many people, so many faces, they hadn't even looked at each other. Suppose that had been all? Suppose one of them had gone another way in the months after that, not the *wrong* way, just another way?

"So much could have gone wrong," she said. "And I don't mean the really bad things. Only little ones. I could have missed my flight. Or you could have missed yours. Sheer chance. That's what it is, right? We're together only by chance."

"Do you really think that?"

"What I think is that in the old days, people held their gods responsible for what happened by chance. And if that's the reason we met—"

Smiling, he put a finger on her lips. "That way you can find connections between anything, and you end up believing in the good Lord or a great world conspiracy."

"Or TABULA."

"Yes, TABULA too."

"Maybe they saw to it that you had the seat behind mine in the plane. Or that my baggage was lost, and I had trouble with the flight attendant. Or that you—"

"Hey," he interrupted her quietly. "It makes no difference now. None at all."

She took a deep breath and calmed down. The wind helped, the sight of the sea, most of all Alessandro. Simply because he was with her. His body so close to hers.

Drowsily, she closed her eyes and a little later felt him kissing their lids. He did that sometimes to make sure she had sweet dreams. She lay in his arms, feeling very supple, even in human form.

The yacht made her way through the waves, westward through an avalanche of spray.

Don't look back.

No, certainly not. Not anymore.

Then she awakened. Everything was as it had been. He was there, holding her. They were lying under the throw, in the warm, gentle sea breeze. The engines hummed deep in the hull. The sky might have been swept clear. All was well.

"I was dreaming," he said.

"Me too."

She had plans for her dreams. And his.

"One day," she said. And fell silent again.

Sometime she would tell him about them.

Not today. Not tomorrow.

But one day, yes.